THE DEFENSE OF THE COMMONWEALTH

JOHN J. SPEARMAN

DEDICATION

To the readers who enjoy my work and encourage me to write. To Alicia, my wife and my strength, who challenged me to pursue it further. To all those who offer me moral support—you know who you are and I cannot be more grateful. Finally, to you, the reader. You are the reason I do this.

OTHER BOOKS BY THIS AUTHOR

The Halberd Series

Gallantry in Action
In Harm's Way
True Allegiance
Surrender Demand

The Pike Series

Pike's Potential
Pike's Passage
Pike's Progress

The FitzDuncan Series

FitzDuncan
FitzDuncan's Alchemy
FitzDuncan's Enlightenment
FitzDuncan's Fortune

ACKNOWLEDGMENTS

Dear Reader,
You are the purpose of this and all my books. Thank you for reading. If you like what you have read, please leave a positive review on Amazon.com or goodreads.com. If you did not like it, I'm sorry.

If you would like to stay abreast of my latest activity, please visit my website: johnjspearmanauthor.com

PART ONE:
BIRTH OF THE COMMONWEALTH

1

Thursday, June 1, 2479, was a great day in Stan Schodowski's life. He was read in as the captain of RLS *Ulysses*, the most powerful ship in the Republic of Lincoln's small fleet. *Ulysses* was a cruiser with a hull composed of walls of a ceramic-titanium sandwich. If she had been on earth, she would have weighed two hundred fifty-five thousand tons. She was three hundred eighty meters long, fifty-eight meters wide, and fifty meters from dorsal to ventral (top to bottom).

Powered by two fusion reactors, *Ulysses* was capable of maximum acceleration of five hundred g, or five hundred times earth' gravity, and it took only thirty-seven minutes for her EM drives to reach that level of boost. She had a crew of two hundred sixty, including fourteen officers. She was armed with four 155mm railguns, twenty-eight 40mm missile defense railguns, and point-defense lasers. In addition, she had sixteen missile tubes, from which Warhammer missiles would launch, tipped with destructive antimatter warheads.

Commissioned only three years ago, *Ulysses* was equal to the best ships in settled space. She was the pride of the Republic of Lincoln's fleet, which now numbered one cruiser, three destroyers, and eight patrol boats. For an individual planet, Lincoln possessed a navy of which they were justly proud.

Lincoln had plans to grow. They had begun settlement of the planet of Aries over a hundred years before. Aries was quickly reaching the point of becoming self-sustaining. Though it was nearly a two-week journey to reach Aries from Lincoln, Aries was well-positioned with regard to other trading partners.

Schodowski's mission was to patrol the hyper corridors into and out of Lincoln. The most heavily-trafficked corridors were one connecting the Lincoln system to the Roosevelt system and another leading to the Aries system. In between the 'named' systems, there were other unpopulated systems. His ship, *Ulysses*, was based in the Lincoln system along with one of the destroyers, RLS *Percival*. The other destroyer, RLS *Aspiration*, was based in the Aries system. The patrol boats were used to keep shipping lanes free from pirates and smugglers.

Schodowski was proud to claim his descent from "originals." His ancestors had been in the first wave of colonists recruited by the Tri-Dolor Group. His parents and grandparents were among the wealthiest and most influential people on Lincoln. Schodowski was one of those born to a life of power and privilege but believed his or her achievements were solely because of ability and effort. With no known military threats, the government of Lincoln saw nothing wrong with promoting Schodowski.

They had reason to doubt their judgment when they received word on July 10 from RLS *Aspiration* in the Aries system that it was under attack by Chinese warships. Sensor data indicated three Chinese 319-type cruisers, and four 162-type destroyers had entered the Aries system. The logs of the battle indicated that *Aspiration* was overwhelmed by the number of missiles launched by the Chinese, and it was presumed that the ship was destroyed. *Ulysses* and *Percival* were put on high alert. On Tuesday, August 4, Schodowski's world came crashing down when the Chinese emerged from hyperspace at the exit from the corridor to Aries. The battle was as brief as it was one-sided.

Schodowski tried to make a run for it, but the Chinese had caught him flat-footed. They were able to close the distance. When they reached missile range, they fired. The seventy-two ship-killer missiles were almost twice as many as *Ulysses* and *Percival* could defend against. Both ships were obliterated.

A few days later, Chinese troop transports arrived in the Lincoln system and began offloading soldiers. Lincoln had only a token number of ground forces to oppose them. The one attempt at resistance was a disaster, as the Chinese ships in orbit dropped kinetic weapons on the Lincoln soldiers. The Chinese Republics quickly announced that the Lincoln system was theirs.

Captain Latasha Polk of RRS *Hillis* was patrolling the hyper corridor in the Roosevelt system that eventually led to the Rodinan Dneiper system. Unlike the Republic of Lincoln's Schodowski, Polk had earned her position by merit. She was proud to command the finest ship in the Republic of Roosevelt's small fleet. Shadowing her on patrol was RRS *Tomahawk*, a destroyer. The *Hillis* was similar in design and armament to Lincoln's *Ulysses*, though a couple of years older.

Polk had no warning from her intelligence services that anything unusual was happening, so when four Rodinan *Navarin*-class cruisers winked into normal space, followed by three *Levchenko*-class destroyers, she was surprised. She immediately ordered *Tomahawk* to run for safety to another system, realizing the battle was already lost. She positioned *Hillis* to block the Rodinans from catching *Tomahawk*. The battle lasted less than thirty seconds. The seventy-six missiles launched by the Rodinans ships were nearly triple the number she could defend against.

Rodinan troop transports followed two days later and began shuttling soldiers down to the planet. Like Lincoln, Roosevelt had only a small number of soldiers. Rather than engage in a foolhardy act of resistance, Roosevelt disbanded the units before the Rodinans arrived and tried to erase all records of who had been in the military. If they were going to mount a resistance effort, they wanted to try to hide their small number of trained soldiers in the general population.

Speaker Harry Monroe, leader of the planet of Carolina, had been on a video conference with the sixteen other leaders of the loosely-aligned planets whose residents were largely from what had been the United States on earth. The Alliance had long ago pledged to support one another in the event of an attack from outside forces. During the conference, Monroe had watched as the planetary leaders bickered and argued, resolving nothing. In his mind, it was clear that none of the other members of the Alliance would allow their navies to depart their systems, let alone submit to the command of someone else.

If you added up all the ships belonging to Alliance members, the combined fleet would have outclassed the Rodinan or Chinese navies. The Alliance had more cruisers, more destroyers, and more patrol boats. They could force the Rodinans and Chinese to vacate Roosevelt and Lincoln if they worked together.

Yet the leaders of the Alliance planets were terrified that they would suffer the next invasion if they sent their ships away to join a combined force.

As Monroe rubbed his temples, trying to massage away his frustration, Debby Johnson, the deputy speaker, was leaning back in her chair, staring at the ceiling. "That accomplished less than nothing," she sighed.

"On the contrary," Monroe replied sarcastically, "it accomplished a great deal. We now know we can count on the other members of the Alliance for absolutely zilch. We might have had some small hope before, but now they've eliminated that."

"What do we do now?"

"I don't know," Monroe admitted. "I'm certainly no Themistocles."

"Who the hell is that?" she asked.

"A leader back on earth in ancient times," Monroe explained. "He was appointed as leader of an allied force similar to what we have, or don't have, considering the results of this meeting. When his allies all wanted to return home, he tricked the enemy into offering battle—a battle he ended up winning. I don't have skills like his to pull this group together."

His console buzzed with an incoming call. The ID on the screen indicated it was President Chychlyk of Alleghany. Johnson tilted her head up in an inquiry. "Chychlyk," Monroe mouthed to her as he opened the connection.

"Hi, Harry," Chychlyk greeted him, "wasn't that a complete cluster?"

"Hi, Steve, I've got Debby Johnson with me," Monroe replied, "and, yeah, that was even worse than I expected, and I didn't have high hopes to begin with."

"Well, I was just talking with Sally Martin. You mind if I bring her onto the call?"

"Go ahead," Monroe replied, looking at Johnson with his eyebrows raised in slight surprise.

"Hi, Harry. Hi, Debby," greeted Martin, president of the planet of New Boston. "Steve and I were talking, and we have an idea we want to run by you."

"Go ahead," Monroe said.

"All three of us border the Brits," Steve explained, "you connect to Caledonia, I connect to Caerleon, and Sally connects to York. They're our biggest trading partners. They've always played it straight with us on Alleghany, which is more than I can say for some members of our so-called Alliance."

"True," Monroe confirmed. "We've never had any complaints. The trade agreements we have with them were actually a pleasure to negotiate."

"What would you think," President Martin suggested, "about approaching them?"

"From the standpoint of defense?" Harry asked.

"Yes," Chychlyk confirmed. "Their navy is bigger than the three of ours added together, so our guys would probably have to take their orders from them. Would that be a problem for you?"

"If it's a problem, I can always find new commanders for whom it's not a problem," Monroe responded. "Do you think they'd go along with it?"

"I can't see why not," Martin stated. "It makes all of us stronger in the long run."

"What about in the short run?" Monroe asked.

"We haven't had much time to discuss this," Chychlyk cautioned, "but I'd imagine they'd pull our ships out of our systems and locate them centrally. If any of us came under attack, it might be ten days or more before the combined navy could respond."

"The same sticking point the Alliance isn't prepared to deal with," Monroe stated, "and one which doesn't matter. The Rodinans or Chinese can land as many damned troops as they want. But they won't be there very long if they don't maintain control of the orbital position."

"So, you're with us on this?" Chychlyk asked.

"Hell, yes, I'm with you on this. Debby?"

"There will be some squawking," Johnson replied, "but there will be no matter what we do. This sounds much better than what we have now, which is nothing."

"If it's acceptable," Martin said, "I'll contact their foreign secretary and get things started."

Ryan MacArthur had just begun his day when his personal assistant interrupted him. "Sir," he said, "you have an incoming call from President Sally Martin of New Boston. Should I put it through?"

"Of course," MacArthur agreed. When the call appeared on his comm, he greeted her. "President Martin, this is an unexpected pleasure. How may I help you?"

Sally quickly explained the situation New Boston, Alleghany, and Carolina were facing. "We talked among ourselves a few hours ago, Ryan," she continued, "and agreed that we would like to approach you guys."

MacArthur fought not to wince at the 'you guys.' The name of his government was the Inter-Planetary Commonwealth. Still, none of the Americans he dealt with ever used the name. It was always, 'you guys' or 'your government' and behind their backs, 'the Brits.'

"What are you proposing, Sally?"

"A mutual defense treaty," she confirmed.

"Don't you have one with the other Alliance members?"

"As I mentioned, it became clear in our conference call yesterday that none of the other Alliance members will allow their ships to leave their home systems, let alone take orders from someone else," she recounted. "We're not like them. So we'd like to add our ships to yours, and, since you're the biggest dog in the fight, we'd permit you guys to command the joint fleet."

MacArthur adjusted his posture, sitting up slightly straighter. This was big, he thought. Big enough that he needed to get others involved immediately.

"And Speaker Monroe and President Chychlyk are in agreement?" he asked.

"Yes," Martin stated. "We just discussed this a couple of hours ago. I've been waiting for you to get into the office."

"Um, this is kind of a big thing to drop on me, Sally," he responded. "I'm going to need to talk with some people."

"I figured you guys would need to talk about it. So do what you need to do and get back to me, please."

After exchanging pleasantries, they ended the call. MacArthur immediately contacted Lewis Suffield, the prime minister. Suffield was the head of the Liberal Democrats, the party currently holding a narrow majority in both houses of the Commonwealth's Parliament.

While the Commonwealth took much of its governmental structure from the old United Kingdom on earth, there were some critical differences. A Parliamentary form of government on the British model had already been established, and the House of Commons was elected similarly to its earthly predecessor. Unlike what had happened on earth, though, the Commonwealth House of Lords became a viable and influential political entity. Eligibility was established based on wealth with essential stipulations. To be a member of the House of Lords, one must have debt-free capital holdings of more than five hundred million pounds and stand for election. A seat in the House of Lords brought with it no official title. However, the members were commonly called 'Lord So-and-So,' indicating they held (or had held) a seat in the upper chamber of Parliament. The new lords were required to reinvest fifty percent or more of their annual income in small business incubators at fair terms arbitrated by the Crown and to pay a flat thirty-five percent tax rate on all income. If the debt-free value of their capital holdings dropped below the five hundred-million-pound figure, they had to relinquish their seat. This made the House of Lords necessary in the Parliamentary procedure for the first time in centuries as they quickly realized they contributed over ninety percent of the tax revenue in the Commonwealth. They re-established authority equal to the House of Commons, and Parliament became a bicameral legislature.

With the resurgence of the House of Lords, the king or queen exercised his or her authority as a tie-breaking vote in the upper chamber. It had rarely been needed, but it reestablished the monarch as a political presence, though relatively minor. After the second Great Uprising on earth, the Royal Family had begun posting the Prince of Wales to Caerleon as a safety precaution if something happened to the rest of the family. When the rest of the Royal Family was killed in the third Great Uprising, Prince William became William VI.

When MacArthur contacted the prime minister, they agreed to sweep their calendars free for the day to meet and discuss this development. They called Admiral Regina Roberts into the meeting as well. The three of them worked into the night and hammered out the basis of an agreement between the Commonwealth and the three planets.

2

Lincoln was one of two planets initially claimed by a consortium known as the Tri-Dolor Group. Tri-Dolor had been a joint venture of three large multi-national corporations based in what was the United States on earth.

During the exciting days of the second half of the twenty-second century, governments and corporations had funded an orgy of exploration in interstellar space. Earlier in the twenty-second century, an Anglo-American corporation— filling the void left when the American government had lost the will to explore space—had pioneered the development of the first workable Alcubierre and EM drives along with the invention of plasma shielding that both contained the immense heat of fusion reactors and captured the electrons produced. The same company brought in additional partners and then developed mass compensators and inertial dampeners, enabling advances in sub-light travel. The leading governments and corporations of earth leased spacecraft from this company to map out hyper-corridors free of dark matter through which the Alcubierre drives could travel.

During this age of exploration, well over a hundred planets had been found that fell into what was commonly called the "Goldilocks" zone with gravity and climate similar to earth. Of course, not all the planets were inhabitable. Those with multiple moons, for instance, usually had enormous tidal forces and were seismically active.

One thing scientists discovered through analyzing these planets and the life forms found on them was the "Goldilocks" nature of earth's Van Allen belts. Earth's Van Allen belts allowed enough solar radiation to penetrate to encourage slight genetic mutation and evolution, but not enough to be deadly. In the planets of the proper size and climate, explorers found that the Van Allen belts were either too thin, meaning the planet was inhospitable for sustaining life, or the belts were too thick, which meant life had not evolved on the planet, usually not much beyond some single-cell organisms.

Those planets with only simple microorganisms were the prime candidates for settlement. In most cases, care was taken to preserve the native species in a controlled environment to keep them free from contamination, while vast spectra of earth's flora and fauna were brought in to 'terraform' the planet.

To spur colonization, the corporations and governments initially offered significant incentives if colonists left earth and moved to one of the newly-discovered planets. One of the lasting incentives, still part of the legal framework of most of civilized space, was incentives for having large numbers of children and penalties in the form of higher taxes for those who did not reproduce. In the early days, widespread egg and sperm harvesting and ex-utero gestation were employed. Children born this way were fostered to colonist families.

As was typical in human history, fortunes were made and lost by speculators during this period. When it became clear that these new ventures would take several generations to become solidly profitable, many on earth lost interest. As a result, the initial wave of colonization, where colonists were recruited by corporations on earth and given financial incentives to move, petered out. Some still wished to leave earth and start over somewhere else, but now they had to buy passage and pay their relocation expenses.

That situation changed following the Second Great Uprising in 2371. This was a coordinated series of nuclear explosions set off by religious extremists in several major cities on earth. Earth suffered a "brain drain" as the best and the brightest of its citizens left as quickly as they were able to find a new home. Most colonies adopted new statutes forbidding the practice of any religion that would not accept the right of other religions to co-exist. In addition, proselytizing, missionary work, and evangelizing were also banned. These measures caused great controversy and unrest for a time.

With the influx of people following the Second Great Uprising, the colonies founded by the western powers quickly surpassed their earthly progenitors in economic strength. As a result, the ties between the colonies and the earth-bound powers became weaker and weaker.

After the Third Great Uprising struck in 2451, earth was left an impoverished, radioactively-polluted, and violent world. Leaders of the former first- and second-rank world powers had largely been killed by the initial attacks of the Third Great Uprising. Within weeks, earth residents who could afford passage to one of the planetary colonies departed on whatever transport they could arrange. This became known as the Last Exodus. Earth's governments collapsed when they could not feed the growing numbers of refugees. Moreover, medical care for those afflicted by radiation sickness of growing severity became increasingly unavailable.

Rescue efforts were mounted by many of the colonies, but when unstable rulers seized control of the remaining stockpiles of weapons on earth and tried to force passage off-planet by shooting down the shuttles the colonists sent to load refugees, these efforts were reluctantly abandoned. Even as the earth's population succumbed to the radioactively-polluted environment, these rulers kept their fingers on the triggers. The last human survivors of earth were rescued in 2466 by an expedition from the planet of Rotterdam.

Lincoln was one of nineteen planets whose colonists had originated mainly in the United States. The original rulers of Lincoln were the Board of Directors of the Tri-Dolor Group, but in 2352, residents of the planet held a referendum on self-rule and ceased to have any further ties. Lincoln's government repaid all debts owed to the Group, and Tri-Dolor had no other recourse.

The nineteen planets of American background were only loosely allied. They were initially claimed and settled by corporations, not governments. They had a mutual defense treaty where they pledged to come to one another's aid if attacked and some trade and monetary agreements. Six of these claimed other planets in different systems and had already begun to settle those planets, though none were self-sustaining yet.

In contrast to the United States, which had left space exploration to the private sector and had exhausted its resources in trying to be earth's policeman, the Russians and the Chinese had made concerted efforts toward settling new planets. The Russians, who now called themselves Rodinans after the destruction of Russia, had colonized twenty planets. The Chinese, who had become the dominant power on earth in its final centuries, had colonized eighteen planets. Moreover, both had unified inter-planetary governments. The Rodinans called theirs the Federation of Rodinan Planets. The Chinese called theirs the Unified Chinese Republics.

In the initial frenzy of colonization, the United Nations had underwritten colonization efforts on three planets: New Delhi, Patagonia, and Nyumbani. Of these, New Delhi was the most successful. The British government had settled three worlds, and those three were now beginning the colonization of three others. The Germans had established two planets and had started settling a third. A joint Japanese-Korean consortium had colonized one world, Edo, as had the French government, with Lutetia. The other planet in civilized space was Rotterdam.

Originally it was discovered by a Dutch multi-national conglomerate, which funded the initial wave of settlement. The corporation was unable to attract large numbers of settlers and reduced its investment in the system as a result. The company's stock price dropped sharply in the market crash that followed the Second Great Uprising. A group of primarily eastern European nations purchased a controlling interest in the company through shell corporations and shadow companies. The leading partner was Poland, but Ukraine, Estonia, Latvia, Lithuania, Finland, the Czech Republic, Slovakia, Hungary, Croatia, Italy, and Spain were all members.

As the worldwide economy recovered, the partners began to divest the parent company of its most profitable assets, amassing a tremendous hoard of cash. This cash was then distributed through the shell corporations back to the countries and used to pay for a massive migration and colonization program. Once the news broke of who the company's real owners were, they filed bankruptcy papers on the remainder of the corporation, keeping ownership of the planet. The money they raised through their deception was enough to pay for nearly thirty percent of the population of some countries to travel to Rotterdam, though a much smaller percentage from Italy and Spain because their investment in the project was more limited. An even greater percentage of the population wished to go, so they conducted lotteries to determine who would get the berths on the colony ships.

The original Dutch settlers, who had been mainly left to their own resources by the corporation, welcomed the newcomers and the increased investment in the planet. As the greatest number of residents came from Poland, Polish was adopted as the official language. Still, an effort in the education system was made to keep all the original languages alive. The economy of Rotterdam snowballed, and the government established two priorities from the start: to invest in the infrastructure to exploit the abundant resources in the system and to provide passage to any citizens of their original countries who had been left behind.

The Commonwealth controlled three established planets: Caerleon, Avalon, and Caledonia. It had also begun settlement of York, Southampton, and New Glasgow. In the initial wave of colonization, the British government on earth had offered significant tax benefits to individuals and corporations wishing to settle on the newly colonized planets. It also provided citizens of the other countries in the earth-bound British Commonwealth free passage. While this was not an important source of colonists initially, it became so later.

With the economic strength of the three existing solar systems, the Commonwealth had built a space-going navy consisting of five cruisers, twelve destroyers, and twenty patrol boats. Adding the ships from New Boston, Carolina and Alleghany would bring three more cruisers, five more destroyers, and a dozen more patrol boats. Admiral Roberts drafted a quick plan of how the combined force would be positioned to respond to an attack on any of the six established planets and the three Commonwealth planets under development.

She also developed a long list of issues that needed to be resolved. She did not want to treat the Americans as second-class citizens since she knew their acceptance of whatever command structure was put in place was vital to the success of the venture. How to deal with issues of seniority was one such issue.

On the technical side of things, the biggest issue was computer system architecture and language. To be most effective, the combined ships needed to communicate with one another. Roberts realized that one of the American planets might have a better computer set-up than the Royal Navy's, so she left that open-ended.

While she was working on those details, the prime minister and foreign secretary were in deep discussion about how wide-ranging the agreement would be. It was tempting for them to think about linking the defense agreement to trade concessions. While they were meeting, the prime minister's personal assistant buzzed them. "King William is here, sir," she whispered. "What should I do?"

"Send him in," Suffield replied.

King William VIII had taken a keen interest in politics, though he was unabashedly non-partisan. He had worked closely with the Conservative government before and was just as involved now that the Liberal Democrats were in power. Suffield had jokingly asked him early on whose side the king was on. "The Commonwealth's" was William's answer.

Both men rose to greet the king, as was customary. He quickly waved them back to their seats and asked what had them squirreled away. He had tried to reach both of them and been told they were unexpectedly unavailable. Sensing that something was happening, he decided to pay them a visit.

MacArthur explained to the king the call he had received from President Martin of New Boston. Suffield then related what other things they might extract from the Americans in exchange for this treaty. William gave the slightest frown when he heard this. Suffield caught a brief glimpse of his expression and stated, "You have a problem with this, Your Highness?"

"I was just thinking if situations were reversed," William replied, "how we would feel about other conditions being placed upon us. I doubt we'd be too happy, even though the conditions might not be so onerous as to make us forego an agreement. It might make future cooperation more difficult, though."

"What would you suggest?" MacArthur asked, knowing that the king would offer his opinion regardless.

"Treat them like family," the king offered. "In fact, treat them like the prodigal son. Welcome them into an alliance."

"May I ask why?" Suffield inquired.

"A great American, Benjamin Franklin, once said, 'We must join or die.' The Rodinans and Chinese are obviously on an aggressive program of expansion. We could not stop them if they came after us. But, with the resources of the Americans, we ourselves are stronger. If we make it an attractive proposition to join us, perhaps some of the other Americans may follow suit. I'd think that is something worth more than a few concessions."

3

While the king had no real authority to dictate public policy, both men recognized the common sense of his proposal. After he left the room, they drafted the basic structure of the agreement. They waited on Admiral Roberts for her part, which came that evening.

The next morning, MacArthur and Suffield contacted the three American heads of state and submitted their proposal. After reviewing the broad terms of the agreement, Chychlyk of Alleghany asked, "No strings?"

"No strings?" Suffield queried, not understanding what Chychlyk was asking.

"No strings attached," Chychlyk explained, "no trade concessions, no leverage, no other hidden items?"

"No," Suffield responded.

"You're kidding, right?" Sally Martin, president of New Boston, commented.

"Someone told me yesterday that Benjamin Franklin once said, 'We must join or die.' This seems to be a time when that statement might hold true," MacArthur replied. "Avalon is only a hop, skip, and a jump away from the Chinese and the Rodinans. Caerleon is right next to it. We are all stronger together."

"So, if I've got this right," Harry Monroe of Carolina said, "the only issues relate to integration of our ships into your fleet—systems compatibility, for instance. We're leaving the patrol boats out of it."

"That's right," MacArthur confirmed. "You use your patrol boats the same way we do—similar to what on earth was called a coast guard in the wet navy days. We don't see any reason to pull them off their regular duties. Of course, there might be times in the future where they can act as scouts and such but that's in the future."

"Hell, I'll issue the orders as soon as we get off the call," Monroe cracked. "Can you get me the contact info for your Admiral Roberts?"

"That's one of the first items on her list," MacArthur reminded, "setting up kewpie links with your ships."

Kewpie referred to Quantum Particle Communications devices that enabled instant communication regardless of distance, provided both quantum particles were in "normal" space and not hyperspace. These systems had been called kewpies almost from the moment they were invented.

"The quickest way to establish that is to have your ships come here to Caerleon as quickly as you can arrange it. But, in the meantime, we can route communication through these kewpie links," MacArthur said.

"How about you, Sally, Steve?" Monroe asked. "Is this going to work for you?"

"Shouldn't be a problem," Chychlyk responded.

"Same here," Martin agreed.

Three weeks later, the last American ship from the three planets, RNBS *Knox*, arrived in the Caerleon system. Admiral Roberts and the American captains worked their way through the biggest issues of integrating the ships into one coherent fighting force over the next month. She could see that the Americans initially had a bit of a chip on their shoulders. Some of those feelings were dispelled quickly when she pointed out that Captain McIntyre of Carolina's RCS *Raleigh* was second to her in terms of time in rank and would take command of the joint force if she were incapacitated during a battle. The rest of those negative feelings were dispelled by her competence at every turn.

Once they solved as many integration issues as they could on paper, she led the combined force through joint maneuvers and began conducting computer-simulated exercises against potential foes. This uncovered more problems which they worked to fix quickly. It also disclosed some weak links in command of American and Royal Navy ships.

Roberts started trying to address those on her end first. She met with the First Space Lord, the cabinet minister in charge of inter-planetary defense. She pointed out three of her captains who were incompetent and asked for the authority to replace them. The First Space Lord hemmed and hawed but would not give her an answer. She then asked to bring the prime minister into the discussion. The First Space Lord seemed reluctant to do so. Finally, she pointed out that she would involve the prime minister regardless, with or without him. The First Space Lord grudgingly agreed to contact the prime minister.

"Prime minister," First Space Lord Robert Hamilton began, "I have Admiral Roberts in my office, and she simply insists on speaking with you."

"Then put her on the line, Bob," Suffield responded.

"Prime Minister," Robert s commenced, "in conducting exercises, I have identified six captains who are clearly not suited for command of a ship at war. Three of them are Royal Navy, and three are Americans. I need them all replaced as soon as possible, like yesterday, and thought it would be better if we cleaned our own house first before we asked the Americans to do the same. Unfortunately, Mr. Hamilton would not grant me the authority to make those changes."

"Who are the captains?" Suffield asked.

"Ours? Or the Americans?" Roberts asked.

"All of them," he responded.

She gave him the list of names and their ships. He winced at hearing one of the Royal Navy captains, Captain Emily Lutella. He rubbed his forehead and nodded.

"You have the authority to replace the three of ours. So, Bob, find some meaningless job in administration for Lutella. Don't worry about the other two."

"Thank you, prime minister," Roberts said.

"Thank you for bringing this to my attention," Suffield sighed. "I'll have Ryan MacArthur contact the Americans."

Roberts had already identified qualified replacements for the three Royal Navy captains she was tossing. However, it took the better part of two weeks for the three American captains to be replaced. As she had suspected with Captain Lutella, the three American captains were politically connected, and some backroom negotiation needed to take place before the changes were made. After the new commanders were installed, she planned more drills, simulations, and exercises. Her early assessment of the new commanders was that they all were at least competent.

Five weeks after making the changes, two Rodinan *Navarin*-class cruisers winked into normal space in the Carolina system, followed by three *Levchenko*-class destroyers. Troop transports accompanied them and began off-loading soldiers three days later. Speaker Monroe and Deputy Speaker Johnson went to a secure location. They advised the inhabitants of Carolina not to resist the Rodinans but to cooperate as little as possible.

It was the middle of the night. A shrill alert tone from her comm unit and the console outside her quarters woke Admiral Roberts. She rose from her bunk and entered her ready room. Sitting down in front of the console, she activated it and accessed the message that triggered the alert.

It was a bulletin informing her of the arrival of the Rodinan ships in the Carolina system. She rubbed her eyes and reviewed the ships available to her. By the time we get there, she thought, they'll reinforce. With that in mind, she determined a force of four cruisers and eight destroyers would be necessary to evict the Rodinans.

Along with her flagship, HMS *Lavall*, she selected the three American cruisers and five destroyers. She added HMS *Enfield*, HMS *Mascoma*, and HMS *Canaan* to the force. That left the remainder of the Royal Navy as the reserve. She checked the astrographics briefly. It would take eleven days for the combined force to arrive in Carolina. She issued the orders to the twelve ships.

On the seventh day of the trip, Roberts received word from the foreign secretary. MacArthur passed along the news that the Carolinians reported the Rodinans had reinforced their ships in Carolina, adding another cruiser and two more destroyers. That brought their numbers to three cruisers and five destroyers. Roberts congratulated herself mildly on her excellent guess regarding the Rodinan numbers. She felt confident she was bringing a strong enough force to Carolina.

On Tuesday, December 5, 2479, Admiral Roberts led the combined force into the Carolina system. The hyper corridor dropped them into the system twenty-six degrees below the ecliptic. The Rodinans were waiting for them, about halfway between that corridor exit and the inhabited planet, Carolina-2.

After reviewing the disposition of forces, Roberts made a minor adjustment to her formation. She ordered her four cruisers into a tight group in the center, with the eight destroyers in a ring around them. The ships were abreast of one another, approaching the Rodinans in unison, traveling at the customary 0.23*c* or twenty-three percent of light speed.

As they moved further into the system, they could determine the Rodinans' course and speed. Roberts ordered her force to decelerate. The slower pace would delay the beginning of the battle but would lengthen the time the enemies were in range of both missiles and railguns. She also communicated the adjustments necessary to intercept the Rodinan ships.

When the Rodinans picked up her change in speed, they began boosting towards her. Roberts responded by slowing her force still further. With the greater weight of armament, a more prolonged engagement suited her purposes. The Rodinans, on the contrary, would prefer to shorten the time they were in range and hope to get lucky on their first pass. If they did and knocked some of the Commonwealth and American ships out of the fight, they might even the odds. As it was shaping up, the closing rate between the two forces would provide only enough time for both sides to fire a single salvo of missiles at each other. The railguns would be in range for only a few seconds. Based on the rate of fire, even a difference of seconds was worth working for.

From the moment she entered the Carolina system, it would take thirty-one hours for the two fleets to come within range. Roberts' combined force was still slowing, while the Rodinans were still accelerating. She recalled reading a quote from an officer of the Royal Navy in the age of sail on earth, "Hours of anticipation culminating in a few seconds of fury." The aptness of the description made her smile.

As the two groups of ships neared missile range, the closing rate between the two groups was 0.18*c*. Roberts saw that the Rodinan ships would be within range of the Commonwealth and American railguns for under twenty-eight seconds. That would be enough time to fire the 155mm railguns nearly fifty times. Over such a great distance, at the maximum range one and a half million kilometers, firing fifty shots might produce only one hit, particularly since the enemy would be engaging in evasive action.

As soon as they reached the maximum range, the railguns in both forces began to fire. Sensors aboard HMS *Lavall* indicated the Rodinans had also fired their ship-killing antimatter missiles. Roberts chose a different strategy. Since there was only enough time for one salvo, her orders were to fire when the range would be its shortest, giving the Rodinans less time to try to knock her missiles out. Both sides began ECM, or electronic counter-measures, to fool enemy missiles.

When the incoming missiles closed to within five hundred thousand kilometers, the smaller 40mm railguns began spitting out shells to try to shoot and destroy the projectiles. Shortly after that, the point-defense lasers began stabbing into space, seeking to destroy the incoming missiles. The Rodinans had fired sixty-eight missiles. The Commonwealth and American force fired ninety-six in return. Admiral Roberts watched this from the observer's chair on the bridge of HMS *Lavall*, wearing the uncomfortable shipsuit and helmet required during combat. She watched as the display showed the red lines of enemy missiles and green and blue lines of the missiles fired by her force.

Her ships' various counter-measures led thirty-five of the Rodinan missiles astray. One-by-one other red tracks disappeared from the display as the 40mm anti-missile defense railguns and point-defense lasers found targets. Only one Rodinan missile survived, hitting RNBS *Ticonderoga* on the port bow. The antimatter warhead detonated, obliterating most of the front third of the ship. The larger railguns employed by the Rodinans also scored some hits, causing minor hull breaches on every ship in her force.

The green and blue tracks of her own missiles had more success. Thirty-eight were led awry by counter-measures, which left fifty-eight for the Rodinan anti-missile defenses. The Rodinan railgun and laser defenses eliminated another forty-nine missiles, leaving nine untouched. Those nine missiles slammed into the three Rodinan cruisers and three of their five destroyers.

Roberts watched the sensor blooms on her display when the missiles hit. A few minutes later, detailed scans showed her that two Rodinan cruisers and one destroyer were largely demolished, with only chunks of metal drifting through space. The other Rodinan cruiser was missing most of its stern. A destroyer was broken in half, and the other destroyer hit by a missile imploded because its mass compensator was knocked out. The mass of the ship increased exponentially in an instant. Scans also showed that the 155mm railguns of the combined force made hits on the surviving two Rodinan destroyers.

Both sides were now out of range. The British and American ships continued to decelerate. The two surviving Rodinan ships adjusted course, heading for the hyper corridor that would lead them back to the Roosevelt system, which the Rodinans controlled. For the time being, they abandoned the sixty thousand Rodinan troops on the surface of Carolina. Roberts watched with frustration as the Rodinan ships pulled away since she had no way of cutting them off.

She watched as damage control reports began appearing on her display. Her force had suffered one hundred and thirty-two dead, most from *Ticonderoga*, with another forty-seven wounded, primarily from the hull breaches caused by hits from the Rodinan railguns. Search and rescue operations were already underway, looking for any who might have survived from the bow of *Ticonderoga* and for any Rodinans floating in space or still trapped on the remnants of the ships that were still drifting outward.

Roberts ordered her force to set course for an orbit of the planet Carolina. RNBS *Ticonderoga* was, amazingly, able to match course and speed with the rest of the force. She would need to spend considerable time in a shipyard, though, before she would be able to return to battle. Roberts sent a message back to the Admiralty indicating the mission had been successful and also a message to Speaker Monroe wherever he was hiding.

4

Speaker Harry Monroe received the message from Admiral Roberts with great satisfaction. Immediately he ordered messages to be broadcast planet-wide to the Rodinan forces urging their surrender. In less than thirty-six hours, the Commonwealth and American ships would be in orbit and have the ability to drop kinetic weapons on the Rodinans. Their position was no longer tenable, and continued resistance would be unwise. Within an hour, he received a message from the Rodinan general, wishing to discuss surrender terms.

Before Admiral Roberts left the bridge to begin her after-action report, she issued orders to a group of freighters that had been waiting for her instructions before proceeding into the Carolina system. The freighters were carrying hundreds of anti-ship mines. Roberts knew a counter-attack by the Rodinans was probable, so she planned to lay those mines at the hyper corridor entrance as a defense against any Rodinan incursion into the Carolina system.

Foreign Secretary MacArthur was unprepared for the deluge of calls he received the next day. All the heads of state of the remaining fourteen American planets contacted him, all inquiring whether they could be added as signatories of the treaty signed with Carolina, New Boston, and Alleghany. When MacArthur was unavailable due to being on a call, seven attempted to bypass him and contacted the prime minister directly. Then, at three o'clock that afternoon, both men received a message inviting them to dine with King William VIII that evening.

At the end of a very long and extraordinary day, MacArthur had just enough time to splash some water on his face before meeting Suffield to go to the palace. Suffield informed him of the conversations he'd had with the heads of state who had reached him, and MacArthur confirmed that he had spoken to all of them by that time. Moreover, MacArthur confirmed they all made the same request.

"Do you think William knows?" MacArthur asked, "and that's why we're invited to dinner.

Suffield laughed. "He knows. I'm not sure how but I'm certain he knows."

The two men arrived at the palace and were shown to a dining room. King William VIII greeted them and offered them some refreshments. Both declined, citing the long day they'd had. They sat down to dinner.

"I understand," the king began, "that you've heard from the other Americans."

"Yes, Your Highness, we have," Suffield responded.

"Lewis, Ryan," the king stated, "for the remainder of dinner can we drop the formality and be casual, like Americans? Please just call me William."

"Yes, Your ... William," Suffield responded with a stutter, chuckling to cover his embarrassment.

"Good. And the other Americans wanted?"

"They wanted to be permitted to sign the same treaty as the three," MacArthur confirmed.

"Good. Will you allow them to do so?"

"We haven't had the opportunity to discuss it yet," Suffield replied.

"Then let's discuss it," William suggested.

Neither of the two was really quite prepared to do this. Both thought the king's active interest was unusual. The king read their expressions and chuckled softly.

"Surprised I'm sticking my nose in it, are we?"

"Well, yes, I am, William," Suffield commented.

"Remember when you asked me whose side I was on," the king reminded, "and I told you I was on the Commonwealth's side? That hasn't changed. I wish I could claim that I predicted this would happen—that the other Americans would contact us and ask to join the agreement—but I didn't. I felt that if we handled it properly, though, we might create the possibility of something like that taking place. It happened much more quickly, though, than I would have guessed."

"Why do you think they changed their minds so quickly?" MacArthur asked. "This came about because of their unwillingness to allow their ships out of their own systems."

"Because we won," Suffield answered. "At least we won this round."

"That's a part of it," the king weighed in. "Another part of it is trust."

"What do you mean?" MacArthur asked.

"Even though they have had this 'Alliance' for quite some time," the king explained, "I don't think the agreement was built on trust—it was built on fear and necessity. Remember, the different American planets were settled by competing private interests. They have always competed fiercely among themselves. They still do. None of them were willing to trust their ships, built at great expense, to one of their rivals. Each of them assumed that, if they did, their ships would be misused or sacrificed by one of their competitors since they would have done the same thing to gain a competitive advantage."

"That's quite a callous view," Suffield commented.

"Perhaps even cynical," the king agreed, "nonetheless, I believe it to be true."

"Then why would they agree to join us," MacArthur asked, "when they wouldn't join with their fellows?"

"If you are a student of history, you would know that their situation calls for compromise. Unfortunately, their fixation on competition between themselves rules that out. None of their heads of state is enough of a leader or has enough stature to be able to weld competitive interests together. They need a George Washington, and they don't have one."

"Wasn't he the one who instigated the rebellion of the Americans against British rule around a thousand years ago?" MacArthur asked.

The king chuckled. "Not exactly. He led their army, and when the war of rebellion ended, he served as their first president, but he did not instigate the uprising. America was thirteen separate colonies, much like the American systems are nineteen different planets now. Among the American colonies, there were two very different interest groups. The northern colonies were traders and were beginning to become centers of manufacturing. The southern colonies were primarily agricultural, with landowners owning large tracts that were worked by slaves.

"The northern colonies were much more eager to separate from Britain, and if you want to find the 'instigators' of the rebellion, that's where they were. The wealthy landowners in the southern colonies resented how they felt the mother country took advantage of them in terms of lending practices, but the smaller farmers really didn't care. The northerners did not trust that the southerners were as committed to rebellion, which was likely true. All the colonies had local volunteer soldiers—militias—that they had formed. They were extremely reluctant to allow their soldiers to serve under the command of someone from a different colony."

"Sounds familiar," MacArthur commented.

"How did they resolve this lack of trust?" Suffield asked.

"One of the primary instigators of rebellion, a northerner, proposed that command of the army formed from the combined militias be given to a southerner, George Washington. It was a brilliant compromise, both in who proposed it and the person he named. It strengthened the commitment of the southerners since one of their own was the commander-in-chief. It calmed the fears of the northerners who were unwilling to give command to someone they viewed as a competitor. Washington was respected by those who knew him. He had military experience. He was physically an imposing figure—he looked like a commander-in-chief—and he was somewhat dull and not a rabble-rouser."

"And the American planets don't have that sort of compromise candidate," Suffield suggested.

"No, they don't," MacArthur stated. "That I can state unequivocally."

"But why would they choose us?" Suffield asked.

"We don't represent a competitive threat," the king stated. "They see us as something 'other,' and we're bigger than any of them individually, though not so much larger as to be frightening. We're not so different as to be alien or strange because we share a common language and culture but different in the sense of not being a part of the competition among themselves. We're an impartial third party. How Admiral Roberts handled that business with the captains is a great example. We cleaned our house before we asked them to do the same."

"She also ensured the three American groups were represented in the action at Carolina," Suffield said.

"Yes, she did," the king concurred, "and from my limited understanding, though one of the American ships took the most severe damage, it was a 'luck of the draw' situation and not her putting an American ship in a more dangerous position than a Commonwealth ship—something I'm sure all the American commanders relayed back home."

"So, we're their compromise candidate," Suffield concluded.

"We're the compromise candidate," MacArthur stated, finally understanding the king's concept, "because we didn't ask for anything in return. So that's why they all want in now."

"I was already leaning towards allowing them to join the arrangement," Suffield stated, "but now I understand better why."

"So, you want me to approve adding them all in?" MacArthur inquired.

"Yes," Suffield confirmed, "but everyone signs the same deal as everyone else."

"You realize that Admiral Roberts is going to need some help?" the king suggested.

Suffield sighed heavily. "I hadn't thought that far ahead. This only came up today."

"I'd recommend keeping the headquarters of the operation here on Caerleon," the king stated. "I'd also suggest you pull her off the bridge of her ship. She's shown a deft hand at managing this, and we can't afford to lose her. With the number of ships that will be added, we have enough to divide into two or three task forces that we can assign to different sectors. Keep her in overall command but promote some people below her to fight the battles. Name a Commonwealth officer to replace her but as you move along, look for the best of the Americans to promote—and only based on merit. I don't want to hear about another Captain Lutella."

"You heard about that?" Suffield asked.

William gave a sly smile. "In an opportunity like this, you'll find that there is very little that happens that escapes my notice. I would suggest that you avoid promoting officers to settle political debts for the duration of this conflict."

5

The next few weeks were a maelstrom of headaches for Admiral Regina Roberts. She was pulled from the bridge of HMS *Lavall* and reassigned to a desk in a government office building on Caerleon. She had to oversee the integration of twelve American cruisers and twenty-six American destroyers into the combined fleet. The combined fleet now had nineteen cruisers and forty-three destroyers. She had to determine where best to deploy those ships to counter potential threats from the Rodinans and Chinese.

Making things more difficult was the astrography. If Admiral Roberts were to split the fleet into three task forces, besides Caerleon, the logical places to locate them centrally would be in the Lincoln and Roosevelt systems. Since that was impossible, she decided her next best option would be to split the fleet in half, with one half based in Caerleon and the other in the Aries system, even though Aries was early in its development.

She was also dealing with the problems of integrating the new ships into the combined force. Their computer systems needed to be changed, kewpie pairs needed to be exchanged, and all the issues they had uncovered with the first group of American ships were now quadrupled. To begin with, she had no staff to assist her. Only after bypassing the First Space Lord and appealing directly to the prime minister was she given the authority to hire the people she needed. She breathed a huge sigh of relief when the prime minister replaced the First Space Lord with someone competent, Wes Stevens. Stevens had run one of the largest corporations in Commonwealth space and had retired just two years before.

Prime Minister Suffield made a personal appeal to him to get him to join the government.

Once Wes Stevens was in charge, her organization began to grow rapidly. She and Stevens had several meetings when he first took over, and he understood what Roberts needed to do, even when she didn't quite realize the next step. Stevens also grasped that the qualities that made an excellent commander at the helm of a ship did not necessarily transfer to a job managing, say, logistics. So, Stevens also took the lead on replacing the handful of incompetent commanders they'd identified on the American ships that had joined the combined force more recently.

Six months after Stevens became First Space Lord, in July of 2480, he suggested to her that it was time to split the fleet. She discussed her misgivings about setting up three task forces, and he deferred to her judgment. She had earlier promoted Archie MacDonald from HMS *Sussex* to rear admiral as her replacement when she was promoted, and she now needed to pick another candidate.

Fortunately, by this time, she had the results of four months of joint operations with all the Americans. When she sat down to go over candidates, there was one who clearly stood out. Akil Brown was clearly the best though he came from a planet, Ithaca, with only two destroyers to contribute to the fleet. He did not have as much time in rank as some other candidates, but the results of the drills and combat simulations showed he stood out.

When she sat down with Wes Stevens to discuss the promotion, she pointed out several potential problems, including time in rank. The biggest problem was that Brown commanded a destroyer, and his planet had no cruisers. She felt a rear admiral needed to be on a cruiser. She didn't know how she would be able to convince any of the Americans to allow Brown to use one of their cruisers as his flagship.

"Then don't," Stevens told her.

"What?"

"Don't go to the Americans. Put him on one of ours," Stevens said. "You told me an admiral doesn't fight his own ship, right?"

"Right…" she said slowly, not understanding Stevens' point.

"Brown will be in command of a task force, based either here or in Aries. I agree he should be on a cruiser. However, this is a combined force, so put him on one of our cruisers."

"Oh," she said, realizing his point, "I gotcha."

"Now the question is, here or Aries," Stevens stated. "Which is more likely to see action in the next few months?"

"Aries," Roberts replied without hesitation. "They are ideally positioned to intercept either the Rodinans or the Chinese going to or from Lincoln and Roosevelt."

"Put him there," Stevens said. "That shows we have confidence in our allies and does not make it look like we're trying to grab all the glory."

"But what about those who would think we were just putting him in harm's way?"

"He's on our ship," Stevens said.

The announcement of the promotion of Akil Brown went over with mixed results. Some of the American planets with captains more senior in date of rank complained, but when Admiral Roberts shared the criteria by which she made the decision, the grumbling faded. The combined fleet was split, with the Blue Task Force under Brown stationed in the Aries system and the Red Task Force under Archie MacDonald based in Caerleon.

Brown's group immediately began to show results. From the Aries system, Brown was positioned to be able to intercept shipments to or from Roosevelt and Lincoln. After the Blue Task Force intercepted the first Chinese freighter, the Rodinans and Chinese avoided Aries. Brown responded by splitting his ships up and sending them into neighboring systems through which the Chinese and Rodinans would need to travel to reach their new conquests. Brown kept his ships on the move between systems.

His luck changed when the Rodinans and Chinese began escorting their cargo ships with destroyers. His previous command, the destroyer RIS *Telemachus*, was poised to intercept in system H2820. However, when the Rodinan freighters appeared, with three Rodinan destroyers escorting them, Brown ordered *Telemachus* not to engage. Afterward, Brown sent a message to Admiral Roberts requesting patrol boats to use as scouts. When the same thing happened with a Chinese convoy in system H2798, he made the request again, despite having not heard back from Roberts on his first request. If he'd had advance notice of how many escorts were accompanying the Chinese or Rodinan freighters, he could have positioned his ships to oppose their passage.

Admiral Roberts had been frustrated with Brown's requests. She could see the value of having patrol boats scouting but the agreement with the Americans excluded patrol boats. So, she went to Wes Stevens with her problem.

Stevens thought for a moment after she explained how useful the patrol boats would be. "Use ours," he stated a few moments later.

"But that will leave us wide open," she countered immediately. "Why can't I ask the Americans? They have all the patrol boats from Lincoln and Roosevelt…"

Stevens cut her off by raising his hand. "Issue a general order to use ours," he repeated, "and make sure the order states that the patrol boat responsible for providing information leading to a successful convoy interception will share in any prize money from the capture of enemy cargo. Naturally, the Americans will demand that they be included."

Roberts issued the order. Stevens ensured that the foreign secretary and prime minister knew what Roberts had done. Within seventy-two hours, the Americans had agreed to put their patrol boats under Commonwealth command.

Three weeks later, the patrol boat stationed in system H2804 signaled that a Chinese convoy was heading from the Chinese Múxīng system towards system H2798. The convoy was escorted by two destroyers. Admiral Brown had enough time to dispatch the cruiser *Ohio* and three destroyers to intercept the Chinese in system H2798.

Captain Jennifer Giersch aboard *Ohio* smiled in satisfaction. Along with the destroyers *Patterson*, *McIntyre*, and *Garza*, she arrived in system H2798 with enough time to cut the incoming Chinese convoy off. She had been able to position her force so the Chinese could not avoid them and would not be able to escape to another system without going through them. Her instructions to the other captains were clear. They were to target the two Chinese 162-type destroyers and leave the freighters alone. They would seize the freighters and take them away to prize court, where they and their contents would be auctioned off.

Right on schedule, the Chinese ships winked into normal space. Giersch began broadcasting a demand to surrender, which would reach them a few minutes later due to the distance. About the time the Chinese would have received the message, sensors showed her how they were planning to respond. The two 162-type destroyers began to change course and accelerate towards her force. At the same time, the freighters frantically tried to decelerate in the hopes of returning to safety.

Giersch had plotted her position carefully and the freighters had no hope of escape. She ordered her force to begin to close with the approaching Chinese destroyers. It would take several hours for them to come within range.

When the Chinese warships reached missile range, they fired eight ship-killer missiles at her ship. Her force returned fire with twenty-eight. Three Chinese missiles were led astray, and the other five were blasted from the sky by the point-defense railguns and lasers. Of her missiles, thirteen went off-course, and eight were eliminated by the Chinese defenses. That still left seven. Three hit one destroyer and four the other. All that was left were two expanding clouds of debris.

Casualties were minor: two dead and eleven wounded due to a handful of Chinese railgun shots. Giersch ordered her ships to close with the Chinese freighters and ordered the Chinese to continue to decelerate until they reached a dead stop and then stand fast. She assigned prize crews to take over the enemy ships, accompanied by marines who would keep the Chinese crews under lock and key.

The most challenging part would be the reinstallation of the computer controls necessary to fly the ships. Standard practice for a surrendering ship was to sabotage the operating system, making it more difficult to fly the ship away. Fortunately, one area where the Americans had a significant advantage was computer science. This would be a delay of at most a couple of hours.

6

As the year 2480 came to a close, the success enjoyed by the combined forces of the Commonwealth and the American planets encouraged them to discuss the liberation of Lincoln and Roosevelt. Based on intelligence, they knew how many ships were stationed in each system. The Chinese and Rodinans had moved over one-third of their navies into the captured systems. When he heard that the politicians were bickering over the issue, Wes Stevens, the First Space Lord, made an appointment to meet with the prime minister and foreign secretary.

After exchanging greetings, Stevens jumped right to the point. "Keep the politicians out of it," he urged. "It's a military problem. Let the military decide the best course of action. The politicians have stayed out of it until now, and things have been going well. Besides, doesn't the treaty say we get to call the shots?"

"It does," Ryan MacArthur, the foreign secretary replied, "but in something of this magnitude, the different heads of state—"

"Sorry, Ryan, but that's crap," Stevens interrupted. "Is it, or is it not, a military problem?"

"It's a military problem," Lewis Suffield, the prime minister, stated, "we don't disagree."

"Fine," Stevens continued. "Now, here's another military problem: suppose we liberate the two planets. What happens after that? Is the treaty over?"

"I suppose—" Suffield guessed.

"This is the bigger issue," Stevens commented. "I have no doubt that we can liberate Lincoln and Roosevelt. It's what happens after that which concerns me most. What will prevent the Rodinans or Chinese from returning immediately and doing it again? MI-6 estimates that both have embarked on fairly aggressive shipbuilding campaigns. If the treaty ends and the Americans revert to what they were doing, it puts us all at risk. Ask your Americans if they are willing to go through this again."

"What are you driving at, Wes?" MacArthur asked.

"I have a couple of things I'm driving at," Stevens explained. "First, we must embark on a shipbuilding campaign in concert with the Americans. I hate to say it, but we're going to be in an arms race. If we don't work together, we're screwed. Second, if we continue to work together, these ships can't just return to their home systems. We need to keep them where they are now. In fact, Roosevelt and Lincoln are ideally positioned as places where I would like to base a task force. As Aries, York, Southampton, New Glasgow, and the other recently-settled planets become self-sustaining, we'd probably want to keep the base in Aries and add one in Southampton.

"You need to talk to these politicians and convince them to keep their fingers out of the pudding and, after you do that, you need them to understand that the treaty is just beginning and not ending," Stevens summarized.

Suffield and MacArthur spent a great deal of time in video conferences with the different American heads of state. The three original chief executives, Chychlyk, Martin, and Monroe, were of great assistance. Convincing the rest of the Americans was more difficult. Chychlyk was the first to point out that some of the executives were planning that they would annex the newly-liberated Lincoln and Roosevelt systems and add them to their own. He shared some surveillance recordings that captured four other American heads of state discussing with their subordinates plans for annexation.

Chychlyk refused to provide the recordings since it would reveal from whom he had received the information. However, he provided written transcripts of the conversations. Suffield contacted each of the four executives, threatening to make their plans public knowledge amongst the rest of the group and the public. All of them attempted to deny it at first. When Suffield provided portions of written transcripts, three of the four yielded somewhat, admitting that there had been some "brainstorming" in their offices. Suffield demanded that such "brainstorming" cease immediately.

The fourth chief executive, Helen Bonham of Washington, was resolute in her denial. She refused to admit anything and accused Suffield of lying. Suffield passed the information back to Chychlyk. The next day, copies of the written transcripts appeared in the leading news media not just on her home planet of Washington but on all the American planets. By the end of the week, the Washington legislature had begun impeachment proceedings. This effectively ended the attempts by the chief executives to influence the military planning regarding the liberation of Lincoln and Roosevelt.

Suffield chose a different method to approach the continuance of the treaty. He asked Admiral Roberts to speak with the captains of the American ships to evaluate their willingness to work together in the future. All agreed that the combined force was significantly more effective militarily than returning to individual planetary forces. Moreover, all felt the way the forces had been combined and managed had been without bias and all expressed confidence in Admiral Roberts' leadership.

Armed with this information, Suffield and MacArthur then began discussions with the different heads of state to gain their assurance that they would not withdraw from the treaty once Lincoln and Roosevelt were liberated. Some tried to argue that, although the Treaty of Caerleon (as it was now known) did not specify an ending date or circumstance, it was understood that the end of this crisis would also bring about the lack of need to continue the arrangement.

With the more obstinate executives, Suffield shared the confidential assessment prepared by the Commonwealth's MI-6 spy agency, showing that the Rodinans had begun constructing six new cruisers and fourteen new destroyers. While he did not have the same information from the Chinese Republics, Suffield pointed out that they would probably attempt to keep pace with the Rodinans.

By mid-May of 2481, Suffield and MacArthur had received guarantees from the different Americans that they would continue as partners in the Treaty of Caerleon. Even more promising, negotiations had begun on a joint shipbuilding program. At the same time, planning on the military side continued.

Admiral Roberts had met with her two admirals, Brown and MacDonald. All three agreed that the best way to liberate the two planets would be to conduct simultaneous attacks on each. If they chose to attack one before the other, both admirals believed it was likely that the occupier of the other system would call for reinforcements and make the battle more costly.

They issued orders for each of the planets to contribute ten thousand ground troops—not because they expected significant fighting to take place once they had established control of space. On the contrary, the ground troops would be needed to gather and control the troops of the former occupiers before repatriating them and would also be playing a role in re-establishing civil order. Ground troops had been one of the issues that had been a sticking point with the heads of state before prime minister Suffield had resolved the situation.

With the planning complete, the date of the attack was set. July 4, 2481, would be the date Task Force Red would invade Lincoln, and Task Force Blue would invade Roosevelt. The Americans were happy about the significance of the date.

Admiral Brown was ready for the biggest day of his career. Sitting on the bridge of the cruiser HMS *Courageous*, his Blue Task Force of nine cruisers and twenty-three destroyers was about to emerge from hyperspace into the Roosevelt system. They would be exiting the hyper corridor early, anticipating that the Rodinans would have laid a substantial minefield near the entrance. Emerging as little as four light-minutes before the end of the corridor would give his ships time for their sensors to identify the mines and eliminate them using their defense railguns and lasers.

According to the latest intelligence, he would be facing six Rodinan cruisers and nine of their destroyers. He had planned, drilled, and practiced with his captains for weeks leading up to this engagement. He had thrown every wrinkle he could into the computer simulations and was confident his people were ready.

When Blue Task Force winked back into normal space, Brown waited anxiously for the sensor data to appear. Scans of the area where he expected mines were waiting would take eight minutes to come back. In the meantime, he looked to see where Rodinan ships were waiting. According to the sensors, the Rodinans were just outside the normal hyper corridor exit, where they would be within missile range if he had taken the corridor all the way to the end.

His ships were traveling at 0.23c, or twenty-three percent of light speed. He would be within range of the Rodinans in just under eleven minutes. He would need to defend against the Rodinan missiles at the same time as he expected to reach the minefield. That was one of the more complicated scenarios he had prepared his task force to face. He quickly activated the microphone in the helmet of his shipsuit.

"Blue Task Force, it seems the Rodinans want to try to make things difficult for us. Remember, we practiced against this same set of conditions before. Targeting parameters are already set. Godspeed people. I'll see you on the other side of this."

The clock ticked down. The scans they started when they emerged from hyperspace came back and indicated there was indeed a substantial minefield waiting for them. As Brown suspected, they would reach the edge of the field at the same time they would need to deal with the incoming missiles.

Before they reached the point in space that marked the end of the hyper corridor, the defense railguns and lasers began lashing out at the mines drifting in space. The Rodinan ships fired as soon as Brown's force came within missile range. Brown had programmed his launch to delay by nearly three minutes. Closing the distance before launching his missiles would give the Rodinans much less time to target them.

He watched the display light up with the red tracks of enemy missiles. Electronic jamming began to lead some of the one hundred thirty-two Rodinan ship-killer missiles off-target. A sensor bloom appeared as one of his ships, *Patterson*, a destroyer, hit a mine. The *Patterson's* computer immediately sent a damage report, indicating the starboard bow had been struck and sixteen compartments were no longer tied into the computer net—substantial damage.

More of the red tracks began to wander off-course. One-by-one, they began to disappear from the display as they were hit by railgun or laser fire. Of the one hundred thirty-two missiles the Rodinans fired, fifty-five went astray. Seventy-four were eliminated by the point-defense systems. Only three would survive to hit their targets. In the meantime, Blue Task Force fired their antimatter missiles, two hundred thirty-six in all. Given less time to employ counter-measures, the Rodinans were able to trick a smaller percentage of the Commonwealth and American missiles off-course. The Rodinan point-defense network had less time to react and find targets. One hundred and eight of the missiles survived to hit the Rodinan ships.

Brown watched the display. The three surviving Rodinan missiles hit the cruiser *Cairo* and the destroyers *Thomas* and *Kowalchik*. *Cairo* and *Kowalchik* suffered substantial damage. *Thomas* blew up when its reactors were hit and broke containment, releasing the power of two tiny suns. Two other ships—the cruisers *Galveston* and *Exeter*—hit mines before clearing the field. Of the Rodinan ships, nothing remained but expanding clouds of debris.

In the Lincoln system, Admiral Archie MacDonald had faced a similar scenario with similar results. He lost two ships—a cruiser and a destroyer—and had two cruisers and two destroyers that took substantial damage from either mines or missiles.

Both admirals began transmitting messages encouraging the surrender of the occupying forces on the planets, giving an estimated time of arrival for when the Commonwealth and American ground forces would be landing. Before either task force was established in orbit, messages were received by the resistance movements on both planets, urging the ground troops to arrive quickly as they were having trouble controlling the mobs of people seeking reprisal against the Rodinan or Chinese troops.

Less than a month after ground troops landed on Lincoln and Roosevelt, provisional governments were already in place. Within forty-eight hours of each other, the provisional governments of both Lincoln and Roosevelt sent petitions to the prime minister asking to be included in the Commonwealth. Upon receiving each request, Prime Minister Suffield and Ryan MacArthur contacted the leaders of the provisional governments. They asked them to conduct planet-wide referenda on the question.

The news leaked out, of course. Suffield and MacArthur fielded calls from the other American heads of state. Some were angry, accusing the Commonwealth of encouraging or fostering these petitions. Others were curious, trying to determine where the idea had come from. When Suffield and MacArthur both denied prior knowledge of the petitions, that information was received with a skeptical ear. Debate was attempted in both Houses of Parliament, but Suffield was able to table any discussion until the results of the referenda were known.

On Lincoln, the referendum was approved by seventy-three percent of the citizens who voted. On Roosevelt, sixty-nine percent approved. With these results in hand, the governments, no longer provisional, resubmitted their petitions to be allowed to join the Commonwealth. At this point, both Houses of Parliament began to debate the issue. Within a week, it was becoming clear the prevailing opinion was in favor of allowing the two planets to join the Commonwealth but not as full partners. Much of the debate began to focus on what restrictions would be placed on the new members. The prime minister was dismayed at how the debate was being framed.

At this point, King William VIII asked the prime minister for permission to address both houses. While the king theoretically had the right to do so whenever he pleased, it was customary to be formally invited. Suffield quickly agreed. The king's address was scheduled for Wednesday, September 3, 2481.

"My Lords and Members of the House of Commons, we have an opportunity without precedent before us. Two planets, having suffered invasion and subsequent occupation by foreign troops, have asked to join our Commonwealth. First and foremost, they seek that most fundamental human desire, safety. But beyond that, they see obvious economic advantages to joining our Commonwealth.

"None have questioned whether our Commonwealth would be stronger due to their inclusion—we can all see that they and we would be better off than we are today. We all see the benefits of adding their resources to ours. Yet our focus had been on trying to exploit their relative weakness. The discussion in both Houses about this matter has focused on what sort of restrictions to place on them as new members of our Commonwealth and what sort of temporary and permanent advantages we can extract from them as the price of joining us.

"What has been discussed is not a partnership but subjugation, not equality but servitude. What has been discussed is not the foundation for a long-lasting association but a guarantee of resentment. When we liberated Roosevelt and Lincoln from their foreign occupiers, did we ask for guarantees of material reward, or did we move forward because it was the right thing to do? If your neighbor's house were on fire, would you charge him to use your hose? If an acquaintance were attacked on the street, would you demand compensation before coming to his aid?

"These two planets have held referenda in which their citizens voted overwhelmingly to join our Commonwealth. They are already linked to us by a shared language and similar culture. They are our friends and neighbors. Centuries before, the two nations from which we sprang on earth enjoyed what was called a 'special relationship.' That 'special relationship' endured as a partnership of equals, not one of master and servant.

"If both parties benefit by joining, what other advantages are necessary? The Crown's position on the petitions from the planets of Roosevelt and Lincoln is that both should be admitted to our Commonwealth without delay. If they are willing to abide by our laws, there should be no further obstacle. Indeed, the Crown's position would be the same in the future if other planets wish to join us—an offer of inclusion for mutual benefit.

"My Lords and Members of the House of Commons, extend the hand of brotherhood to Lincoln and Roosevelt and to any others who follow their example. Welcome them to our Commonwealth. Add their strength to ours without reservation or qualification.

"May God bless our Commonwealth."

Led by the prime minister, a few of the leading Liberal Democrats from both Houses stood to applaud the king's speech. Others joined them, and shortly afterward, both houses were giving him a standing ovation. The king nodded in recognition, then left without ceremony.

The prime minister quickly introduced a resolution by which Lincoln and Roosevelt would be admitted to the Commonwealth, provided they adopted current Commonwealth laws, regulations, and electoral practices for the Commonwealth Parliament. They would be allowed to keep whatever form of planetary government they wished, but in matters of trade, currency, and foreign policy, they would be a part of the Commonwealth. They would be expected to contribute taxes on the same basis as the existing Commonwealth planets. It was passed with little dissent by both houses by the end of the day. That evening, the foreign secretary transmitted the formal offer to Lincoln and Roosevelt.

7

Over the next thirty-six years, one by one (and occasionally, two by two), the other American-settled planets joined the Commonwealth. Under the Treaty of Caerleon, the navies continued to work together. However, there had been issues between the members in terms of funding. Once everyone joined the Commonwealth, the combined forces were renamed the Royal Navy of the Inter-Planetary Commonwealth and solved those issues and many other lesser problems.

Now in his nineties, Wesley Stevens continued as First Space Lord. Admiral Regina Roberts had long since retired. One of the priorities Stevens insisted upon was an aggressive budget for research and development of new weapons. Military technology had not advanced since the beginning of the interstellar age, and he believed there were many opportunities for improvement.

Stevens finally stepped down at the age of ninety-six, handing the reins to Linda Marshall. Marshall continued Stevens' emphasis on research and development and made a breakthrough ten years later, in 2527. But unfortunately, the Rodinans and Chinese made the same discoveries within months of the Commonwealth. This generated a frenzy of activity within the MI-5 and MI-6 agencies. Both looked to see whether someone had leaked the Commonwealth's secrets.

In the Royal Navy, there was a division known as Advanced Warfare. The Director of Advanced Warfare was Nancy Filson. A physicist by training, Filson had been focused on the idea of being able to alter the shape of plasma shielding. Plasma shields, which made fusion reactors possible, had only been generated in hemispherical form. Putting two of them together made possible the containment of fusion reactions. Ships had long had a plasma shield generator on the ship's bow as a navigational aid. Traveling at speeds as great as 0.3c, or thirty percent of light-speed, impact from even a tiny piece of dust could be catastrophic. The plasma shields on the bow provided the front of ships with a hemisphere of protection from impacts.

Filson's intent was to be able to wrap plasma shielding around an entire ship. Since the invention of plasma shielding, little research had been devoted to the subject. Physicists generally believed no further refinements were possible. Filson refused to accept that. First Space Lord Marshall and Admiral of the Fleet Daniel Freshley supported Filson in her endeavors.

Before solving the problem of creating plasma shielding in a different shape, Filson learned that extending plasma shielding to cover an entire ship would require enormous power. While she moved ahead with the shielding issues, she also convinced the First Space Lord to divert some funding into scholarships and fellowships for graduate students in the field of nuclear engineering. The area of nuclear engineering had become un-sexy to scientists. It was no longer attracting the best and brightest young minds. She hoped the increase in funding would attract some students to the field who might have chosen other areas of study.

Filson was fortunate that two students, at opposite ends of the Commonwealth, decided to take advantage of the increased funding for nuclear engineering that the First Space Lord authorized. Nate Naginata and Bill Guisarme, at Roosevelt and Southhampton, respectively, began pursuing the problem of reactor efficiency. They learned of one another when their dissertations were published. They met when they came to Caerleon to interview with Filson for jobs.

Filson hired them both and assigned them to work together. The results astounded even her most optimistic hopes. Less than six months after being hired, the two men came to her with a new design that would produce nearly double the energy from existing reactors. Naginata and Guisarme's innovation focused on transferring energy from within the plasma containment sphere to outside. As they moved forward, building a prototype, she urged them not to stop there. She suspected subsequent developments in weapons and shielding would require even more power.

Over the next five years, her team focused on trying to create plasma shields in shapes other than circles. Finally, on August 13, 2527, they formed plasma shielding in a paraboloid shape. By the end of the year, Advanced Warfare had designed plasma shield generators that could enclose a ship from bow to stern with overlapping elliptic paraboloid shielding. Filson's team tested the shielding and found it was entirely invulnerable to antimatter warheads and railgun projectiles. The one area of weakness was the stern. The overlapping paraboloids of the shields could not protect against an attack from directly behind a ship.

Another part of Advanced Warfare concentrated on weapons development. Since the plasma shielding was totally effective against projectiles and antimatter weapons, the Commonwealth needed something that would be able to penetrate that shielding. Director Filson did not delude herself that the Commonwealth was more forward-thinking than the Rodinans and Chinese. They were likely working to solve the same set of problems.

The only successful way to break through plasma shielding was to overwhelm it with energy. The energy build-up would then reverse the flow of the plasma, like reversing the flow of a river, sending it back into the shield generator and burning it out. The first concept Advanced Warfare delivered was a plasma torpedo. These torpedoes were twelve times the size of the current antimatter missiles—almost the size of a small ship. They were easily identified by existing defense sensors and would be eliminated quickly by railgun and laser defenses.

A young man named Adrian Wowk was one of the initial designers in the earliest stages of the photon torpedo project. However, he became disillusioned when the leaders of the design team became enthralled with the idea of breaking down the shields with a single shot. Wowk remembered his grandfather's advice when he was overwhelmed with work. "How do you eat an elephant?" his grandfather had asked. "One bite at a time," was the answer.

Rather than try to cause critical failure of a shield with a single discharge, Wowk believed that multiple shots delivered in a short period would accomplish the same goal. While plasma shielding could shed excess energy, it took time. If he could increase the energy build-up faster than the shield could bleed it off, he could cause the shield to fail.

The leaders of the torpedo design team attempted to fire Wowk, claiming he was "not a team player" because of his lack of support for their single-shot concept. Filson interviewed Wowk and, instead of terminating his employment, turned him loose to pursue his ideas. Wowk concentrated on methods of delivering multiple blows quickly. Under his direction, Advanced Warfare developed the first photon cannon. This high-energy laser used capacitors to build up a charge and then release it instantaneously. Though a single shot from a photon cannon could not burn through a shield, repeated impacts on the same shield section would cause the shield generator to fail.

Filson's decision to back Wowk turned out to be proven correct when the torpedo project failed miserably. With Wowk's development of photon cannons, attention turned back to Naginata and Guisarme since photon cannons were another considerable power drain. The two scientists had continued to work on the efficiency of the transfer of power from the contained nuclear explosion at the heart of a fusion reactor to outside the enclosure where the energy could be used. As a result, energy captured from their next generation of new designs nearly doubled again.

With the power issues solved for the time being and the new photon cannon weapon in development, attention turned to the hull construction of the ships. With antimatter missiles, there had been no reason to try to armor-plate military vessels. The nature of an antimatter/matter explosion made armoring a negative as the increased mass would have augmented the amount of destruction. However, thicker hulls provided more protection if photon cannons breached the plasma shielding.

Research quickly focused on the relative merits of reflective armor versus ablative armor. Reflective armor was designed to 'bounce' the laser blast from a photon cannon away. Ablative armor was designed to absorb the shot's energy, causing the armor to melt or boil away at the point of impact but preventing or at least delaying the penetration of the hull interior. Testing quickly showed that a combination of ablative armor with a reflective surface was easily the most effective.

The combined effect of these new developments meant that every ship in the Royal Navy was now obsolete. The issue of funding a new shipbuilding campaign caused a change of government, with the Conservative party gaining enough seats to control Parliament. The new prime minister, Bob Eubank, was the first to come from one of the planets which joined the Commonwealth after the Offer of Inclusion. Eubank announced that his agenda was not one of Conservatives versus Liberal Democrats but instead of safeguarding the Commonwealth. He kept Linda Marshall, the First Space Lord, in place because of her track record of success in developing the new reactor technology and weapons and defense systems.

Shortly after Eubank was elected, King William died. His daughter, Charlotte, inherited the throne as the eldest child. Charlotte earned a Ph.D. in economics and was a careful student of her father's example.

Shortly after the election, MI-6, the foreign intelligence service, reported that the Rodinans and the Chinese had also developed the same technology of plasma shielding. It was assumed they also created a new weapon at the same time. An arms race began. While the Commonwealth had no aggressive intentions, it did not want to be vulnerable to attacks from its rivals. Ship designs were approved rapidly, and construction began quickly.

The new ships were much more attractive than before. The last generation of ships was angular and boxy. The new ships were curved, and their reflective armor made them gleam. It also resulted in the creation of both armored and un-armored cruisers. The un-armored cruisers were now known as light cruisers. They and the destroyer class had a reflective coating, but their hulls were no thicker than ships of the previous generations.

The heavy cruisers received a laminate of ceramic and metallic layers. They required larger powerplants because of the greater mass due to the armor. They ended up being twenty percent larger than the light cruisers. They also carried heavier artillery with four 105mm photon cannons. Light cruisers had four 90mm photon cannons, and destroyers had four 75mm cannons.

Three destroyers and two light cruisers with paraboloid shielding were going to be commissioned in less than two months. Admiral Freshley needed to select their commanders. Already some of the more senior officers were jockeying for position, hoping to get one of the new ships. None of them were on the shortlist Freshley was reviewing on his desk.

This was the dawn of a new era for the Royal Navy. Freshley was determined that these ships would go to the best and the brightest young officers he could find. He wanted commanders who would not only embrace the new technology but who would look for new ways to deploy it and take advantage of its potential. He went through the list one last time, then sent it to his yeoman with instructions to summon those officers to Caerleon.

PART TWO:
PERSEVERANCE ANDREWS

8

Commander Perseverance Andrews of the Royal Navy sat nervously outside the office of the Admiral of the Fleet. Her ship arrived at Caerleon Station the day before. It was a routine stop for resupply after four months of patrol duty. Her current posting, her first with the rank of commander, had another eight months to run, so the summons to see Admiral Freshley was unexpected. For the last sixteen hours, she wracked her brain, trying to anticipate the reason for the meeting. Perseverance knew she was not in trouble, so the only thing she could think of was a new assignment. The rumor mill said that mysterious new ships were due to be commissioned soon, but she did not dare hope for command of one since she was so junior.

As she entered the outer office, a commander who looked familiar was leaving the admiral's office. He nodded at Andrews pleasantly and left. Andrews did not get a look at his name badge. Then, at 11:00 precisely, the yeoman sitting next to the admiral's door nodded to her. Andrews stood, went to the door, and knocked. "Enter," came the call from within.

Andrews opened the door and stepped inside. She strode to three paces before the admiral's desk and saluted. Admiral Freshley, already standing, returned the salute.

"Commander Andrews, reporting as ordered," she said.

"Grab a seat, commander," the admiral said, gesturing to some armchairs off to the side.

Freshley and Andrews were of nearly equal height and similar build. Perseverance was one hundred eighty-three centimeters tall, while Freshley was two centimeters taller. Both were slim with broad shoulders. Freshley's hair was mostly gray, with a few black strands remaining. Andrews' hair was raven black.

The admiral came around the desk. Andrews picked an armchair but did not sit until the admiral chose a chair. When the admiral sat, Andrews followed suit but did not relax. Instead, she was perched on the edge of the cushion, her posture rigid. The admiral sat more comfortably.

"Relax, commander," Freshley said. "This is a good meeting. At least, it's meant to be a good meeting."

"Sir," Andrews replied, nodding in acknowledgment but not relaxing.

"I have to ask," the admiral said. "You probably get this question a lot and are sick of it, but how did you come to be called Perseverance?"

"My parents," Andrews replied. "All my siblings have unusual names. My sisters are Felicity and Prudence. My brother's name is Steadfast. I'm lucky to be the second youngest. So people were used to our odd names when I came along."

"They are unusual," Freshley commented, "but I wouldn't use the term odd. Back to the business at hand. We're pulling you off the *Addison*. You're assigned to a new command. How much do you know of the research that Advanced Warfare has been conducting?"

"Just the rumors, admiral," Andrews answered. Her hopes began to soar.

"What does the rumor mill say?" Freshley asked.

"That they've developed a way to generate a defensive shield around ships that makes antimatter weapons useless," Andrews answered.

"What do you think about those rumors?"

That topic had been the center of discussion in the wardroom two nights before. Andrews' executive officer, Lieutenant Commander Louis Lopez, had claimed that it was theoretically impossible. Andrews spent the better part of an hour trying to convince him he was wrong and explaining why she believed it could be done.

"I think it's possible, sir," Andrews replied. "If it is, it makes all our existing weaponry useless. Kinetic and antimatter warheads would have no effect. With even one small ship like that, I could destroy the Chinese and Rodinan navies, as long as I didn't run out of ammunition."

"Well, we won't be asking you to do that," Freshley said with a chuckle. "Though the Rodinans and Chinese might implement that strategy."

"They have ships of this type, too?" Andrews asked. "I suppose that's a reasonable assumption," she continued, answering her own question.

"It is a reasonable assumption," Freshley confirmed. "MI-6 has proof the Rodinans are about as far along as we are in shield design. As you will learn, the bigger problem is power generation. From what we know, we have a significant advantage there. We don't have good intelligence from the Chinese Republics, but I expect them to be not far behind the Rodinans. That brings us to the reason you are here. We have five ships with the new shielding, either complete or nearly so. I'd like to offer you command of one of them. Interested?"

"Yes, sir!" Andrews replied with enthusiasm.

"Good," Freshley replied. "Your ship, HMS *H.E. Rowen*, is due to be commissioned in five weeks. She's a destroyer, the second of a new class. Her sister ships will be commissioned in the same ceremony. This afternoon you have an appointment with Advanced Warfare, where you will begin to receive a complete education on all the new systems. Your XO and chief engineer will join you and your counterparts for the other four ships."

Admiral Freshley dismissed Andrews shortly after that. On Andrews' way out, she saw a friend from her first posting sitting anxiously outside Freshley's office. She and Commander Ken Berger were ensigns on their first assignment after receiving their commissions. They became good friends as a result.

Neither of them attended the Naval Academy. Instead, both enlisted in the Reserve Officer Training programs offered at their universities: Andrews on Alleghany and Berger on Lincoln. Their first posting was on the aged cruiser HMS *Exeter*. The *Exeter* was a Royal Navy ship before combining the various fleets. Most of the *Exeter*'s crew came from a British rather than an American background. As a result, Andrews and Berger were two of the small handful of people aboard who "talked funny," according to the rest of the crew.

The good-natured teasing they received helped forge a bond of friendship. It helped that Berger was one of the nicest people Perseverance Andrews ever met. Of course, it didn't hurt that Berger was handsome, with an air of youthful innocence. Underneath that pleasant exterior, though, Berger was tough as nails, as several crew members learned when they tried to test him.

Perseverance and Ken stayed in touch since then, maintaining their friendship. Dating was out of the question since Berger explained early on that he would never become involved with anyone in the navy. Seeing him sitting on pins and needles outside the admiral's office brought a big grin to Perseverance Andrews' face. Before she could say anything, the admiral's yeoman called Berger into the admiral's office.

"Catch up later?" Perseverance whispered. Berger nodded briefly in response.

Andrews went and checked into the Bachelor Officers Quarters on the station. Once in her room, she used the console to contact the Executive Officer on *Addison*. She connected immediately.

"We heard the news already, skipper," Lieutenant Commander Louis Lopez said.

"What did you hear?" Andrews asked.

"Only that you were reassigned, and we are getting a new CO," he replied. "Can you tell me anything more?"

"I wish I could, but you know how things are," she sighed. "I'm sorry I didn't get to say goodbye. Please let everyone know I think we were a first-rate crew."

"Affirmative."

"Would you please get the ensigns to pack up my stuff and send it to the BOQ?"

"Will do, skipper."

"Thanks. Please stay in touch, Louis. I enjoyed working with you, and I hope our paths cross again."

"I'll do that, skipper. Gotta scoot. New CO is on her way."

No sooner did that call end than she heard from Commander Berger. "Give me a few minutes, and I'll meet you in the mess," he said.

Perseverance left her room, went to the Officers' Mess and took a table. About ten minutes later, Ken Berger entered. He looked around briefly, caught sight of her, and came over. The grin on his face was apparent from across the room.

Perseverance rose, and they gave each other a kiss on the cheek. They both sat and waited for the server to take their orders. When he left, they both began to speak at the same time. They caught themselves, laughing.

"You first," Andrews said.

"I just got command of a new destroyer, the *Burke*," Berger said.

"He gave me *Rowen*," Andrews replied.

"Damn, Persie, who'd a thunk it? You and I getting two of the newest ships in the fleet?" he stated. "Who got the *Simpkin*?"

"I think I saw him leaving when I arrived," Andrews said. "He looked familiar, but I couldn't make out his name tag. I know I've seen him before. I suppose we'll see when we have our meeting at 14:00."

"We'll find out who our XOs and engineers are, too," Berger said. "Unless I can find them on the system first."

Berger pulled out his comm unit and tried to access the personnel roster for his new command. Then, shaking his head in disappointment, he commented, "It's not posted, or I can't access it yet."

"It doesn't matter. They'll be at least as good as we are," Andrews said jokingly. "When I was summoned to the admiral's office, I didn't even dare to hope for this. I mean, comparatively speaking, we're awfully junior."

"I know," Berger agreed. "Maybe they'll explain their thinking in the meeting."

The server delivered their meals. Noticing they were short on time, Andrews and Berger ate quickly. They limited their conversation to getting caught up on each other's personal lives.

Entering the conference room, Andrews saw five tables arranged in a horseshoe, with three name cards in front of each. At the center of the table on the furthest end, she saw the commander who was leaving Admiral Freshley's office when she arrived. Perseverance's table was next to his, and Ken Berger's was across the open end of the horseshoe. Andrews headed to her table and introduced herself.

"Perseverance Andrews," she said, offering her hand in greeting.

"Hank Boyd," the man responded. "I've seen you around."

"Likewise," Perseverance replied. "Good to meet you."

Andrews waved Berger over. "Ken Berger, Hank Boyd," she said, introducing them. "Hank, Ken."

Boyd grinned. "You look familiar, too," he said.

"Same," Ken said, smiling.

While they began chatting, Perseverance discretely checked the name cards at her table. In addition to her own, there was one for Lieutenant Commander Elizabeth Schneider and another for Lieutenant Commander Constantino Diaz. She recalled meeting Schneider before. She, too, was tall, she remembered—about the same height. Diaz was someone whose name seemed familiar, but she couldn't remember his appearance.

A large group of people entered the room. Perseverance noticed Schneider right away. She was the tallest. She cleared her throat to get Boyd and Berger's attention and nodded at the newcomers. The three of them retreated to their places at the different tables.

When Schneider approached, Perseverance welcomed her, reminding her of their meeting. Almost hidden behind her was Diaz. He was short and slight, only one hundred seventy centimeters in height. Despite his lack of stature, there was something arresting about him. Diaz seemed to crackle with energy and good humor. Perseverance found herself liking the man before they even finished shaking hands. Before they had a chance to begin talking, Admiral Freshley strode to a podium at the open end of the horseshoe.

"Welcome to the future of the Royal Navy," he said.

Freshley kept his remarks short and turned the meeting over to Nancy Filson. She gave them a briefing on paraboloid plasma shielding, photon cannons, and powerplant development. It lasted the rest of the afternoon.

Dinner was brought in. Perseverance turned her attention to her officers, trying to get to know them better. Schneider would be the chief engineer on *Rowen*. Diaz would be Perseverance's executive officer and second in command.

Perseverance found it challenging to maintain a conversation with Schneider. She was friendly enough but seemed a person of few words. After she received information on the new powerplant developments resulting from the work of Naginata and Guisarme, her attention was riveted on her comm unit as she began reading the material immediately.

Diaz was the opposite. In no time at all, Perseverance felt as though she and Tino Diaz were friends. Once they realized they'd lost Schneider's attention, they began to discuss how the new technologies would affect battle tactics.

When dinner was over, Perseverance and Tino adjourned to the Officers' Club. Eight other officers had the same idea, including Ken Berger and his new executive officer. They settled in a corner of the bar, and the larger group took up the topic of conversation Perseverance and Tino had been pursuing. When it reached 22:00, Perseverance said her goodbyes, reminding everyone their first session would begin at 08:00 the next day.

The following morning, MI-6 conducted the first briefing. Agent Koromoah, a dark-skinned woman, opened by explaining that the information MI-6 gathered was not complete and was culled entirely from the Rodinan Federation. She admitted that MI-6 had little success in penetrating the security of the Chinese Republics, and any information they obtained was second-hand.

With those warnings issued, she stated that MI-6 was confident that the Federation and the Republics were close to launching ships with their own versions of paraboloid plasma shielding. MI-6 was slightly less sure but still reasonably convinced that neither the Federation nor Republics had made the same advances in powerplant efficiency.

"That means our rivals will likely not have the same offensive weaponry. They have probably worked to develop some offensive capability," Koromoah said, "but it will likely take a different form—one that is not dependent on generated power."

"They won't have photon cannons," Boyd interjected.

"We believe it is unlikely," Koromoah confirmed. "That does not mean they will be weaponless. There are alternative strategies they have probably pursued—as we have. Since the availability of power is likely a limiting factor for them, they have probably pushed the development of these alternatives further than we have."

"Do we have other weapons under consideration?" Berger asked.

"Yes," Koromoah answered. "That's all I'm willing to say at this time."

Koromoah continued, giving estimates of when the Federation and Republics might be putting their new-design ships in service. Finally, after providing a range of estimates based on the information gathered, she stopped.

"Quite frankly, they could be ready today," she admitted. "Whichever one finishes first is likely to attack the other, or us, immediately."

It was a sobering thought with which to conclude her portion of the program. There was a short break after. Perseverance was struck by how quiet her fellow officers were compared to the night before. The previous evening, they were excited about new ships, weapons, and opportunities. After hearing Koromoah, the excitement was tempered by the realization that they might need to deploy their new ships immediately in a battle for the defense of the Commonwealth.

They spent the next ten days learning every feature of the new ships. Then they moved aboard their new commands and began training the other officers, both commissioned and non-coms. The last two weeks were spent training the crews of the new ships.

Every member of the five crews was hand-picked from the rest of the Royal Navy. Perseverance was pleased to have two officers and a senior chief petty officer she knew from previous postings. Lieutenant Martha Leen was *Rowen*'s second officer, and Lieutenant Harry Piacquad was the fourth officer. SCPO Patricia Carroll was the Chief of Boat or COB.

A week before the commissioning ceremony, Perseverance was summoned suddenly to a meeting on Caerleon Station. When she entered the briefing room, she saw the other commanding officers of the new ships— Commanders Berger and Boyd—and Captains Danforth and Tasker of the light cruisers *Albany* and *Cairo*. Tasker was the last to arrive. When she sat, Agent Koromoah appeared.

"The Rodinans were the first to complete their new ships," she stated. "Thank God they decided to attack the Republics first. We believe they chose the Republics because the Chinese Second Fleet was closer than ours. The Rodinans attacked in the Tǔxīng system with a force led by their two newly-completed heavy cruisers. Chinese Admiral Xie Haiming led a heroic defense of his system, ramming his own ship into the Rodinan heavy cruiser *Bayan*. The *Bayan*, the namesake of its class, was destroyed. The Rodinans departed after losing *Bayan*. Their other heavy cruiser, *Ustinov*, is believed to be undamaged. All of the Republics' Second Fleet is wiped out. The Rodinan attack group, comprised of most of their First Fleet, is largely intact, though not undamaged."

"Did the Republics employ any of the ships with plasma shielding?" Boyd asked.

"No. The Chinese Second Fleet had none," Koromoah answered. "We assume the Republics will use their new construction to retaliate against the Federation, though there is a possibility they will come after us. We will need to wait and see."

After the briefing, they returned to training. The news that the Rodinans already had ships with plasma shielding meant MI-6's estimate was now a reality. How soon the Republics could deploy their suspected new ships and against whom, or whether the Rodinans would follow their attack on the Chinese with one on the Commonwealth were looming questions.

The Commonwealth commissioned the first of their ships to feature plasma shielding and photon cannons in secret. Though Queen Charlotte presided over the ceremony, there were no media allowed. There were three destroyers of the *Simpkin*-class—*Simpkin*, *Rowen*, and *Burke*, and two of the new class of light cruisers, the *Albany*-class, which were *Albany* and *Cairo*. *Albany* and *Rowen* were sent to the Avalon system in the event of a Chinese or Federation attack. *Cairo* and *Simpkin* were sent to the Roosevelt system to face a possible Rodinan incursion, and *Burke* was held back at Caerleon.

Nine days after Andrews and *Rowen* arrived in the Avalon system, the questions were answered when the Republics entered the Automedon system with a force led by one of their new 401-type heavy cruisers and one 164-type destroyer, both defended with plasma shielding. The Automedon system had no inhabitable planets but was a critical hyper corridor junction, linking parts of the Commonwealth and providing access to the Chinese and Rodinan systems and some non-aligned worlds. *Burke* was sent from Caerleon to join *Albany* and *Rowen* in the Avalon system, which "bordered" the Automedon system. Admiral Freshley traveled aboard *Burke* and would take command, using *Albany* as his flagship.

Sensors also reported the speed and course of the Chinese ships. The sensors also provided information on their design. The new ships the Republics developed had an awkward bulge in the middle. MI-6 and Advanced Warfare surmised that the swelling accommodated larger reactors needed to provide enough power for the shielding. This confirmed their belief that the Chinese had not developed more efficient reactors as the Commonwealth did.

The Chinese entered the Automedon system at $0.23c$, or twenty-three percent of light-speed. They were accelerating slowly on a direct course for the hyper corridor leading to Avalon. Automedon Station was on the side of the ecliptic near their passage and would be within their missile range. Admiral Freshley figured the Chinese would destroy the station on their way through. The next evening, he was proven correct when the Chinese launched four antimatter missiles at the station, blowing it to smithereens. Before it was destroyed, the sensors in Automedon reported the mass of the two new types of ships, fleshing out the profiles.

9

Admiral Freshley was still aboard HMS *Burke* when sensors reported the arrival of the Chinese ships into the Avalon system. The captain of HMS *Albany* quickly transmitted the information back to the admiral. *Burke* was in the Avalon system but only just arrived. *Albany* and *Rowen* were on the far side of the ecliptic from *Burke*, awaiting the arrival of the Chinese. There were nine other ships with *Albany* and *Rowen*, three conventionally-armed cruisers, and six conventionally armed destroyers. In addition to the two new Chinese ships, there were seven others—three older 319-type cruisers and four 162-type destroyers.

Freshley ordered the Commonwealth ships to move to a position where they would be able to defend Avalon Station. Losing one planetary station, Automedon, was terrible. Losing two would be inexcusable. He knew his conventionally-armed ships would match up well against the older Chinese ships but had no idea what the capability of their new ships would be. As he watched, via sensors, the Chinese changed course for Avalon Station. He noted that their new heavy cruiser and destroyer were very slow to the helm. Their movement seemed ponderous.

One thing the Royal Navy had insisted upon in the new ship designs was no loss of performance. *Rowen* could match the acceleration of any destroyer in the Royal Navy. *Cairo* and *Albany* were slightly quicker than an *Ithaca*-class cruiser, the last class built without the new defense system and weaponry. On the other hand, the new Chinese ships seemed to be quite a bit slower than the older models.

The Chinese changed course to intercept the Commonwealth ships and began to slow. Freshley ordered his ships to decelerate as well. Ideally, they would meet in open space, with the Chinese well out of missile range of Avalon Station. Monitoring the progress of both forces, it appeared they would be easing into range of one another in about twenty-eight hours.

He called his captains together using the holographic communications projectors. Though the captains stayed on their ships, the projectors made it appear like they were in the same room. Freshley went over the plan of attack he wanted to use. His conventionally-armed ships would take on the conventionally-armed Chinese ships, concentrating on the three 319-type cruisers. *Albany* and *Rowen* would focus on the Chinese heavy cruiser and the new destroyer type. He asked the captains to adjust duty schedules so their best teams were in place at the beginning of the engagement and to ensure crews were fed beforehand. *Albany* and *Rowen* also carried conventional antimatter missiles and would be firing against the Chinese along with the rest. Freshley did not know whether the new Chinese ships were equipped to do the same.

Watching the clock tick down was one of the most frustrating things Commander Perseverance Andrews experienced. She found herself pacing the corridor between the bridge and her quarters repeatedly. Sitting still was an impossibility. Hours before, she toured the ship. Due to the early training they underwent, she already knew most of the crew by face and name. There was a definite level of excitement in the crew. Part of it was normal apprehension before a battle. Part of it was eager anticipation regarding what the new technology would do. Once they were within minutes of engagement, Perseverance took her seat on the bridge and ordered the ship to begin evasive action.

When the two forces drew within range, both sides launched antimatter missiles. As the distance between the two groups closed, railguns opened fire. The two new Chinese ships launched missiles along with the older ships, but these missiles were aimed at *Rowen* and *Albany*.

When they came within range, *Rowen* and *Albany* began firing their photon cannons at the two new Chinese ships. With the missiles on the way, both sides commenced counter-measures, with electronic jamming and false signals to distract enemy missiles. Point-defense networks on the two forces lit up, with railguns and lasers trying to shoot down incoming missiles. *Albany* and *Rowen* were fully integrated into the point-defense network for the Royal Navy ships.

The Chinese fired eighteen missiles at *Rowen* and *Albany*. The twelve from their heavy cruiser targeted *Albany*, and the four from the destroyer were aimed at *Rowen*. The Commonwealth's point-defense network eliminated all but two, one aimed at each ship. They detonated fifty thousand kilometers before the missiles reached the two Commonwealth ships.

Perseverance was looking at the sensors, trying to figure out what the hell the Chinese missiles did. Immediately, damage control indicated a shield failure midships on the quadrant facing the missile. Rather than try to scroll through the screens, she called out, "Sensors! What *was* that?"

"X-ray laser, sir," the petty officer at the sensors station called back. "Crazy powerful."

In the command chair, Andrews was watching the battle unfold. The conventional missiles launched by both sides ran the defense gauntlets. Chinese counter-measures led forty-eight of the Royal Navy's missiles astray. Still, their unlinked point-defense network was not as effective. Eight Commonwealth missiles survived to hit the seven older Chinese ships. One of the 319-type cruisers was hit by two warheads and was blown into small pieces. The others all suffered significant damage and were unable to continue offensive action.

She saw the Royal Navy's counter-measures distract forty-six of the Chinese missiles off course. The combined point-defense network eliminated another thirty-one. That left three Chinese missiles. One was aimed at *Rowen*. Perseverance held her breath, waiting for the impact. The shudder she expected to feel never happened. *Rowen* was undamaged. The antimatter warhead of the Chinese missile was ineffective against the plasma shielding. The other two Chinese missiles hit two conventional Royal Navy cruisers, leaving them heavily damaged and out of the fight.

Andrews noticed from the sensor readings that the two new Chinese ships were not joined with their older ships in the point defense network. All the Royal Navy ships treated incoming missiles as a threat. In contrast, the new Chinese ships focused only on missiles explicitly aimed at them. Since none of the Royal Navy's missiles were aimed at the new ships, their point-defense networks were silent.

While this was going on, *Albany* and *Rowen* were engaged with the new Chinese ships. The 90mm photon cannons on *Albany* and the 75mm cannons on *Rowen* were breaking through the plasma shielding on the Chinese ships. The Chinese fired another salvo of the new type of missiles from those ships, but the Commonwealth's point-defense network was able to distract or eliminate all of them.

Both *Albany* and *Rowen* were able to fire thirty salvos per minute from their photon cannons. The repeated hits of the Royal Navy's guns quickly made the battle lopsided. In less than five minutes, both of the new Chinese ships were disabled and radioed their surrender. There had been shield failures on both HMS *Albany* and *Rowen* from the initial missile attack, but the Chinese had been unable to penetrate the hull.

Perseverance ordered the ship to stand down from general quarters after receiving word from Admiral Freshley. *Albany* and *Rowen* maneuvered closer to the crippled Chinese ships and sent marines over to take control of them. The video feeds from the marines' combat armor told the extent of the damage the Commonwealth's photon cannons caused. Both ships took a savage beating, and it was apparent quickly they were unsalvageable. Freshley decided to bring the Chinese survivors to *Albany* and *Rowen* before their ships fell apart.

Perseverance and Diaz reviewed the battle in her ready room afterward. The sensor logs were converted into a holographic projection displaying the entire engagement. Of most interest to them was viewing the impact of the antimatter missile on their shielding and seeing the effect of their guns on the Chinese shields.

"Madre de Dios!" Diaz muttered under his breath when he saw the antimatter missile explode harmlessly. The shield swallowed the entire detonation like snuffing a candle. They then watched the effect of their guns.

The Chinese destroyer did not engage in any sort of evasive action. Instead, the ship rolled to move damaged areas away from the point of impact. Shot after shot hit home. Sensor readings showed the shields failing section by section. Generally, three salvos by the *Rowen*'s cannons in succession were enough to cause shields to drop in each paraboloid section. After that, the cannons started to gouge into the hull.

When she finished writing her after-action report, Perseverance went to the ship's shuttle bay to oversee the arrival of the Chinese crew. She saw the first two shuttles arrive. Each shuttle held thirty of the Chinese. Only one of the shuttles went back to the Chinese ship.

"Sergeant, how many more remain aboard their ship?" she asked Sergeant Clemons of the Royal Marines.

"Only twenty-three, sir," Clemons responded. "They lost over eighty percent of their crew. We brought back the largest group just now. The rest are scattered through the rest of the ship, isolated from the main bunch. We're conducting EVAs to bring them back into atmosphere. Their captain will be the last one to leave."

My God, Perseverance thought. Though she and Diaz had viewed the sensor data, Clemons' report made it hit home in a different way. The photon cannons had caused much greater destruction than she imagined. Her train of thought was interrupted when her comm buzzed. Looking at it, she saw Admiral Freshley called for a conference in fifteen minutes.

Perseverance returned quickly to her ready room and activated the holographic display software that allowed everyone to appear in the room with her and Lieutenant Commander Diaz.

Freshley opened the meeting. "The Chinese government had only declared war a few days ago when they attacked Automedon Station. They just sued for peace through diplomatic channels. The Foreign Service is handling things now. I understand that Queen Charlotte has suggested that the Chinese pay only for the destruction of Automedon Station, with no other terms. Obviously, our first test in this new form of war was successful. Don't become complacent. I suspect the Chinese and Rodinans will not cease in their efforts to leapfrog over us in terms of technology."

Having communicated the surrender of the Republics, Freshley closed the meeting quickly. HMS *Burke* was already adjusting course to return to Caerleon. Perseverance received orders to remain in the Avalon system until a transport arrived to remove the Chinese survivors. Then she and *Rowen* would join HMS *Albany* in the Automedon system on an extended patrol.

In the debrief on Caerleon that followed this engagement, Director Filson pointed out that the superiority of the Royal Navy's powerplants and point-defense network integration proved to be the difference. Filson urged that the Royal Navy not only maintain its ongoing research but actually needed to increase budgets. She pointed out that the Chinese and Rodinans realized they were lagging behind the Commonwealth's technology and would increase their efforts. Filson also warned that planning for the next generation of ships should already begin, anticipating further improvements.

10

I t was almost three years later that now-Captain Perseverance Andrews saw action again. Still in command of HMS *Rowen*, she was part of a screen of three destroyers stationed in the Aries system. The other two destroyers alongside her, HMS *Symes* and HMS *Funnell*, were newer than the *Rowen*, part of the shipbuilding campaign that continued in the Commonwealth. The Royal Navy no longer deployed unshielded ships. Andrews was the senior officer of the three commanders and commanded the small force.

The last three years were a hectic time for all of the large multi-system governments. All three moved quickly to solidify their hold on currently unpopulated and un-terraformed systems claimed in the initial phase of exploration. The Commonwealth had six of these and promptly began the decades-long terra-forming process on all of them. The Rodinans and Chinese Republics had only five each. Not only did they have claims on fewer systems, but those systems were also less abundant in natural resources compared to the ones the Commonwealth was beginning to exploit.

This imbalance could be traced back to the initial wave of exploration. The planetary claims of the Americans and British came from private enterprise in the never-ending search for exploitable profit opportunities. The governments of the United States and the United Kingdom had no role. The settlement of space by the Rodinans and Chinese, on the other hand, was entirely government-controlled. Private corporations moved at a much quicker pace than governments.

In addition to terra-forming activity, MI-6 was confident the Rodinans and the Chinese had been building ships at an aggressive pace. Intelligence had little success in penetrating the veil of security in the Chinese Republics but a much better idea of the state of affairs in the Rodinan Federation. According to what they gleaned, the Rodinans were nearing completion of a group of ships that would increase the size of their navy to near-parity with the Commonwealth and outnumber the navy of the Republics.

The biggest question was what the Federation would do. Would they be content to maintain a defensive posture, confident their navy could withstand an attack by either the Republics or the Commonwealth? Would they go on the offensive and attack one of their rivals, and if so, which one? MI-6 had no firm answers, just guesses and assumptions.

Perseverance Andrews had her own ideas. She was confident the Commonwealth still possessed a technological advantage. The Federation was still struggling with powerplant development. According to MI-6, there were several catastrophic accidents related to this over the previous three years. If the Republics faced the same issue, then both would consider the Commonwealth a mutual threat.

Andrews knew the last successful attacks the Republics or Federation made against the Commonwealth (which actually occurred before the planets coalesced into the Commonwealth) were when they attacked in concert, capturing Roosevelt and Lincoln. Though they did not work closely, they put their rivalry aside for a time. Perseverance reckoned they were smart enough to figure that out and try again—not necessarily creating a combined force but both choosing to attack the Commonwealth and not each other.

Unlike when they took control of Roosevelt and Lincoln, Andrews believed the Federation and the Republics would try to seize the underpopulated Commonwealth systems. She thought they would test the will of the Commonwealth. Snatching underpopulated systems did not present the same threat as subjugating populated worlds. Given that the Commonwealth would need to defeat the Federation *and* the Republics to win them back, it might raise the political cost to an unacceptably high level and erode public support.

Andrews had studied the astrographic projections repeatedly. She came to believe the current Commonwealth strategy of defending the borders of its space was doomed to fail. The day before, she tried to plead her case privately to Rear Admiral Melba Kenard but was told politely to sit down and be quiet. Andrews presented a plan of defense in depth, withdrawing from the border systems and concentrating the fleets in three different locations where they could respond to incursions by either the Republics or Federation.

"Five of the six border systems we are defending have inhabited planets. Only Automedon does not, though it is at least as important from an economic standpoint," Kenard stated. "You and I might agree that defense in depth is a better option, militarily. From a political standpoint, it's impossible. Those five planets are inhabited by voters—voters who will not understand why it would be better for the Commonwealth to pull back. Abandoning Automedon Station, which is just now nearing completion after the Republics destroyed it, would likewise be viewed poorly by the taxpayers. The inevitable loss of ships if war breaks out is slightly less awful than beginning a conflict with confidence in the government damaged. You obviously feel an attack is imminent?"

"I do, sir," Andrews stated. "When the Rodinans complete their latest round of shipbuilding, I reckon they'll come as soon as those ships complete shakedown. As for the political realities that stand in the way of a more effective defense, I understand, sir."

Andrews knew the opening days of a conflict would result in the sacrifice of good ships and crews. If the enemy decided to attack through the Aries system, her force of three destroyers would not be enough to stop them. The best she could hope for would be to slow them down and bloody their noses. After that, the space above the planet would be occupied by the enemy (probably the Federation, based on the astrography) whether the Commonwealth defended it or not.

At the same time, though, she could also understand how angry the residents of Aries would be if the navy pulled out of the system. Most civilians possessed little knowledge of military strategy and would not understand how pulling back would be of any benefit. They would feel abandoned. Their unhappiness would spread throughout the Commonwealth.

Having heard Kenard's explanation, Andrews suspected the Admiralty understood the losses they would suffer in the event of an attack. It would be a setback to begin a war, but Andrews also understood the importance of public opinion. This conflict would probably drag on for a couple of years or more. If it did, the superior industrial capability of the Commonwealth compared to either of the other rivals would play an increasingly critical role. Coupling that with the solid support of the citizenry, Perseverance could understand the long-term logic, even though it was her and her crew's butts on the line.

Andrews adjusted her thinking after the meeting and tried to develop a plan to enable her three ships to do as much damage as possible to the enemy. First, she analyzed the most probable routes the Rodinans and Republics might follow. The Republics faced a six-jump trip that would last over a month. The Federation's path was quicker. Their path would take three jumps and seventeen days.

The Federation path started in their Venera system, then went through system H2813, which was unpopulated, and into the Commonwealth's Hercules system, also unpopulated. Perseverance wrote her findings in a report and sent it to Admiral Kenard. Along with her report, she also requested a patrol boat be sent to H2813 immediately. In addition, she included a request for enough mines to create thick minefields at two hyper corridor termini, to be provided as quickly as possible.

His comm unit lit up the following morning. "Captain Andrews," a yeoman asked, "please stay on the connection for Admiral Kenard."

Moments later, Kenard's face appeared on the screen. "My flag lieutenant read your report and urged me to contact you, captain. He suggested you would be able to explain your ideas more quickly than he could summarize your findings and that you believe time is critical. Give me the overview."

Andrews summarized the astrography. "A patrol boat will warn us in advance which path the Federation selects. We would then have either fourteen or seventeen days to lay minefields at both the entrance and exit to an intermediate hyper corridor on their path to Aries. The mines won't affect their shielded ships but should be effective against the older ships ONI tells us are still in service."

Kenard looked at Andrews quizzically. "An intermediate corridor? Which one?"

"The corridor from H2813 to Hercules," she replied.

"At the entrance and the exit of an intermediate corridor. Interesting. Makes sense, even though I don't think anyone has done it before."

"Yes, sir," Andrews confirmed. "I doubt they'll expect them there or scan for them."

"I'm going to cut the orders to get the patrol boat headed your way and get you as many mines as possible. I hope you don't mind, but I'm planning on taking your idea and sharing it with the others. Might as well use all the mines we have—they'll be obsolete soon. "

"Yes, sir. Thank you, sir," Andrews replied.

Perseverance Andrews hoped there was enough time to at least position the patrol boat. Knowing which hyper corridor the Federation would use was critical to her scheme. If she could get the mines laid in time, that would increase the amount of damage she might inflict on the Rodinans.

Andrews had few illusions. If the Federation wanted to press the attack, they would be successful. Her goal was to make them pay the highest price possible. If her idea worked, the Federation might decide the price was too high, knowing that the deeper they traveled into Commonwealth space, the more difficult and costly it would become in terms of ships and crew.

A few hours later, she learned PB 59 was on its way. She directed them to proceed at best possible speed to system H2813. Once there, they were to find a place where they could observe and remain undetected. After the Federation force came through, the patrol boat would follow at a great distance, if possible staying out of range of the Federation's sensors.

A few days later, Admiral Kenard informed Andrews that ten fast military transports carrying five thousand mines were in transit. Andrews directed half of them to enter the corridor to system H2813 as slowly as possible since they would be creating a minefield just before the hyper corridor terminus. The other five would lay a second field on the Hercules side of the corridor. Andrews ordered them to begin laying mines before the terminus of the corridor. One of the transport commanders contacted the admiral, questioning Andrews' orders.

"Commander," the admiral replied, "I am aware of this and suggest you follow the orders you were given."

When Perseverance drafted her earlier report, she explained her reasoning. With a minefield at the entrance to the hyper corridor, the Federation would expect to find one at the exit. As a result, they would probably exit hyperspace before the corridor terminus to have time to clear a path through the mines they expected to encounter. Andrews estimated they would drop out three light-minutes before the terminus.

When the admiral's flag lieutenant queried Perseverance on why she felt it would be three light-minutes, Andrews could only answer, "Honestly, I'm just guessing. At three light-minutes, it will take their sensors just under six minutes to give them a read on where they expect the mines to be. They would then have slightly more than six minutes to clear a path. I figure they are as competent and confident as we are and I would choose three light-minutes."

That was a good enough explanation for the flag lieutenant. He called it out for the admiral in case Kenard had a problem with it. Kenard approved the idea, and the other wrinkle Perseverance proposed.

Almost seven weeks later, PB 59 reported the arrival of a Federation force in system H2813. A group was on the way consisting of one heavy cruiser, two light cruisers, and two destroyers possessing the new shielding, plus five cruisers and four destroyers of the older unshielded type. The Commonwealth transports had laid their minefields and departed weeks before. Captain Andrews ordered her three destroyers into deep space beyond the terminus of the hyper corridor from Hercules to Aries. Then, based on the information received from PB 59, which would shadow the Rodinans, they would reverse course and attempt to be right behind the Federation ships when they re-entered normal space.

The advances in plasma shield design still had not found a way to protect the area dead astern of a ship. Andrews hoped that her three destroyers would be able to damage the drives of some of the shielded Federation ships before being knocked out of action themselves. She had no illusions that she could win this fight. Perseverance just wanted to extract the highest cost possible from the Federation. If everything worked out just as she planned, perhaps the severity of the damage would be enough to convince the Federation to abandon this attack.

Admiral Kenard shared Perseverance Andrews' ideas with her counterpart, Rear Admiral Al Czervik, in command of Blue Fleet, and the other front-line commanders in her command, Red Fleet. One of them, Ken Berger, grasped the concept and implemented similar plans in his own sector. One did not. Admiral

Czervik ran into the same problem. Hank Boyd followed a plan similar to Perseverance's. Boyd was the only one of the three who transferred to a new ship, HMS *Mellon*. His previous command, *Simpkin*, was now under a different CO, far from the front lines.

One problem the Royal Navy encountered due to the development of plasma shielding was the immediate obsolescence of every non-shielded ship. The navy needed new ships and needed them immediately. That required vast amounts of money. The government, Parliament, in particular, controlled budgets. The funding needed to rebuild the fleet required Admiral Freshley and First Space Lord Marshall to hold their noses and make certain compromises. There were several recently promoted officers whose chief qualification for higher rank was a connection to a politician with influence over the navy's budget. Two of those commanded border sectors. They had decided not to adopt any of the ideas shared with them.

In addition to the force approaching Andrews, patrol boats in other sectors identified a second Federation force and one from the Chinese Republics. Freshley suspected a second Chinese force would attack one of the two commanders who chose not to send a patrol boat out to scout. Freshley was already preparing contingency plans to backstop those areas.

When these attacks hit home, Freshley knew he would lose half the destroyers in the navy. He hoped like hell he could save as many members of their crews as possible. However, he did not know how he would address the problem of the politicals.

11

The first reports from PB 59 were encouraging. The patrol boat shared sensor data showing the speed and maneuverability of the Federation ships. Like those of the Republics three years earlier, the shielded Federation vessels moved ponderously. Later, PB 59 reported the Rodinans flew unaware into the first minefield. Four of the unshielded ships were damaged enough that they could not continue. PB 59 shut down her drive out of range of the Federation sensors. It coasted to the hyper corridor entrance, using passive sensors only to assess the damage to the Rodinans. The Rodinans would detect her transition into hyperspace, but it would be too late to do them any good.

When PB 59 entered the Hercules system, it reported that four of the remaining five unshielded Rodinan ships were disabled and drifting. In addition, there was a debris field suggesting another ship was entirely obliterated. Andrews congratulated herself on guessing their entrance point correctly. She figured the Rodinans emerged into normal space smack into the middle of her minefield from the damage PB 59 observed.

Now came her part. PB 59 tracked the course and speed of the five shielded Federation ships. Perseverance needed to guess when her opponent would exit hyperspace. Since the remaining Rodinan ships were shielded, they had little to fear from antimatter mines. In discussing the matter with her second in command, Lieutenant Commander Marc Marlotte, she decided they would travel all the way to the terminus.

With PB 59 able to report the exact time of the entrance of the Rodinans to hyperspace, it then became a simple question of astrogation to direct her three ships so they would be in the best possible firing position when the Rodinans returned to normal space. She wanted her ships to be well within range of the Rodinans. After all, Perseverance had only three ships, and she needed to disable the drives of five of her enemy.

Little information was available to her regarding the range of the Rodinan weapons. However, ONI suspected it was similar to the laser warhead missile used by the Chinese Republics three years earlier. Advanced Warfare reported the Chinese warhead contained a small atomic bomb that generated a powerful, focused x-ray laser. It lasted only a fraction of a second but even so was powerful enough to burn out a shield generator and leave that section of a ship's hull bare. The Royal Navy had not yet developed their own version of missiles with laser warheads, but the rumor mill said they were close.

Her three ships had a point-defense network capable of dealing with twelve enemy missiles per salvo. She suspected the Rodinan ships could launch at least thirty-two. The Chinese missiles detonated at fifty thousand kilometers, and she reckoned the Rodinan missiles would be similar. What the flight range of the missiles was, she did not know. This attack would provide the first hard intelligence the Commonwealth would have on the Rodinan offensive capability.

To be close enough to make sure of disabling the Federation ships, Perseverance knew she would probably be within missile range long enough to receive plenty of damage. In her mind, it was not a question of surviving the attack. Instead, it was a question of surviving long enough to thwart the Federation's plan.

Aries was lightly populated. The Rodinans would have little difficulty subduing the inhabitants and establishing control. Gaining a new system, already terraformed, within an economically viable distance to their own Venera system would be a massive win for the Federation. The force the Rodinans sent would be powerful enough to defend Aries against any efforts by the Commonwealth to recapture it, unless the Royal Navy was willing to take a big risk.

Andrews' three ships were approaching the hyper corridor where they determined the Rodinans would emerge. The calculations were correct, and the five Federation ships appeared in normal space precisely where she figured. Perseverance issued orders to the other captains earlier to fire as soon as their guns achieved target lock. Her ship, *Rowen*, would focus first on the drive nacelles of the Federation heavy cruiser. *Symes* and *Funnell* would aim for the two light cruisers.

The four 75mm photon cannons on each of the Royal Navy destroyers could fire salvos every two seconds—the time it took to build up the necessary charge in the capacitors. How many shots they would be able to fire before the Rodinan missiles reached detonation was anyone's guess. Andrews reckoned she had more than ten seconds but less than thirty. Every shot needed to count.

Once the Federation ships emerged, it took less than a second for the guns to lock onto them and begin firing. *Symes* and *Funnell* switched targets at the ten-second mark and began firing at the two destroyers. *Rowen* continued to fire on the heavy cruiser.

Though she would not know until much later, Andrews' tactic of firing up the unprotected stern of the Federation ships was devastatingly effective. Unfortunately, she had no time to spare to evaluate sensor readings on the damage she caused since the Rodinans fired their first salvo of missiles three seconds after emerging from hyperspace. As she figured, they fired thirty-two missiles.

The point-defense network of the three Commonwealth ships eliminated the twelve enemy missiles Andrews estimated. Another seven missiles went astray, influenced by electronic countermeasures. That left thirteen Rodinan missiles untouched to reach detonation range. Three targeted *Symes*, while *Funnell* and *Rowen* each drew five.

Symes reported shield failures but no hull damage from this first salvo. *Rowen* and *Funnell* were not as fortunate. One of the powerful x-ray lasers reached the reactors on *Funnell*, breaching the containment of the controlled fusion reaction. The ship was consumed in a nuclear fireball as the miniature sun at the heart of the reactor expanded instantly. The damage to *Rowen* was less catastrophic but still severe. Two of the lasers penetrated the hull, exposing compartments within the ship to the void of space.

Andrews gave the order to reverse thrust to try to pull out of range. *Rowen* and *Symes* continued to fire on the Federation ships. The Rodinans had flipped their positions, trying to pull their unprotected sterns away from the fire of the

Commonwealth destroyers. It was too late, though, as the drive nacelles or housings were damaged or destroyed on all five ships.

The photon cannons from *Rowen* and *Symes* began to overload the shield generators on the Federation ships. As the shields failed, the shots started to chew into their hulls. One hundred and fifty seconds after launching their first missile salvo, the Rodinans fired another. This comprised only twenty-six missiles due to damage received from the Commonwealth cannons.

Rowen and *Symes* together could only defend against eight missiles if their point defense networks were intact. As it was, they eliminated five, with six missiles going astray due to countermeasures. Eight of the Rodinan missiles pursued larger fragments of the destroyed *Funnell*. Four remaining missiles headed for *Symes*, with three aiming for *Rowen*.

Three missiles aiming for *Symes* expended their lasers on still-shielded portions of the hull. The fourth, however, came from dead astern and destroyed her EM drives, almost reaching the reactor. Likewise, two of the three missiles targeting *Rowen* hit unprotected sections of her hull.

The front third of *Rowen* was sheared off by one x-ray laser. Another dug deep into the ship, narrowly missing the bridge. As it was, the bulkhead collapsed, exposing the bridge to the vacuum of space. With helmets and shipsuits on, the worst effect was being yanked against the harness strapping everyone into his station.

Rowen and *Symes* were now out of photon cannon range. *Rowen* continued to reverse thrust while *Symes*, without drives, was trapped by her earlier momentum. She was unable to increase her distance from the Federation ships.

One hundred and fifty seconds after the second missile salvo, a third, of twenty-three missiles, was launched by the Rodinans. With the distance between the Commonwealth ships growing, the point defense was less effective. Twelve of the Rodinan missiles unleashed their powerful lasers, all against *Symes*. The Commonwealth destroyer did not survive the onslaught. One of the lasers hit her reactors, unleashing a nuclear blast that consumed the ship.

Apparently, *Rowen* was out of range. Andrews immediately ordered sensors to scan the wreckage of the front third of the ship, beginning to drift away as the rest of *Rowen* continued to decelerate. The petty officer manning the sensors station reported she could not—those sensors were offline. However, she did report that six emergency lifepods were ejected from the bow section.

Andrews then inquired if the ship's tractor beam was still operable. When that was confirmed, she ordered them to pull the lifepods aboard. She instructed the marine gunnery sergeant in command of the ship's two squads of marines, to take two of her men and use the shuttle to look for any other possible survivors.

"The shuttle is destroyed, captain," Gunnery Sergeant Arango replied.

Andrews thought quickly. Figuring she was out of the range of the Rodinan missiles, she ordered the ship to close on the drifting piece of wreckage. "Gunny, can you have your men investigate if I pull the ship closer?"

"Affirmative, captain," Arango responded. "Our combat armor can scan for life forms as well."

Twenty minutes later, four marines were in space outside the remnant of the front of *Rowen*. One after another, they reported they could detect no signs of life. When Arango confirmed there was no one left alive, Andrews ordered them to return. By the time the marines returned, the last of the six lifepods was being brought aboard.

While waiting, Andrews surveyed the damage control reports. They did not paint a pretty picture. The front third of her ship was sheared off. Only one of her 75mm cannons remained. There were two deep holes in the ship where the x-ray lasers penetrated, both roughly three-quarters of the way through the ship. To say *Rowen*'s structural integrity was compromised was an understatement so extreme it bordered on humor. Broadcast communications were gone, as were external sensors of radar and lidar. The only remaining outside communication was through the kewpie link to the Admiralty on Caerleon Station. Through this, she could reach Aries Station.

Twenty-eight of her crew of ninety-three were missing, presumed dead. Another seventeen were listed as wounded, though that number included the twelve members of the crew now emerging from lifepods. The medical corpsman was reviving them.

When the marines and lifepods were secure, Perseverance inputted the course change necessary to bring *Rowen* gently into orbit around the inhabited planet. When that was done, she gave the command to leave the bridge. *Rowen* could be controlled in a rudimentary fashion from engineering. Any sort of complicated maneuvers would need people to return to the bridge.

The section of the companionway connecting to the bridge was also exposed to vacuum. Entering the next section, though, would require venting it to space, then restoring atmosphere after the hatch was closed again. Perseverance was the last to leave the bridge and enter the companionway's next section. She dogged the hatch shut and restored the atmosphere. When the indicator next to the hatch showed green, she opened her helmet.

Marlotte, her XO, was already giving instructions to the bridge crew with updated damage control assignments. He reminded them to keep their shipsuits and helmets on, as bulkhead failure was still possible. She waited for him to finish.

"I'll be in engineering," she said.

Her first priority was to find out what was happening outside the ship. In what condition were the Rodinan ships? What course were they following? How successful was *Rowen* in damaging their drives? Would the Rodinans be able to hit Aries Station? Some of those answers would not be immediately available. Aries Station was far enough away that the light from the encounter that just took place would not reach it for another twenty-five hours.

Her path to reach engineering required a significant detour over and around the damage. It took her nearly twenty minutes when it would ordinarily be a walk of fewer than five minutes. Upon arriving, she greeted Lieutenant Commander Choe, the head of engineering, and asked if she could take his seat.

Choe yielded the chair in front of the main engineering console. Perseverance sat down and identified herself to the computer with her thumbprint. Once recognized, she placed a call to Rear Admiral Kenard at the Admiralty. A flustered marine lieutenant answered.

"Um, Captain Andrews," he gulped.

"Lieutenant, where is the admiral's yeoman?" Perseverance asked.

"In a meeting with the admiral and admirals Czervik and Freshley," he answered. "Things are kind of crazy around here."

"Is there someone who can brief me on what is happening?" she asked.

"Um, everyone who really knows what's going on is with the admiral right now," he explained.

"What about you?" she asked.

"Me? I don't know anything. I was just walking down the corridor, and the admiral grabbed me and told me to answer any calls and take notes. I guess all hell is breaking loose," he said.

"What kind of hell?" she asked.

"The Federation and the Republics attacked in four different places. So, um, I don't think it's gone too well for us so far," he shared.

"Where did they attack us?" she asked.

"Ilium, Automedon, Aries, and Southampton, I think. I really don't know much past that," he said.

"Very well, lieutenant. Please let the admiral know I called."

Less than five minutes later, the console alerted her to an incoming call from the admiral.

"Captain Andrews, status?" she demanded.

"*Symes* and *Funnell* both destroyed, sir. *Rowen* is heavily damaged but still mobile. We have one cannon still operable. I don't know where the enemy is because we lost all our outside sensors, and Aries Station is too far away to have received any information from their scans. We damaged them, but I cannot say how severely. Currently, we are heading to orbit the planet," Andrews stated.

"Analysts are examining your sensor feeds from while you still had them," the admiral replied. "You may have disabled the drives on all five, but we cannot confirm that. In the absence of any better intelligence, continue on your course."

"Sir, what is happening?"

"The Republics attacked Automedon and Ilium. The Federation entered Aries and Southampton. Ilium and Southampton are under enemy control. Automedon Station is again destroyed, but we may have prevented the Chinese from continuing to Avalon. We don't know yet. Right now, we're trying to move assets to backstop Avalon and possibly Aries, and try to drive the enemy away from Ilium and Southampton," the admiral stated.

"What are our losses?" Perseverance asked.

"*Rowen* is the only ship to survive in all four attacks," she said, "and it sounds like you're pretty much out of the fight. You did well, captain. We could not ask for anything more. Someone will be back in contact once we know more. Kenard out."

With that call over, Andrews then contacted the Admiralty office on Aries Station. The lieutenant on duty had no other information. It would be many hours before sensor data reached the station. Perseverance asked the lieutenant to leave instructions to contact *Rowen* as soon as any information arrived.

12

Perseverance then turned her attention to damage control. For the next ten hours, she and her XO worked to stabilize the ship's condition. When they felt they had the worst problems under control, she turned her attention to the after-action report. Unfortunately, her ability to write a thorough account was constrained by the lack of sensor data. As a result, she could not determine how badly damaged the enemy ships were. Having done the best she could, she needed sleep.

Her quarters were destroyed. The best she could do was a bunk in officers' country that belonged to one of the ensigns who was missing, presumed dead. After being in a shipsuit for so long, she also needed a shower and a change of clothes. She was able to draw a new uniform from stores and headed for a shower and rest.

Her sleep was interrupted four hours later by a call from Aries Station. She brought it up on her personal comm unit. It was the lieutenant she spoke to earlier. The console identified her as Lieutenant Broadbent.

"Captain," she said, "we still have no sensor information, but an ore carrier further out picked up this—a broadcast message in the clear."

He played the recording for Perseverance: "Attention, Aries Station. This is First-Rank Captain Kurschenov of FRS *Donetsk*. We are without drive capability. We surrender and require immediate assistance."

"The message is repeating on a loop, captain," she said.

Andrews blinked to get the sleep out of her eyes. "Right," she said, taking a deep breath. "Are there any ships in the system with any sort of tractor capability?"

The lieutenant frowned in thought. "Only the tug, captain."

"What kind of tug?"

"I don't know, captain."

"Find out. Now," Andrews snapped.

The lieutenant hollered over her shoulder, asking someone for the information.

"Lieutenant, I'm going to dress and buzz you back in a few minutes. Get me the make and model of the tug. Get the ore carrier to give us a feel for where the Rodinans are. They probably don't have any sophisticated sensor capability, but they can take reads of the broadcast message, and we can triangulate. Andrews out."

Perseverance pulled aside the blackout screen of the bunk. She pulled on the khaki undress uniform she pulled from stores. Her first steps took her to the bridge before she remembered the bridge was unusable. She headed for engineering. When she arrived, the ship's third officer, Lieutenant Coulton, was seated at the console that commanded the ship. Coulton yielded her chair to the captain. Andrews contacted the lieutenant on Aries Station.

"What kind of tug, lieutenant?" she asked.

"A Church & Graham 87, sir."

Perseverance quickly looked up the specifications of that type of tug. The key factors she needed were its tractor beam's strength and the ship's acceleration. She then looked at a system map. Aries Station orbited the inhabited planet, Aries-2. It was on the far side of the ecliptic, meaning on the other side of the star from *Rowen* at the center of the system. She then added the last known course and speed for the Rodinan ships, factoring in a purely ballistic trajectory. The readings she hoped to receive from the ore carrier would confirm this.

With that information entered, she created a holographic map of the system, showing the projected path of the Rodinan ships. The good news was that the Rodinans would not fall into the star on this pass. The bad news was it wouldn't matter—they would all die when the speed of their ships exceeded the $0.3c$ threshold and their mass compensators failed. When that occurred, the mass of the ships would increase exponentially in an instant, and they would implode—collapsing in on themselves.

Andrews marked the point at which the current model showed that would happen. She then began to draw a course for the tug, leaving Aries Station and proceeding at top speed to intercept the Rodinans. Her first attempt showed the tug would arrive too late. It was close enough, though, to merit further inspection.

"Lieutenant, commandeer that tug immediately," Andrews barked. "Every minute counts. I'm working up course and speed but for now, send them on a path to slingshot around the star in the direction of the ore carrier. Get that tug moving. Contact me to confirm when it is done. I will refine the course and give them further instructions once I know they are underway."

The tug had a tractor capacity of one hundred and eighty kilotons. From the sensor readings Perseverance had of the Rodinan heavy cruiser, its mass was approximately the same. With only one tug, they could save only one vessel. The Rodinans could transfer all their people onto that ship and avoid being crushed if she could shave some time off from the tug's transit.

Perseverance returned to the tug's specifications. In particular, she was looking for a "max boost" acceleration figure. EM drives had a normal full acceleration figure. It was possible to exceed that number by as much as one hundred percent for a limited time. This was called "max boost." Doing so would increase wear and tear on the drive nacelles dramatically. Running in excess of the normal maximum for too long could also lead to failure of the drive or, even worse, the creation of a sudden harmonic tremor that could literally shake a ship apart. If a ship's max boost was greater than 500G, it would also be too much for the standard inertial dampeners to handle, and the crew would be subject to a portion of the excess G force.

Andrews guessed that the tug's drive could only tolerate max boost for four hours. She entered those numbers into the console and drew a course tighter to the central star, using the star's gravity to increase the tug's acceleration further. She tapped the key to produce the calculated course. This showed the tug would arrive with seven minutes to spare *if* it departed at that moment. She sent the course information to the lieutenant and then tried to contact her.

"Where's that tug, lieutenant?" Andrews demanded.

"Sir, the owner refuses to comply," the lieutenant replied helplessly.

"Get 'em on the call. *Now*," Andrews snapped.

Less than a minute later, a man with a porcine face appeared on the screen. His skin looked oily, as though he was sweating. His expression was smug.

"Who am I speaking with?" Andrews demanded.

"Finley Hooper," the man answered.

"Mr. Hooper," Perseverance said, trying to control the irritation that started when the lieutenant informed her the owner would not cooperate and increased once she saw his face, "the Royal Navy needs your tug and needs it this instant."

"As I told your lieutenant, I can't release the tug without a contract," Hooper replied. "We need to discuss rates and insurance coverage, liability for damages—"

"Mr. Hooper," Perseverance said through gritted teeth, "we don't have time for that. We need to get your tug moving *now!*"

"It isn't going anywhere without—"

"Hooper, I don't have the appropriate legal citation at my fingertips to prove to you that the Royal Navy can confiscate your ship at any time, but I know such a law exists. I can promise you that if you don't release that tug to me this instant, I will make sure you are tried on over six hundred counts of being an accessory to murder, in addition to whatever the war crimes tribunal comes up with," she snarled.

"What are you talking about?" Hooper protested.

"There are five Rodinan ships adrift right now. Without your tug, everyone on board them will die. The Rodinans have already communicated their surrender. That makes those deaths a civil issue and a war crime since they are prisoners of war. Therefore, I will hold you liable for those deaths. Now, give me that tug!"

"Alright, already," he whined.

"Give the lieutenant the kewpie link," Andrews stated. "She will transmit course information that *must* be followed. Every second counts. Any more foot-dragging, and it's your ass on the line, Hooper."

Perseverance ended her connection. She was furious. People like Hooper annoyed her to no end. So she waited until she cooled down before contacting the lieutenant again.

"Lieutenant Broadbent," Andrews asked, "keep the kewpie connection with the tug open. We need precise telemetry. I will send course adjustments to make sure this works."

"Yes, captain. I'll set that up and establish a link for you," Broadbent replied.

"I'm going to record a message for you to transmit to the ore carrier as well," Andrews stated. "I will send it to you in a few moments."

"Yes, captain."

Perseverance recorded a message for First-Rank Captain Kurschenov of FRS *Donetsk*, informing him that help was on the way. In the message, she instructed him to gather all his people on the heavy cruiser. It would be a near thing, but the tug should arrive with roughly ninety seconds to spare before the Rodinans crossed the threshold of 0.3c. When she finished that, she wrote up what she planned to do with the tug to save the Rodinans and transmitted it to the Admiralty.

Later that day, she received the first briefing from the Admiralty on what had happened. Forces from the Chinese Republics entered the Ilium and Automedon systems. In both cases, they attacked with a force consisting of a heavy cruiser, two light cruisers, and three destroyers, all equipped with plasma shielding, accompanied by four cruisers and five destroyers of the older, unshielded type. In Ilium, the Commonwealth force of three destroyers was wiped out, with very little damage to the Chinese. In Auromedon, the Commonwealth force was eradicated but caused enough damage that the Chinese did not continue into Avalon, the next Commonwealth system. The Rodinans attacked at Aries and Southampton. The entire Federation force of shielded and unshielded ships entered the Southampton system, and the Royal Navy was able to cause only minor damage if any.

To counter these incursions, the Royal Navy now possessed only twenty-one shielded ships—three heavy cruisers, six light cruisers, and twelve destroyers. The most immediate threat to the territorial integrity of the Commonwealth was the Chinese force in Automedon. It was also the most heavily damaged enemy force, so it did not take a genius to figure out Admiral Freshley's next move.

Following the briefing, Andrews received official approval of her plan to rescue the Rodinans. It included orders to tow the Rodinan ship to Aries Station, where arrangements were made to transport the prisoners to an unspecified detention facility. Perseverance smiled to herself. There was no detention facility on Aries-2. It was probably being constructed at this moment. In addition, the Commonwealth did not have military personnel in place to guard the Rodinan prisoners. Admiral Kenard also commented on her after-action report, stating, "Good job!"

It was mid-morning the next day when Perseverance would learn if her attempt to save the Rodinans succeeded. She watched the display of the tug's progress. When the tug came close enough to seize the Federation ship in its tractor beam, Lieutenant Broadbent opened the live voice communication channel to the tug.

The man commanding the tug knew the countdown and latched onto *Donetsk* with thirty-nine seconds to spare. Instead of a normal approach, he was going to "crack the whip" because of the lack of time. This meant the tug would sail past *Donetsk* to the limit of the tractor beam. When it reached the end, the tug's forward momentum would stop instantly, and it would be dragged behind *Donetsk*.

This maneuver would subject the tug to a massive G-force, far beyond what the inertial dampeners could counter. The dampeners would allow a fraction of the excess g-force to bleed through. It meant that the occupants of the tug would face a brief moment experiencing as much as twenty-five g. The tug's crew were all wearing g-suits and had injected themselves with the necessary precautionary drug cocktail to allow them to survive. It would be painful for them but not life-threatening. It would also reduce the momentum of the *Donetsk* instantly.

Perseverance heard the explosive grunt from the tug's crew in the instant their momentum reversed. A few seconds later, the commander reported, "We got 'em, and the other ships just turned into lumps."

At the same time, *Rowen* was nearing Aries Station. Perseverance and the remaining crew received orders to leave the ship and report to Caerleon. A transport was already on the way to collect them.

Rear Admiral Al Czervik of Blue Fleet led a force of two-thirds of the Royal Navy's ships into Automedon. Perseverance was the last to leave *Rowen* since she was watching Czervik's entrance into the Automedon system with great interest. She continued monitoring the situation on her personal comm all the way to the transport ship.

She was disappointed to learn only three of the Republics' ships were still in the Automedon system—the heavy cruiser and two light cruisers. Apparently, they were too heavily damaged to make the jump to hyperspace. Her old friend Ken Berger had been in command of the three Royal Navy destroyers. Though he did not survive the battle, he ensured the Chinese would advance no further.

When the Royal Navy ships drew to within five million kilometers, the Chinese ships launched a salvo of twenty-one missiles. Perseverance guessed some of their launch tubes were damaged and unrepaired. The Chinese continued to fire salvos every three minutes. The point defense of Czervik's ships was able to counter these missiles, and only one reached detonation range. The Chinese surrendered as soon as Czervik's ships pulled within the range of their photon cannons.

On the second day of the journey to Caerleon, Perseverance received notice to join a call from Admiral Kenard at 14:00. It would be a welcome break from her primary duty during the trip—writing condolence letters to the parents or spouses of the twenty-eight members of the crew who died. *Rowen* had a small crew. As a result, Perseverance knew every member. Writing the letters was emotionally wrenching. While she could not say she liked every crew member, she certainly knew them. For those of whom she was fond, the letters were tough to write.

Just before the appointed time, she positioned herself at the console in her small cabin. At 14:00 precisely, the console alerted her to the incoming call. She pressed the key to respond.

"Admiral," she greeted her, noticing she was the only other person on the call. She had thought it would be a conference.

"Captain Andrews," Kenard replied. "I apologize for the long delay in contacting you."

"Sir," she protested, "things have been rather busy."

"Nevertheless, I wish to congratulate you and thank you for your successful defense of Aries. I know you were unhappy with the political reality of mounting our defense as we did, and the losses were every bit as horrible as you predicted," she said. "That only adds to the luster of what you and your force accomplished. The crews on *Rowen*, *Symes*, and *Funnell* will be granted Royal Unit Citations. I have nominated you for the Conspicuous Gallantry Cross."

"Thank you, sir," Perseverance replied.

"You will be joining Admiral Freshley's staff for the next six months," he continued. "Your next command will not be available before then. She's still under construction—a heavy cruiser, HMS *Manitoba*."

"What will I be doing on his staff?" Perseverance asked.

"Working with Parliament and helping promote the war effort in the media," Kenard explained. "Like it or not, you're the only hero we have so far. So we're going to trot you out in front of the politicians and the press."

"So, I won't really be *doing* anything," she surmised. "Just dealing with imbeciles."

"That's unfortunately close to the truth," Kenard stated. "A sad reality is that it is hard for the Royal Navy to maintain its funding unless there's a war on. Then it becomes all too easy, even though it's too late. According to what Admiral Freshley told me, you're going to help ensure that we scoop up as much as we possibly can while we can. This war won't last forever. We want to make sure we are far stronger at the end of it than we were at the beginning."

"How long do you think the war will last, sir?"

"Three, maybe four years," she replied. "We have two advantages. First, we have a technological edge in terms of our powerplants. MI-6 estimates our enemies are more than three or four years away from matching us. The other advantage is our industrial capacity. Compared to our enemies, we can build more ships, faster."

"Don't our enemies know this?" she asked.

"The Republics and the Federation have been more aggressive in their shipbuilding in the last few years than the Commonwealth," Kenard said with a frown. "As I said, it has been difficult to maintain funding. In the next twelve months, they will launch a wave of new ships while our cupboard will be bare. We will have a bit of a storm to weather then. Three years from now, the situation will be reversed when the keels we lay down in the immediate near future become ships joining the service. If we can hang on until then, we'll win."

"And our enemies believe they can win before that happens?" she suggested.

"They hope," Kenard clarified. "Unfortunately for them, their one tactical advantage is soon to be eliminated. By the time you take command of *Manitoba*, you'll have missiles with bomb-pumped lasers similar to those of the Republics and Federation. They still won't have anything to match our photon cannons. That's classified, by the way, even though the rumor mill is all over it. Regardless, as I said, we will need to weather a bit of a storm, but I am confident we will."

13

As soon as the transport emerged into normal space in the Caerleon system, Perseverance's comm unit lit up. Someone from the Royal Navy Office of Public Affairs tried to reach her while the ship was in hyperspace. Perseverance looked at the screen. The computer identified the contact as Commander Saint John Powell. She returned the call. A man with video star good looks answered.

"Ah, Captain Andrews. Thank you for returning my call," he said.

"Commander," she replied neutrally.

"Captain, I'm going to be your liaison with the Office of Public Affairs for the next several months," he said. "I'll be the one coordinating your interaction with the media and public at large."

Andrews rolled her eyes at this.

"I understand your reaction," Powell said, "but these orders come from Admiral Freshley himself. Though you now are part of his staff, most of your time will be spent far away from the Admiralty. You and I are taking a media tour of all twenty-five settled Commonwealth systems."

"Really?" Andrews asked in a disbelieving tone, her face screwed up in distaste.

"Really. And your first press conference will be when your transport docks at Caerleon Station," he said. "Would I be correct in guessing that you do not have a formal dress uniform with you?"

"My quarters were destroyed in the battle," she replied, "so, no—I don't have a dress uniform."

"Are your sizes in the system?" he asked.

"They should be."

"Fine. I'll have one prepared for you and delivered aboard once the transport docks. You'll need to change quickly and then come meet the media."

"What the hell am I expected to say?" she asked.

"Not much, actually. Best to keep it to general platitudes and not take any questions," Powell replied. "Something along the lines of, 'I'm happy to be back, owe it all to my crew.' Maybe ask for a moment of silence for those who lost their lives in defense of the Commonwealth and leave it at that. This is more to get your picture in circulation. Take a few minutes to jot something down and run it by me. Otherwise, I'll prepare a script for you."

"Why is this even necessary?" Perseverance protested with a hint of whining in her tone.

"C'mon, captain. You're an intelligent woman," Powell answered. "The Royal Navy just got its ass kicked. You are the only hero we have. You will be the navy's public face for the next few months. You're going to inspire the Commonwealth to support the war effort. Of course, it helps that you are physically attractive—you will be that much more effective. Besides, these orders come from Admiral Freshley. We don't have to like our orders, but we do need to carry them out. You should have learned that in ROTC."

"Fine," she said with a sigh.

"I'm sending you a preliminary itinerary for the next few days," Powell said. "Let me know if you have any questions."

Powell ended the call, and almost immediately, Perseverance's comm unit indicated she received a file. She opened it and began to look it over. The first event was her arrival at Caerleon Station. According to Powell's schedule, the news conference was scheduled for 17:00.

Caerleon Station, and the Royal Navy, kept Caerleon Standard Time. This was the same time as in the city of Caerleon, the capital of the Commonwealth. The planet Caerleon had a twenty-three-hour and fifty-six-minute day and a year of just over three hundred and seventy days. The Commonwealth maintained the old earth calendar. With twenty-five inhabited planets, each with their own planetary axis, rotation cycle, and orbital period, it would have been impossible to create a calendar that matched the months to the seasons, so the decision was made long ago to simply maintain the earth calendar.

After the press conference, Perseverance was scheduled for dinner with Commander Powell. The next following days were blocked out for briefings. Her third day after arriving showed a visit to Caerleon Yard and HMS *Manitoba*. That was the only thing she saw on the schedule that made her smile.

Perseverance was not frightened by public speaking. She actually considered it a strength. The press, however, was a different proposition. Her view of the news media was that they much preferred setting up a "gotcha" moment, where they could lure someone into a misstatement, than reporting news.

In her mind, she reviewed her conversation with Commander Powell. She was aware they got off to a slightly negative start. It was not his fault—he had a job to do. She considered that if the two of them were traveling to all twenty-five settled Commonwealth systems, they would probably be forced to spend up to six months in close company.

She looked him up in the navy database. Powell was an academy graduate in the top quintile of his class. His first postings were line positions. All his promotions to higher ranks came in his first year of eligibility, which spoke to his performance. While serving as a lieutenant commander aboard HMS *Darling*, he earned the Distinguished Service Cross for bravery. After that, Powell transferred to a staff position in the Office of Public Affairs, coinciding with his promotion to Commander. There was obviously more to Powell than she suspected initially. Perseverance thought it would be better to clear the air now than let any bad feelings linger. She tapped out another message.

Commander Powell: Please understand my lack of enthusiasm for our upcoming assignment in no way applies to you or reflects any fear of public speaking. My negative view of the news media is the source of any reluctance. I look forward to meeting you and working together.
   Andrews

She then began to draft her "statement." When she felt comfortable with it, she set it aside. She would review it in the morning and transmit it to Powell after making revisions.

Two days later, the transport docked at Caerleon Station. As soon as the gangway was secure, a courier appeared, bearing Perseverance's new number one dress uniform. Taking the bundle to her tiny cabin, she quickly changed, donning the black hosiery, white shirt and black tie, navy blue double-breasted mess jacket and skirt, and white hat. She put on the shoes that were included and breathed a sigh of relief that they fit. After she stowed her undress khakis in her bag, she checked her appearance in the mirror.

Even though she was her own worst critic, she admitted to herself she wore the uniform well. Something about wearing the "number ones" made her stand a bit straighter and lift her chin slightly higher. The uniform fit well. She was tall and broad-shouldered, angular and not curvy. Her coal-black hair fell straight to just short of her collar, and she usually wore it tucked behind her ears. She had strong facial features with expressive eyebrows. A former boyfriend once told her she was "damned attractive but not pretty." That description suited her just fine. She jammed her hat on, grabbed her bag, and headed for the gangway.

After a brisk walk, she joined the dwindling queue of members of her crew from *Rowen* waiting to disembark. She shared farewells with handshakes and hugs as the line moved forward. Waiting at the hatch was her executive officer, Lieutenant Commander Marlotte.

"Looking sharp, skipper," he commented, holding his arms open for a hug.

After a quick clasp, they released. "Good luck and Godspeed, Marc," she said, then headed down the gangway.

Commander Powell was waiting at the bottom, next to the station hatch. He, too, was in dress uniform. He saluted, and Perseverance returned it. Then he reached for her bag. She pulled it off her shoulder. Powell took it and handed it to an enlisted man.

"We're in conference room A," he said, gesturing to the left.

They began walking. Also dressed in number ones, Powell was as good-looking in person as he appeared over the comm. He was about five centimeters taller than Perseverance. Powell smoothly adjusted his position so he was on her left, to the outside of the corridor. When they had nearly reached the security checkpoint where crew members were meeting their families, Powell pointed to a door on the right. He beat her to it by a step and opened it.

"I'm sorry to drag you away from your crew," he said. "We are right on schedule."

Perseverance noted he used the British pronunciation, though he did not have a British accent. They continued down the corridor, turning left at the next intersection. The first door on the right was marked "A." Before opening the door, Powell stopped.

"You have your remarks?" he asked.

Perseverance pointed to her head and nodded.

"Good. I'll introduce you. You deliver your remarks, and then I'll close. We will not be taking any questions this time," Powell said. "Ready?"

Perseverance nodded. Powell opened the door, and she strode in, stopping just short of the dais. She set her face in a neutral expression, then turned to face a room full of reporters and cameras. At least the lighting in the room was bright enough that the camera flash mechanisms were not needed. Otherwise, she would be blinded. Powell walked behind her and ascended to the lectern. He cleared his throat and began.

"Members of the press—may I present Captain Perseverance Andrews, late of Her Majesty's Ship *Howard Earl Rowen*. Under Captain Andrews' leadership, the *Rowen* was the only Royal Navy ship to survive the recent attacks, though not without cost. In addition, Captain Andrews successfully thwarted the Federation's attack, disabling all their ships and saving Aries Station, despite being outnumbered. Finally, Captain Andrews took command of the rescue effort that saved the lives of five hundred and ninety-one Rodinan prisoners. Ladies and gentlemen, Captain Andrews."

Polite applause greeted Perseverance as she climbed the two steps to the lectern, but it died down as soon as she faced them.

"Before I deliver my remarks, I would like to request a moment of silence on behalf of all the brave men and women of the Royal Navy who gave their lives in defense of our Commonwealth."

Perseverance bowed her head and counted slowly and silently to fifty. She noticed that the crowded conference room fell completely quiet. As she counted, the faces and names of her crew passed through her mind, as well as her friends Ken Berger, Jimmy Brighenti, the captain of HMS *Symes*, Tadhg Cokeley, captain of HMS *Funnell*, and other friends and acquaintances she knew who perished. Tears welled in her eyes.

Raising her head, she said, her voice lower-pitched than before, "Thank you."

Perseverance drew herself to her full height and looked out at the reporters as a tear rolled down her right cheek. "I'm grateful to be here, in front of you today. Without my crew, and without the support of the other members of our force in Aries, the *Symes* and the *Funnell*, I would not be here. We lost twenty-eight members of our crew on *Rowen*—men and women I knew well. *Symes* and *Funnell* lost all hands, as did every other ship which stood to face this unprovoked attack by the Republics and the Federation."

As she spoke, her voice climbed back to its normal register. Then, with a few blinks, the moisture in her eyes gave way to a steely glare. The track of the lone tear which escaped evaporated under the lights focused on her.

"I'm grateful that I survived because I intend to continue the fight—to my last breath, if need be, just like my friends and shipmates. It was a black day for the Royal Navy and for our Commonwealth. That battle is over, but it was not the end. Many battles remain to be fought. I would like to close with a quote from a great leader in our Commonwealth's past on earth, Winston Churchill. During the darkest days of a war where we suffered defeat after defeat in the early days, he said, 'We shall not fail or falter. We shall not weaken or tire. Neither the sudden shock of battle nor the long-drawn trials of vigilance and exertion will wear us down. Give us the tools and we will finish the job.' Ladies and gentlemen of the media, fellow citizens of our great Commonwealth, that is my pledge to you—we shall not fail or falter. That is my request of you—give us the tools so we can finish the job. Thank you."

Perseverance stepped down from the lectern. Powell moved behind her and took his place in front of the crowd. Several members of the media were already trying to shout questions. Powell raised his hand for silence and began to speak over the shouts.

"Please," he said. "That's all for today, folks. We will schedule a full press conference in the next few days. You will have the opportunity to ask questions then."

Powell left the podium and escorted Perseverance out through the door they entered. The press continued to shout questions as they walked away. Even when the door shut, it still took a few seconds for the tumult to die down.

"That was brilliant," Powell commented. "The draft you sent was good, but your delivery made it powerful."

He took her to the BOQ on Caerleon Station, where she obtained a room. When the clerk asked how long she would be staying, she looked to Powell.

"Four days," he replied.

Before Perseverance went to her room, he told her, "I'll be back to pick you up for dinner in an hour, at 19:00. You can change into casual clothes."

She laughed. "I don't have any—unless you count undress khakis as casual clothing."

"Right," he said with a soft chuckle. "Remind me to give you some time to buy some. We have a long haul in front of us, and you won't need to be in uniform the whole time—unless you prefer…"

"Perhaps over dinner, you can give me an idea of what our upcoming tour will look like. That will help me figure out the clothing piece. Unfortunately, my quarters on *Rowen* were vaporized, so I don't have much."

"Will do," he said. "I'll be back at 19:00."

14

Powell met Perseverance in the lobby of the BOQ. He was wearing undress khakis. She raised an eyebrow at this.

"Since you don't have anything else to wear, I thought I should match," he said. "It did mean changing my idea of where to eat. So we'll dine in the Officers' Mess here. It's quite good."

"Where were you going to take me?" she asked.

"Somewhere more fun. I'll just save it for another time. The Officers' Mess offers one advantage. We can speak relatively freely," he said.

Shortly after they were taken to a table, he asked, "I'm not much of a drinker, but I do enjoy a glass of wine now and then. If you'll join me, perhaps we could split a bottle? I only ask because it will keep interruptions down."

"That makes sense."

"Red or white?"

"That depends. Is the beef they serve real four-legged beef or…?" Perseverance asked.

"It's real."

"Then red. I'll be ordering a steak."

The server arrived and asked if they wanted anything to drink. Powell looked at the wine list quickly. He paused, thinking.

"A bottle of the Bristol Mills Cabernet," Powell said.

As the server retreated, Powell said, "It's good, not great, but my expense account doesn't allow great. It comes from New Boston—one of the better mass-market vineyards."

"You know wine?"

"Only a little," he said with a shrug. "I don't drink alcohol often, so when I do, I'd rather not drink crap."

"Why tonight?" Perseverance asked.

"A couple of reasons. Since we are just getting to know one another, I figure a glass of wine might help us relax a little."

"You said a couple of reasons," Perseverance reminded him when he mentioned nothing else.

"Please don't take this the wrong way," he cautioned, "but watching you today, I got the sense you could use a glass of wine or two. You've been under great stress, and this assignment seems to have added to it. It shouldn't. Based on how you handled yourself earlier, the next few months will be easy as pie."

"That's an expression I haven't heard in a long time. And, you're probably right about the stress," she admitted.

The server returned with the bottle of wine. He went through the process of opening it and presenting the cork to Commander Powell. He then poured a small amount into Powell's glass for him to sample. Powell took a sip and nodded. The server then filled Powell's wineglass halfway and did the same for Perseverance.

"Since we are going to be spending a great deal of time together," Perseverance said, "I reckon it would be rude to call you 'Commander' all the time. What is your first name? Saint?"

"My mother's curse strikes again," Powell chuckled. "It's pronounced Sinjin."

"Why is that your mother's curse?"

"She is very British. She delivered me on June twenty-fourth, which is Saint John's Day. He is the patron saint of love, loyalty, friendship, and authors."

"I noticed you don't seem to have an accent," Perseverance remarked, "but you do pronounce certain words the British way."

"Would you pwefeh it if I spoke moah wike this?" he replied, adopting a drawling aristocratic English accent made famous by a bumbling character on a long-running video comedy series.

Perseverance laughed. "No," she said between chuckles, shaking her head.

"Mother isn't quite that bad," Powell commented. "My father is American, and I grew up on Carolina, where they still live. In addition to my strange first name, some of her British pronunciation stuck in my head. Growing up, the kids in school beat most of it out of me, but some still lingers, tucked away in my brain."

The server took their orders. Perseverance ordered a porterhouse steak with a baked potato and asparagus. Powell told the server he would have the same.

"So," Perseverance began, "I did some checking up on you. How does an academy graduate with a Distinguished Service Cross end up in Public Affairs?"

Powell closed his eyes for a moment. "Right to it," he commented under his breath. "Captain, I promise I will share the story behind my switch but not tonight. My current position is not as farfetched as you might think. My father is a partner with Meldrum, Fewsmith and Powell, the biggest advertising agency on Carolina and one of the biggest in the Commonwealth. My mother is a copywriter for them. Advertising and public relations were the usual dinner table conversation topics while I was growing up. Turning the tables, how does a preacher's daughter from Alleghany end up in the Royal Navy?"

"Haven't you heard about preachers' kids?" she said. "We're all rebellious as hell and have daddy issues—or mommy issues if she's the minister."

"Is that why you joined the navy?" he asked with a smile.

"Partly. Why did you? You went to the academy. You were far more committed than I was," she said.

"I'll answer you in a minute," he said. "First, are you close with your family? There's a reason I'm asking."

"Not close, but not estranged," she replied. "I contact my parents and my sibs on their birthdays and at Christmas, and they return the favor. We're past the gift-giving stage. Why?"

"It might come up during our travels," he said, fudging the truth slightly. "You wanted to know why I went to the academy?"

She nodded

"A lot of reasons," he said. "One was that I didn't want to spend my life thinking about ways to convince people to buy one brand of toilet paper over another. Another was foolish romantic notions I had in my head from stories I read as a boy. I thought the uniforms were sharp. The structure and discipline appealed to me… I could go on, but it's your turn."

"Isn't what you're doing right now trying to convince people to buy a brand of toilet paper?" she retorted.

"If I have to be a shill for something, what better product than the Commonwealth and the Royal Navy? I'm still serving the Commonwealth and get to wear the snazzy uniform," he replied. "Your turn. Quit dodging the question, captain. Why did you join the Royal Navy?"

"If we're going to be spending so much time together, you can call me Perse," she said. "If we get to be friends, I'll even let you call me Persie without punching you in the nose."

"Thank you, Perse," he said, smiling at her continued attempts to deflect. "The question?"

"I already told you—rebellion and daddy issues," she said, "at least, in the beginning. All of my siblings rebelled in their own way. Thankfully, we all survived the rebellious phase. I think I chose the least destructive path. As soon as I arrived at college, away from home, I immediately wanted to do something to prove my independence. If it pissed my father off, so much the better. Joining the officer training program accomplished that. He's still not over it."

"That's a good reason to start," Powell admitted, "but you stuck with it after you learned what was actually involved. Why?"

"I haven't spent too much time thinking about it," she said. "You're going to keep pressing me for answers, though, so give me a minute."

Fortunately for Perseverance, the server brought their food. With a flourish, he placed their plates in front of them, then hovered nearby, waiting for them to sample the food. Perseverance quickly cut into her steak and sliced a small bite. It was every bit as delicious as she hoped. She gave the server a thumbs up.

By the time she finished chewing and swallowed, she thought up her answer. "Despite our desire to rebel against our father, all four of us were indoctrinated to a life of service to others. Sublimating my own desires to pursue a common goal, as the navy demands, resonated within me. Instead of something abstract, like religion, the navy's goals are concrete. I like that. The structure and predictability were appealing. The uniforms are snazzy, like you said. However, what really convinced me was that I thrived in this new world. Being in the navy makes me happy, most of the time."

"Most of the time," he commented. "When does it not?"

"When I'm forced to deal with the jackals and hyenas of the news media," she retorted.

"That's already been communicated," he said. "Give me another."

"Okay," she replied, wiping her lips. "Being put into an impossible situation and not being able to fix it."

"I suspect you're talking about recent events?" he inquired.

"Yeah. We all knew the Republics and/or the Federation would be coming for us. The proper thing to do, strategically, would be to prepare a defense in depth, pulling out of the border systems and positioning our forces to respond to an enemy incursion. I know why we didn't, and I accept the decision, but I don't have to like it."

"Why do you think you were stuck in that position?" he asked.

"Politics," she replied. "The residents of the systems we left would not understand the strategic reasons for doing so. They would feel that they were abandoned. Then, if the enemy entered and gained control of the system, even temporarily, they would feel betrayed. The news media would fan the flames and create a political crisis. So instead, we sacrificed twelve ships and their crews. From an ethical, moral, and financial standpoint, that loss is greater than a temporary occupation of our systems. We weighed the political complications more heavily. And now, you want me to visit every settled system in the Commonwealth to 'sell' the idea that we did the best we could. Sorry, commander, but that's bullshit."

"Sounds to me like you don't accept the decision," Powell said. "Not trying to pick a fight..."

Perseverance took another bite to give herself time to think and cool down. Calming down was easy. Her steak tasted divine. The thinking it through took a bit longer.

"I do accept it," she said. "Part of what makes the Commonwealth a better place to live is our system of government. You've never heard of refugees trying to escape the Commonwealth to live elsewhere—it's always the other way around. In this case, the cost of maintaining political stability in a crisis bigger than any we faced before is the sacrifice of twelve ships, like pawns in a chess match. I accept the necessity, but that doesn't mean I have to like being a pawn in a bigger game."

"So, not a pawn," he commented. "What do you see yourself as?"

"A knight," she replied with a grin. "Swooping in from some unlikely place and creating havoc or saving the day."

"Do you still have a problem with 'selling' our cause?" he asked.

"You're going to need to give me a few days, Saint John. I just lost some of my crew and some good friends," she said. "Plus, I nearly got my ass blown up. I'm not in the greatest frame of mind. The necessity of winning the war—no problem. Defending our opening action? Give me some time."

"Next question—do you have any skeletons in your closet? Any deep, dark embarrassing secrets I should know before the media airs them out?" he asked.

Perseverance almost spluttered out the mouthful she was chewing. "What the hell?" she exclaimed once she swallowed.

"You mentioned you are a preacher's daughter," he said with a sly grin. "There's a certain preconception—"

"No," she stated firmly. "Not me. Don't ask about my brother and my sisters, though."

"They match the stereotype?"

"Sex, drugs, piercings, arrests, keeping bad company—oh yeah, they did it all, except for tattoos. I'm the only one who got one, but I skipped the other stuff. As I said, they all survived and made it through to the other side. One is a nurse, one is a teacher, and one is a psychologist. All of us leading lives of service to others," she said.

"You have a tattoo? Where?"

"You don't know me well enough yet."

"How do your parents feel about their children?"

"They are mostly pleased with how we turned out—though I ended up the black sheep of the bunch."

"How?"

"Because I might kill people in doing my job," she said.

"But what you do might result in saving thousands more," Saint John exclaimed.

"I tried that argument. Didn't fly," she said. "What about you? Your folks happy with your choices?"

"They were."

"They aren't now?"

"It's more than they don't understand why I haven't left."

"Would this have to do with your DSC?"

"It does. And I promise I'll tell you but not tonight," he said. "Anything else I should know?"

She looked at him quizzically while she ate another bite. One of her eyebrows lifted. She chuckled quietly while she finished chewing.

"You're trying to ask if I'm involved with anyone without asking, aren't you?"

"I would never..." he mock-protested. "It's against regulations."

He paused, then continued. "But if I were trying to learn that, it would only be so you could warn him or her before the media show up on their doorstep. There is also a ceremony on Friday that you might want to invite a significant other to attend."

"Ceremony? For what?"

"You're being awarded the Conspicuous Gallantry Cross," he said.

"Admiral Kenard mentioned she put me up for it but normally those things take months, if not years."

"When Queen Charlotte learned of it, she insisted the process be shortened."

"The queen is involved?"

"The queen is very involved," Saint John said. "Even though her constitutional authority is virtually nil, she wields a great amount of indirect influence. She keeps herself well-informed. From what I heard, she persuaded Admiral Freshley that the Commonwealth needed a hero. He agreed."

"Was it her idea to have us gallivanting around the Commonwealth?"

"I don't know, but it certainly might have been. Now, is there anyone you would like to invite to the ceremony?"

Perseverance shook her head. "You asked me, so what about you? Any significant other?"

"Not for a while," he answered neutrally. "Would you like to invite anyone from your family? By the way, you should also alert your family about the media possibly contacting them."

"You don't need to invite any of the family. As far as my father is concerned, I'm still the rebellious daughter. My brother and sisters wouldn't be able to get here in time. Will the media really contact my family?" Perseverance asked.

"Did I, or did I not tell you that you were going to become the public face of the Royal Navy?" he asked.

"You did," she said glumly.

"If I'm any good at my job—and I should tell you, with all due modesty, I am damned good at it—you are about to become one of the most recognized people in the Commonwealth, second, perhaps, only to Queen Charlotte," he said.

"Bullshit."

"Oh, ye of little faith… I'll remind you that you said that in a couple of months," he teased.

"But… I'm just me," she protested. "I'm not—"

Powell held up his hand for her to stop. He pulled out his comm unit. After searching for a moment, he handed it to her.

"It's already begun," he said.

She looked on the screen. There was a picture of her from the press conference, showing the tear on her cheek and the determined set to her jaw. Though embarrassed, she had to admit it was one of the better snapshots ever taken of her. She scrolled down. The headline of the article that went with the picture read, "We shall not fail or falter."

"You're kidding, right?" she asked.

"Nope. You don't even know the best part."

She raised an eyebrow.

"This is from the *Clarion*. Their normal stance is to vehemently oppose any position the government takes—doesn't matter which party is in power. However, they seem to hate the Tories just a bit more," he explained. "Their coverage of this afternoon is amazingly positive. Not only is their article positive, but they also chose a flattering photo of you. With no makeup and the crappy lighting in the room, they probably have hundreds that make you look awful."

"But I'm not that special," she objected.

"Wrong," he said flatly. "We lost eleven of twelve ships last week, and only yours survived, though it might as well be scrapped. You might say that your survival was a matter of luck, and you might be correct. What is not a matter of luck is that the group under your command is the only one of four that prevented the enemy from obtaining its objective. That's not luck. That's competent leadership. Add to that the fact that you are arrestingly attractive—"

"Shut up," she interjected.

"You'll see," he said.

15

They finally agreed to disagree on that subject. The rest of the meal was spent discussing the topics that would be covered in the next day of briefings. He also warned her that she would be expected to make some "off the cuff" remarks during her visit to Caerleon Yard to see her next ship.

The first briefing was the following day, Tuesday, from Advanced Warfare. An older woman whose name Perseverance did not catch conducted the briefing. The woman's appearance was unkempt, with long, frizzy gray hair and rumpled clothing. She spoke in a monotone, making it even harder to pay attention. Nevertheless, Perseverance was able to learn of two significant developments.

First, there were advances in electrical conduit composition and in capacitor design that would reduce cycle time for the Royal Navy's photon cannons, increasing the rate of fire. The new technology would be included on all ships under construction. Existing ships would require a refit, and there was no timetable for that.

The other piece of news was the introduction of the Cyclops anti-ship missile. Like the Chinese and Rodinan missiles, the warhead contained an expendable x-ray laser powered by a nuclear fission bomb. The Cyclops missile had a range of five million kilometers. The warhead would detonate at fifty thousand kilometers from the target, similar to the Chinese and Rodinan missiles. The Cyclops was already in production. Though numbers were limited, the first of them were already on the way to the remaining ships in the navy, along with a software update to control them. They fit in existing launch tubes.

By the time they broke for lunch, Perseverance's head ached. The woman from Advanced Warfare was so relentlessly dull that it had been a strain to pay attention, especially after two glasses of wine the night before. The information shared was wonderful, but the mumbling delivery and the lack of any eye contact from the presenter made it an ordeal.

The afternoon briefing began with a presentation from a lieutenant on Admiral Freshley's staff. She gave an update on current ship construction. In Caerleon Yard, there were currently five ships nearing completion—one heavy cruiser, HMS *Manitoba*, two light cruisers, and two destroyers. There was another group of five ships that were still two years away from completion.

When the lieutenant finished, a member of MI-6 entered and provided estimates of the construction underway in the Federation. The Rodinans had twice as many ships under construction as the Commonwealth, due at roughly the same time. The presenter apologized for the lack of firm information regarding shipbuilding efforts in the Chinese Republics, but MI-6 was confident their numbers were similar to the Federation.

When the briefing wrapped up at 15:00, Commander Powell pulled Perseverance aside. "You have the next few hours free," he advised. "Do you have dinner plans?"

She shook her head.

"I'd be delighted if you would join me again," he said. "I did not want to presume—you might have friends you would like to catch up with while we're here on the station. We'll spend a lot of time with one another over the next few months. I don't want you to get tired of me right away."

"I had not even thought about it," she admitted. "There might be, but I'll have to check. In any case, I'm free this evening."

"Why don't you take advantage of a few hours free and buy some civilian clothing. The place I have in mind for dinner tonight calls for a dressy casual look. For me, that will be slacks, dress shirt, sport coat, and no tie," Saint John said.

"I'll see what I can do. What time?"

"I'll pick you up at 19:00," he said. "If you want to make other plans, tomorrow night and Thursday night, you're free. Friday night, you have a commitment."

"What commitment?"

"I'll tell you over dinner," he said, strolling away.

Commander Powell might have thought he was giving Perseverance permission to indulge herself by shopping, but the truth of it was she hated it. One of the things she liked about the Royal Navy was the uniform since it eliminated any choices. Her figure—tall and slender, with wide, square shoulders—meant ready-to-wear clothing rarely fit properly, except for athletic wear, which she usually found in men's sizes.

She consulted her comm unit to determine what options there were on the station. Leaving the navy section, she headed for a mass merchant. She figured she would begin with the easiest things and work her way up. She bought comfortable workout clothes first. Rather than lug her purchases around with her, she opted to pay the small charge to have them delivered to the BOQ.

From there, she decided to visit a boutique named "Anton's." The shopping directory she accessed gave it the highest reviews, though it cautioned that it was expensive. Cost didn't matter to her much. She hardly spent any of her income, so had a sizeable cash reserve in the bank. Besides, in her experience, stores like that were quite accomplished at kissing their customers' butts. Since she expected to find nothing that would fit, her disappointment would be tempered by someone fawning over her obsequiously.

When she reached Anton's, one glance in the window confirmed her guess. Opening the door, it made a tiny bell tinkle. There were two stunningly attractive women, both on the cusp of middle age. Perseverance figured they were in their late forties though most people would think they were a decade younger. Both women turned to approach her but were stopped by a hiss, "Ssst!" A short and slight man with thinning dark hair slicked back and a pencil-thin mustache came trotting up from the rear of the store.

"No, no, ladies. I will assist Capitana Andrews," he called. "Buon, pomeriggio, Capitana," he said, bowing deeply. "I am Anton. You honor us with your presence."

Perseverance wanted to laugh out loud. Anton was probably no more Italian than she was. He knew how to kiss butt, though, and judging by the appearance of the two assistants, he knew his business.

"Why, thank you, Anton," she said, playing his little game and adopting a suitable persona. "I'm flattered that you know who I am."

"Everyone knows la Capitana Andrews," he protested. "Such a speech you made… But you don't want to hear that. How may we help you?"

"In the attack, my quarters were destroyed, along with everything I owned," she said, making a 'pfft' sound and gesturing with her fingers as though a balloon just flew away from them. "All my civilian clothing—gone. And tonight, my friend wants to take me to dinner somewhere 'dressy casual,' and I have nothing to wear except uniforms."

"You have come to the only shop on Caerleon Station that can help you, Capitana Andrews," Anton stated.

"Ah," she sighed sadly. "If only that were true, but I am too tall, too square," she said, wiggling her shoulders, "but not big," she added, cupping her hands in front of her chest. "Nothing fits."

"Nonsense!" he exclaimed emphatically. "You have una bella figura. I know designers who would fight for the chance to dress you. Come. You will see."

Anton turned and strode to the rear of the shop. As he turned, he snapped his fingers, and one of the assistants hurried to follow him. Fighting to hide her smile, Perseverance followed. Anton spun around again and looked Perseverance up and down. He scurried over to a rack, his assistant close behind. Anton began by pulling two dresses and handing them back to his assistant without looking. After skipping a few racks, he pulled another. He darted across the room and pulled two more. Anton then looked at Perseverance's feet.

"Nine?" he asked.

Perseverance nodded.

"Becky, the Vittorio 'kittens' size nine, black," he ordered the other assistant.

Turning back to Perseverance, he instructed, "Go with Laura and try these on. Wait for the shoes to get the full effect."

Perseverance really wanted to laugh. She found the whole thing comical. If the dresses Anton selected really did fit, she knew she wouldn't be able to contain herself.

Laura was waiting outside a dressing cubicle. The dresses were hanging inside. Becky had already brought the shoes, black patent leather pumps with a short heel. She had also left two of the nylon slip-ons one wears when trying on shoes, along with a shoehorn.

Perseverance entered the cubicle and examined what Anton had selected. They were roughly the same length and would hit her just above the knee. The styles were different, as were the colors. The one which seized her eye and that she hoped most would fit was a metallic gray. She would try it on last. She stripped off her uniform and took the burgundy dress from its hanger.

Perseverance pulled it on over her head, then reached behind to pull up the zipper. She then bent down and slid on the nylon footies, and tried on the shoes. The shoehorn was a help, as the shoes fit perfectly—snug but not tight. She then turned to look in the mirror.

Her laughter bubbled out before she could stop it when she saw her reflection. She clapped her hand over her mouth quickly. Perseverance turned to one side, then the other to see how she looked. The dress fit close to perfect. It was tasteful and though a bit demure, was undeniably classy. She looked down at her feet. Perseverance did not usually wear heels due to her height, but these weren't too bad, bringing out the definition in her calf muscles.

Still chuckling softly, she muttered, "Son of a bitch."

"Is everything alright?" Laura asked anxiously.

Perseverance laughed again. "Everything is good," she replied. "I'm just not accustomed to finding clothes that fit me so well."

"Let's take a look," Laura suggested.

Perseverance opened the curtain. Laura beckoned her into the room, then indicated Perseverance should turn around. When Perseverance completed her slow spin, she saw Laura was scribbling down notes on a pad of paper. Laura sent her back in for the next dress.

This one was royal blue. Again, it fit just as well as the first. When Perseverance opened the curtain, though, Laura took one look and said, "No. Not a good color."

The next dress was kelly green. Laura again made Perseverance come out and spin, making notes. The next one was teal and Laura rejected it immediately, also based on the color. The last was the gray. Perseverance crossed her fingers. This was the most daring of the five dresses. The front was conservative enough, with a yoke collar showing her collar bones. The back was almost non-existent, exposing nearly the entire expanse from shoulder to shoulder and dipping almost to the point of scandal. She tried looking over her shoulder, but it was difficult to get an accurate picture. She liked what she could see, though.

When she opened the curtain, Laura drew her breath in sharply. Laura circled her finger, requesting Perseverance to turn. When Laura saw her back, she murmured, "Oh, yes."

"Take a picture?" Perseverance asked.

Laura used her comm unit to do so. Perseverance turned, and Laura handed her the comm. The photo showed Perseverance's near-naked back.

"Damn!" she muttered.

Laura called Anton in. He took one look at Perseverance and smiled. Then, he circled his finger, calling for her to turn around.

"Magnificent," he whispered, his pretend Italian accent disappearing.

Laura made Perseverance try on the burgundy and the green for Anton to see. He pulled the fabric in a few places, securing it with pins. When he was finished, he instructed Perseverance to dress in her uniform and meet him out front.

"The gray is too dressy for tonight," Perseverance said. "How quickly can you make the alterations to the burgundy?"

"When will you need it?" Laura asked. "Will you be taking all three?"

"Just the gray and the burgundy, and my friend is picking me up at the navy bachelor officer quarters at 19:00—uh, seven o'clock."

Laura checked the time. "We can have it done by six if that's not too late."

"That will work if it is no later," Perseverance said.

Anton cleared his throat to get her attention. He spoke quietly when she turned to him since it was about money. Perseverance guessed his excitement at being able to dress a public figure was now tempered by the realization that she was a government employee and might not be able to afford the dresses.

"Uh, Capitana, the total comes to just over thirty-eight hundred pounds," he almost whispered.

Again, Perseverance wanted to laugh. She held it in, saying, "That's fine."

She withdrew her comm unit and keyed up the financial interface. She raised an eyebrow to Anton, asking where his reader was. He grabbed it, and the transaction was complete with a brief wave of the two devices close to each other. Anton's look of relief nearly made Perseverance laugh again.

"Laura or Becky will deliver these to you by six o'clock," he said.

While leaving the shop, she checked her comm and noted it was already 17:00. For Anton to make the alterations to the dress, he (or someone) would need to scramble. She returned to the BOQ to find a bag containing her athletic wear. After carrying it to her room, she sat down at the console and decided to check the news feeds.

What she saw was a bit of a shock. Her picture appeared in a prominent position on the opening page of the five major news sites. Three of them used the image Powell showed her the night before. Two of them used a slightly different but equally flattering one. Scanning the copy accompanying the picture, she saw the coverage was entirely positive. Her brief remarks were praised, especially her use of a quote from Winston Churchill. Moreover, the media compared Churchill's situation to the one the Commonwealth now faced.

She quit reading when the front desk buzzed her to inform her of a delivery. She went and collected the two dresses and the shoebox. Returning to her room, she decided to shower before dinner.

At the appointed time, Commander Powell arrived to escort her to dinner. He was dressed as he said he would be. When he noticed Perseverance approaching, his expression brightened. Wearing the short heels, she was now the same height.

"Shall we?" he said, gesturing to the door.

Neither of them spoke while still in the navy section of the station. As soon as they were outside, Saint John could contain himself no longer. "Holy smokes, Perse!" he exclaimed quietly. "You look terrific."

She smiled, enjoying the compliment. Other than muttered directions, they did not speak until they reached the restaurant Powell chose, "Turner's." Powell had made a reservation, and they were escorted to the table immediately. The server appeared quickly and asked if they wanted anything to drink.

"Water is fine," Perseverance replied.

"Sparkling or flat?" the server asked.

"Oh, hell. Live it up, I guess. Sparkling," she answered.

"Same," Powell added.

"The wine last night made it awfully difficult to follow what that woman was saying this morning," Perseverance stated.

Powell laughed. "I don't think anything would have helped. Damn, she was dull. I think she must have taken the navy's course in Advanced Dullness."

"Will tomorrow be as bad?" Perseverance asked.

"No," Powell replied. "We start with Admiral Freshley. He will discuss what he thinks the navy needs in terms of new construction. After that, Lord Gilchrist will brief you on the leaders of the Social Democrats and the Conservatives. Then, in the afternoon, you will meet them, as Admiral Freshley will conduct the same briefing for them that you will see in the morning."

"Who is Lord Gilchrist?"

"The best way I can put it is that he's the queen's advisor for political affairs," Powell answered. "He doesn't really have an official title or position. Lord Gilchrist is sort of the ultimate go-between. Everyone knows him, and they respect and trust him. He doesn't take sides, and he stays out of view. Even when things get heated, as they do, both sides can talk with him. I know several occasions where he has helped smooth things out, and he keeps the queen informed of everything. No one is better qualified to give you a crash course on Commonwealth politics."

"So, that's tomorrow," Perseverance said. "Thursday, we visit Caerleon Yard."

"Yes, you'll need to prepare some remarks," Powell reminded.

"Right. What's Friday?"

"Friday is a big day but not a busy one," Powell answered. "At 10:00, there is a ceremony at the palace where Queen Charlotte will present you with the Conspicuous Gallantry Cross. Immediately following, there is a reception. We depart a couple of hours later. For the ceremony, wear the trousers included with the uniform I sent over. We will not have time to change. When we leave Friday morning, give your baggage to the desk clerk. I'll make sure it gets to the right place."

Changing the subject, he continued. "I see you successfully found some attractive civilian clothing this afternoon. Was it fun?"

Perseverance laughed. "It was fun but not in the way you think. It was… comical."

She then proceeded to tell him about the experience at Anton's. Her retelling had him laughing. She did not describe the gray dress, wanting to save that for a later time.

"I'm guessing you can take it or leave it on the girly-girl stuff," he commented.

"Well, clothes shopping has always been an ordeal," she explained. "It's hard to find things that fit. Regarding the rest of it, make-up and such, I know how to do it but don't bother. It's probably been three years since I last wore lipstick."

"Some people need it," he said. "You don't."

"Who is going to be at this ceremony?" she asked.

"Everyone important in the Commonwealth," he answered. "Plus foreign dignitaries. One or two reporters from the media pool plus their cameras."

"Will I get to meet the queen?"

"I don't know. For some reason, the ceremony is being conducted at the palace instead of the Admiralty, so it's possible."

16

The next morning was the briefing with Admiral Freshley. Though two aides accompanied him, he led the discussion himself. The topic was the current and projected size of the Royal Navy and the situation they now faced. Lord Gilchrist was present in the meeting. Gilchrist was a distinguished-looking black man with a bald head. What little hair he possessed was white—a fringe around his head, a thick mustache, and the bushiest eyebrows that Perseverance had ever seen.

Freshley got right to the point. "At the moment, the Royal Navy consists of three heavy cruisers, six light cruisers, and twelve destroyers. We should have triple those numbers. To win this war, we will need five or six times what we have now. We will need even more ships to prevent the next war from following right on the heels of this one. Convincing Parliament of the necessity of building and maintaining a proper navy is difficult in peacetime. It becomes much easier when people are shooting at us. But of course, the same people who denied us funding during the last decade are now the ones screaming the loudest about how unprepared we were."

Freshley then went on to list, in detail, the steps needed to provide the Royal Navy with the ships it needed to defend the Commonwealth. His presentation included every detail, from shipyard capacity and advisability of expanding or reactivating existing shipyards to systems, timetables and budgets, manufacturing capacity, resource availability, and labor force projections. Perseverance thought that if Admiral Freshley got what he asked for, Rear Admiral Kenard's predictions would come to pass easily.

"The constraints on us are money and time," Freshley summarized. "To a certain extent, more money can alleviate some of the time barrier, but not all of it. We need Commonwealth defense spending to immediately increase a staggering amount, to approximately forty-two percent of GDP. You can bet that will cause many of our politicians to go into brain-lock. However, if we don't do this, there might not be a future for the Commonwealth. Fortunately, there is historical precedent."

Freshley accessed a different set of charts. "These charts show military spending as a percentage of GDP in the last major war in earth's past, involving the nations that became the Commonwealth. Though military spending during the war increased to more than forty percent of the combined GDP, the post-war period brought a long-lasting period of strong economic growth. The growth was so strong that within five years, the percentage of debt to GDP fell to a pre-war level, despite the massive borrowing the war required. The economic expansion lasted more than twenty years. That is the message we need the politicians to understand—they need to vote to save us now and establish the foundation for future growth."

With that, Freshley was finished. He asked for questions. Perseverance raised her hand.

"Why did neither the Federation nor the Republics follow up their attacks?" she asked.

"We believe they don't have the ships," Freshley answered. "Beyond what they have in the systems they captured, their numbers are equivalent to ours. They have not retired their unshielded ships yet. They have equipped their older ships with the new missiles. Anything else?"

Powell asked for a copy of the presentation.

When Freshley left the room, Lord Gilchrist said, "Let's take a brief break and then gather again in ten minutes."

When they reconvened, Gilchrist started things off. "That presentation will be shared with the senior leadership of both parties this afternoon. When the Emergency Defense Spending Bill comes before Parliament next week, I expect it to pass easily. It's future spending that is of most concern, and that is why you have been tasked with making this tour of the Commonwealth."

Gilchrist pulled a piece of paper from his jacket pocket and slid it across to Powell and Perseverance.

"This is a list of the members of Parliament who we predict will be the most significant opponents of maintaining the level of increased spending necessary for our success. You'll note there are members of both parties, though there are quite a few more Liberal Democrats than Conservatives. The MPs on the list are concentrated in five of the twenty-five settled systems. Your tour includes all twenty-five planets because we don't want these MPs to feel they are being singled out, even though they are. Plans are in development to attempt to neutralize these MPs."

"That sounds ominous," Perseverance commented.

Gilchrist chuckled. "It did, didn't it? No harm is intended for them. Instead, we will work to find ways for their constituents to benefit from the increased spending—perhaps more than they deserve. If you want to know, captain, I'll tell you more, but I would advise you that politics is a lot like a sausage factory. If you like sausage, never visit the factory to see how it is made— you'll never eat it again."

Gilchrist continued to give them background information on the party leaders they would meet in the afternoon. He was witty, informative, and humorous. Finally, he ended the meeting with a prediction.

"The Liberal Democrats are in power now, but that won't last," he said. "The Conservatives will call for a vote of no confidence before the end of next week. They have already been advertising amongst the citizenry, painting the Liberal Democrats as the party that most often opposed increased military spending in the past. Enough of the Liberal Democrat MPs will jump ship to avoid drowning. The no-confidence vote will carry, and we'll be having elections six weeks after that."

"What do you expect out of this afternoon's session?" Perseverance asked.

"You won't see much of the usual bickering and posturing," Gilchrist stated. "This is neutral ground, there are no media present, and both sides share a portion of the blame for our current situation. Don't be surprised if Admiral Freshley calls out your presence. If the opportunity calls for it, he will mention your plan for defense in depth rather than in the border systems. I doubt you will be asked to speak. If you are, you can mention that you felt it was a sacrifice we should not make again and leave it at that. If any of them press you to say whose side you are on, just say you are on the side of the Royal Navy of the Inter-Planetary Commonwealth and opposed to our foes. That will embarrass and silence them. By the way, your speech was superb."

"Thank you."

"Referencing Winston Churchill was particularly appropriate. Not only was he a brilliant leader in a time of crisis, he was not elected by the people but named to the office by the consensus of the major political parties. That type of consensus approach is a great model for our current leaders to study."

Perseverance circled back to something Gilchrist mentioned in passing. "You know of the proposal I made?" she asked.

"Yes. I have a copy. You made a strong case," Gilchrist said.

The afternoon session with the politicians was remarkably dull. Perseverance was expecting some sort of animosity to surface. But instead, the leaders of both parties were quiet and meek. James Larson, the current prime minister, and leader of the Liberal Democrats, made the only comment that could be perceived as negative when he pointed out that support for such massive spending increases would be difficult to obtain from some of his people.

The thing Perseverance found most odd was the desire of every politician to have his or her picture taken with her. She complied graciously. She asked Powell about it over dinner that night, once again in the Officers' Mess.

"Protection," he said. "For instance, if you're an MP who has a record of voting against navy appropriations bills, when a member of the media points that out, you display the picture and claim you always supported the Royal Navy, just not wasteful spending. If at some point you, Captain Andrews, throw your support behind one party or the other, the party you did not choose will use the pictures to show your duplicity."

"That's awful," she replied.

"Agreed," Powell confirmed. "That's why Lord Gilchrist advised you to stay out of it and declare your support only for the Royal Navy of the Inter-Planetary Commonwealth and your opposition only to our foes."

Changing the subject, he added, "This evening, you're wearing make-up and perfume."

"I look bizarre, don't I?" she said.

"Not at all," he said, shaking his head. "If I weren't used to seeing you without it, I wouldn't have noticed. It looks good. You didn't use much and chose to accent some of your better features—your lips and cheekbones."

"You know a lot about make-up?"

"Only the bare basics," Saint John replied. "I was in many plays during high school and needed to learn how to apply my own stage make-up. That's all."

"I went out this afternoon and bought some since I figured I might need it on our travels. Perfume, too."

"It's a nice scent," he commented. "Not heavy, just... nice."

"My sophomore roommate in college used to wear it. I always liked it. For pretty much the same reason you just mentioned. So, what's on the agenda for tomorrow?"

"We head to Caerleon Yard. Wear undress khakis. The tour of your new ship begins at 08:00. After that, it will be lunch hour, and you'll deliver some informal remarks to the yard workers. We can stay and have lunch with them if you want."

"I'd like that," she said.

"Tomorrow afternoon at 14:30, we are due at the palace for a brief rehearsal of the medal ceremony. No need to change clothes. Then you're free until Friday morning when we are due at the palace at 09:00. The ceremony begins at ten sharp. You'll be in your number ones. Remember you must wear the trousers, not the skirt. We should be done by 11:00. Then there's the reception. That will last at least another hour. Our ride departs at 15:00 from the station, so we should not be rushed."

"Why do I need to wear trousers for the ceremony?"

Saint John knew the reason but also knew it was meant to be a surprise. "Queen Charlotte's request," he answered. It was true enough.

"So she is going to be there!" Perseverance said triumphantly.

"Yes, she is. For our trip, we'll be on a courier boat and generally will be the only passengers beside the steward and the pilots unless someone needs a lift to where we are headed next. I think it will prove to be the most luxurious duty you'll ever be assigned in your navy career and possibly the most boring. By the end, we'll either be the best of friends or never want to see one another again."

When they reached Caerleon Yard the following day, Perseverance saw her new ship, HMS *Manitoba*, for the first time. Her spirits soared. The ship would have weighed three hundred thirty-five thousand metric tons if she had been on earth. She was four hundred twenty-three meters long, sixty-two meters wide, and fifty-one meters from dorsal to ventral (top to bottom). Next to the slip where she was being finished was a viewscreen. The display could show either the actual view of the ship or, because the lighting was so variable, a compensated image that showed how the ship would appear under uniform illumination.

Though *Manitoba* was classified as a heavy cruiser, that designation was due to the weight of her armor and not her appearance. Perseverance thought her new ship looked sleek and vaguely predatory, like a shark without fins. The hull gleamed a silvery tan due to the reflective armor coating.

Work on the hull was essentially complete, and the ship's interior had atmosphere, heat, and gravity. On the outside, the two double turrets for the 105mm photon cannons remained to be installed, as well as the shield and Alcubierre field generators. The inside of the ship, she was warned, was chaos. Before being allowed inside, she and Powell were issued safety helmets. The tour began at the rear of the ship.

Because no way was known to extend the defensive plasma shielding over the stern of the ship, most of that area was taken up by the holds and the shuttle bay. *Manitoba* was large enough to carry both a shuttle and an MAS—a Marine Assault Shuttle, which could carry an entire platoon of marines in combat armor. Right down the ship's central axis were two huge electrical conduits carrying power to the two massive EM drives at the stern. Because of the vulnerability of the stern, the bulkheads perpendicular to the ship's long axis were composed of thick layers of ceramic alloy composites.

One-third of the way forward was the engineering section, dominated by the two fusion reactors. The reactors were not scheduled to be ignited for several more months. The first missile tubes were to the right and left of the engineering section. Above engineering were the waste recycling facilities, while below was the atmospheric recycling area.

Continuing forward, at midships along the central axis was the missile magazine. On either side of the magazine area were two more missile tubes. Above the magazine was marine country, the quarters for the short company (three platoons) of marines. Their commanding officer held the rank of captain, but while on board *Manitoba*, he or she would be given a "courtesy promotion" and be addressed as "Major." This was in deference to the long-standing custom (and naval superstition) that there could only be one captain on a ship. Below the magazine was the exercise facility for the entire ship. Later, when they were installed, a double turret of photon cannons would be placed on the top and bottom of the hull.

The bridge was just ahead of the magazine, along the central axis. There were missile tubes on either side. Above the bridge was the sickbay and the officers' mess. Below was the enlisted mess.

Forward of that, extending to the bow, were the crew quarters, both officers and enlisted. With a full crew complement, *Manitoba* would carry eighty-three marines and one hundred and forty-two naval personnel, including twelve officers. Of the officers, four were assigned to engineering, while six were part of the bridge crew. There were also two ensigns who would be rotated through every different area of responsibility during their year-long posting.

Perseverance felt like it was her birthday and she kept receiving presents. After living on the destroyer *Rowen* for three years, everything on a heavy cruiser was bigger. The companionways were wider, the ceilings were higher, and the bridge was more spacious. Even the sickbay was a real sickbay instead of a glorified closet. The hatches were still the same size, though.

Seeing her quarters took her breath away. She now had an actual ready room with a massive wooden conference table that would seat all the officers aboard. The construction superintendent allowed Perseverance to register her palmprint for the door lock. Next to her quarters was a duplicate set of rooms, the so-called flag quarters where an admiral would reside if *Manitoba* was chosen as a flagship.

The complete tour took almost three hours. It might have lasted even longer, except Powell reminded Perseverance of her obligation to speak to the workers. The construction supervisor led them to the large cafeteria where the yard workers were gathering for the lunch hour. A podium was set up at the far end of the room.

As she and Powell walked to the podium, Perseverance noticed something unusual. A hush fell on those nearest to her as she crossed the room. Once she passed a few meters beyond them, a quiet buzz of conversation arose. It seemed like the progress of a wave approaching a shore. When they reached the podium, Powell gestured for her to go ahead.

She climbed up the two steps and turned to look out at a sea of faces. Perseverance tapped the microphone and heard it was on. "Can everyone hear me?" she asked. Shouts of "yes" or "yup" or the thumbs-up sign came from the far end.

"Wow!" Perseverance said. "I was just on a tour of *Manitoba*. I'd still be there, but they yanked me away to interrupt your lunch."

She paused for the chuckles that came, as she hoped they would.

"I want to thank you for your hard work. Have you ever heard of love at first sight? I know what it means now. That ship you're building for me is a beauty. My name is Perseverance Andrews. Until recently, I was captain of HMS *Rowen*, which you built a few years ago. Thanks to your hard work in building a sturdy ship, and a hell of a lot of luck, most of my crew and I survived the recent battle in the Aries system. I wish my counterparts on the *Symes* and *Funnell* and the three other forces that were wiped out were as lucky. If you don't mind, I'd like to ask for a moment of silence for them."

Perseverance bowed her head. The entire cafeteria joined her. The silence was so profound that she could hear when someone nearby adjusted the posture on the bench where they were sitting. Beyond the surface level of sensation, she was thinking about the people she knew and cared for who were now gone. She lifted her head and cleared her throat.

"Thank you. I appreciate that. Now, some of you may have seen that Commander Powell here forced me to speak to the news media when I returned to Caerleon."

Murmurs of assent rose from the crowd.

"Oh? You watched it?" she asked.

Stronger acknowledgment came from the group.

"I'm not hearing any booing, so I hope that means it didn't suck too bad. Either that or you guys are really polite."

Laughs followed her comment.

"In those remarks, I said I was glad I survived because I want to continue the fight. I asked for the tools to finish the job. What you have built is exactly the right kind of tool I was talking about. I can hardly wait until I can put *Manitoba* to work."

Cheers greeted this remark. Perseverance paused until the crowd quieted some.

"We didn't ask for this war. The opening round did not go our way—not at all. But all of us who have faced tough challenges know that it is not how you start but how you finish that matters."

More cheers erupted from the workers. Perseverance waited again until they died down.

"The next few years will be tough. Our Commonwealth will be challenged and tested in ways we have never encountered. Things began badly, and I know there will be some dark days ahead. I wish I could promise differently, but I'm not here to blow sunshine up your skirts."

Perseverance spoke over the laughter that came from that comment. "We've all heard the expression, 'Anything worth having is worth fighting for,' right? Our Commonwealth and our way of life are worth fighting for. I'll give my life for it if I have to, like my friends and some of my shipmates did just a few days ago. But having seen the ship you're building for my crew and me, I'm liking my odds a whole lot better now. Thank you."

Perseverance was not prepared for what happened next. She was expecting some polite applause. But instead, it was almost deafening. The people nearest the podium began to stand, and the rest of the workers quickly joined them. She had started to take a step away, and the noise stopped her. she waited until it began to tail off, bowed her head in acknowledgment, and gave a wave.

She and Powell stayed for lunch. They went through the serving line like anyone else, though most of the workers had already passed through. When Powell paid the workers for their meals, he turned to her.

"Where do you want to sit?" he asked.

"Don't worry," she replied. "I got this."

She stepped away from Powell and hollered, "Anyone here from Alleghany?"

A group of three workers seated not far away raised their hands.

"Mind if I sit with you?" she hollered.

They beckoned her over.

Perseverance turned to Powell. "Saint John, you can come with me or find your own people. Up to you."

Powell looked at her with a grin. "Anyone from Carolina?" he yelled.

A couple of groups responded, gesturing for him to join them. Powell gave Perseverance a smirk.

17

They returned to the navy section of Caerleon Station just before 13:00. Powell told her she had an hour and a half to spare, and it would be a good idea for her to shop for anything she might need for the trip. At 14:30, they needed to board the special shuttle that would deliver them to the palace for the rehearsal of the ceremony.

She was waiting for Powell at 14:25. He led her to the security checkpoint within the navy section that controlled access to the shuttle gangway used by the palace. After passing through, they boarded the shuttle. A minute later, Admiral Freshley joined them. Perseverance and Powell both started to rise to give him a salute, but he waved them down. The admiral strapped himself into the seat facing them.

"Nice job at the yard today," Freshley commented.

Perseverance wanted to blush and shrink herself into the seat from embarrassment. She used some language that she would never use in front of the highest-ranking officer in the Royal Navy. Freshley sensed her discomfort.

"Don't worry, captain," he said with a smile. "I'm a sailor, too. Once or twice, I may have used language in public even saltier than anything you said today. I know all the words and have used them often. With certain audiences, they enhance communication."

His comment brought a smile to Perseverance's face. There was a small shudder and an audible clunk as the shuttle disengaged from the station. A few minutes later, Perseverance dared to ask the admiral a question.

"Sir, is it usual to have these ceremonies at the palace?"

"No, not really," he said. "Usually, they take place at the Admiralty. But, given the current circumstances, the queen wants to make a bit of a spectacle."

"Sir, I heard she put a bit of pressure on you to approve this award," Perseverance said. "That makes me uncomfortable."

Freshley looked surprised at this. "Why? Do you think you don't deserve it?"

"A little," Perseverance admitted. "I feel like I'm being granted the 'lucky survivor' prize."

"Hm. I can see how you might feel that way, but you're wrong," Freshley stated. "The facts are known and not in dispute. Of the four border sectors that were attacked, yours was the most prepared, and your defense was the most effective. You are the only one who prevented the enemy from completing any part of their objective. On top of that, you asserted your authority. As a result, you are responsible for saving five hundred and ninety-one souls who would have died without your strong determination to rescue them. There is no doubt in my mind you deserve it. All the queen did is speed things up. Normally these things drag out because people like to have meetings where they can hear themselves talk. Instead, the queen eliminated what would have been wasted time."

"Commander Powell has said the same things, sir, but hearing it from you carries more weight," she said. "Sorry, Saint John."

When they arrived on the shuttle pad at the palace, a page took them to the Throne Room, where the ceremony was to take place. The Throne Room was enormous, with marble columns and a marble floor in a checkerboard pattern of black and white. The walls were faced with marble. The only decorations were portraits of the kings and queens, beginning with William of Caerleon. The only other decoration was the strip of red carpet leading from the entrance, up the steps of the dais, to the throne. The throne itself was a massive wooden chair without ostentation. The scale of the room and the person sitting on the throne were meant to inspire, not the décor.

The Royal Seneschal first cautioned them to ensure their comm units were set in silent mode while in the palace. He then showed them how to process, where to stand, proper etiquette for addressing the queen, should she wish to speak with any of them, and other matters of protocol. The seneschal then led them to a reception hall just off the Throne Room. He showed Perseverance where she would position herself to receive greetings.

"Ordinarily, I would call this a receiving line," the seneschal said, "but there can't be a line if there's only one person in it, heh heh."

Perseverance, awed by the surroundings, realized he was trying to make a joke and managed a faint smile. Her heart was pounding just from being in the palace. The realization that she was the focal point of all this made her almost nauseous.

"Do you have any questions?"

"None that I can think of at the moment, but then, I am scared to death," Perseverance said.

"Don't be," the seneschal said. "Queen Charlotte is very nice, for a queen. She hasn't ordered anyone to be executed for at least a couple of weeks now."

"Ha ha," Perseverance said, not amused.

"Don't worry," the seneschal said. "You'll do fine. I'll even wager you end up enjoying yourself."

"Finished?" Freshley asked. "Then let's head back."

Freshley led the way back to the shuttle pad. He chose the seat facing Perseverance again. "Any questions?"

She shook her head. "I'll admit to being nervous, though," she said.

The admiral smiled. "You'll do honor to yourself and the service, captain," he said. "I'll even go so far as to agree with the seneschal. If you can relax a bit, you'll have some fun."

Later that evening, during dinner in the Officers' Mess, Perseverance was quiet. Powell respected her silence and didn't try to force conversation or jolly her out of her mood. One thing Saint John liked about her was her direct nature. He would learn what was bothering her when she felt like mentioning it. Finally, after he ordered a piece of triple-layer chocolate cake for dessert, she spoke up.

"Sorry. I'm not very good company this evening."

"It's fine. You're entitled," he said with a shrug.

"What do you mean by that?" she snapped defensively.

"You nearly got your ass blown up less than two weeks ago. You lost more than a quarter of your crew. You had friends, acquaintances, and former shipmates on the ships that were lost. I did, too, by the way, so I understand better than you might think. Then, just as you're coming to grips with that, you're thrown into this."

"This?"

"Making statements to the press, giving a speech to the yard workers, high-level briefings with the political leaders of the Commonwealth, and tomorrow the ceremony with the queen present," he listed. "I can't imagine these are part of your normal comfort zone. Yet, you take it all seriously and want to prove yourself as capable in these unusual situations as you do in the ones you've mastered. I can tell you to relax and not to worry, but you will, regardless. All I can say is that so far this week, you've been near-perfect, but the only time I've seen you happy and relaxed was during our tour of the ship."

"Near-perfect?" she protested. "Where have I fallen short?"

"Your speech when you arrived—perfect. How you handled yourself with the bigwigs—perfect. Your remarks in the cafeteria—perfect. The way you found workers from your home planet—genius. The only less-than-perfect thing was this afternoon. You were as nervous as a long-tailed cat in a room full of rocking chairs," he said.

"And all this foofaraw seems normal to you?"

"Nope. Never been in the Throne Room before. It's as alien to me as anyone," he said.

"Then how come you aren't concerned? Or are you, and you're just hiding it well?"

"Some advice my father gave me a long time ago about how to handle situations like this," he said. "He told me, 'Fake it until you make it.' He meant that entering a tricky spot like this would proceed more smoothly if I took my customary confidence with me and pretended there was nothing unusual I couldn't handle. He was right."

"So, I should pretend that being awarded medals with the queen right there is normal? Ri-i-i-i-ight," she said sarcastically.

"Exactly."

"It's not that simple."

"It *is* that simple."

Perseverance leaned back, considering what Saint John was saying. While she was contemplating, the server brought his dessert. As the server placed it in front of Powell, Perseverance frowned.

"Where's my fork?" she asked.

"I'm sorry, sir." The server went to the neighboring table and retrieved a fork, handing it to Perseverance.

"I never said I would share," Powell complained.

"Just employing my customary confidence in an unusual situation," she replied, lifting a bite of cake to her mouth.

When she finished the last bite of his dessert, she said, "Mm—this was really good. Thanks for sharing."

"I think you ate more of it than I did," Powell whined a few minutes later.

"That's okay. I outrank you. You should consider yourself lucky I let you have a couple of bites."

At 08:30 the following morning, Perseverance met Powell at the security checkpoint as they agreed. After passing through, they boarded the shuttle. Admiral Freshley's flag lieutenant was just inside the hatch, checking names off a list. Freshley was already seated, as was General McAuliffe, the commandant of the marines. There were more than a dozen other officers. All were in their formal dress uniforms.

Perseverance leaned over and whispered, "You know this kind of thing—hanging out with the top brass—it happens to me all the time."

Powell snickered in response.

When they landed, they proceeded to a large anteroom next to the Throne Room. The seneschal was there. He went over the order of the ceremony and arranged the different officers in two columns. Commander Powell was placed near the end of one column. When the two columns entered the Throne Room, Perseverance was to remain behind at the threshold until summoned by Admiral Freshley.

After the seneschal finished and left, men and women drifted from the two columns to introduce themselves to Perseverance and offer their congratulations in advance. A tone sounded in the room, warning them the ceremony was about to begin. Perseverance sidled over to Powell.

"I'm telling ya, Saint John, this shit happens to me all the time," she whispered out of the corner of her mouth.

He snorted. Just then, the doors opened. The two columns straightened up. Perseverance heard the marine commandant whisper, "Forward...March"

On "march," both columns advanced, left foot first. The column on the left was on the outside as they turned to the right to enter the Throne Room. The column on the right stopped, then turned when their counterpart in the other column reached them. They did this again once they entered the Throne Room. Perseverance grudgingly admitted that they did well, for a bunch of officers who marched only rarely, if at all. She followed them, making a knife-sharp turn in the center of the hallway. She stopped precisely at the threshold.

Once the two columns of military personnel took position on either side of the strip of red carpet down the center of the room leading to the throne, the politicians entered. Most were dressed in what was considered "business formal"—suits. A handful of them were wearing the dress uniform of the branch of the military in which they once served.

Once everyone was in place, Admiral Freshley stepped forward from the head of his column. "Captain Perseverance Andrews, front and center," he ordered.

Perseverance stepped off smartly. She executed a flawless turn when she reached the center of the red carpet. Reaching Admiral Freshley, she turned to face him and snapped a salute. Freshley's return salute was offered just as sharply. She held hers until after he lowered his hand.

"Your Majesty, ladies and gentlemen," Freshley began in a stentorian voice. "We are gathered today to recognize acts of conspicuous gallantry during active operations against the enemy. Recently, our enemies invaded four Commonwealth systems without prior notice or declaration of war. In each of these systems, a Royal Navy task group comprised of three destroyers was on patrol. In only one of these four did the task group prevent the enemy from achieving its objective—the task group assigned to the Aries system, commanded by Captain Perseverance Andrews.

"The task group, comprised of Her Majesty's Ships *Rowen*, *Symes*, and *Funnell*, is hereby awarded a Royal Unit Citation in recognition of this accomplishment. Sadly, over two hundred members of that task group lost their lives in that engagement. Their citations are being awarded posthumously. We are well aware that an award for bravery does not come close to compensating for the loss of a loved one. However, we hope that, with time, this citation can provide solace to their families, knowing that their loved one died performing at the highest level in defense of the Commonwealth.

"In addition to leading the effective defense of the Aries system, Captain Andrews was conspicuously gallant after the engagement. After Captain Andrews' task group rendered the five attacking Federation ships powerless, our enemies communicated their unconditional surrender and pleaded for assistance. Without the ability to control their speed, these ships faced certain death. When they exceeded the maximum velocity, and their mass compensators failed, all five ships would be crushed instantly.

"Despite losing more than one-third of her crew and the other ships in her task group, and despite the significant damage to her ship, when Captain Andrews learned of their fate, she took charge of organizing a rescue. Her unshakeable determination and careful direction ensured that help reached them in time. As a result, five hundred and ninety-one people were saved.

"Her actions are in keeping with the highest and most noble traditions of the Royal Navy. Moreover, they serve as concrete examples of what conspicuous gallantry is. Therefore, on behalf of the Royal Navy of the Inter-Planetary Commonwealth, Parliament, and Her Majesty, Queen Charlotte, it gives me great pleasure to award the Conspicuous Gallantry Cross to Captain Perseverance Andrews."

The audience began to applaud enthusiastically. Perseverance bent forward in a slight bow. Admiral Freshley leaned forward to drape the medal around her neck.

As he did, he whispered, "Something wonderful is about to happen. Remember to stop three paces short of the steps and curtsy. Then listen to the seneschal."

The two of them straightened. Admiral Freshley took one step backward. He saluted first. Seeing the puzzlement in Perseverance's eyes, he gave her a wink.

18

Perseverance was trying to interpret what the hell the admiral just told her. When he winked at her, her bafflement increased. The applause was dying down, and she heard the herald thump his staff on the floor three times. The crowd hushed instantly.

"Perseverance Esther Andrews," called a clear contralto voice, "advance and be recognized."

Admiral Freshley, wearing a broad smile, gave the slightest jerk of his head toward the throne. Cold fear swept through Perseverance's veins. Nonetheless, she turned sharply and advanced to the foot of the steps.

A band, tucked into an alcove Perseverance could not see, began to play the "God Save the Queen." In their "Beefeater" attire, the Queen's Bodyguard formed on the queen. Queen Charlotte rose from the throne and was handed a gleaming sword by one of the bodyguards. A page scurried from the side and placed a small stool with a rail in front of Perseverance. Holding her sword, the queen began approaching Perseverance, walking down the steps.

The seneschal, who appeared behind Perseverance on her left side, whispered, "When the queen finishes speaking, curtsy, then kneel on one knee with your head bowed."

When the queen reached the last step, she stopped. Perseverance was standing ramrod straight at attention, staring straight ahead. She thought she detected a hint of mischief in the queen's expression. After a brief pause, she began to speak.

"Perseverance Esther Andrews, with whom we are well pleased, it is our great pleasure to name you a Knight Grand Cross of the Royal Victorian Order in recognition of your great service to us and the Commonwealth. Your extraordinary heroism and gallantry in action are in keeping with the highest traditions of the Royal Navy of the Commonwealth, reflect great credit upon yourself and your service, and serve as an inspiration to us all."

"Now," the seneschal whispered.

Perseverance curtsied, then knelt, placing her right knee on the small stool. The queen lifted the sword she was carrying and tapped Perseverance on the left shoulder, then the right. Queen Charlotte made a discreet gesture, indicating Perseverance should stand. On the queen's left, a page handed her an emblem on a ribbon. Perseverance bowed her head slightly for the queen to drape it around her neck.

When Perseverance straightened up, the queen added, "As a further token of the esteem in which we hold you, please accept this sword."

A member of the queen's bodyguard approached Perseverance from the left. With a murmured, "Pardon me," he moved behind Perseverance. He reached around her front, buckled the sword belt on, then retreated quickly to the left. Attendants then scurried in from the right. They draped over her shoulders a cloak of blue with red trim, with an enormous star on the left breast. The attendant on her left made sure the cloak was tucked behind the sword.

As the attendants slipped away, the seneschal whispered, "Withdraw the blade about ten centimeters and hold it."

When Perseverance did this, the queen spoke. "Dame Perseverance, I exhort and admonish you to use your sword to the glory of God, the defense of our Commonwealth, the maintenance of your sovereign's right and honor, and for equity and justice for all, to the utmost of your power."

The seneschal whispered, "I solemnly swear so to do."

When Perseverance repeated the phrase, loudly and clearly, the queen turned and started climbing the steps to the throne. As the queen was ascending, the seneschal instructed Perseverance to take one step back and one step backward to the right. When the queen reached the top of the stairs, the herald thumped his staff three times.

"Dame Perseverance Esther Andrews, Captain of the Royal Navy of the Inter-Planetary Commonwealth, Knight Grand Cross of the Royal Victorian Order," he announced.

The crowd broke into applause. As the applause began to diminish, the queen departed to the right. When the queen was no longer in sight, the seneschal approached Perseverance again.

"You lead the procession out. Go to the reception hall. Congratulations, Dame Perseverance," he whispered.

Perseverance turned sharply and started down the red carpet. Two-by-two, the other members of the military stepped out and followed her, in step. She stopped where the seneschal instructed her to stand the day before.

A queue formed, beginning with the members of the military who had just followed her from the Throne Room, followed by all the other guests, waiting for their turn to meet her."

Everyone offered congratulations. Many addressed her as "Dame Perseverance." When the line was finished, a page appeared and asked Perseverance if he could take the mantle now. She nodded.

"We'll keep this here until you need it again," she said.

Commander Powell approached.

"Did you know about this?" Perseverance demanded.

"Yes," he replied.

Perseverance punched him hard in the shoulder. She thought about it, then hit him again.

"The second one was for Admiral Freshley since he knew about it, too. I can't hit him because that would be assaulting a superior officer, so I hit you twice."

Powell asked, "Are you really mad? Because I wasn't allowed to tell you."

"I suspected," Perseverance said. "There was a naughty look on Queen Charlotte's face. I think she enjoyed her little surprise."

"Can I see your sword?" he asked.

"I haven't even looked it at myself," she replied.

"That's okay. I can look over your shoulder," he said.

Perseverance withdrew the sword from the leather scabbard, tipped with gold trim. Once it was out, she held it with both hands horizontally. The blade was engraved with an intricate design. The engraving began near the tip, with the initials C.R., the mark of Queen Charlotte's reign. Near the hilt, the words "Dux Femina Facti" were written.

"What does that mean?" she asked.

"It's Latin," Powell answered, "from the *Aeneid*, the great epic poem about ancient Rome. It means, 'A woman was the leader of what was done,' I think."

Damn right, she thought. "Huh," she grunted. "I like that. How do you know Latin?"

"I went to a private school where they still teach it," Powell explained. "My father insisted."

Perseverance continued examining the sword. The curved hilt was covered in gold, but she suspected it was merely gold-plated. Solid gold would be too heavy and not strong enough for a weapon. The curve of the hilt attached to the pommel. The pommel was a stylized head and upper body of a griffin, the symbol of the Commonwealth. The sword's grip was covered with what looked like white leather but rougher and tackier than any leather Perseverance ever felt.

"What's this stuff?" she asked, running her index finger over it.

Powell reached around her to touch it himself. "I don't know," he said. "I'll look it up."

He pulled his comm unit out of his pocket and tapped on the screen. A moment later, he announced, "Some sort of fish skin. It could be from a fish, a ray, or a shark. I don't know enough to be able to tell the difference. It's so your hand won't slip if it gets sweaty."

"Well, that's another thing I never knew before," she said, sliding the sword back into its scabbard.

"I think it's beautiful," Powell commented. "I'm jealous."

"Be careful what you wish for, Saint John," Perseverance warned. "I'm sure there will be times I'll be tempted to give it to you—pointy end first."

"Yes, Dame Perseverance," he replied, performing a sweeping bow.

When he straightened, Perseverance hit him in the shoulder again. They spent time at the reception. A few people began to leave to return to their regular lives. Noticing the first departures, the reception hall cleared quickly.

Perseverance was just about to ask Powell if it was time to depart when the seneschal appeared.

"Dame Captain Andrews, your presence is requested," he said. "Please come with me." Then, turning to Powell, the seneschal added, "You don't mind waiting, do you, commander?"

Powell realized it was not a request. The seneschal led Perseverance out of the reception hall and through a maze of corridors, eventually reaching an unmarked door. He knocked.

"Enter," came the queen's voice.

Before opening the door, the seneschal whispered, "Just be yourself."

He opened the door to reveal a small dining room. The table was set for two. The queen was standing next to one chair. Queen Charlotte was an attractive woman. She was roughly ten centimeters shorter than Perseverance. She was slender, with light brown hair now arranged in a ponytail, and blue eyes, wearing a tan suit with a skirt. Perseverance walked stiffly toward her and was about to curtsy when the queen shook her head.

"Please, Captain Andrews, don't. I thought it would be nice to have an informal lunch with you. So informal, in fact, that I insist you call me Charlie until you leave. What shall I call you? Captain?" she asked with a twinkle in her eye.

"If we're going to be informal, Perse will be fine."

"Good. Sit. You might want to unbuckle the sword first."

"Thank you for the sword, uh, Charlie," Perseverance said, stumbling over the concept of such informality. "It's beautiful."

"Have you looked at it closely?"

Perseverance nodded.

"What do you think of the inscription?"

"When Commander Powell told me what it meant, I thought 'Damn right' to myself."

The queen laughed. "Exactly. I apologize for putting you on the spot. Being queen can be pretty boring. I like to spice things up when I can get away with it. You handled it well."

"Well, I punched Commander Powell for not telling me, then I hit him again since I can't do the same to Admiral Freshley. I could see you were enjoying it, though," Perseverance said.

"I did. I've heard you're concerned that I applied some pressure on the Admiralty and the Armed Services Committee about your medal. Don't be. Admiral Freshley and the prime minister both agreed that delay would serve no useful purpose other than to provide some politicians with an opportunity to pontificate. Accelerating the process is better for the Commonwealth."

Perseverance nodded. "I just don't want anyone to think the only reason I got it is because I have friends in high places."

"Well, that's partly true," the queen said with a smile. "You do have friends in high places, or, should I say, I hope we will become friends or friendly, at the very least. As far as earning the Conspicuous Gallantry Cross, no one could possibly question that. I understand you depart on your speaking tour of the Commonwealth in a few hours. How do you feel about that?"

"I understand the reasons for it and will do my best," Perseverance said. "That said, I'd rather be aboard a ship, involved in the efforts to remove the Federation and the Republics from Ilium and Southampton."

They were interrupted when the first course was delivered. The queen waited for the servers to leave before resuming.

"I understand you'd rather be where the action is, Perse. But though you might not believe it, what we hope to accomplish with your tour will be far more important in the long run than what happens in Ilium or Southampton. Anything else bothering you?"

"It looks like there will be a lot of idle time, just traveling from system to system. I don't think I've had that much free time since I was a child."

"I thought you were attached to Admiral Freshley's staff?" the queen asked.

"I am."

"Don't be surprised if he throws a couple of projects in your lap," the queen said. "You didn't hear that from me, by the way."

The queen put her finger beside her nose in the signal to keep this information quiet,

"What do you think of Commander Powell?" the queen asked.

"We're getting to know one another," Perseverance replied. "So far, so good."

"Well, he looks absolutely scrumptious," the queen commented. "That's why I picked him to accompany you. I certainly wouldn't mind being forced to spend time with that for five or six months."

"Your M—" Perseverance began to say, stopping when the queen lowered her eyebrows at her. "Charlie, you're married!"

"Yes, I am. Quite happily, I might add. Not dead, though. No, Perse, not dead. And Commander Powell is a feast for the eyes. The best part is that you outrank him. So, if he's annoying, you can order him to be quiet and just look at him."

Perseverance laughed. It was an attractive option. The queen began to eat, so Perseverance followed her example.

"Speaking of Commander Powell," Perseverance said, "I feel guilty that I'm being fed, and he isn't."

"Oh, he's being taken care of," the queen replied. "Don't worry."

A few minutes later, the queen said, "I understand you lost a dear friend. Captain Berger."

Surprised the queen knew this, Perseverance answered, "Yes. I wouldn't expect you to know something like that."

"Oh, Perse, you would be amazed at the things I know," the queen replied with a smile. "I have my fingers in every pie worth sticking a finger into and quite a few that aren't but might be someday."

While Perseverance was considering this, staff entered. They removed the plates from the first course and delivered the second. Perseverance waited for them to leave.

"Please excuse my asking, Charlie, but why?"

"Because the health and welfare of the Commonwealth is my life. My constitutional authority is indeed almost nonexistent. That does not mean I am powerless. If I use it wisely, my position provides me with a great deal of what the ancient Romans called *auctoritas*, which is the ability to influence people behind the scenes without having authority over them. In addition, I have 'the bully pulpit' as a great American president, Theodore Roosevelt, described it. I can speak up on any public issue, and the media and public will pay attention. I erode my influence if I do this too often or don't use it at all. The key is knowing when to weigh in and on what issues."

The rest of the lunch passed pleasantly. When they finished, the queen gave her a hug. As she was being led to the shuttle pad, where Powell was waiting, Perseverance tried to review the conversation. She came to the conclusion that Queen Charlotte was an extremely skilled interviewer. In the course of an hour, the queen sucked her dry of information—everything from how Perseverance felt the war would unfold, her ambitions for the future, the state of her nonexistent love life, and her political leanings. At no point did Perseverance sense she was being grilled. In fact, she remembered feeling flattered that the queen was so interested.

19

Commander Powell was waiting at the shuttle pad. They returned to Caerleon Station. Aboard the shuttle, Perseverance checked her comm unit. There were messages from her brother and sisters and her mother. She would wait until she was aboard the courier boat to return those calls.

Remembering the queen's comments, Perseverance snuck a look at Powell. Not for the first time, she thought he looked like an actor playing the part of a naval officer. In her experience, ordinary people were rarely that handsome.

"How was lunch with the queen?" he asked.

"Interesting," she replied, knowing this response would be unsatisfactory.

"Oh, c'mon," he complained.

"It *was*," she stated. "You want to know why?"

"Yes, please."

"The most overwhelming thing, besides the realization that you're sitting there with the *queen*, is how comfortable she makes you feel. She has a sense of humor and isn't stuffy at all. The breadth of her knowledge is unbelievable, and she is very, very sharp. You feel... no, you *know* you are the center of her attention, the most important person in her universe. It's intoxicating, like being enveloped in a fog of charm. Not until later did I realize she controlled the entire conversation and extracted every piece of information from me she wanted. It seemed effortless, and I was thrilled that she was so interested in me."

"Ah," Powell said. "I heard rumors, but this confirms it. You have just met someone who possesses true charisma."

Perseverance pondered his statement for a moment. "If that's what it is, I think people misuse the word. I've heard 'charisma' as a substitute for 'charming' many times, but 'charming' doesn't begin to cover it."

Powell laughed. "I agree. There was a man who was a competitor of my father's. Dad used to complain about this fellow constantly. Then, once when we were out, we ran into the guy. My father insisted on introducing me. For the minute or two I spoke with him, I experienced what you described. Later, my father explained about the man's charisma. 'His work is crap,' Dad said, 'but damn, he can sure sell it.' I've never met anyone since who gave me the same feeling."

Once on the station, Powell led them to where the courier boat was docked. They went up the gangway, and the steward shut the hatch behind them. He saluted them.

"Petty Officer Klaus Daimler," he said. "Captain, your cabin is the second of the two. Commander, yours is the first. Your luggage is aboard. What time would you like dinner?"

Powell looked at Perseverance with a shrug to indicate he didn't have a preference. "Let's eat at 19:00 if you don't mind."

Klaus departed. Powell said, "You'll need to look up the regulations for proper placement of the medal and emblem you received."

"Will do," she said. "If you don't mind, I have some calls to return."

When Perseverance was back in the privacy of her room, she started to return the calls she missed. She looked at the list. Then, figuring she would get the most difficult done first, she called her parents.

Her father answered, saying, "Let me get your mother." That was typical for when Perseverance called.

Perseverance waited. She heard a door shut in the background. Then her mother spoke.

"Congratulations, Dame Perseverance!"

"Thanks, mom."

"From the video, it looked as though you weren't expecting that," her mother commented.

"I wasn't. It was a complete surprise."

"Then you handled it quite well, I thought. I want you to know I am very proud of you. Your father is too, but he's too darned stubborn to admit it," she said. "Now, I know you probably have a great many calls to return, so I won't keep you. I just wanted you to know we saw you on the video, and I am very happy for you."

Perseverance was not surprised by the tenor of the call. Her mother's attitude was generally mildly positive toward her and her career. Her father refused to speak with her.

The calls she made to her siblings following that were much more positive. While she and her brother and sisters were not close, they all supported one another. This pattern began when they were all in their rebellious phases. Though they might only speak to one another once or twice a year, it was understood between them that if one of them needed help, the others would rally around.

After finishing those calls, she scrolled through the other messages left on her comm. She was quietly pleased that so many reached out. Reviewing the list, however, reminded her of the one person she would not hear from, Ken Berger.

From the time they served together as ensigns, Ken was her closest friend. She knew she could talk to him about anything and had repeatedly put it to the test. He did the same with her. If there was anyone who would be ecstatic about her recognition today, it would have been him. For the first time in many years, Perseverance felt lonely.

She rarely succumbed to what her mother long ago called the "megrims." Since she enjoyed her life as a naval officer so much, she seldom had cause. Her career did not leave much room for self-indulgence like this. Unfortunately, the next few months would not be filled with the usual routine and the many tasks that filled her day.

She wondered if what she was feeling was a sort of "hangover" from how she felt when talking with Queen Charlotte. She changed into undress khakis, then left the cramped cabin and returned to the common area of the boat. She flopped down on the sofa.

"Perse, you look like you're heading to your execution," Powell commented. "What can I do to help?"

She sighed heavily. After a moment, she looked him in the eye. "It has been a crazy day," she said. "There's a lot my brain is trying to process right now. Just now, I called my parents and my sibs. That went fine. When I finished with them, I realized the one person I really wanted to share the news with is gone," she said. "Ken Berger, captain of the *Burke*, died in the battle at Automedon."

"I'm sorry," Powell responded. Then, after a pause, he added, "I actually know how you feel. It's part of why I'm in Public Affairs, and I already promised to tell you the story, but I'm not ready yet. Were you and he involved?"

"What?"

"Were you and Captain Berger, uh, intimate? I don't remember seeing a 5602 in your file, but—"

"No. Not that way," she said. "He was my best friend. He always said he would never be involved romantically with anyone in the navy."

"I get that. Even so, it sucks to lose a friend like that," Saint John said.

They sat in silence for a time.

"I know we haven't figured out whether we're friends yet," Saint John said, breaking the quiet, "but I can tell you, I think I would like to be friends. For what it's worth, my opinion is that you're an impressive person. You're smart, you're cool under pressure, you're attractive, and you have a good sense of humor. If being friends is not something you want, that's your decision. On a professional level, I want nothing more than your success, if for no other reason than it reflects well on me. You can rely on me to do everything I can to smooth the way for you over the next few months and defuse the tension when I can, regardless."

Perseverance looked him in the eye for what almost became an uncomfortable time. "You're serious," she decided.

He nodded.

"Okay. I'm still thinking about it," she said, exhaling noisily. "I have a lot I'm sorting out right now. Not that I'm opposed, just not ready to deal with it at the moment."

He nodded.

She faced forward again. What she knew of Saint John, she liked—so far. She admitted to herself that it was possible, even somewhat likely, that they would become friends. Of course, it helped that he was, as the queen said, "absolutely scrumptious" to look at.

"Can you share our itinerary with me?" she asked. "I don't know why I haven't asked before now. It's kind of important."

"You've been distracted," Powell said. He sent her the file containing their planned itinerary.

Perseverance opened it and began to examine it. According to the document, they would average between five and six days in transit from each planet to the next. They would spend only about twenty-four hours at each stop. The total, start to finish, was one hundred and sixty-five days. Today was Friday, March sixteenth. They were due to return to Caerleon Station on Tuesday, August twenty-eighth. If Caerleon Yard stayed on schedule, she was due to take command of HMS *Manitoba* on Monday, September tenth.

She realized she and Powell would celebrate their birthdays on this trip—his, on April twenty-third, and hers, on July seventh. She would turn thirty-six. Powell, if she remembered correctly, would be thirty-four.

On each planet, they generally made only one stop, to meet the leader of the local government. On the majority of the planets, that individual held the title of president. On the planets colonized initially by British settlers, that person was the Governor-General. On Carolina, the leader's title was Speaker.

After meeting with the leader, Perseverance would make a speech to the planetary legislature. She wondered why she would speak to them instead of the general public. Then she realized that if the Commonwealth was asking for massive amounts of money to be spent on building new ships, that request would need the approval of these legislatures as well as the Commonwealth Parliament.

"Saint John," she asked, "can you get me a list of who died in the opening battles, sorted by home system?"

"Sure. Why?"

"I was just thinking. I obviously don't know everyone who died—it's over a thousand people. But I'll bet I know or was shipmates with someone on the list from every system. So, when I talk with these folks, I think it will help to have a local connection."

"That's a great idea."

"Here's a better one," she said. "Find examples of businesses in each system that will contribute to the war effort, even if it's just mining or food production."

"That's also a great idea," Powell said. "It's such a good idea that I'm going to ask my boss to let Admiral Freshley know we're going to be mentioning it. Once we get the budgets approved, someone needs to ensure every system benefits in some way. The politicians will certainly make demands, so it's better if the navy is prepared in advance so they can direct things and not just respond."

20

They had been on their journey for eight weeks. Already they had visited nine of the twenty-five planets on the schedule. They celebrated Saint John's birthday by sharing two bottles of wine and getting slightly drunk. Perseverance's speeches were well-received. Her status as a celebrity was diminishing. One reason was Admiral Kenard's attack on the Federation forces in the Southampton system.

The Rodinans had fourteen ships in the system, five of which carried plasma shielding. In the initial attack nearly two months earlier, they destroyed the Royal Navy force without suffering any significant damage. Since Southampton was a planet that only recently opened for settlement, there were fewer than five hundred thousand Commonwealth residents. The Rodinans could seize control with a token force of ground troops.

Admiral Kenard brought a force of two heavy cruisers, four light cruisers, and six destroyers, all shielded. Facing him, the Federation had one heavy cruiser, two light cruisers, and two destroyers—all equipped with plasma shields. Their other ships were of the older type.

In addition, Kenard carried the new Cyclops missile. However, he only was supplied with enough for one salvo, or sixty-four missiles. Kenard concentrated on the shielded Rodinan ships. The combination of the Cyclops and the Royal Navy's photon cannons overwhelmed the Rodinans quickly.

Unfortunately, the Rodinans thought to equip their unshielded ships with laser warhead missiles. Their initial salvo was more than the point defense network of the Royal Navy ships could handle. All the Rodinan missiles targeted the Royal Navy's two heavy cruisers. Eighteen of the missiles survived to detonate and unleash their x-ray lasers.

Admiral Kenard's flagship, HMS *Springfield*, was destroyed. The other heavy cruiser, HMS *Cardiff*, was so heavily damaged the Admiralty had her towed back to Caerleon Yard. The only purpose was to strip the more valuable components from her. The other Royal Navy ships were untouched. As soon as the shielded Federation ships were knocked out of the fight, their remaining unshielded ships surrendered.

On the way to Lincoln, their most recent destination on the tour, Perseverance and Saint John watched the battle in real-time, accessing the sensor feeds through the Admiralty. Though it was a victory for the Commonwealth, it came at a high cost. Perseverance edited her usual remarks to take it into account. As a result, her presentation on Lincoln was much more somber than the others before.

Through the eight weeks they spent together, Perseverance and Saint John grew closer, though both were holding something back. Someone observing them would categorize them as "work buddies" but not as friends. Since she was a member of Admiral Freshley's staff, he assigned Perseverance to the task of reviewing various reports. When they were on the courier boat, she would retreat to her cabin and immerse herself in the tedium of reading the reports queued up for her.

The week before had been entertaining. As Lord Gilchrist predicted, right after they left on the tour, the conservatives called for a vote of no confidence shortly after Perseverance departed. The prime minister lost, and elections were scheduled six weeks in the future. When they arrived on Boreas, the stop before Lincoln, the election was two days away, and there was a great deal of pre-election energy in the air.

On the second night after departing Lincoln, on their way to the York system, Saint John asked Klaus, their steward, for a bottle of wine with dinner. By the time they finished the meal, Saint John had finished two glasses and was well into the third. He was not drunk and didn't even seem tipsy. When Perseverance started to rise from her seat, his arm flashed out and clasped her wrist.

"Please stay," he said quietly. "After Klaus clears the table, I think it's time I tell you how I won the DSC."

"You don't have to," she countered.

"I want to," he replied. "I was close to telling you on my birthday but chickened out.

A few minutes later, after Klaus cleared the table, she suggested, "We could go sit—"

"No. Here is better," he said. "So—how I earned the DSC and ended up in Public Affairs instead of on the bridge of a ship."

He drained the last of his wine.

"It was roughly two and a half years ago, in November. I was the executive officer on HMS *Hunter* under Captain Kathleen LeFerrier. *Hunter* was one of the destroyers finished in the next batch, right after you got *Rowen*. LeFerrier was given command because she was politically connected. Her father is the most senior MP from Caledonia. Shortly after I was posted to the ship, Captain LeFerrier pursued an intimate relationship with me. I put her off as gently as I could, but she persisted. Finally, after I refused her several times, I thought she got the message and gave up. She didn't bother me about it anymore, at least."

Saint John poured the last few drops of wine into his glass. It was barely enough for a sip. He gave a sad smile about it.

"The following year, Lieutenant Helen Showalter joined us as our second officer. You've heard the expression, 'love at first sight?' I don't know if what I felt was love but seeing her for the first time definitely affected me. Working with her only reinforced my attraction to her. She was intelligent, capable, and confident. I fought my feelings for her for nine months. It was clear she liked me, but we avoided flirting and any sort of innuendo. Shipboard romances are dangerous. Even when they work out, they disrupt a ship. When things don't work out, it can be toxic for a whole crew."

Perseverance nodded in agreement.

"One day, about nine months after she joined us, I was in a compartment in the hold, checking the inventory of food supplies. Helen walked in, shut and locked the door, and confessed that she had strong feelings for me and needed to know if I felt the same. I admitted I did. Things escalated extremely quickly."

Saint John reached for his glass but realized it was empty, so he stopped.

"I was worried, wondering if we were indiscreet. Helen assured me that the compartment we were in was one of the few places on the ship where the security cameras had no view. We met there many times. Outside of that compartment, we acted as though nothing had changed. Eventually, my conscience dictated that we do things the right way. Helen agreed, and we filled out the 5602 form required by regulations if you want to have a relationship with another member of the service."

"I know what the 5602 is," Perseverance said.

"We filled it out and submitted it to Captain LeFerrier. Three days later, on our way from Lincoln to Ilium, we picked up a power signature from a large asteroid in M7601, the last system before Ilium. We diverted from our course to go check it out. When we reached the asteroid, we determined the power signature was coming from a full life-support setup—atmosphere, heat, and gravity. There was even a short-range beacon to what looked like a hangar door. Captain LeFerrier called me to her ready room and ordered Helen and me to put on EVA suits and investigate. I asked if marines would be escorting us since that's standard procedure."

Saint John leaned over and took Perseverance's wine glass, where a sip or two remained. He tilted it up but only wet his lips.

"LeFerrier said there was no need for a marine escort. That she scanned the rock, and there was no one home. I protested, and she told me to shut up and do my job. I found Helen and told her what the captain had ordered. We both had a bad feeling about it, so we made sure to take sidearms."

He wet his lips again before continuing.

"We left the ship and floated over to the asteroid, using the beacon to guide us. I figured there would be an airlock near it, and I was right. We went through the airlock and found ourselves in a corridor. There was a normal door on either side and a hatch about fifteen meters ahead, just like a ship. We checked the two rooms, and they were empty. I was reporting our progress over the comm to Lieutenant Hastings, who was on duty on the bridge. We went through the hatch and saw two more rooms and another hatch. These two rooms were crew quarters. After going through them, there was nothing of interest. On the other side of the next hatch, we entered what seemed to be a control room. There were two consoles. Helen went to one, and I went to the other to see if we could pull any useful information from them."

Powell emptied the glass with a sad look.

"The next thing I knew was Lieutenant Hastings yelling, 'Oh, shit!' over the comm. As I spun around, I heard the snick-snap of fléchette rounds. When you hear them, it's too late, you know. Helen was already dead. For some reason, they did not see me right away. Four of them emerged from a compartment on the other side of the control room. I got a couple of shots off and then ran down the other corridor that was nearest to me. I figured it would lead to the hangar."

Perseverance, riveted by his account, noticed that Saint John had clasped her hand. She let him.

"I found out later I hit one of them right off. I got through the first hatch, dogged it, then ran to the next one and went through. I pushed it shut but didn't seal it. When I heard the other hatch open, I pulled mine out of the way and fired at the man who had just entered the corridor. I slammed it shut, dogged it, and went to the next. That was the hangar. It was just big enough to hold an FT, a fast transport. There wasn't much cover, but that's not what I was looking for. I was looking for the emergency button for the hangar door. They came through the hatch just before I reached it. I felt the fléchettes hit me on the left side just as I smacked the button to open the door. The three of us were sucked into space. My head banged on something on the way out, so I don't remember what happened next. The bad guys were dead—they didn't have any protective gear on. I was just as bad off since my EVA suit was shredded on the left side. Lucky for me, Lieutenant Hastings sent four marines after me as soon as he saw I was in trouble. They had almost reached the airlock when I blew the hangar door. Two marines flew out, snagged me, and zipped me back to *Hunter*. The other two went through the facility and retrieved Helen's body."

Saint John stopped speaking. Perseverance waited for him to start again. Instead, he just sat there, clasping her hand.

"You can't leave me hanging," she complained. "That's only half the story."

Saint John took a deep breath. "They put me in a med pod when they brought me back to the ship and put me in a medical coma. I was in bad shape. My left arm was shredded from mid-bicep down, and they couldn't save it. I'm holding your hand with one that's been regrown. My left side was also somewhat chewed up, but my arm protected me from having anything vital destroyed. By the time they brought me back to consciousness, more than a month had passed. One of the first things that happened was ONI began to interview me. Lieutenant Hastings nominated me for the DSC. His nomination was seconded by Senior Chief Petty Officer Millicent Downey, the COB. She was on the bridge at the comms station during the incident. Captain LeFerrier neither supported nor opposed my nomination. Ordinarily, that lack of support would have killed it."

"But it didn't," Perseverance said.

"Right. Remember, LeFerrier told me scans showed no one was present on the asteroid. When ONI went to check the records, as they do in any medal inquiry, those scans had been deleted. The ensign assigned to sensors that day was blamed for 'accidentally' deleting them and censured for not detecting the presence of the four men. Remember, Lieutenant Hastings yelled, 'Oh, shit!'? That's because as officer on duty, he was monitoring the different action stations. He had just pulled up sensors and saw the four men when he shouted. The ensign on sensors could not have overlooked them since Hastings saw them immediately."

"Where is that ensign now?" Perseverance asked.

"He left the service immediately after this. I have no idea—probably sipping fruity drinks on a beach somewhere. Anyway, ONI questioned Captain LeFerrier. She claimed I volunteered to investigate the facility. When she advised me to wait for a marine escort, I refused. When ONI tried accessing the security footage showing her ready room, it showed her sitting at her console. ONI also noticed the timestamp had been altered. They suspected she deleted the footage, replaced it with something non-incriminating, and fudged the timestamp."

"This keeps getting worse and worse," Perseverance commented.

"In the last visit from ONI, I asked if the Admiralty had a record of the 5602 that Helen and I submitted. They are very good at not showing any reaction, but I could tell they were surprised by this. After that meeting, no one came to see me for a week. I was stuck in the hospital with no access to the outside world. I found out later my parents had not been notified. Then after a week, Admiral Freshley showed up. He asked me some questions, mainly to verify what ONI included in their report. He then dug into my dealings with

Captain LeFerrier. I told him about her desire for an intimate relationship during my first year aboard. That was something that I had not mentioned before. He thanked me for my time and left."

"Damn," Perseverance whispered. "I think I know how this ends, but keep going."

"Four days later, Admiral Freshley reappears. He activates a field suppressor to counter any listening devices. Then the admiral tells me the cameras in the room have been turned off so he can speak freely. 'Here's how it's going to go, commander,' he said. 'You deserve the Distinguished Service Cross. You'll get it. When the promotion list comes out in a couple of months, you'll be on it. The bad news is I can't touch Captain LeFerrier. In fact, I'm getting pressure to promote her to command the task group we will station in Ilium. I'll probably go along with it since I think it will expose her weaknesses more clearly and more quickly. I hope like hell you decide to stay in the navy because we'll need you in a couple of years, but I can't blame you if you leave.' We talked after that. Perse, I've wanted to be in the navy since I was eight. I didn't want to leave. At the same time, I realized that what happened really screwed up my head. Admiral Freshley offered me the Public Affairs slot to give me a chance to sort things through. He's also responsible for me being assigned as your tour guide. So that's where we are."

"Tell me about Helen," Perseverance asked.

"I'd rather not if you don't mind," he said.

He released Perseverance's hand and stood. Looking down at her, he smiled, but it was a pained smile. He left and went to his cabin.

21

After Saint John left, Perseverance went to the console in the common sitting area. First, she looked up Lieutenant Helen Showalter in the Bureau of Personnel (known as BuPers in the Royal Navy) database. Unfortunately, the file was inaccessible, citing "Killed in Action" as the reason. There was an ID picture, though.

Even from the terrible quality of an official ID picture, Perseverance could tell that Showalter was striking. The lieutenant was blonde, her hair cut in a style very similar to how Perseverance wore hers, with eyebrows that were hard to see in this awful picture. Her eyes were large. She had prominent cheekbones and a thin nose. The overall effect was dramatic, like that of a high-fashion model and not one of "girl next door" prettiness.

Her curiosity not satisfied, Perseverance began searching social media sites. Here, Perseverance found what she was looking for. Showalter had been a volleyball player in college at the University of New Boston. There were pictures of her in action, her hair long and in a braid. She was tall, broad-shouldered, and slender. From the pictures, it looked like a knee injury ended her volleyball career. There were pictures of her commissioning ceremony, her hair now cut shorter as in the ID picture. There were snapshots of her in various social settings, from the beach, to nightclubs, to what looked like being a bridesmaid at a wedding. Her smile was big and wide. Several of the pictures seemed to catch her laughing.

Finally, there was one picture of her with Saint John. It was taken by someone else aboard HMS *Hunter*. Saint John was looking straight ahead, with the awkward "I'm getting my picture taken" smile on his face. Showalter's smile was more genuine. Her eyes were aimed off-center, in Saint John's direction, as though she wanted to keep him in her peripheral vision.

Perseverance returned to the Royal Navy site, then scrubbed her searches from the console's history. It would not do for Saint John to find out she'd been looking into his past like this. His story touched her. Losing a lover had to be horrible. To have your commanding officer possibly orchestrate it was even worse. Perseverance had never lost a lover. She lost her best friend, Ken Berger, but they were never lovers.

She entered her cabin and undressed for bed. Sliding between the sheets, she thought about her relationship with Ken. A few years before, she had been talking to Ken, crying on his shoulder (even though it was over a comm) about another failed relationship that she had just ended. During the conversation, she experienced a revelation.

About halfway through the call, she became aware that she wasn't that upset about her recent break-up. She was crying because it was the usual and expected reaction in these circumstances, but she realized she was not sad. That stopped her tears quickly.

After ending the call, she conducted a self-examination to try to determine why she was not upset. She decided her lack of grief was because she still had her relationship with Ken. No matter what happened with this latest clown, she knew Ken still loved her in his way, and she could count on it. He was her safety net.

From there, the idea germinated in her brain and her heart that someday, down the road, she and Ken would come to the same realization—that they were perfectly suited for each other, were best friends, loved each other and they should be together. They would get married and live happily ever after. She never mentioned this to Ken. There were a couple of relationships she attempted after coming up with this idea, but when they ended, she was almost unaffected. Similarly, when Ken told her about a woman he was seeing, Perseverance was unconcerned. She knew it wouldn't lead to anything because, in her heart, she knew that she and Ken were somehow destined to be together.

That all came crashing down when Ken died in action. Lying in bed and conducting a self-examination, Perseverance started to think about it. His death hit her so hard and was still bothering her. Now she began to understand that the rational part of her brain was puzzled by why she was still troubled and felt it was wrong to feel such grief over the loss of someone who was just a friend. Meanwhile, her emotional side, which she kept hidden from everyone, had every right to mourn the loss of the person she always relied on and with whom she planned to be even more closely linked in the future.

She began to weep. Saint John's story of the loss of his lover had touched her. She now understood she, too, had lost a lover, even though they were never physically intimate. That understanding now gave her soul the permission it had been seeking. Perseverance sobbed herself to sleep, doubly sad that the two of them didn't figure things out in time to share the happiness they would surely have enjoyed.

When she woke in the morning, she looked in the mirror. She looked awful. Anyone could tell from her red, puffy eyes that she had cried extensively the night before. She also felt like all her emotional juice had been squeezed out of her. There was a lingering sense of loss and of emptiness. She now understood why she felt so lonely not long before.

She washed her face vigorously to try to eliminate the signs of her emotional evening but was only partially successful. She sat down and joined Saint John for breakfast. He looked worried at first, fearing he had overshared the night before. That feeling went away when he looked at Perseverance.

"You look as bad as I feel," he commented. "What did I do?"

She smiled. Saint John did what Ken used to do, immediately trying to take the blame for something absolutely not their fault. "You didn't do anything. It's… me. I don't want to go into it now, but I promise I'll tell you when I'm ready."

"Sounds familiar," he said.

"Steal from the best, I always say," she replied. "I have to ask, what happened to Captain LeFerrier?"

"She's dead. Admiral Freshley did end up promoting her. She was in command of the task group in Ilium—one of the two that disregarded the advice brought forward by an extremely savvy captain. Let me tell you a story. It doesn't have a happy ending yet, but I think you'll be interested. There's some humor in it, in a way."

"Fine. Go ahead."

"Once upon a time (since that's the way all good stories start)," Saint John began, as though he were reading a bedtime story to a child, "there were five captains in the Royal Navy. Three of these captains were hard-working, industrious people who earned the position on their own merits. Two of these captains were incompetent boobs who were blessed by having powerful and influential relatives. How do you like it so far?"

"I think I know how this turns out," she said.

"These five captains were placed in command of defending the border. Enemies were threatening the Royal Navy, so the borders were important. Since the enemy would come with a greater force than any of the five had, one of the hard-working captains made a suggestion. They should send out scouts to learn if and when the enemy was coming and prepare traps to bother the enemy on the way. That way, even though they might be outnumbered, they would still be ready to do their very best. Three of the captains thought that was a great plan and did just that. The two incompetent boob captains said, 'pooh-pooh' to the idea."

"Does one of these bad captains have a name that rhymes with LeFerrier?"

"Indeed, clever Persie. She was one of the incompetent boobs. Anyway, the enemy decided to attack. One of the hard-working captains was lucky, and the enemy stayed away from him. One of the hard-working captains fought a good fight and prevented the enemy from getting past him but sadly, he died. One of the hard-working captains disabled all the enemy ships and then, if that wasn't enough, rescued all the enemies from certain death. The kind and generous queen rewarded this captain with a medal and made her a knight."

"But what happened to the incompetent boobs?" Perseverance asked, playing along with the story time idea.

"Oh, what happened to the incompetent boobs isn't very pretty, I'm afraid, Persie. They and their ships were destroyed within minutes, and they barely even scratched the paint on the enemy ships. They left a big mess for everyone else to clean up."

"I hope that's not the end of the story," she said.

"The end of the story hasn't been written yet."

"So now I know why I didn't have a good feeling about LeFerrier," she said. "Who was Crawford Larson related to?"

"You just met with him two months ago or thereabouts—the prime minister. Or I should say, the former prime minister, since the Liberal Democrats were spanked so soundly in the election."

"I should have figured that out on my own," she said. "This story cheered me up more than the one last night, even though it doesn't have a happy ending either. It's bad enough that people died but what's worse is that more will be sacrificed to make up for the incompetence of LeFerrier and Larson."

"Admiral Freshley and I spoke about this issue," Saint John said. "He said it's a difficult problem during peacetime since budgets are always at risk. However, a shooting war gives him the chance to get rid of them since budgets aren't subject to the same wheeling and dealing. We'll see."

Two months later, they were approaching Alleghany. It would be the twentieth planet on the tour. The day before, Parliament announced the passage of an emergency appropriations bill. Construction of eight heavy cruisers and twelve each of light cruisers and destroyers was to begin immediately. Also passed was an emergency powers act, giving the government the authority to commandeer civilian shipbuilding facilities and other manufacturing resources necessary for timely completion of the work. Nevertheless, it would still be thirty months before the first ship was finished.

The last system they visited, New Boston, was the first time Perseverance faced anything resembling a hostile question from the media. Up to now, they had been better behaved than she expected. At the usual Q&A following her speech in New Boston, a reporter asked why it was taking the Royal Navy so long to recapture the Ilium system from the Chinese Republics.

Perseverance wanted to say the complete failure of Captains Larson and LeFerrier to defend Southampton and Ilium made recapturing them more difficult, as seen by the losses taken in Admiral Kenard's attack on Southampton. The Royal Navy lost both the heavy cruisers in that battle *and* Admiral Kenard. They could not afford to suffer the same losses in retaking Ilium. If they did, the Commonwealth would be left wide open to an enemy attack, with insufficient ships to mount an adequate defense.

She knew she could not speak so plainly. Instead, she tried to dance around the question. Both she and the reporter knew she wasn't giving a straight answer. She and Saint John discussed it later. Both agreed that her non-response practically guaranteed that other reporters would follow up. Saint John had been communicating back and forth with the Admiralty. The officially approved answer the Admiralty sent was that the situation was a high priority, and strategies were being considered to retake the system while avoiding the losses suffered in Southampton.

"That response is going work with the media the way blood in the water does for sharks," Saint John said. "It's true enough, as far as it goes, but there's not enough *mea culpa* in it."

"*Mea* what?"

"Sorry. It's Latin. It means 'my fault.' What the Admiralty is trying to do is avoid blame. I think you and I know there is plenty of blame to share. The Admiralty is to blame for putting bad officers in critical positions. The politicians are to blame for playing games with the budget, forcing these people on the navy, and for our current state of unpreparedness. Hell, even the average citizen is to blame since no one wants the higher taxes needed to pay for an effective military."

"So, what do I do?" Perseverance asked.

Saint John sighed. "You have two choices. You can spit out the Admiralty's message or tell the truth. The Admiralty's response will just send the media into a feeding frenzy. On the other hand, telling the truth may well get you fired. They'll haul us back to Caerleon, cut off your epaulet, break your sword, and cast you out of the service."

Perseverance was not a rule-breaker. She loved the navy. She did things the "navy way." When her plans for defense in depth were rejected, she followed orders, even though she knew they would result in avoidable losses. She accepted that the political fallout from withdrawing from the border systems was unpalatable. That situation was bad enough. Two incompetent but politically connected captains made that bad situation far worse. For the next day and a half, Perseverance wrestled with this.

They arrived at Alleghany Station with four hours to spare before they needed to board the shuttle that would deliver them to the capital, Pittsburgh.

Perseverance had already arranged for her brother and sisters to be invited to attend her speech, and she would see them afterward. However, she had not invited her parents because she doubted her father would come. Nevertheless, it was her father she called, after checking to make sure it was not the middle of the night where her parents lived.

He answered in his usual way. "Hold on. Let me get your mother."

"Wait, Dad. It's you I need to talk to," Perseverance pleaded.

"Me?"

"Yes, Dad, you. I have a dilemma."

"And you think *I* can help you?" he asked, his tone full of scorn.

"I think so," she said. "I hope so."

"Very well. What is this dilemma you face?"

Perseverance did the best she could to explain her problem. Her father listened.

"Why don't you want to do what your superiors order?" he asked.

"Because it doesn't feel right, Dad. Beyond the fact that it will make my day unpleasant because it will cause every other reporter to ask a version of the same question, it just isn't sitting well with me," she said.

"And your superiors will fire you if you speak the truth?" he inquired.

"I don't know that for certain," she admitted. "They will undoubtedly be unhappy with me. If they don't fire me, they probably will put me in unpleasant circumstances until I decide to leave on my own. I doubt they will appreciate me telling the whole, unvarnished truth."

"This calling you have pursued… If the leaders do not appreciate the truth, perhaps this organization is not the best place for you. This goes beyond me being right or you being right, do you understand?" he asked.

Perseverance considered his words carefully. "Yes, Dad. I do."

"One last suggestion," he said. "Proverbs eight, verses seven through nine. I'm glad you called, Persie."

He ended the call. How he closed the call stunned her momentarily. Perseverance quickly looked up the Bible verses before she forgot them. As she did, she reflected that this was the most pleasant conversation she had held with her father for nearly twenty years. She found the quotation he referenced.

For my mouth will utter truth; wickedness is an abomination to my lips.

All the words of my mouth are righteous; there is nothing twisted or crooked in them.

They are all straight to him who understands; and right to those who find knowledge.

22

After Perseverance delivered her prepared remarks, she opened the session to questions from the crowd of legislators and the media. She usually took questions from the legislators before responding to the reporters. One of the members of the New Boston Congress raised her hand.

"Why is it taking the Royal Navy so long to recapture Ilium from the Chinese Republics?" she asked.

"I assure you the situation is a high priority for the Admiralty. Strategies are being considered to retake the system while avoiding the losses suffered in Southampton," Perseverance began, spouting the line the Admiralty wished for her to say. She then went beyond those approved remarks, saying, "Retaking Southampton was difficult, and we suffered unacceptably high losses. With the ships we've lost so far, if Ilium proves to be as difficult as Southampton, we will leave the Commonwealth with an inadequate defense."

"This is worse than I thought. How did we get into this situation?" the legislator asked, following up on her original question.

"There's plenty of blame to go around," Perseverance said, knowing she was likely committing career suicide. "The root of the problem is that building and maintaining the ships the Royal Navy needs is expensive. No one in his right mind wants to pay higher taxes, right?"

Her comment drew a laugh. She continued, "The navy asks Parliament for X amount of money, based first on its analysis of its needs. It then revises the request downward to what it feels is a reasonable figure that Parliament might possibly approve. Parliament agrees to provide an amount. Let's say it's X minus a hundred. The navy tries to negotiate. During the negotiations, a member of Parliament might say, 'My niece has always wanted to be in the Royal Navy. Let her into the academy and make her an officer, and I'll vote for X minus fifty.' Another MP might say, 'My biggest financial supporter's son wants to attend the academy. Let him in, and I'll support X minus fifty.' The navy holds its nose and agrees to these requests to get the appropriation passed at X minus fifty. Keep in mind that the X figure was already reduced from what the navy felt it *needed*— not wanted but *needed*–to maintain an adequate defense of the Commonwealth. Remember that the navy is not composed of children who only want shiny toys. We're adults, tasked with what we feel is the most important job in the universe—protecting the Commonwealth."

Perseverance paused to drink a sip of water. She held up her finger to indicate she was not finished. She glanced over at Saint John. His expression was a mix of admiration and sympathy. He admired Perseverance for her courage in telling the truth and compassion because he suspected the cost would be her career.

"Now, it might be that the one MP's niece or so-and-so's son is perfectly well qualified. That happens. Unfortunately, it also happens that they sometimes are not. In either case, the navy decides accepting one or two officers who might not be qualified is an acceptable price to pay for getting a bigger portion of the budget requested."

"This budget dance happens every year," Perseverance continued. "Maybe it turns out that so-and-so's son is an incompetent idiot who can't even tie his shoelaces. If the navy holds him accountable, they lose that MP's vote in the next round of haggling over the budget. They might also lose the votes of other MPs allied with the first. To protect those votes, the idiot enjoys the same career progression as a well-qualified officer. Eventually, he will command a ship and achieve enough seniority to be considered for an even more advanced position. This gives the navy the first chance to control the problem. Suppose the navy promotes the idiot into a position where his inadequacies will be exposed. Finally, the navy can eliminate him without political backlash. If it's clear that so-and-so's son is a fool, the MP will withdraw his or her support because no one can afford to be associated with a disaster. Unfortunately, that's what happened in Southampton and Ilium."

Several of the legislators began clamoring to be heard next. Perseverance picked one.

"What are you saying about Southampton and Ilium? Will you please explain?"

"Sure. Before I go on, please keep in mind I am speaking as only one person. I do not speak for Admiral Freshley or Admiral Czervik. In Southampton, our force of three destroyers assigned to protect that border system was commanded by Crawford Larson, nephew of the former prime minister. In Ilium, the commander was Kathleen LeFerrier, daughter of the most senior MP from Caledonia. I was in command of the Aries system. Ken Berger commanded the force in Automedon, and Hank Boyd was in New Wales. Following the attack, the Chinese Republics made three-and-a-half years ago, we knew it was only a matter of time before they or the Federation came back and tried again."

Perseverance paused for water again.

"Three of us did everything we could think of to prepare. Hank, Ken, and I sent out patrol boats to act as scouts and inform us when the enemy was coming. We laid minefields in case the enemy tried to bring some of the older, unshielded ships. These same ideas were shared with LeFerrier and Larson. They chose not to implement them. The Federation did not choose to come through the New Wales system, so Hank Boyd faced no action. In Automedon, Ken Berger prevented the Republics from advancing further. However, it cost him his life and the lives of everyone in his force. I described my experience in Aries earlier. In Southampton and Ilium, our forces were unprepared. Our ships were destroyed quickly—within minutes. In return, we inflicted no significant damage on the enemy. When Admiral Kenard entered Southampton, he faced a virtually untouched Federation force. Though we regained the system, the cost was high. We lost two heavy cruisers and Admiral Kenard."

Perseverance now called on the most strident of the legislators, who jumped out of her seat and was shouting, "Captain Andrews! Captain Andrews!"

"Are you blaming Captain Larson for the losses we suffered later in retaking Southampton?"

Perseverance paused before answering. She considered her words and how to phrase her response.

"I suppose I am, though it is not my desire to single out a fellow officer this way. I would prefer to cast blame on the whole process of procurement and appropriations. In order to get a larger portion of a still inadequate budget, the navy made compromises that led to Captain Larson being in command of our defense force in Southampton. The most important reason why the navy sent me out to every populated system in the Commonwealth was to generate goodwill and prepare you all to support the budget request that Admiral Freshley will be presenting to Parliament. Our situation is dire—I am speaking of the Commonwealth, not just the Royal Navy. Our reluctance to spend the money needed for a proper defense in the past created the circumstances we now face. The Royal Navy will do its best. I promise you that. Over a thousand men and women gave their lives a few months ago in proof of that. I will reiterate what I said then. Give us the tools, and we will finish the job. And when the war is over, and the Commonwealth emerges victorious, do not forget the absolute necessity of maintaining a proper defense."

The next questions Perseverance took were from legislators who clearly were only trying to get on the record. When she began calling on the media, they only requested clarification of what she said earlier. Saint John stepped in and closed the meeting at that point. He later told Perseverance that the media were too busy filing their stories to bother her in their customary way.

She and Saint John went to the waiting room offstage. "It's been nice knowing you, Saint John," she said.

"You're still stuck with me a few more days," he said. "They'll yank our butts back to Caerleon, so we'll be together for that trip."

Perseverance's brother and sisters entered the waiting room. After exchanging hugs, Perseverance introduced them to Saint John.

"Steadfast, Felicity and Prudence, this is Commander Saint John Powell."

After introductions, her two sisters pulled her aside. Steadfast, out of politeness, stayed with Saint John, attempting to make small talk. He wanted to be part of the conversation with Perseverance as well but figured his sisters would get him caught up later.

"What the hell, Persie!" Prudence exclaimed. "It was like you dropped a bomb in there. We were seated with the media, and they were going crazy."

"Yeah," Felicity agreed. "They were commenting that you were really brave or really stupid to talk about such things. One of them said, 'Enjoy it while it lasts, folks, because we'll probably never see her again.' I'm guessing the navy will not be pleased with what you said."

"Have you decided to leave the navy?" Prudence asked.

"I hope not," Perseverance replied, "but I think they will probably get rid of me."

"That will be hard for them to do," Felicity commented. "They just gave you a medal, and the queen just knighted you, or whatever that was."

"Oh, they'll probably say I was upset because of the losses we took, which made me mentally unbalanced. Of course, they'll phrase it sympathetically, but the end result will be the same."

"Then why did you do it?" Felicity demanded.

"The situation is as bad as I said, and it bothers me. So, I talked with Dad," Perseverance said. That drew gasps from her sisters since they knew how distant Perseverance and their father were. "He suggested that if the navy can't handle the truth, perhaps it's not something I want to be a part of. I thought about it. He's right."

"So what will happen now?" Steadfast asked, having wandered over when Saint John was interrupted by the buzzing of his comm unit.

"I turned my comm off, but I can imagine they are already trying to reach me," she said. She turned and saw Saint John speaking to someone on his comm. "See?"

"Changing the subject," Prudence said, "you've been traveling with *that* the last four months? He's certainly easy on the eyes. How is he in the sack?"

"Prudence!" Felicity exclaimed.

"Oh, c'mon, Felix! Like you aren't thinking the same thing," Prudence replied.

"I haven't... We haven't—" Perseverance began.

"Bullshit!' Prudence said fiercely, "unless maybe you are stupid like the one reporter thought. Or is he a jerk? People that good-looking usually are. Or is he...?"

"He's not," Perseverance interjected promptly. "And he's not a jerk. He's a really nice person. It's complicated because we're in the navy. They have rules—"

"Screw the rules!" Felicity said. "The two of you, by yourselves—"

"We're not by ourselves," Perseverance interrupted. "There are two pilots, plus Klaus, the steward."

"Big deal," Felicity said.

"Please tell me you've thought about it, at least," Prudence inquired.

"Of course, I've thought about it!" Perseverance replied, exasperated. "It's just—"

"Sorry to interrupt, Perse," Saint John said, appearing at her side suddenly, "but we're wanted on a call in a couple of hours. We are also instructed to return to the ship immediately. Sorry."

Perseverance said her goodbyes with hugs all around. Her sister, Prudence, whispered in her ear, "If you're leaving the navy, you ought to jump his bones before you go." Perseverance blushed brightly.

Her brother Steadfast was last. After they hugged, he held Perseverance by her upper arms. "Persie, it's not often I agree with Dad, but in this case, I think you made the right decision by following his advice. I hope it works out, but if it doesn't, it just means there's something else you are meant to do," he said.

"Now you do sound like Dad," she commented.

"Well, he's not wrong *all* the time," Steadfast replied.

Perseverance and Saint John returned to the spaceport and caught the next shuttle to Alleghany Station. It was not until they boarded the courier boat that Saint John said anything. Perseverance wanted to talk about it earlier, but he shook his head, waving his finger at all the other people around.

"Grab a seat," he suggested once they were aboard. "We have about forty minutes before the call."

"I'm doomed, aren't I?"

"Well, my boss was none too happy. Captain Rosen probably needed to clean the spittle off his comm when he finished with me. Who knows how the top brass feel?" Saint John said.

"Probably at least that furious," Perseverance said with a sigh.

"I'm sorry to drag you away from your family. It looked like you were having an interesting discussion."

"Did you listen to any of it?" Perseverance asked fearfully.

"No. I was busy being yelled at by Captain Rosen. I must say, I've been in the navy awhile, and I've grown accustomed to hearing certain words. He put them in some combinations I never heard before," Saint John said with a smile.

"Sorry."

"I have your back, Perse. You said things that needed to be said. It's a shame you had to be the one to do it. When did you decide?"

"After I spoke with my father this morning. It's the first time I can remember that I asked his advice about anything, and the longest we've spoken in a long time. He suggested that if the navy can't handle me telling the truth, maybe it isn't as great a place as I thought," Perseverance said. "He also quoted scripture, of course."

"What passage?"

"Here. I'll show you," she said. She looked up the passage on her comm unit and handed it to Saint John.

"That's certainly appropriate," he agreed after reading.

Just then, his comm unit buzzed. He glanced it.

"Huh," he grunted. "Our call is postponed."

"How long?"

"Another two hours," he said.

"What do you think that means?" she asked.

23

Not long after, Perseverance's comm alerted her to an incoming call. She looked at the screen, seeing the contact ID for Admiral Freshley. She jumped up and sprinted into her cabin, shutting the door.

"Yes, sir," she answered.

"Captain Andrews," Admiral Freshley began, "did Lord Gilchrist share with you his 'sausage' analogy to describe the Parliamentary process?"

"He did, sir."

"You just gave the entire Commonwealth a close look at part of the sausage factory," Freshley said. "It's going to be a few days before we can gauge how the public feels about it. Here on Caerleon, some people want your head on a plate. I'm not one of them, by the way. You also have some influential people who support you vigorously. Even more people can't decide whether to be furious with you or ashamed of themselves. Time will tell. Regarding your assignment, I've instructed the pilots to proceed to New Glasgow, the next system on your itinerary. We will know how to proceed by the time you arrive."

"Yes, sir," she replied. "And sir, I'm sorry I did not warn you in advance. I imagine you did not appreciate being caught by surprise. For that, I apologize."

"Hmm," Freshley hummed. "You're not apologizing for what you said?"

"No, sir. I believe what I said is true, and I will not apologize for that. I'm apologizing for not letting you know in advance what I planned to say," she said calmly and firmly.

"Very well, Captain Andrews," he stated. "By the time you reach your next destination, we will know better how we want to proceed. Freshley out."

Perseverance returned to the common area. Saint John was not there. He appeared a couple of minutes later.

"Who was your call?" he asked.

"Admiral Freshley. Who was yours?"

"Captain Rosen. Our conference call is now canceled. Rosen is still mad as hell. He now blames me for not 'controlling' you. When I reminded him that you outrank me, he shouted that it didn't matter and he would see to it my career was over," Saint John reported.

"I'm sorry," Perseverance replied, "but you know what? Fuck Rosen."

"What did Admiral Freshley have to say?"

"He said there were people who wanted me punished, but he wasn't one of them, that there were people on my side—he did not say he was in that group—and public opinion is all over the place. We're heading to New Glasgow, and they'll make up their minds by the time we get there," she related.

"Well, it's not as bad as I first thought," Saint John said. "We haven't been dismissed from the service yet."

"Yet," she said.

Perseverance checked her comm unit. There were a dozen messages from former shipmates. She began to read them. Eleven of the messages were positive. Only one was not. The sender was not mad at what Perseverance said but that she might have ended her career.

Perseverance tapped out short replies. She thanked them for their support and admitted she did not know what would happen to her. She kept her return messages short and general since she had no additional information. She had just sent the last one when Saint John knocked on her cabin door.

"Dinner," he said. "Or do you want to eat in your cabin?"

"I'm coming," she replied. "Have Klaus give us a bottle of wine. We both could use it, I think."

They sat at the small table. Klaus brought the food out, along with the wine. When their glasses were filled, Perseverance raised hers and held it out toward Saint John.

"Here's to telling the truth," she said.

They clinked glasses, had a sip, and began eating. After one bite, Perseverance stopped.

"Mr. Daimler?" she called.

Klaus stuck his head out of the tiny galley. "Yes, sir?"

"Is this real chicken?" she asked.

"Yes, sir. Some supplies were delivered," he said. "For the next two weeks, we'll eat real food and not processed soy imitations."

"Wow! That's great, Mr. Daimler," she said. "How did you fit it into your budget?"

"Alleghany is your home system, sir. One of the leading grocery chains donated the food as a gift to you," he said. "We were only limited by what we could fit in the freezer. They also refilled our wine rack."

"Good job, Mr. Daimler," she said. "Thank you for taking them up on their offer."

"Not a problem, sir. The pilots and I benefit too. And, sir, if you don't mind my saying, thank you for speaking up today. I've served under some of the kind of people you mentioned, and I always wondered how they got to where they were. Now I know."

"Thank you, Mr. Daimler," she said.

Klaus disappeared behind the galley door. Perseverance and Saint John made short work of their meal. A real roasted chicken breast, real sautéed potatoes, and real green beans were not the typical fare aboard ship. Most often, they would have processed soy, colored, flavored, and shaped to look like the real thing. As someone told her on her first posting, "It's not very close to the real thing, but it's close enough that you can tell what you're missing."

After dinner, they finished the bottle of wine. Neither of them was much affected. They went to the small sitting area and shared the sofa.

After a minute, Perseverance looked at Saint John and asked, "Saint John, can I ask you for a favor?"

"Sure. What?"

Perseverance scooted down to his end of the sofa. She pushed him so he was leaning toward the arm of it. She then moved right next to him, pulling his right arm over her shoulder, and putting her head on his chest.

"If this makes you uncomfortable, say so," she said, "but I would really appreciate it if you would hold me for a little while. Just hold me."

"Um, sure," he replied. "Just let me get a little more comfortable."

He shifted his position slightly. Perseverance put her head on his chest again. He laid his arm on top of hers. Neither of them spoke.

Within a few minutes, Saint John realized she had fallen asleep. When Klaus entered to clear the table, he saw the two of them. Saint John held his finger to his lips, asking Klaus both to be quiet, to not wake her, and to keep his mouth about this. Klaus nodded his head with a smile, then mimed zipping his lips shut.

Saint John looked down at Perseverance's face. He gently gathered a stray lock of hair that had fallen forward and tucked it behind her ear so he had a better view. He wanted to stroke her hair or arm as a reassuring gesture but did not want to wake her up and especially did not want her to think he was taking advantage. Eventually, he fell asleep as well.

A twinge in his back from maintaining the unaccustomed position woke him. Perseverance had slid down his chest. Her head was in his lap, and she had pulled the arm he draped over her earlier down and was holding his hand to her breast with her hand on top. As gingerly as possible, he tried to extract his hand in a way that wouldn't wake her. Instead, she clutched it tighter to herself in response to the slight movement. Saint John then struggled to pull his comm unit from his pocket so he could check the time. It was 06:30. Saint John took a moment to gaze at her. He never saw her look so vulnerable or more attractive. He took a deep breath, then quickly pulled his hand away from her chest and used it to give her shoulder a gentle shake.

"Hey!" he whispered. "It's time to wake up."

Perseverance's eyes snapped open. It took her a moment to figure out the situation. When she did, she launched herself off Saint John first, then the sofa. Her face was already flushing red.

"Shit!" she exclaimed. "I feel asleep."

"*We* feel asleep," he responded.

"I'm so sorry—"

"Don't worry about it. It's 06:30, though. Time for us to get moving."

"Right," she agreed, then almost sprinted to her cabin.

Perseverance avoided him as much as she could, given that the courier boat was so small. She stayed in her cabin most of the day, emerging only to grab a sandwich from the pantry and take it back to her quarters. Dinner was silent, and she kept her eyes on her plate. When she finished, she stood quickly, about to dart back to her cabin.

"Stop!" Saint John demanded. "Sit down! I don't know why the hell you're acting like this, but we didn't *do* anything."

She sat back down but still would not look him in the eye.

"Perse," he said, "you had an incredibly stressful day. You needed a friend and a cuddle. There's nothing wrong with it—we could all use that from time to time. And, in case you missed it, I've been trying to be your friend for over four months and have gotten nowhere."

"I think of you as a friend," she said meekly.

"Then throw away the ten-meter pole you've been using to keep me at a distance."

"I'll... I'll try," she said.

"What's the problem, anyway?" he asked. "Is it me? Did I do something?"

Perseverance paused, then lifted her head. "It's you, but nothing you did. You're just too handsome. Every guy I've met who was even half as good-looking as you was an arrogant, self-absorbed prick."

"So that's what you think of me," he said scornfully.

Perseverance shook her head vigorously. "No. You haven't acted like that at all. But a part of me is holding back, waiting to see it."

"You'll be waiting a long time, then, I hope," he said. "But that frightened part of you doesn't believe what I said and is thinking, 'That's just what I expected him to say.' What about you? I could say the same about you. In my experience, women as attractive as you are usually turn out to be narcissistic bitches. I haven't seen any indication you're that way, and it's been long enough that it would have come out by now."

"I don't think I'm a narcissistic bitch," she said.

"You're not," he replied, exasperated. "You're a nice, honest, genuine person, just like I try to be. Not an arrogant, self-centered prick."

"Self-absorbed," she corrected, smiling faintly.

"Fine! Whatever!"

"You've been nothing but nice since I met you," she admitted.

"Good. My mother and father would be pleased to hear it."

"Why aren't you an arrogant, self-absorbed prick?" she asked.

"Because my mother and father brought me up to not be that way. My dad is an older version of me—picture me in thirty years, with a few lines on my face and gray hairs at my temples, and you have my dad. My grandfather, however, looks nothing like us. I mean, he's not ugly. He's just normal. By the time my father was six years old, grandpa had noticed people were treating his son differently because of how he looked. He pulled my dad aside and told him, 'Damned few of the people who are attractive on the outside are just as pretty on the inside. If you can be one of those few, you'll have a happy life, and I will be proud of you.' Grandpa repeated that message to my father countless times. He and my grandfather have told me the same thing my whole life."

"Is your dad a good person too?" she asked.

"I think so. After all, mom agreed to marry him, so I think he had it figured out by then," he said. "He pestered her for almost a year to go on a date with him. When she finally agreed, all she would consent to was 'just coffee.' She told me she knew she would marry him by the time her coffee grew cold. She heard from others earlier that he was a genuinely nice person and told me she saw the proof at the coffee shop."

"Is she pretty?"

"Yes, but she doesn't promote it. Her work wardrobe is made up of the most unflattering clothes she can find. She says as a copywriter, her ideas should win the day, not her looks. Dad is a bit more on the 'If you've got it, flaunt it' side of things. What about you? How did you avoid becoming a stuck-up bitch?"

"Are you kidding?" she snorted. "You saw my sisters. I'm the ugly duckling compared to them. Plus, until my junior year of high school, I was taller than most of the boys. Beyond that, it took another couple of years for me to grow into my looks—a late bloomer. It wasn't until my sophomore year of college that things changed. The first time a boy asked me out in college, I thought I was being pranked again."

"Wait a minute. 'Again?' What do you mean?" he asked.

"Every year in November, my high school had a big celebration called, 'Homecoming.' My junior year, there was a boy on the basketball team I really liked," she explained. "He was handsome and tall, so I was thrilled he asked me. When we left the dance, he took me to a secluded spot, and we started making out. I'd never even kissed a boy before, so you can imagine how exciting it was.

I didn't let him do anything other than kiss me, but he certainly tried. After he took me home, I thought I was in love. On Monday, all that came crashing down. When I arrived at school that morning, people were snickering behind my back. Finally, a girl I didn't like very much pulled me aside and asked me if I enjoyed being a part of the heifer contest."

"The what?"

"Heifer contest," she said. "The boy who took me to the dance and his friends had a contest to see who could bring the ugliest girl to the dance. The ringleader of that little bunch convinced the others that the ugly girls would be so grateful for the attention that they would all get laid."

"That's awful!" Saint John exclaimed.

"I marched right up to that boy and slapped his face," she said. "Then I smacked him on the other side, remembering God's advice to turn the other cheek. Afterward, I went to the office and told them what I had done and why since I thought I would get suspended for slapping him. The principal listened to my story, told me not to do it again, and sent me back to class—with a note excusing my tardiness."

"Well, I'm not that guy," Saint John stated.

"I know," she confirmed. "I'll try. I promise."

24

Two and a half days later, her comm buzzed upon exiting hyperspace and emerging into normal space in the New Glasgow system. The tone indicated she missed a call when they were in hyperspace. There had been no further communication with the Admiralty since her call with Admiral Freshley and Saint John's with Captain Rosen. The ID of the missed call read: Communications Maintenance. Puzzled, she tapped the key to return the call.

"Gilchrist," she heard. "Hello, Captain Andrews."

Stunned, Perseverance took a moment to respond. "Uh, hello, Lord Gilchrist."

"Please, it's Alfred. Or else I shall be forced to address you as Dame Captain Andrews. I take it the caller ID threw you off?" he said.

"Yes, sir—uh, Alfred," she responded. "Um, please call me Perse. Why did it read: Communications Maintenance?"

"Charlie—Queen Charlotte's little joke," he explained. "I don't have any sort of official title. However, the queen decided that since most of what I do is smoothing communications between different groups, she would name me director of political communications. I argued that having a title would be counterproductive, and I thought she agreed. Since then, comm units have identified me as 'Communications Maintenance.' She likes her fun. Now, you're probably wondering why I am calling."

"Yes."

"In the three-plus days since your 'truth bomb' exploded, public opinion about the content of your speech has gelled. It's hard to believe the public could have a lower opinion of politicians than before, but that is what the polls show. Approval ratings for the Royal Navy have risen slightly, held in check by the sentiment, 'Why didn't they admit this sooner?' As for you, the latest numbers show that ninety-one percent of those contacted know who you are, and seventy-nine percent have a favorable or highly favorable opinion of you."

"What does this mean?" she asked.

"It means that leaders of both parties are in a panic since members of both groups are guilty of leveraging appropriation votes for favorable treatment within the Royal Navy. The Liberal Democrats have much more reason to be concerned since eighty-two percent of these politically connected officers are linked to Liberal Democrat MPs. Still, the Conservatives have some, so their hands are also dirty—just not as dirty as the Liberal Democrats. The public wants these officers removed from the navy immediately, and there will probably be public hearings in both chambers of Parliament," Gilchrist explained. "Leaders of both parties are pressing their people to identify these officers. Admiral Freshley already has a list but has not shared it with the politicians."

"That's good, isn't it? It means they'll address the issue. Do these polls show whether people are more or less willing to support the navy financially?" she asked.

"That's the biggest positive to come out of this for the Royal Navy," he said. "The answer is yes. But, of course, we are at war, and everyone knows the need for more ships is great, so it is difficult to determine how much influence your most recent speech made. Your speech of four months ago, which you've been repeating in various forms since then, has also influenced this."

"Then that's very good," she said.

"It is, but…" he began. "Perseverance, in the world of politics, into which you have just thrust yourself, there is always a big 'but.' In this case, the 'but' involves you. Before I go any further, let me say I admire your boldness and courage. It took guts to speak up like that. As someone older and much more experienced in politics than you are, I will also say that there were ways you could have accomplished the same objective without putting yourself in so much risk. And now we get to the purpose of my call."

"Which is?"

"If you had thought to contact me," he said, "we could have arranged for the same information to reach the media without your name being involved. Unfortunately, you did not know that speaking with me was even an option. That is why I am calling now. If you ever run into a situation like this in the future, contact me, and together, we will develop a strategy. I say this not to stifle you—that is not at all what we want—but to protect you."

"We? Who is 'we?' And do I need protecting? I've been thinking I pretty much ended my navy career a few days ago," Perseverance said.

"As for the 'we,' it is me and some friends you have in high places," he replied. "More than that, I will not say. Regarding protection, with public opinion of you so favorable, the Royal Navy cannot cashier you right now. That does not mean you are forgiven. There are some who feel you betrayed the service by airing dirty laundry in public. Some will be jealous of the attention you have received. Remember, the navy is also a government bureaucracy. Bureaucracies are full of small-minded petty tyrants. In the navy, these petty tyrants control little fiefdoms as far away from danger as they can get. People like you, bold and unafraid to speak the truth, frighten them. With what you have started, they are afraid the navy will seek out every incompetent officer, not just the politically connected ones. When this tour ends, and you return to active duty, you will probably face a hundred minor indignities. I can't say what form they will take. Just know to expect them. Take a long-term view. Remember, time wounds all heels, shit sinks to its own level, and the big wheel of karma may move more slowly than we would wish, but, eventually, it does work its way around."

Perseverance paused, considering his words.

"So, you're saying I'll still have a job, still take command of HMS *Manitoba*, but I will have to deal with annoyances, irritations, and interference?" she asked.

"Yes."

"For how long?"

"I can't say, Perseverance," Gilchrist answered. "Usually until you can prove there is a pattern. If you can do that, even with only one person, the rest will stop, fearing they might also be caught. My advice to you is to document everything you do. Every order you give, every order you are given, every request you make, every report you file. Get used to using your comm unit to record every conversation. Every document you submit should have a backup copy on your personal comm. Keep a log, using paper and ink, of everything. I know it's a pain in the ass, but the better job you do of documenting everything, the less time you will have to put up with it. When you reach a point where you are confident you have evidence to accuse someone of malfeasance, come to me."

Perseverance groaned. "I hate playing the 'cover-your-ass' game."

"They are counting on that," Gilchrist said. "Most of them got to the positions they now enjoy by playing that game. It doesn't mean they are all that good at it. It just means they were better than the people they brought down."

"Why are you telling me all this?" she asked.

"Because the future of the Commonwealth is at stake," he said, "and we feel more confident in that future if you get to play a key role in it."

Later that day, Perseverance spoke with Admiral Freshley on a call he scheduled. Though reassured by what Lord Gilchrist said earlier, she was still apprehensive about her status with the navy. She also expected some form of discipline would be forthcoming.

"Captain Andrews," Freshley opened the call, "I'm going to jump right to the heart of things. When they ask you about the subjects you brought up in the recent Q&A, please refer them to the navy's Office of Public Affairs on Caerleon. When you receive a negative response to that, as you will, you may tell them that Admiral Freshley promised you that they would get straight answers. Our purpose is not to silence you. Otherwise, we would not allow your tour to continue. We want to channel the message through Public Affairs, so we speak with one voice. You may admit that you do not know everything about the situation since that is completely true. Do you understand, Captain?"

"Yes, sir. Understood," she replied.

"When you return to Caerleon in four-and-a-half weeks, you will still be taking command of HMS *Manitoba*. Your role will be different, though. When we lost Admiral Kenard in Southampton, it created a vacancy. We just announced the promotion of Gretchen Smith-Clark to rear admiral in command of Red Fleet. You will be her flag captain. I will tell you, off the record, that you were under consideration for that post despite your lack of seniority compared to other candidates. However, your recent 'revelations,' which many others call an 'outburst,' removed you from the list—despite a record of success none of the other candidates can match." Freshley said.

"Yes, sir. Thank you for telling me, sir," Perseverance replied, swallowing her emotions.

"Very well. Continue your speaking tour. Speak of what you know. Refer any sensitive questions to public affairs," he said. "Is that clear?"

"Yes, sir. Quite clear."

"Good. That is all. Freshley out."

With the call ended, Perseverance let the air out of her lungs. She sat and began to parse the things Admiral Freshley said. On the good side, she would still take command of *Manitoba*. On the bad side, the ship would no longer be entirely hers. She would have an admiral aboard.

Even worse, she knew Gretchen Smith-Clark, having served under her before. Perseverance felt that Smith-Clark was the sort whom clueless managers valued and employees despised. No doubt, she thrived in staff positions where interpersonal skills were not entirely necessary. From her earlier exposure to Smith-Clark, Perseverance knew she was a micro-manager and suspected she was paranoid.

When one of Smith-Clark's employees came to her with legitimate questions on an assignment, her first reaction was to treat the inquiry as a challenge to her authority and competence. Smith-Clark insisted on approving even the most routine matters, yet it was never her fault if something went wrong. If she saw two or more of her subordinates chatting, she invented an excuse to join the conversation or break it up. Perseverance attributed this to a fear that Smith-Clark thought her employees were conspiring against her. Smith-Clark's background before Perseverance served under her was in staff positions. After her only line assignment to this point, Smith-Clark returned to a staff position afterward. Perseverance did not pay attention to her later career, preferring to forget the woman.

Perseverance admitted to herself that Smith-Clark was intelligent enough. Despite never having served on a ship, Smith-Clark adapted quickly and learned from her mistakes, even though she never admitted to them. Perseverance, to her regret, had seen others like Smith-Clark in her career, both men and women. They were obsequiously compliant to their superiors and delivered the requested work on time without fail. Of course, underlings did the job and received none of the credit—only blame. Perseverance imagined that Smith-Clark's official record would be spotless.

Serving as her flag captain would be an unpleasant challenge. Perseverance imagined she would be blamed for every shortcoming or misstep in Red Fleet. So Gilchrist's advice to document everything would be critically important.

Perseverance's outlook did not improve by the dinner hour. Once again, she was glum. Saint John noticed and waited until the end of the meal to comment.

"What is it now?" he asked.

Perseverance thought about giving him a non-answer but remembered her promise that she would try to reduce the emotional distance she was keeping. She sighed and told Saint John about her conversations with Lord Gilchrist and Admiral Freshley. Perseverance then shared her previous experience with Smith-Clark. Saint John frowned while considering what she said.

"I don't think they chose Smith-Clark to target you," he said. "Admiral Freshley was the final authority on that promotion, and he told you a few days ago that he is not one of the ones who want your scalp. Consider his situation."

"What about it?"

"You just exposed the problem with politically-connected officers. He cannot choose you because people would view it as a reaction to your speech. In choosing someone for a high-profile position like this—one of two rear admirals in the navy—he needs to select a candidate with no taint whatsoever. Let's look at Smith-Clark from a different perspective. Are there any black marks on her record?"

"No. Probably not."

"Would she have earned positive evaluations from her superior officers?"

"Yes, but that is only because the review process does not include any input from subordinates," Perseverance protested.

"That's not likely to change. The process is supposed to be as objective as possible. Subordinate feedback would be entirely subjective. If I'm her superior officer, even though I might not appreciate her personal style, the objective measure is whether she got the job done. In the absence of any formal complaint, the objective results overweigh any subjective feelings I may have."

"I guess so," Perseverance grudgingly admitted.

"Has she been anyone's 'favorite?' Has there been someone above smoothing her path?"

"Not that I know."

"So, what Admiral Freshley sees is an officer with the rank of captain, fairly senior. I'm going to assume she earned her promotions in her first year of eligibility along the way—another positive. She has served in both staff and line positions, she gets the work done, there are no complaints, no one would accuse me of favoritism for promoting her, and she probably presents herself well in public settings. Do you see why she is a safe, non-controversial choice?"

"I suppose," Perseverance replied with a hint of a whine.

"There's one more thing to consider," Saint John added. "Whom did Admiral Freshley ask to draw up a list of candidates?"

Perseverance shrugged. "His staff?"

"Correct. People who reached their positions acting in ways similar to Smith-Clark. She's one of their own. You'll be wise to follow the advice Lord Gilchrist gave you, especially the part about paper and ink. If Smith-Clark is a paranoid micro-manager, as you say, she might track every keystroke you make."

"Ugh," Perseverance groaned.

"Hey, it could be worse," Saint John pointed out.

"I know, I know," she replied. "I still have a job."

"I was going to say, 'It could be me.' But, yes, you still have a job. And in whatever we do to retake Ilium, *Manitoba* will likely play a part, given that she will be one of our two remaining heavy cruisers. However, Admiral Czervik has seniority *and* experience, so Smith-Clark will either sit it out or be limited to an observer role," he said.

"I doubt she will leave the ship," Perseverance replied. "She'd be terrified that her officers might plan her downfall in her absence."

"Still, *you* are captain of the ship. She won't have a meaningful role unless something happens to Admiral Czervik. Let us all pray he avoids any mishaps," Saint John said.

"Amen."

That night, Perseverance lay in bed, her mind racing. She tried to focus on the positives, but the negatives of her situation kept intruding on her thoughts. After what seemed like hours, she realized she simply did not want to think—about anything. She knew something that would give her some peace of mind. It probably took another hour before she talked herself into it.

She rose from bed and crept to Saint John's cabin. The door was unlocked. From the dim light of the clock on the table, she could see he was sleeping on his left side, facing the center of the bed. Slowly, gently, she lifted the covers and slid under them carefully. Then, trying to make no sudden or jarring movements, she positioned herself in front of him. She took his right arm and smoothly drew it over, clasping it to her breast.

The warmth of his body and the feel of his arm holding her chased all thoughts from her brain. She let out a soft sigh. Sleep claimed her almost immediately.

In the morning, she woke first. She realized where she was. She was snuggled up to him and still clutching his hand to herself. Not wanting to move and disturb the calm comfort she felt, she shut her eyes again. She could feel him pressed up behind her. Remembering what her sisters said, she smiled to herself. She started to feel frisky and was thinking about wiggling into him to see what would happen.

"Um, good morning," he said, his voice gravelly from sleep.

Her naughty thoughts flew away, replaced by embarrassment. "Good morning," she replied, sounding as though she squeaked.

"To what do I owe the honor of having you here?" he asked.

"I couldn't sleep," she said. "My mind was racing, and I couldn't get it to stop."

"Did this help?"

"Yes. I slept like a log," she said.

"It is very comfortable," he said. "I wouldn't mind staying like this for a couple of hours. Unfortunately, nature calls. Will you still be here when I come back?"

"Probably not," she said. Then she giggled.

What the hell was that? she thought. *I haven't giggled for a boy since I was six years old.*

She felt him get up. When she heard the door to the head shut, she jumped from the bed. Her leg got caught in the covers, so she hopped around to free it. Once untangled, she bolted from his cabin to her own. When she closed the door behind herself, she wanted to laugh out loud.

A few hours later, she was standing in front of the New Glasgow Parliament. She delivered the same general speech she had given twenty-one times before. However, the way she concluded was vastly different.

"Before we get to the Q&A, I realize many of you would like to ask me about my remarks a few days ago on Alleghany. I hate to tell you this, but I'm not prepared to answer them."

Groans of disappointment rose from members of the audience. Perseverance held up her hand to silence them. Then, when quiet returned, she spoke.

"The reason for this is not because the navy ordered me to shut up," she said. "Things are in motion, and I am here, in New Glasgow, and not in Caerleon, where they are taking place. Please contact the Office of Public Affairs—"

Louder groans and some muttered complaints came from the crowd. Perseverance again held up her hand for quiet. It took longer this time.

"Admiral Freshley himself promised me that you would get straight answers," she said.

Sarcastic comments came from the media section. Perseverance talked over them.

"The simple fact is a great deal has happened and is happening very quickly," she said. "I am not aware of everything that has been decided or is taking place. You listened to what I said a few days ago because I told the truth as I saw it. If you ask me about what is taking place now, I would have to guess. That would be foolish on my part, and I would be a completely unreliable source for you. Public affairs is closest in time and distance to what is happening. Admiral Freshley has promised straight answers. The reason he has asked that you go through public affairs is not to conceal information from you. It is so that the information shared with you is accurate."

She opened the assembly to questions, beginning with the legislators. Several tried to ask her questions about what was happening with personnel decisions. Perseverance politely but firmly directed them to public affairs. The fifth question asked was different.

"Is your career in jeopardy as a result of you speaking up?" the woman asked.

Perseverance wanted to smile because she anticipated this question. "Not to my knowledge," she said. "When I set out on this tour of the Commonwealth, I was told I would take command of a ship upon my return to the Admiralty. That was confirmed yesterday. That is the most concrete acknowledgment of my status with the Royal Navy I can ask for."

"No repercussions at all?" the woman followed up.

Perseverance gave a small laugh. "I'm willing to bet my performance from this point forward might be subject to detailed scrutiny, wouldn't you?"

That remark generated the laughs Perseverance hoped it would. She saw several members of the audience nodding in agreement. There were no more difficult questions after that.

25

When they returned to the courier boat, docked at New Glasgow Station, Perseverance checked her comm unit to see if she had received any messages. There was only one, from "Communications Maintenance." It read, "Good job."

She checked with Saint John. "Any blowback?

He shook his head.

"Lord Gilchrist said I did a good job," she reported.

"I thought so," he said.

"Um, hey—can we talk?" she asked.

"Sure."

"Your cabin or mine?" she asked.

"You would probably feel more comfortable in yours if my guess about the topic is correct," he said.

In her cabin, there were only two places to sit. One was the chair in front of the small desk with a computer console. The other was the bed. Perseverance took the chair.

"So, what's on your mind?" Saint John said with a smile.

"You... me... us," she answered. "I can tell from the slightly smug look on your face that you guessed correctly."

"It wasn't that hard," he admitted. "It's been on my mind too. Before you say anything, I want you to know that I'll do my best to abide by your wishes."

"I don't think you'll find it too difficult," she said. Perseverance took a deep breath. "I think I'd like to explore what this is between us. We have a bit more than three weeks before we return to Caerleon, and I think that's enough time to learn whether we should just be friends or if there might be something more. If we decide to keep going, we can fill out the 5602 then. How do you feel about that?"

"Pretty damned happy," Saint John admitted.

"Um, so, how do we start?" she asked, blushing.

"Most couples start by kissing before they reach the sleeping together phase," he teased. "We seem to have gotten out of order. How about we backtrack a little? May I kiss you?"

She nodded, biting her lip as she rose from the chair. Saint John stood up from the bed. They started modestly. Things progressed quickly after that.

A few days later, forty-four officers in the Royal Navy resigned their commissions. There was no press release and no public announcement. The list of the resignations was closely held. None of the politicians who could usually be counted on to supply information shared a single name.

The next time a reporter asked the Office of Public Affairs, Captain Rosen replied, "The matter has been addressed."

This answer, of course, whipped the media into a frenzy. Reporters did everything they could to ferret out more information. They had no success. The main reason they ended up empty-handed was a verbal agreement Lord Gilchrist negotiated between the leaders of both political parties and Admiral Freshley.

The officers in question would resign. The explanation offered to their shipmates or members of their department was, "they received new orders." That was enough to eliminate most questions. The navy would make it difficult for the media to identify who those officers were—not by hiding the information. The navy simply would not release the names. If a diligent reporter was willing to dig and patient, he or she could eventually compile a list. While there were undoubtedly some reporters who would have devoted the time and effort, their bosses did not possess that sort of patience. In exchange, both party leaders agreed to support the navy's requests for funding, at least through the end of the war. Further, the leaders of both parties agreed not to use this information against each other for political advantage in the future.

Lord Gilchrist considered the agreement a success since all three groups felt slightly dissatisfied with the outcome. That, he felt, was the mark of a successful compromise. Queen Charlotte was satisfied because it offered hope that the navy would get the resources it needed without any further argument.

The last three stops of the tour were uneventful. Legislators and reporters quit asking Perseverance about her earlier remarks since she repeated the same statements, referring the questioner to the Office of Public Affairs. Aboard the courier boat, things were going well. Klaus noticed immediately that only one bed was being used. Saint John knew the first time Klaus noticed when he heard the steward mutter, "About damn time."

Perseverance spent much of the time reviewing personnel files for the crew assigned to HMS *Manitoba*. Her executive officer was Commander Joe Sullivan. She knew Sullivan and was looking forward to working with him. The head of engineering was Commander Feng Lu. She did not know him. The senior petty officer was Linda Redjacket. She would serve as COB from the acronym. Perseverance also worked with Redjacket before and thought highly of her. Redjacket was perhaps the most taciturn person Perseverance ever met. In spite of that, she possessed a wicked sense of humor, though it was incredibly dry.

Perseverance drew up a personnel schedule based on the yard's construction plans. There was no sense in having everyone report when the ship was not ready. She issued orders regarding when each officer and each section of enlisted should arrive.

After a week of intimacy between Perseverance and Saint John, they separately came to the same conclusion—they wanted to pursue this further. Saint John actually mentioned it first, over dinner. Perseverance agreed. She had not experienced emotional, intellectual, and physical compatibility like this with any previous partner, not that she had a wealth of experience.

The only regret either of them had at the end of their journey was that they delayed getting together for so long. They were happy to be seeing the last of the courier boat, though. Five-and-a-half months was a long time to spend in such close quarters, even with someone you were crazy about. Together they filled out the 5602 form. Saint John also applied for a transfer back to a line position. He did not inform Perseverance until after he filed the request. Her reaction was a mild surprise.

"Good," she said.

"I was worried you would be upset with me. That's why I didn't let you know ahead of time," he admitted.

"Why would I be upset? There can't be that many people on active duty who have earned a DSC. We could use everyone we can get," she commented.

Klaus saved the last of the real steak, potatoes, and vegetables they received at Alleghany for the last meal aboard the courier boat. After serving the meal, he told them he was heading to his quarters until morning. After they finished eating, sharing a bottle of wine with the dinner, they sat on the sofa, reminiscing about some of the funnier and more unusual moments they shared over the past five-and-a-half months. They ran out of things to say at the same time and retired to Saint John's cabin without a word.

Tomorrow they would dock at Caerleon Station. This would be the last night they could spend together until the 5602 was approved. Perseverance already received orders from Admiral Smith-Clark, instructing her to report to HMS *Manitoba* the next day. Saint John would return to public affairs, where he suspected Captain Rosen was waiting to deliver an epic ass-chewing.

The yard was completing the finishing touches on *Manitoba*. The reactors were lit, and the engineering staff would already be living aboard; according to the schedule Perseverance drew up weeks before. In a day or two, depending on the progress of the yard workers, they might take *Manitoba* away from Caerleon Station and tune her massive EM drives. They would then return to complete anything that remained to be done and for the formal commissioning ceremony. After that, *Manitoba* would spend two weeks in neighboring systems, ensuring all of the ship's systems worked without flaw.

They docked at Caerleon Station the following day. Perseverance and Saint John had already said their goodbyes privately. They both thanked Klaus for taking such good care of them. Saint John headed to the Office of Public Affairs.

Perseverance left the navy section of the station searching for a paper journal. With a duffel, garment bag, and a sword belted around her waist, she drew a lot of stares. She took Lord Gilchrist's warning to heart. She had seen plenty of court cases get bogged down by arguments over whether records stored in the cloud were altered. Materials she saved to a private and secure cloud account, with a paper backup, would hold up much better.

It was more challenging to find something she could use for a journal than she anticipated. She went to five different stores on the station before finding something suitable. Each one only held a hundred pages, though, so she bought three. She stuffed them in her duffel and returned to the navy section.

Once there, she found a shuttle that would take her to Caerleon Yard, where HMS *Manitoba* was docked. An electric cart drove her along one of the long construction booms where the gangway to *Manitoba* was located. Perseverance carried her bags to the end of the gangway. That was where trouble first appeared.

Waiting at the hatch was Lieutenant Kleinschmidt. Marcia Kleinschmidt would be the ship's sixth officer. According to Perseverance's schedule, Kleinschmidt was not due to report for three more days. Perseverance greeted her with a salute and asked permission to come aboard.

"Lieutenant, I appreciate your eagerness, but what are you doing aboard?" Perseverance asked.

"Following orders, sir," Kleinschmidt responded nervously.

"Whose orders?" Perseverance asked calmly. "My orders did not require you to report for three more days."

"The admiral's orders, sir," Kleinschmidt replied.

"Which admiral?" Perseverance asked.

"Admiral Smith-Clark, sir."

"Tell me, lieutenant, are all the officers aboard?"

"Yes, sir. Except for you, but you're here now," Kleinschmidt replied.

"What about enlisted?" Perseverance asked.

"We're still missing about two dozen, sir. They are still en route."

"And our marines?"

"All of them are here," the lieutenant answered.

"Thank you, lieutenant. Carry on," Perseverance said.

As Perseverance headed to her quarters, she was fuming. Having the entire ship's complement aboard served no useful purpose. In fact, since the crew would most likely get in the way of the workers trying to finish the remaining construction tasks, it might be detrimental and slow things down.

When she reached her quarters, she pressed her hand onto the palm lock that controlled access to her quarters. A red bar appeared. Perseverance thought that was odd. During her tour of the ship a few months ago, as a favor, the construction supervisor allowed Perseverance to register her palmprint for the door. She tried again. The red bar appeared. A moment later, the door opened. A lieutenant appeared.

"Yes, captain? How may I help you?" she asked.

"Lieutenant, who are you, and what are you doing in my quarters?" Perseverance asked, fighting to stay calm.

"Oh, I'm sorry, captain," called a saccharine voice from inside. "The flag quarters aren't ready yet, so we moved in here. I hope you don't mind switching?"

As she spoke, she came within view. As soon as Perseverance saw her, she snapped a salute. Admiral Smith-Clark did not return it.

"Oh, and this is my flag lieutenant, Wendy Foxcroft," Smith-Clark added.

"Lieutenant," Perseverance said, acknowledging her.

Perseverance reached into her pocket and thumbed the "record" feature on her comm unit.

"Sir, you were not to report on board until we completed trials," Perseverance said. "May I ask why you are here?"

"I can do my work here as well as anywhere," Smith-Clark replied easily, "and I missed being aboard a ship, so I thought I'd move in early."

"Yes, sir. Did you also issue orders for the crew to report early?" Perseverance asked.

"Yes. Why?" the admiral said in the same sickly-sweet tone of false innocence.

"Sir, were you aware I worked with the construction supervisor to develop the reporting schedule?" Perseverance asked. "The arrivals, including yours, were staggered to give the workers unhindered access to the areas that they need to complete. The schedule was approved by Admiral Freshley."

"You no longer report directly to Admiral Freshley," Smith-Clark snapped. "The yard can adapt. I felt it was important to get the crew aboard so they could begin to familiarize themselves with the ship."

"Sir, my concern is that this will delay the timely completion of the ship," Perseverance stated.

"Complaining again? I would have thought you got it all out of your system back on Alleghany," the admiral asked, her tone slipping from sweet to sly.

"Sir, you are my superior officer," Perseverance said. "You command Red Fleet. I am the captain of HMS *Manitoba* and command this ship. Assigning quarters aboard HMS *Manitoba* is my responsibility. As my superior officer, you have the authority to countermand my orders. You have the authority to change the reporting assignments I already made, but I need you to give me copies of those orders for the record."

Smith-Clark rolled her eyes. "Fine, captain. Consider yourself so ordered."

"Sir, I'm afraid I must request written copies. For the record."

The admiral turned away. The door slid shut, leaving Perseverance about ready to explode in the companionway. Perseverance walked to the flag quarters. The door was open because the flag quarters were not finished. According to the labels she could read on some of the cartons, it looked like many of the components that would be installed were present, but the work had not begun.

Still carrying her bags, Perseverance set off to find her XO, Joe Sullivan. After stopping and asking two crewmembers she encountered, she found him on the bridge. As she entered, a petty officer called, "Captain on the bridge!" A few looked her way, but most continued what they were doing, as was expected. Sullivan was one of those who looked.

"Skipper," he said in greeting, noting that Perseverance was still carrying her bags and wearing her sword.

Perseverance positioned herself so her back was facing the two bridge cameras. "Commander, I need an update on the status of all the construction projects remaining to be finished," she said out loud.

Silently, just moving her lips, she formed, "We need to talk. No cameras."

"Yes, sir," he replied. "I was just about to go meet with the construction supervisor. Would you like to join me?"

"I think that would be best, commander," she said.

"Why don't we drop your things off in my quarters, captain, until we find a better place for them?" Sullivan said as he rose.

"That would be nice," Perseverance agreed.

As soon as they were in the companionway, out of earshot of the bridge, Perseverance muttered without moving her lips, "What the fuck, Joe?"

"I'll tell you in a minute," he muttered back, also not moving his lips. "Not here."

They reached his quarters. "Here you go, skipper. Leave your stuff right here. I'll take you to the construction supervisor now."

She followed him down two levels and to the stern of the ship. He took her to the shuttle bay. Once inside, he led her to a spot at the center of the interior wall.

"This is a blind spot," he said quietly. "There are still microphones but if we speak in not much more than a whisper, they won't pick it up."

"Are you sure?" she asked.

"Look, I just arrived yesterday," he said. "One of the first things the admiral did was order me not to contact you. She said she wanted to judge how you handled an unexpected stressful situation. As far as blind spots, I haven't had the chance to walk the ship thoroughly yet, but Linda Redjacket served on *Springfield*, Admiral Kenard's flagship. She rotated off before Southampton. It's the same class as *Manitoba*. I checked this one out, and she was correct. There are a couple of other places but not as easy to reach."

"Good to know," Perseverance said. "I don't think we'll need them because we're going to be strictly business. Let's make this the one and only time we meet like this. I served under Smith-Clark before. If you didn't figure it out already, she's bad news. She got where she is by it always being someone else's fault. You probably heard I'm sort of in the doghouse—"

"I figured," he interrupted.

"Yeah. So, I can't do anything other than be an obedient captain," Perseverance said. "Anytime you want to bitch about the admiral, don't come to me. I'm going to make sure I get every order in writing, I'm going to try to record every conversation I have with her or her flag lieutenant—I got a bad feeling about her instantly—and I'm keeping a journal with pen and paper, so it's not anywhere on the system. I suggest you and Linda Redjacket do the same. Otherwise, we'll just be among the many she's stepped on along the way. Now, did you really have a meeting with the construction supervisor?"

"Yes," Sullivan replied. "He should be in environmental right now."

"Let's go see him. While we're walking, you can figure out where I'm supposed to sleep until the flag quarters are finished," Perseverance suggested.

26

The next two months were, as far as Perseverance was concerned, like being assigned to one of the seven circles of hell. The biggest problem was having the entire crew aboard with the ship unfinished. Keeping everyone busy and productive, while keeping them out of the way of the workers, was her biggest challenge. For the most part, Admiral Smith-Clark stayed out of Perseverance's way. The admiral never failed to miss an opportunity to make a snide remark about Perseverance addressed to Lieutenant Foxcroft, who seemed to have attached herself to the admiral like a lamprey. She delivered these remarks just loud enough so Perseverance would hear.

Joe Sullivan offered to give Perseverance his cabin until the flag quarters were finished, but she turned him down. Instead, she slept in the sick bay. Perseverance did request to use his small office space in the meantime. When the flag quarters were finished three weeks after her arrival—as on the originally approved schedule—Admiral Smith-Clark decided she would actually prefer to be there. Perseverance simply said, "Yes, sir."

It took Perseverance five requests to obtain a copy of the orders Smith-Clark issued. The one instructing the crew to report early and the other demanding the construction supervisor change the palm lock on the captain's quarters. The flag lieutenant claimed there was no written order regarding the change of quarters and that one was not necessary. Perseverance documented all this in her paper logbook and maintained recordings on her comm unit of every conversation she held with either Smith-Clark or Lieutenant Foxcroft.

Smith-Clark's insistence on having the crew report early did interfere with the yard workers' progress. The yard fell behind schedule, and the ship was not finally complete until eight days past the scheduled delivery date. Nevertheless, the commissioning ceremony took place as scheduled, even though *Manitoba* was not finished. Perseverance suspected Smith-Clark wanted to blame her for the delay. The existence of the reporting schedule Admiral Freshley approved probably prevented her from doing so.

The only unequivocally good news Perseverance received was the notice that the 5602 she and Saint John filed was approved. They spoke daily, though Perseverance could say nothing about her current situation. Saint John was clever enough to read between the lines and had a good idea of the challenges facing her. His request to return to a line position was granted. He could not tell Perseverance about his assignment, though.

Once *Manitoba* began trials, Smith-Clark became a regular presence in the observer's chair on the bridge. She was frequently disruptive, holding discussions with her flag lieutenant in which she frequently commented in a voice everyone on the bridge could hear, as though offering Foxcroft a tutorial on how to command a ship. Smith-Clark would refer to Perseverance as the "so-called hero of Aries," using her fingers as imaginary quotation marks.

In all their interactions, Smith-Clark's tone and demeanor conveyed mild disapproval of everything Perseverance did. She remarked on the quality of food in the officers' mess, the performance of the mess steward she and Perseverance shared, and the type of drills Joe Sullivan conducted and their frequency. Joe Sullivan shared with Perseverance that Foxcroft spent a couple of hours daily reviewing the security camera footage from the previous twenty-four hours.

When Perseverance began conducting combat simulations, Smith-Clark tried to issue commands regarding the operation of *Manitoba*. This confused the bridge personnel since they did not know whose orders to follow. Oddly enough, it was Foxcroft who spoke up about this first, questioning whether Smith-Clark should be trying to manage the ship while also guiding Red Fleet. The admiral told her to shut up and not make any further stupid statements. However, Smith-Clark did stop trying to command the ship.

Through all this, Perseverance kept her expression neutral and responded crisply to every order. After each combat simulation, she hurried to her ready room to make a copy of the bridge recordings showing the admiral's interference and save it to her personal comm unit. Up to this point, while there was plenty of evidence showing the admiral's unpleasant pattern of behavior, there was no individual action that was damning enough to merit a confrontation. The admiral had not done anything that could be construed as a mistake. Smith-Clark would simply claim that her style differed from Perseverance's and that personalities often clash in the navy. Testing a subordinate's ability to manage challenging circumstances was a superior officer's prerogative. Any board of inquiry would give the admiral the benefit of the doubt, and Perseverance's career would be over.

Perseverance gritted her teeth, determined to outlast the unpleasantness. She repeated Lord Gilchrist's advice to herself so many times that they became almost a mantra. Her occasional calls with Saint John helped maintain her sanity and her patience. He still was unable to tell her about his assignment, but she could see from the background behind his face that he was aboard a ship.

A bit more than two months after *Manitoba* was commissioned came the news Perseverance had hoped for. The Royal Navy would be attacking in the Ilium system to regain it from the Chinese Republics. Admiral Czervik would command the task force, but *Manitoba*, as one of only two heavy cruisers in the Royal Navy, would take part, seconded to his task force.

The Republics had six shielded ships in Ilium—a heavy cruiser, two light cruisers, and three destroyers. In the initial attack, they also brought six unshielded ships. The Admiralty suspected the Chinese had added to that number. The Royal Navy's plan of attack included two heavy cruisers, three light cruisers, and three destroyers that were shielded, plus eighteen unshielded ships pulled from retirement—six cruisers and twelve destroyers.

The unshielded ships carried only skeleton crews. Before entering the hyper corridor to Ilium, all but three of those crew members would depart the ships on shuttles. The unshielded ships would proceed to close within missile range of the enemy, fire one salvo, and make sure they were tied into the point defense network. Then the remaining three people would exit the ship using the emergency lifepods.

The Royal Navy's shielded ships would close to within photon cannon range of the enemy as quickly as possible and hammer them into submission.

Perseverance thought it was a good strategy. It showed that Admiral Freshley was not above using the enemy's tactics against them. Both the Federation and the Republics used their unshielded ships to increase the number of missiles they could launch—why not do the same? When the plan was shared, Perseverance figured out where Saint John was and why he could not tell her about his assignment earlier.

In their next conversation, she said, "I'm pretty sure I know what you're doing and why you couldn't tell me."

"Of course, you did," he responded, "because you're clever."

"I'm guessing you and the others in your situation volunteered?"

"As I said, clever," he responded. "But look at it this way, I'm commanding a cruiser! That was a goal I had that I can now check off the list."

"Promise me you won't do anything stupid—beyond what you've already done?" she asked.

"I can't promise that, Persie," he said. "I plan on living a long time, and I'm sure I have many more stupid things to do before I'm through. As far as this goes, I plan to do my bit, then run like hell."

"That's a good plan," she agreed. "Do that."

Thirteen days later, the task force under Admiral Czervik exited the hyper corridor into the Ilium system at a speed slower than the usual 0.23c. He suspected the Chinese planted a minefield near the terminus of the corridor in the event the Royal Navy brought unshielded ships. As a result, Czervik ordered his force to travel at 0.10c and to drop out of hyperspace thirty light-minutes short of the terminus. That would give his force time to see and clear the minefield, enabling the unshielded ships to proceed without damage.

The slower speed would expose his force to an additional missile salvo from the enemy as they approached the range of the Royal Navy's photon cannons. His ships would also be able to launch an additional salvo, and, most important, the slower speed would increase the time the Chinese would be within range of the photon cannons.

Upon entering the system, Admiral Czervik ordered active scans. It would take nearly an hour for radar to return with any information regarding what was waiting for them at the terminus. It would take five hours to reach that point at their current speed.

Perseverance waited on the bridge until the radar returns came in. As expected, there were mines in abundance. Not long after that information was received, radar returns also showed the presence of the Chinese ships. They were waiting near the limit of missile range from the terminus of the corridor. The scans showed they reinforced the six shielded ships with six more unshielded ships. There were now five cruisers and seven destroyers, unshielded.

Given that it would be three hours or more until *Manitoba* and the other Royal Navy ships came within range of the minefield, Perseverance decided to show her face around the ship. Along the way, she encountered Linda Redjacket, the senior petty officer aboard. Linda was a woman of few words—very few. Her appearance was like no one else Perseverance had ever met. Redjacket had angular features with deep-set eyes, coppery skin tone, and straight black hair. She explained once to Perseverance that she was descended from the indigenous inhabitants of the North American continent on earth.

Perseverance had always enjoyed Linda's company. Despite her quiet nature, she possessed a strong sense of humor. It was very dry and came in the form of muttered comments. But, if you paid attention, you were treated to some of the most hilarious (and devastating) wisecracks Perseverance ever heard.

With a crew of one hundred forty-two (plus the admiral and her flag lieutenant) and eighty-three marines, Perseverance knew everyone aboard by name at this point. She and Linda wandered through the ship. While their path might have seemed aimless, Perseverance tried to show her face to as many of the crew as possible without making it seem like she was checking departments off a list.

Perseverance made a point of saying hello. Linda merely gave slight nods. Nonetheless, they were greeted warmly everywhere. "Hey, skipper. Hey, COB," would be the usual. Perseverance greatly preferred the informal "skipper" to the more formal "captain." Linda had no choice. As the senior non-commissioned officer aboard, she was the COB.

When they reached the bow of the ship, Redjacket gave Perseverance an almost imperceptible nod, the barest hint of a smile and a meaningful look before walking away. Perseverance understood the message Linda was conveying. *I'm glad you did this, and I was happy to join you.*

Perseverance went to her quarters and put on her shipsuit and helmet in preparation for the battle, then returned to the bridge. Admiral Smith-Clark appeared shortly after and took her position in the observer's chair behind and to the left of the command station. The rest of the bridge crew was suited and helmeted, watching the countdown clock Commander Sullivan started, showing the range to the closest mines.

There was no sound or vibration when the clock reached zero. The fire control displays lit up. Sensor blooms appeared where the point defense lasers hit mines. It was over in a couple of seconds.

"Looks like we got 'em all," reported Lieutenant Kleinschmidt on fire control.

"Three minutes to missile range," Joe Sullivan stated.

"Captain! Engage full reverse thrust now," Admiral Smith-Clark ordered.

"Sir? What do you see?" Perseverance asked, turning to the admiral.

She saw a look of panicked fear on the admiral's face, like a trapped animal. Her skin was pale. Her eyes were wild.

"Don't question my orders," Smith-Clark snarled. "Full reverse thrust now!"

"Sir, my orders are to maintain position with the rest of our ships," Perseverance replied.

"This is *my* flagship," the admiral barked, "and I will position it where I wish. Full reverse thrust now!"

Perseverance was dumbfounded at the admiral's behavior. Lieutenant Pettengill, at the astrogation post, looked to her for clarification. Perseverance shook her head slightly.

"Captain! How dare you countermand my orders! You've been working against me and undermining my authority since you stepped foot aboard! Consider yourself relieved. Astrogation, full reverse thrust *now!*" the admiral snapped, on the edge of hysteria. "Captain, get out of the goddamned chair and go to your quarters, or I will have the marines take you there!" Smith-Clark yelled.

Almost in a daze, Perseverance rose from the command chair and began crossing to the hatch. Lieutenant Pettengill reluctantly engaged full reverse thrust. Commander Sullivan sat in stunned silence. Admiral Smith-Clark crossed to the command station and began to strap herself in.

"May I ask the reason for these orders, admiral?" Sullivan asked.

"Czervik is a fool," Smith-Clark spewed. "His plan is ridiculously dangerous. He'll get us all killed. I can save *this* ship from annihilation, at least."

Sullivan saw a communication request from Admiral Czervik. Smith-Clark saw it at the same time. "Don't you dare answer that!" she screeched.

"Sir, if we pull away from the other ships, we reduce the effectiveness of the point defense network," Sullivan said.

"That's Czervik's problem, not ours. If he wants to go down with the ship, let him," she said.

In her quarters, Perseverance linked her comm unit to the camera feeds from the bridge. She began uploading the recording, starting with Sullivan's announcement of three minutes to range. She saw the incoming communication from Admiral Czervik, but then it disappeared. She suspected Smith-Clark cut off her outside comm access.

A sense of dread began to overcome Perseverance. Whatever came out of this incident was probably going to be extremely ugly. She was confident she would be exonerated, but even the slightest association with something like what just happened could stain her career. Coupled with her earlier outspokenness…

After the initial moments of stunned disbelief, Sullivan's wits returned. What Smith-Clark did was contrary to one of the most basic tenets of the navy. He quickly keyed a note to Major Embleton of the marines, requesting armed marines to come immediately to the bridge and seize the admiral, then confine her to quarters.

Manitoba began to pull away from the other ships. Messages were pelting Sullivan's console. He looked at the other members of the bridge crew. Every single one wore an expression of confusion and fear.

Two marines in combat armor burst onto the bridge. Before anyone could react to their arrival, they reached the command station. They grabbed the admiral's arms, keeping her hands away from the keys of the console. Smith-Clark glared at Sullivan with a look of absolute fury.

"You fucking weasel," she snarled. "I'll make sure you pay for this if we don't all die first. You and your precious Captain Andrews. You've been plotting against me from the beginning, haven't you? I'll get you both. You'll see."

Meanwhile, the marines unbuckled her safety harness and began to lift her out of the chair. "Get your hands off me, fucking assholes!" she screeched. The marines did not relinquish their hold of her upper arms and guided her off the bridge.

"Reverse course, lieutenant. Rejoin the others," Sullivan ordered Lieutenant Pettengill.

Sullivan then answered the comm request that had just arrived on his console.

"What the fuck is going on with *Manitoba*, commander?" Admiral Czervik demanded.

"We're returning to the fight, sir," Sullivan replied. "Admiral Smith-Clark has just been taken to her quarters. I was about to recall Captain Andrews to the bridge."

"Explain, commander," Czervik demanded.

Sullivan tried to explain what just happened in as few words as possible.

"Holy shit!" Czervik exclaimed in frustrated amazement. He sighed heavily and rubbed his face with his hands. "Here's what you're going to do, commander. Regain position. You missed the first salvo. Don't waste your missiles now—they'll just get picked off. Make sure you're tied into the point defense network. I don't know if you'll be close enough to help with what we have coming at us in a few seconds. Keep Captain Andrews and the admiral in their quarters until I figure out what to do. No visitors. Cut off their outside comm access. You're in command. Czervik out."

Seconds after Admiral Czervik ended the call, the remaining Chinese missiles reached detonation range. The shielded and unshielded Chinese ships launched one hundred missiles. Three survived the Royal Navy's point defense to fire their x-ray lasers. All three targeted HMS *Northumberland*, Admiral Czervik's flagship. The lasers caused shield failures but were not able to penetrate the hull.

The Royal Navy, even without *Manitoba's* contribution, launched one hundred and thirty-four missiles. Twenty-three survived the Chinese point defense efforts. Ten were aimed at the heavy cruiser, seven at one of the light cruisers, and six at the other. The results were dramatic. The bridge of the Chinese heavy cruiser was vaporized and, with it, the command structure of the Chinese force. A Royal Navy missile hit one of the light cruisers in its reactor, creating a fireball that consumed the ship. The remaining light cruiser was heavily damaged and out of the fight. The remaining ships broadcast their surrender.

27

The battle ended without *Manitoba* playing a part. Admiral Czervik sent marines to take control of the Chinese ships. He also ordered search and rescue operations for the Royal Navy personnel who ejected in lifepods from the unshielded ships after firing their missiles. He ordered Admiral Smith-Clark transferred to *Northumberland* and Captain Andrews to the light cruiser, HMS *Howland*. That done, he contacted the Judge Advocate—Fleet and turned the case over to him.

Before being taken to HMS *Howland*, Perseverance gave her personal comm unit and her written journal to Commander Sullivan. She asked him to copy all the recordings and documents in the folder marked "Project Reports." She also asked him to take pictures of every page of her hand-written journals. When he finished, he was to surrender them to the Judge Advocate's attorneys.

Lawyers from the Judge Advocate quickly contacted every crewmember present on the bridge of *Manitoba* during the incident. Each member of the bridge crew was interviewed three separate times by pairs of attorneys. Commander Sullivan turned over Perseverance's comm unit and journals during his second interview.

From the time of the incident, Sullivan issued standing orders that Lieutenant Foxcroft was barred from accessing the security camera footage. In addition, her information access was restricted. A keystroke and activity monitor was established on her Royal Navy account. During the same interview when he handed over Perseverance's comm unit, Sullivan informed the lawyers of these steps and provided access for them to log into the monitoring program he set up.

The Judge Advocate ordered Admiral Smith-Clark and Captain Andrews to be returned to Caerleon. Admiral Czervik transferred the two onto destroyers for the journey. Captain Constantino Diaz was placed in command of HMS *Manitoba* and flew to meet the ship on a courier boat.

Admiral Freshley was informed of the incident immediately. His attention was elsewhere for the time being. He would let the Judge Advocate investigate and wait for the preliminary report. Freshley's concern was with Ilium. At the time of the initial attack, fewer than two hundred thousand citizens of the Commonwealth were living on the planet. Since gaining control of Ilium, the Chinese Republics sent nearly a half-million people to the system while holding the Commonwealth citizens in concentration camps.

Freshley's first task was transporting the Commonwealth's First Army to the planet to gain control of the situation. The army would need to keep the two groups on the planet separate, or else violence was likely to flare up. The easiest solution was to build camps to contain the Chinese until the end of the war, but politics reared its ugly head. The Liberal Democrats were howling that this violated human rights and wanted to offer the Chinese asylum.

Within the Commonwealth government, MI-5 opposed this vehemently. Offering so many people asylum when there was no possible way to investigate their background would open the Commonwealth to an almost ready-made spy network. The Conservatives saw the truth of what MI-5 feared. Still, they realized it would be politically unpopular for anyone to oppose the noble humanitarian offer of asylum. The solution they floated up in a trial balloon was to restrict the "refugees" to residence on Ilium for a generation. That suggestion was deemed discriminatory, and the Conservatives gave up any opposition.

From the time she was removed from the bridge, Admiral Smith-Clark maintained she did nothing wrong. During the journey to Caerleon, she complained about being held in the brig "like a common criminal." She demanded her communications be restored. She insisted she should be allowed to meet with her flag lieutenant. Smith-Clark told anyone who would listen that the necessity of removing Captain Andrews from the bridge for insubordination led to her order for HMS *Manitoba* to reverse thrust. She claimed she did so

THE DEFENSE OF THE COMMONWEALTH

because she needed time to evaluate the situation internally before proceeding further and that she always intended to return to the battle as soon as possible.

In contrast, Perseverance kept quiet. She never complained. She was polite and made no demands. Convinced that her navy career was effectively finished, she thought about what job she could pursue after this. In a particularly dark moment, she reckoned that the queen would revoke her membership in the Royal Victorian Order, and the navy would take back her medal for conspicuous gallantry. While she wished she could speak with Saint John, she wanted more to have him hold her. She feared that any personal contact would not be allowed until after her court-martial, except with her lawyer.

She was interviewed by three different lawyers from the Judge Advocate's office. One informed her that Smith-Clark accused her of conspiracy, insubordination, and failure to obey a lawful order. Perseverance laughed upon hearing this. The attorney looked at her quizzically.

"If you review the camera feeds, you'll see that all my meetings with my officers were in the course of performing normal duties. You will find no instance of insubordination. I will let the court decide if her order was lawful. For my part, I hope the navy charges Smith-Clark with harassment and failure to engage the enemy. Commander Sullivan will have turned over to your people my personal comm unit and the paper-and-ink log I kept. That should help you prove her accusations are false."

Arriving at Caerleon Station, she was escorted from the ship by two members of the SP. Someone once told her that the initials stood for "Shore Patrol" in the wet navy days on earth. Today, everyone thought it was for "Service Police." At least the SP did not make her wear restraints. Reaching the end of the gangway, carrying the small bag that contained her one change of clothes, an unadorned khaki undress uniform, and a few of the most basic toiletries, she was stunned to see Lord Gilchrist waiting. Another man in an SP uniform arrived from the gangway carrying Perseverance's duffel, garment bag, and sword. The SP left her with Gilchrist.

"You have been released into my custody until the court-martial," he explained. "You will be under house arrest, but your communication privileges are restored. The Judge Advocate's people still have your comm unit. You may never get that back. I will lend you one until the navy replaces your old one."

Perseverance snorted derisively. Lord Gilchrist raised one of his impressively bushy eyebrows at this. Perseverance shrugged.

"Even though I didn't do anything wrong, I'm still screwed. After speaking out the way I did, just being associated with something like this now is the end of my navy career," she said flatly. "It doesn't matter that Smith-Clark is a complete idiot who rose as high as she did by clawing her way over the bodies of others."

"I think you don't have an accurate read on how you are perceived, either within or outside the navy," he commented. "This is neither the time nor the place, however, for this discussion. So, let's get out of here."

Lord Gilchrist led her to the security checkpoint marking the divide between the navy's portion of the station and the public area. An imposing figure of a man was waiting for them. He led the two of them to an electric cart. Lord Gilchrist indicated Perseverance should take a seat. When he sat, they drove off, leaving the main concourse and along a corridor leading toward the center of the station. Before they reached the end, a door opened to the left, and they drove inside a passageway.

They stopped at a spot where two similar carts were parked. Lord Gilchrist rose from his seat, as did the man. Perseverance followed. The man pressed a button, and the wall split open, revealing an elevator. The doors shut, then opened a minute later. Perseverance did not feel any sensation of rising or falling, one of the side effects of an artificial gravity environment.

Perseverance followed. After a couple of turns, they reached a small waiting area with a gangway. The man opened the hatch and waved them forward. A small shuttle with only four seats was waiting. The man went forward into the tiny cockpit. Perseverance sat next to Lord Gilchrist and strapped in.

"I feel like I'm in one of those spy thrillers," she commented.

"Why?" Gilchrist said,

"Secret corridors, a disguised elevator, a bodyguard who is one of the scariest people I've ever seen, and a private shuttle so far," she replied.

"Not a spy thriller," Gilchrist said. "Just rich, powerful, and incredibly well-connected." He tried to look smug, but the effect was ruined when he began to laugh.

"Humble, too," Perseverance cracked. That made them both laugh harder.

Thirty minutes later, they touched down on a shuttle pad behind an enormous brick house. In front of the house was a sweep of lawn. In the rear, a swimming pool with a huge garden beyond that. Thick woods were roughly fifty meters away on either side. Grabbing her bags and sword, she followed Lord Gilchrist into the house.

"You know, it's funny," she said. "Every time I'm put under house arrest, I stay in a place just like this."

Lord Gilchrist laughed as he opened the door. A pleasant-looking dark-skinned woman was waiting. She reached for the bags Perseverance was carrying.

"This is Samantha," Lord Gilchrist explained. "She takes care of me and this house."

Hearing this, Perseverance let Samantha have the bags.

"Go on," Gilchrist encouraged. "Follow her. She'll take you to your room and answer some of your questions. We'll have dinner in about ninety minutes. I'll see you then, and we'll resume our discussion."

Perseverance followed Samantha to a flight of stairs, then down a corridor to a bedroom. At least, Perseverance thought it would be described as a bedroom since there was a bed in it. There was also a sitting area with a sofa, two armchairs, and some tables. The sitting area was as large as her parents' living room and took up less than half the floor space in the room. There was also a work area with a large wooden desk. Opposite the bed was a vanity.

Samantha opened the door to what Perseverance thought was a closet, except that Samantha disappeared inside. Leaning her sword against the vanity, Perseverance scurried to follow. Behind the door was indeed a closet—bigger than most bedrooms Perseverance had ever seen. She started to laugh. Samantha cocked an eyebrow at her.

"When we were still outside, I told Lord Gilchrist I stay in places like this all the time," Perseverance said between snorts of laughter.

Samantha merely smiled. She opened the garment bag and withdrew the two dresses and the dress uniform. It still left almost ten meters of space when she hung them up.

"It's Tuesday," Samantha said. "Lord Gilchrist likes to dress for dinner on Sundays, Tuesdays, and Thursdays. Your dress uniform or either of these dresses would be appropriate. If you let me know which you would like to wear, I'll get the wrinkles out while you bathe."

Perseverance shook her head in amazement. "Samantha, you're going to have to give me a minute. An hour ago, I was in the brig on a destroyer. Now, I'm in the biggest damned closet in the biggest damned bedroom I've ever seen, and you're acting as my valet or something. I'm having trouble filtering all this. By the way, before I forget, what is your relationship to Lord Gilchrist? I don't want to embarrass myself more than I have to."

"Lord Gilchrist is my employer," Samantha replied with a kindly smile. "As far as my role, it varies. I'm his housekeeper, his maid, his cook from time to time, his masseuse, his confidant, his personal trainer, and his valet. I'm probably forgetting something, but you get the idea. Now, if you're worried that you're putting me to too much trouble, relax. It won't take but a minute to get the wrinkles out, and I'm happy to do it. Is there anything else?"

"Um, two things. Lord Gilchrist mentioned he would lend me a comm unit until I get mine back, and where is the bathroom you mentioned?"

"The comm unit is on the desk. The bathroom is the next door on this wall," Samantha said, pointing. "You should find everything you need in there."

"Right. Oh, the burgundy dress, please. Thanks. Sorry if I'm acting a bit weird," Perseverance said as she started to leave the closet.

"I understand, Dame Perseverance," Samantha replied.

Perseverance was tempted to march over and grab the comm unit so she could call Saint John. Unfortunately, she knew if she did, they would talk for hours. From what Lord Gilchrist mentioned briefly on the station, she reckoned he might have more information for her, so it would be better to call Saint John later. Besides, she didn't know whether he was still aboard a ship out in the Ilium system or somewhere else. She decided to investigate the bathroom. A shower would feel mighty good.

She paused outside the door. *I'll bet it's enormous*, she thought. She opened the door. *Winner!* she congratulated herself. Stepping inside, she saw a sunken tub with what she thought were water jets. Opposite the tub was a shower that could easily hold six people, with more nozzles than she could count. Both tub and shower had computer touchpad controls. There was a stack of towels on a small table. A sink in the middle of a counter was surrounded by every sort of

THE DEFENSE OF THE COMMONWEALTH

luxury soap, shampoo, or bath product she could imagine. On the back of the door was a robe. She reached out and felt the robe. She rubbed the thick, soft fabric between her fingers and sighed involuntarily.

I stay in places like this all the time, she thought. *Especially when I'm under house arrest.* She began to laugh again.

She decided she would take a shower. Looking over the array of products near the sink, she chose a soap and a shampoo she'd heard of before. She stripped quickly and pressed the touchpad next to the shower.

"Manual or voice control," it asked.

"Voice," she responded.

"Main menu," it stated.

"Options," Perseverance requested.

"There are three sub-menus from which to choose," it said. "Shower, moisturize, dry."

"Shower options," she asked.

"Shower options are rainforest, waterfall, heavy mist, deep tissue massage, gentle massage, standard," it stated.

What the hell, Perseverance thought. "Rainforest," she said.

A few seconds later, Perseverance felt like she was caught in a heavy but gentle downpour of warm rain. She had never been in a rainforest, but this certainly seemed like she imagined one would be. "Waterfall," she said.

A slot opened on one end near the top of the enclosure. A solid strip of water flowed out, about two centimeters thick and a meter wide. Perseverance moved to stand under it and began laughing in delight at the feeling.

By the time she finished, Perseverance had tried all the different shower options—some twice. She used the drying feature, which blew warm, dry air on her from all angles. Some of them tickled. She even used the moisturize option. The machine gave her several options, and Perseverance chose one without knowing what each would do. From the neck down, the machine sprayed her with a lightly scented body oil. For a moment, she worried that she would be so covered in oil she would need another shower. Her skin absorbed the material quickly, though, and felt as soft as she could ever remember. *Yup*, she thought, *all the time.* She snorted.

She noticed Samantha picked up her clothes where she'd dropped them. Perseverance put on the robe and tied it around her waist. Entering the bedroom, she saw the burgundy dress laid out on the bed, with her underwear on top. Her black shoes were next to the bed. She dressed, then checked herself in the mirror she remembered seeing on the back of the closet door.

Satisfied that she looked presentable, she left the bedroom. She retraced her steps to where Samantha was waiting when they entered the house. Perseverance figured she could puzzle out where the dining room was from there.

28

I t took longer than she expected, but she did find the dining room. Lord Gilchrist joked he was about to send a search party. He sat at the head of the long dining room table and placed her on his right. He quickly reminded her to call him Alfred, and he would address her as Perse.

"Perse, I must say you look lovely in that dress. It flatters you," he said.

"Thank you," Perseverance replied, blushing slightly.

"You're not accustomed to compliments?" he asked.

"Not really," she admitted. "Not regarding my appearance."

"I'm surprised," he said. "You are quite striking. I would have thought men would be falling all over themselves to be with you. If I were forty years younger, I know I would be."

"Alfred, you're flirting with me, aren't you?" she realized.

"A little, perhaps," he admitted with a grin. "Perse, when you spend decades trying to learn how to do something well, you get a certain pleasure from exercising that skill. Don't worry. I'm too old. I wouldn't be able to handle you when you caught me."

"When *I* caught *you*?" she asked.

"Perse, I'm far too old to be able to chase you properly. The effort would probably kill me. Therefore, I would need to make you chase me. You would catch me quite easily but then… oh, well."

Perseverance laughed. Lord Gilchrist did not have the mesmerizing presence that Queen Charlotte did. Still, he was skilled at making people feel comfortable. The small amount of tension that remained in her after that marvelous shower disappeared.

He waited until Samantha served the first course to take up the subject he dropped when they were on the station. "Perse, I think you underestimate the esteem in which you are held. This applies both to the public and within the navy. You feel you tarnished your image irreparably within the navy by speaking out. In the navy, like any familial group, there is a strong taboo against revealing family issues to the rest of the world. In your case, it does not apply."

"Why not?"

"What you revealed was not some family secret," he said. "You spoke up against a form of blackmail. Other than Admiral Smith-Clark, whom I will discuss in a minute, did you feel any of the officers aboard *Manitoba* were colder, more distant, or resentful toward you?"

"No."

"Do you feel the officers aboard *Manitoba* are much different from the rest of the navy?"

"Maybe a little better than average," she said uncertainly.

"Why? Because they were on your ship?" he teased.

"Maybe," she admitted, smiling.

"Would it be reasonable to say that the officers aboard *Manitoba* were a fairly representative sample of the navy at large?" he inquired.

"I want to disagree," she said, "but I'm having difficulty coming up with a sound reason."

"Perse, I'm willing to bet you that I could pull any ship in the navy and interview their officers. Nearly all of them—more than ninety percent—would have a highly favorable opinion of you. The others wouldn't have any opinion at all. Let's shelve that for now," he said. "Who was the one officer aboard *Manitoba* who did resent you?"

"Admiral Smith-Clark, but—"

"Even before this, did you think Smith-Clark was a shining example of a Royal Navy officer?" he asked.

"No."

"Why not?"

"I served under her before. She did not trust her subordinates to do their jobs, so she constantly checked up on them, interfering in what they were doing and altering her original orders. It was never her fault whenever something went wrong—according to her. It would come down to her word against her subordinates, and the superior officer always wins, especially when the subordinate has not documented the interference or changes demanded. She was also a lurker."

"A what?"

"A lurker. Someone who stands behind the corner listening to the conversations of others. She would use the information she gathered in two ways. Any good ideas she heard she would steal. Any of her subordinates who spoke against her would find their words repeated back to them in their performance reviews."

"Did you know that when you reported to her earlier, that was her only line position before her promotion to admiral?" he asked.

"No."

"She did it only to get her ticket punched, so to speak. Do you remember when we spoke, and I mentioned petty tyrants and suggested you document everything?" he asked.

"Yes. I kept track of everything. It was a pain in the ass, but I think I'll be glad I did," she said.

"Yes. I'll get back to that," he said. "I'm telling tales out of school now, and you'll need to pretend you never heard this, right?"

She nodded.

"There were four candidates put forward for admiral of Red Fleet. Admiral Freshley's staff submitted three names. Admiral Freshley added you to the list. When you spoke out on Alleghany, his staff convinced him to withdraw you from consideration. I should tell you his staff is made up of the sort of bureaucratic moles I mentioned to you. When you brought to light the political blackmail the navy was subject to, they began to fear their own little schemes would be exposed. You see, they've been doing the same thing, only on a much smaller scale than the politicians."

"What do you mean?" she asked.

"I'll bet you've been sucked into it without even knowing," he said. "When you were in command of *Rowen* and came in for supplies, did the supply officer ever say something like, 'An extra container of real steak came in by mistake. You want it?' Of course, you do. The supply officer then mentions he has a nephew, or the daughter of a friend, or something like that. He sure would appreciate it if you would keep your eye on them, mentor them and help guide their careers. Nothing like this has ever happened?"

Perseverance cleared her throat. "Um, well, yes, it has. That's just doing someone a favor."

"No, it's not," Gilchrist argued. "Do you really think a full container load of real steak arrived by accident? Or is it more likely someone will be shorted, and the supply officer will say, 'Gosh, I don't know what happened.' Which is it?"

"Damn," Perseverance muttered. "I never thought about it."

"Of course not," he replied. "Never look a gift horse in the mouth, right? Besides, the person you were asked to check up on probably wasn't that bad— not like the politicals. Now imagine that supply officer a decade or more later. He is now a part of Admiral Freshley's staff. They're finally addressing the problem with the politicals. Are you concerned that the dozens, or hundreds, of 'favors' you've traded might be exposed?"

"I see your point," she said.

"Back to choosing an admiral for Red Fleet. Admiral Freshley's staff convinces him to pull your name. The other three candidates are people *they* put forward. They all have *immaculate* records," he said sarcastically. "The only one with any line experience is Smith-Clark. Admiral Freshley, relying on the recommendations of his staff, approves her. Now, when I warned you, I did not know which of the three candidates would be picked. I simply knew they were of a type that views you as a threat, hence my advice."

"You make it sound like some sort of mass conspiracy," Perseverance remarked.

"It's not," Gilchrist said. "Each of these individuals is operating independently. It's only after they reach a certain level that they realize their peers have been doing the same thing. It's definitely not a topic for conversation."

"I understand," she said.

"That's only half of why Admiral Freshley came to make such a bad choice," Gilchrist explained. "The other reason is that he has more on his plate than he can chew right now. Fortunately, he knows he made a mistake. The candidates for the position now are all line officers. Your name is not one of them. Are you disappointed?"

Perseverance gave him an incredulous look. "While somehow you have helped me relax, I still think my career is over."

"You're wrong," Gilchrist stated firmly. "I've seen what the Judge Advocate has—at least, as of this morning. I doubt there is much, if anything, still outstanding. It includes all the materials you compiled, which paint a damning picture. It will be an open and shut case. The bridge cameras show that Smith-Clark panicked and usurped Admiral Czervik's authority. You behaved properly. If the navy wanted to, they could hang Smith-Clark for 'failure to engage.' They won't. Instead, they will discharge her and bind her up with the Official Secrets Act. *Manitoba's* bridge crew who witnessed the encounter have been advised by the Judge Advocate's people to keep quiet. You will be completely cleared."

"That's nice to hear you say," Perseverance said. "I'll believe it when it happens."

"Then I get an 'I told you so' when it does," he teased.

"That's fair."

"You are not being considered for the Red Fleet position because Admiral Freshley wants to see what the rumor mill generates," Gilchrist said. "Despite the gag orders being issued, word of the incident is already spreading. So far, the rumors are of the 'Smith-Clark lost her frickin' mind' variety, and your involvement was unimportant—it could have been anyone."

"Alfred, how do you know all this?" Perseverance asked.

He laughed. He began to recite:

"The time has come," the Walrus said,
"To talk of many things,
Of shoes—and ships—and sealing wax—
Of cabbages—and kings—
And why the sea is boiling hot—
And whether pigs have wings."

"That's an old poem Charlie teased me with, the first time we met after she inherited the throne," he said. "She claimed I knew everything, like the walrus. She calls me that behind my back—the walrus. I don't see the resemblance, myself."

Perseverance almost laughed out loud since he looked very much like a walrus with his bald head, thick mustache, and impressive girth, but she kept her mouth shut.

"I used to be in politics," he continued. "I was a Conservative MP, but I voted my conscience and according to the wishes of my district. I probably voted against my party more than forty percent of the time. It drove the party leaders crazy, but over time, MPs on both sides began to respect my 'middle-of-the-road' pragmatism. About twenty-five years ago, I chose not to run for re-election, thinking I was too old."

"If you don't mind my asking," Perseverance inquired, "how old were you?"

"Sixty. Anyway, it wasn't even a month into the new session of Parliament when I got a call from the prime minister, asking me to meet with the opposition to explore a possible compromise on a bill currently under debate. That was the first of many such requests from both sides of the aisle. Sometimes I could help them find common ground, sometimes not. Either way, I always strove to keep things grounded in common sense and what was best for the Commonwealth and kept my mouth shut about anything in which I was involved. Over the years, I began to be included in discussions outside of Parliament. As a result of all this, people in both parties and the government willingly share information with me, trusting that I will use the information at the appropriate time or not at all. In addition, they have confidence I will keep it to myself."

"So, what's next?" she asked.

"The court-martial is scheduled for Thursday. An attorney from the Judge Advocate's office has been assigned to you. He will meet with you tomorrow. Your part in the proceedings will probably be resolved by noon. After that, it depends on the Admiralty. They may have orders for you," he said.

"May have? Or will have?" she asked.

"May have. A lovely woman like you should never try to take advantage of a defenseless old man like me by asking such a question," he teased. "Now, you've been very patient, listening to my ramblings, but I know a part of your mind is well aware that Samantha left a comm unit on the desk upstairs. You haven't spoken to Commander Powell in all the time since this blew up. It would be inhuman of me to keep you here any longer. Go ahead."

Perseverance managed to find her way to the marvelous bedroom. She picked up the comm unit and began synchronizing it with her accounts. It seemed to take forever though she knew it was only a minute or two.

After all that, she thought, *he'll probably be tied up.* She accessed his number and initiated the call. Sure enough, the call went to the message bank.

"Hi," she said. "I'm allowed to talk to people now, and I'll have you know the first call I made was to you. Call me back when you get this, even if you think you'll wake me up. There's nothing better than waking up to talk with you."

When she closed the call, she accessed her own message bank. He had left five messages for her. She accessed the first one.

"Hey Persie, they just woke me up from the lifepod. Not fun. I feel like I have the worst hangover of my life, and I'm freezing. I love you. Call me."

Perseverance was stunned. *He used the "L" word*, she thought. *He went first! I win! Oh shit! That was nearly ten days ago! He's probably... Shit!*

"Persie, I know you're very perceptive and picked up on my use of a certain word in my last message. I said it on purpose. Please don't leave me dangling in the wind like this. Please call."

Perseverance called him back, knowing she would go into the message bank. "I love you, too," she said. "I just listened to your first two messages. They took away all communications from me until I landed on Caerleon. I called you as soon as I set up the comm, so I didn't know I left you hanging. I love you, too, but I'll always remember you said it first."

She closed the call and returned to Saint John's messages.

"Persie, I just heard that something happened on *Manitoba*, and you're being held without communications access. They're calling it 'protective custody' instead of whatever they usually say, so I'm hoping for the best. I hope you heard my first message before they locked you up. You can disregard the second one."

That was nice, she thought.

"Persie, the rumor mill is saying the Smith-Clark went nuts just as *Manitoba* was about to enter missile range and ordered you to reverse course. When you didn't do it, she confined you to quarters after calling you a bunch of names. Your XO, Sullivan, called the marines and had her dragged away kicking and screaming. Anyway, I still feel the same about you as I did in the first message I left, but I'm not saying it again until I hear it from you."

She smiled at his last remark and then started listening to the last message.

"Persie, I'm guessing you're still being held without comm access. I heard you were being taken to Caerleon, and you should arrive there soon. More information has come out. I may have helped it along. I shared with someone how she screwed with the crew reporting schedule and your quarters. It came back to me a couple of days later with embellishment. Is it true she was openly mocking you on the bridge in front of the crew before the incident? That's what they're saying, at least. I wish you had told me about it. Not that I could have done anything but be sympathetic. I'm currently taking my horse back to the barn, so to speak. Call me when you can."

29

Her comm unit woke her in the middle of the night. She glanced at the screen to make sure it was Saint John. She connected.

"Nothing better than to wake up to talk with you," she said, repeating her earlier message.

"Hi, Persie, I listened to your messages before I called you, so I'm all reassured," he said. "How are you?"

"I'm a lot less gloomy than I was a day ago. Lord Gilchrist is my host for my house arrest. He shared some background information that made me feel better about my predicament. In the morning, I meet face-to-face with my lawyer from the Judge Advocate's office. Friday is the court-martial," she replied. "How are you? Can you tell me where you are?"

"I'm fine. It took a couple of days to get over feeling cold from being in the pod. But, yes, I'm allowed to tell you where we are. I checked. We just entered normal space in an uninhabited system, one jump away from the Oregon system. It's where the navy keeps obsolete ships and ones too badly damaged to repair. They call it the Twelfth of Never. Once we park the ships, we'll hop a transport back to Oregon and, from there, a liner to wherever we've been assigned. Some folks have orders already. Some, like me, are still waiting. So, how accurate were the rumors?"

"Pretty close to the truth, in this case," she said. "The admiral panicked as we neared missile range and ordered reverse thrust. I thought she saw something to which she was reacting at first. However, when I saw her expression, I realized that wasn't the reason. The rest of it was pretty much as you described."

"Was she really mocking you in front of the crew?" he asked.

"Yeah."

"I wish you told me."

"Would you have beaten her up for me?" Perseverance asked, teasing.

"Probably not, though I would have wanted to. If it's any consolation, the emphasis of the rumors is more about the admiral losing her mind than you. A couple of people who have shared it with me didn't even mention your name," he said.

"Huh," she grunted. "That's what Lord Gilchrist said. I think that's the desired outcome, as far as the Admiralty is concerned."

"What do you know about your court-martial?" he asked.

"Not much. I think I'll know more after meeting with the lawyer. Lord Gilchrist thinks my part will be resolved before noon," she said. "If that's the case, then I wait for orders."

"If it drags on?" he asked.

"Then I'm stuck at Lord Gilchrist's house, which is not a bad place to be," she said. "The bedroom I'm in is humungous. You wouldn't believe the shower. It does everything except scrub your back, though I bet it does that, too, if you know how to work it."

Saint John laughed. There was a long silence. "Sooo—I said it."

"You certainly did," she replied. "And I said it back. But you said it first. Nyah, nyah. What inspired you?"

"Being in the lifepod," he said. "When they revive you, you feel like... death. That's the best I can describe it."

"Beats the alternative," Perseverance quipped.

"I suppose. The pod only warms you to just above freezing to extend battery life. Normally, there are two people in each one, and the only way to fit is to hug one another. That's supposed to help maintain body heat and reduce the drain on the battery as well," he explained. "The drug that is injected puts you in a coma and slows your pulse and respiration to about a third of normal. That's to reduce oxygen demand. The drug also overrides your body's reaction to the cold, preventing it from shutting off blood flow to your extremities. When you regain consciousness, you experience the worst hangover symptoms you can imagine— spins, dry heaves, the works. On top of that, there is this sense of cold that goes all the way into your bones. The hangover lasted about twelve hours. The cold took three days to shake. Since I felt like I was going to die, in between the dry heaves and after my teeth stopped chattering, I told you I love you."

"I love you, too."

Perseverance slept better that night than she had since Ilium. Samantha woke her at 07:00. That was sleeping in, as far as Perseverance was concerned. She navigated the shower again, which gave her the giggles. Samantha was waiting for her in the kitchen and cooked a breakfast of real bacon and real eggs.

According to Samantha, Lord Gilchrist had already left for the day. The attorney from the Judge Advocate's office would arrive at nine o'clock. That left Perseverance with an hour. She spent that time reviewing the news sites to see the coverage regarding Ilium and then anything that might be of interest in the Commonwealth.

The lawyer, Alex Papadapoulos, arrived five minutes early. He was one of the three lawyers she spoke with during the journey back to Caerleon. Papadapoulos was young. Perseverance guessed mid-twenties. He was short, mostly bald, and showed the beginning of a pot belly. At the same time, his face was lively and expressive, and he smiled easily. His eyes indicated intelligence. He seemed full of energy.

Samantha directed the two of them to a study and shut the door. Papadapoulos set his leather case down and pulled a tablet from it. He perched on the very edge of the wingback chair and rubbed his hands as though eager to begin. Perseverance matched his upright posture but sat more comfortably.

"Okay," he said. "First, I apologize for not being in more regular contact. After speaking with you initially, I was assigned to your case and have reviewed all the evidence the Judge Advocate compiled. You can relax. This is going to be a piece of cake."

"If you say so," Perseverance commented gloomily.

"It will be. Trust me. Now, logistics. Court begins at ten sharp tomorrow in the Admiralty headquarters here—dirtside. Lord Gilchrist has already let me know his driver will deliver you in plenty of time. I will meet you there. There will be three officers as judges—no jury. The officers will be Admiral Freshley, Admiral Czervik, and Captain Boyd. Czervik will be presiding remotely via comm. A holographic projection of him will appear where he would be sitting. All three are line officers—good for you, bad for her. You will wear your number ones. Enter the courtroom carrying your sword, not wearing it, and place it on the table parallel with the way the judges are seated. Smith-Clark will not be present. Understand so far?"

Perseverance nodded.

"Good.

"Your hearing is first. It will begin with the charges being read. Smith-Clark has accused you of conspiracy, insubordination, and failure to obey lawful orders. The Judge Advocate must prosecute those charges whether they believe they have merit since they were made by a superior officer. I will defend you against those charges. Let me go over the charges one by one. Is that acceptable?"

"That's fine," she said.

"Conspiracy," Papadapoulos stated. "Smith-Clark has stated that she believes you have coerced the other officers aboard *Manitoba* to ally against her. She offered no evidence of any orders that were not carried out in a timely manner, or any disrespect shown by those officers. The only evidence the Judge Advocate's people found that even remotely supports her accusations are video clips showing you interacting with the ship's officer in the course of your normal duties. All communication between you and the ship's officers was proper and concerned with only topics related to the performance of your duties. I will move to dismiss these charges. The officers will grant my motion."

"Good. That's one."

"The next, insubordination. It will take longer but should end up being more fun," he said.

"Define *fun*," Perseverance asked.

"Smith-Clark provided the Judge Advocate's office with a handful of dates when the supposed insubordination occurred. She could not recall the specific time of day," Papadapoulos said. "In reviewing the security camera feeds from the days she referenced, we found no evidence supporting her claims. We did find gaps in the recordings on each of the days in question. The recordings you saved on your personal comm overlap these gaps in every case. Even more, in checking your recordings against the camera feeds, there were other gaps that your saved files cover. None of them show insubordination on your part. On those recordings you saved where the audio portion is clearly understandable, the recordings document a pattern of harassment instead. This is also corroborated by your written journal. At this point, I expect the prosecution to object."

"To what part?" Perseverance asked.

"The prosecution will object, claiming your documentation proves Smith-Clark's accusation of conspiracy, which will already have been dismissed. Who advised you to document everything so thoroughly?" he asked.

"Lord Gilchrist," Perseverance replied. "Plus, I served under Smith-Clark before. I knew what sort of person she is."

"The Lord Gilchrist answer is great," he said. "For the other, *if* you are asked—when asked a question, answer only the question asked and don't volunteer any additional information—so *if* you are asked, you should say that having served under Smith-Clark before, you felt it would be in your best interest to maintain thorough and accurate records. That way, it comes across that you were only covering your butt, and you aren't accusing her of anything—even though you are in an oblique way. Got it?"

"In my best interest," Perseverance repeated. "Got it."

"Smith-Clark will probably also have accused you of deleting the camera footage. That won't stick. The Judge Advocate has forensic evidence showing you copying the footage from the console in your ready room but not deleting it. That evidence also shows Lieutenant Foxcroft was responsible for the deletions. She has since been arrested and charged. I will move that charges against you for insubordination be dismissed. I will ask if there are charges of harassment against Smith-Clark filed. The presiding officers will then confirm that charges of harassment are already pending against Smith-Clark. They will approve my motion to dismiss the insubordination charge."

"Two down, one to go," Perseverance said.

"Right. Failure to obey lawful orders," he said, rubbing his hands together again. "From the moment *Manitoba* was seconded to Admiral Czervik's task force, it ceased to be a member of Red Fleet. Therefore, it could not serve as Smith-Clark's flagship during that time. Smith-Clark's presence on board was superfluous. She was, for lack of a better word, no more than cargo. Any order she gave during that time was not a lawful order. She may claim that other orders she issued during the mission were obeyed, and our response is 'courtesy to the rank.' That means anyone who obeyed an order from her during this time was doing so as a courtesy to her rank and not out of legal obligation. Since one of the charges against her is the issuance of an unlawful order, when I move to dismiss the charges, the motion will be granted."

"Then what?" Perseverance asked.

"One of the officers, probably Admiral Freshley, will, at a minimum, tell you that all charges against you have been dismissed, and your sword is hereby returned to you. I'm hoping for more, but I won't say anything because I don't want to jinx it."

"Then I'm free to go?" she asked.

"Yes. They'll probably recess for lunch at this point and begin with Smith-Clark at 13:00. You might find it entertaining to watch, in the same way that dropping a watermelon from the roof of a building can be entertaining," he said.

Perseverance frowned. "I think I'll skip it."

"That's probably a good idea, for you," he said. "I have to be there. I'll try to enjoy it for the both of us."

Perseverance laughed. Papadapoulos stood, sliding his tablet back into his leather case. He offered his hand.

"I'll see you tomorrow, just before ten," he said. "Remember, number one uniform, and carry your sword, don't wear it. You'll have to take it off to get through security anyway. Don't worry about anything related to this. It's strictly a formality."

Perseverance spent the rest of the day full of nervous energy. She wanted to do something, but there was nothing to do. Samantha reminded her that it was Thursday and Lord Gilchrist would like her to dress for dinner.

Since Perseverance only had the two dresses and her formal uniform, and she needed the uniform for the next day and already wore the burgundy, she wore the gray dress she bought at Anton's. Lord Gilchrist was properly appreciative.

"Damn!" he said. "If I were forty years younger, I'd be chasing you around the house right now. Did you buy this with someone in mind or in the hope it would help you find a someone?"

"My wardrobe usually consists of uniforms or extremely casual clothes," she answered. "Commander Powell asked me to find something that was 'dressy casual.' Shopping for dressy clothes is not fun for me. Most stuff doesn't come close to fitting properly. I got lucky and walked into what was probably the only shop on the station that had clothes to fit me."

"Dominic's or Anton's?" Gilchrist asked.

Perseverance's eyebrows shot up in surprise. "Anton's," she replied. "How would you know something like that?"

Gilchrist laughed—a low, rolling chuckle. "Remember? According to Charlie, I know everything. The real answer is that I pay attention," he said. "Both Dominic and Anton cater to the same customers, though each prefers different styles from the other. Both specialize in *haute couture*—high fashion— from designers you may have heard of. Both used to be located here, on Caerleon but moved to the station when they realized most of their business was from other systems. You have the same figure as many of the couture models who buy from them—tall, broad-shouldered, and slender. Both Dominic and Anton would carry things that fit you. Was it expensive?"

"Yes."

"Was it worth it?" he asked.

Perseverance paused in thought. She remembered that the time in Anton's shop was actually fun. Blushing, she also remembered how quickly the gray dress was left in a heap on the floor, the first time she wore it for Saint John during the last week of their trip.

"It's not something I'm going to make a habit of doing," she said, "but, yes, it was worth it."

Saint John called her in the evening after dinner, and she reported the conversation with the lawyer. Saint John expressed confidence that it would go her way and asked her to call when it was over. For some reason, his calm confidence influenced her. After the call, she realized she was not as concerned. She simply wanted it to be over.

30

Perseverance woke at six the following day, rested and ready. After another decadent shower, she dressed in her formal uniform. When she arrived downstairs, both Lord Gilchrist and Samantha were there.

"Today's the big day," he said, "though I hope you will have bigger and better days to look forward to in the future. David will be here at nine to drive you to the Admiralty. When you are finished and need a ride, contact him. The number should be in the comm unit I lent you."

"Will I be staying here after my house arrest is over?" she asked.

"I hope so," he replied. "Though we have not seen much of one another, your presence at dinner has been delightful. You are welcome to stay until duty pulls you away."

Lord Gilchrist departed shortly after breakfast. Perseverance began to pace. Samantha put a halt to it.

"If you're going to act like a caged animal, do it in the garden," she said. "Just having you in the house is making *me* antsy."

The bodyguard arrived just after nine. He held the door of the groundcar open for Perseverance, and he sat up front at the controls. He wouldn't actually drive the vehicle. Traffic control computers would guide the vehicle after he input the destination. He would only take control of the vehicle in an emergency by overriding the system.

Papadapoulos was waiting for her. They went through the security checkpoint. One of the security guards did not want to allow her sword, but the supervisor told him not to worry.

"The queen gave it to her, remember? She ain't likely to use it on anyone, are you, Cap'n?"

Perseverance shook her head.

"Alright then," he said, waving for the guard to return it to Perseverance.

"It's not that important," Papadapoulos commented. "I could have told you not to bring it, but it's an old naval tradition, and I like to respect and honor those. It's also a small piece of staging for the presiding officers—you show respect for the service, plus you were granted the sword by the queen for bravery and coolness under fire. Admiral Smith-Clark has no sword. The case against you is so feeble, you don't need any extra sort of help, but it does help illustrate further the difference between you."

They reached the room where the court-martial would take place. A lieutenant wearing a sword was waiting for them. Other than the lieutenant, there was no one else in the corridor. Papadapoulos stopped.

"The lieutenant will draw his sword and escort you in. When you reach the table where I will be standing, place your sword across the table with the hilt to our left, which will be the officers' right," he said. "Remain at attention until ordered to sit. One of them will ask you how you plead after reading each charge. You respond, 'Not guilty,' crisply and firmly. Don't move until one of them orders you to sit. Once you sit, it's my show. When I rest the case, you will stand at attention. The three officers may leave the room to deliberate if the charges have not all been dismissed. When the door shuts behind them, you can relax. In this case, I expect all charges to be dismissed so no deliberation will be needed. If they do leave, it will be less than five minutes, so I would recommend parade rest. They will be able to see you in the camera feed. When they enter, it's back to attention. Got it?"

Perseverance nodded.

"If they ask you any questions, answer only the question asked. Do not volunteer any information. If they ask why you documented so thoroughly, what's your answer?" Papadapoulos inquired.

"Having served under the officer before, it seemed in my best interest," Perseverance replied.

"Excellent. You're ready. See you inside."

Perseverance heard four bells. The doors of the room swung open. She straightened her posture to stand at her full height.

The lieutenant said, "It's time."

Perseverance stepped off smartly. She walked with her head high and eyes straight ahead. Her turn to the table where Papadapoulos stood was crisp. She laid her sword on the table with the hilt to her left, took one step back, and stood at attention.

The room was quite empty. The only people present were the three presiding officers, the prosecutor, and Papadapoulos, two petty officers wearing SP armbands, the lieutenant who escorted her, and Perseverance herself. Captain Boyd read an administrative summary of the reason for the court-martial and listed the presiding officers. He then read the charges against Perseverance and asked for a plea after each one. Perseverance responded, "Not guilty," three times.

"You may sit," Admiral Freshley stated when that was finished.

Perseverance sat, maintaining a stiff, upright posture. The prosecuting attorney moved out from behind his table. He cleared his throat quietly and began.

"We will attempt to prove today that Captain Andrews is guilty of conspiring against Admiral Smith-Clark, that Captain Andrews is guilty of repeated acts of insubordination, and that Captain Andrews failed to obey a lawful order," he said.

Admiral Czervik snorted and muttered to the other two officers. Perseverance thought she heard him say, "Good luck with that," but she could not be sure. Now it was Papadapoulos' turn.

"We will demonstrate conclusively that Captain Andrews acted at all times and in all ways in keeping with the highest standards of conduct in the Royal Navy. There was no conspiracy. At no point did Captain Andrews ever display insubordinate behavior, though Admiral Smith-Clark should be accused of harassment. Finally, the order that Admiral Smith-Clark claims Captain Andrews failed to obey was not a lawfully given order. Indeed, by attempting to give that order, Admiral Smith-Clark could be and should be charged with failure to engage, one of the most serious offenses possible," he said.

The prosecutor took over, claiming the video records showed repeated meetings between Perseverance and the other officers as proof that they were conspiring against Admiral Smith-Clark. Captain Boyd asked if there was any other evidence supporting the claims of conspiracy. The prosecutor admitted there was none.

Papadapoulos then moved that the charge be dismissed for lack of evidence since the recordings showed Captain Andrews in routine interaction with the officers during the course of duty. Admiral Freshley looked at the other two officers. Both nodded.

"Charge dismissed," Admiral Freshley stated. "Next?"

The prosecutor referenced the dates Admiral Smith-Clark provided when the alleged insubordination took place. He mentioned that the camera footage documenting the insubordination had been deleted from the system. While video recordings found on Captain Andrews' comm unit appeared to cover the missing time, those recordings could not be trusted as they might have been altered.

Admiral Czervik broke in. "So, all we have is Admiral Smith-Clark's word that insubordination took place, is that correct?"

"Yes, sir."

Papadapoulos took over, producing a forensic analysis where the experts ascertained that the recordings of Captain Andrews' device were unaltered. He mentioned the trail left by Lieutenant Foxcroft and her subsequent arrest for tampering with official records. Then he noted that the audio recordings on Captain Andrews' comm demonstrated a pattern of harassment by Admiral Smith-Clark, supported by entries in her written journal.

As Papadapoulos predicted, the prosecutor objected. "Documentation to this degree is unusual and supports Admiral Smith-Clark's accusation of conspiracy. Accordingly, I move that the conspiracy charge be reinstated."

At this point, Admiral Freshley spoke directly to Perseverance.

"This is an extraordinary level of documentation. Have you ever kept track of your interactions with a superior officer so thoroughly before this?"

"No, sir."

"Why did you do it in this case?"

"Sir, Lord Gilchrist suggested it."

"Any other reason? Perhaps your earlier assignment serving under Smith-Clark?"

Papadapoulos mouthed, "Best interest," to her.

"Sir, my earlier experience led me to believe that it would be in my best interest to follow Lord Gilchrist's advice and document my interactions with the admiral thoroughly," she said.

Admiral Czervik laughed out loud at this. "Motion denied," he said, looking at the prosecutor dismissively. Freshley looked at Boyd, who nodded. "Motion denied. The conspiracy charge remains dismissed," Freshley stated.

Sensing that the moment was right, Papadapoulos stood. "If it please the court, I would like to move that the charge of insubordination be dismissed."

Admiral Freshley looked at the other two officers. Both nodded.

"Charge of insubordination is dismissed. Next?"

"In the moments leading to the engagement in the Ilium system, Admiral Smith-Clark claims she lost confidence in Captain Andrews' ability to perform her duties adequately due to her belief that Captain Andrews was conspiring against her. For this reason, she ordered the ship to reverse thrust immediately so as not to expose the ship and crew to unnecessary danger with an unfit captain. For this reason, Admiral Smith-Clark's order to reverse thrust was a lawful order, which Captain Andrews clearly refused to obey," the prosecutor stated.

"Objection," Papadapoulos said, standing. "From the moment HMS *Manitoba* was seconded to Admiral Czervik's task force, the ship ceased to be a part of Red Fleet and therefore was no longer Admiral Smith-Clark's flagship. Admiral Smith-Clark's scope of command is strictly limited to Red Fleet. Admiral Smith-Clark's presence on the ship and on the bridge was superfluous. She had no more legal authority than a bag of beans in the galley. Any orders she gave during this time that were followed demonstrate courtesy to the rank. That makes her order on the bridge to reverse thrust an unlawful order that no officer should obey. Further, her attempt to reverse thrust on the cusp of the engagement is clear evidence of failure to engage. I move that the charge of failing to obey a lawful order be dismissed."

For the third time, Admiral Freshley glanced at the other two. As before, both nodded. Admiral Freshley then beckoned the other two with his finger to draw closer. The three men leaned their heads together and whispered quietly.

Admiral Freshley then rose. Perseverance leaped to attention in response. The admiral came around from behind the table where he had been sitting and crossed in front of Perseverance. He turned the sword on the table so the hilt pointed to her.

"All charges against you are dismissed, Captain Andrews," he said. "Your sword is returned to you. However, before we allow you to depart, the court would like to state for the record that it believes that, since taking command of HMS *Manitoba*, your performance of duties was flawless, and your conduct and deportment in difficult circumstances were exemplary and in keeping with the highest standards of the Royal Navy."

"Thank you, sir," Perseverance replied.

Then, feeling it was the proper thing to do, she saluted. The admiral returned her salute. The faint trace of a smile graced the corners of his mouth.

Dropping the salute, he stated, "This court is in recess until 13:00."

The admiral turned away. Czervik and Boyd were already halfway out the door. Perseverance turned to Papadapoulos and extended her hand. He shook it enthusiastically.

"Thank you," she said.

"My pleasure," he replied.

31

When she returned to Lord Gilchrist's house, she changed into undress khakis. Her mood was odd. With all the charges against her dismissed, she thought she ought to feel happy, or relieved, at least. She didn't. She didn't even feel justice was served since the whole thing should never have happened. Smith-Clark had ruined the joy Perseverance expected to feel when taking command of *Manitoba*. She'd forced Perseverance to pay close attention to every single step she took aboard her own ship. The experience was degrading and unpleasant. She hoped she never faced anything like it again.

She contacted Saint John. The comm rolled to his message bank immediately. From what he told her earlier, she figured he was in hyperspace, on the way to the Oregon system. She left a message, letting him know all the charges were dismissed. She wondered if he knew his ultimate destination yet. As of their conversation the night before, he still did not have orders.

For that matter, she did not know what was in store for her. HMS *Manitoba* was in Tino Diaz's hands now. She was pessimistic about being given command of a ship—she didn't know if any were available. Ordinarily, that was information on which she tried to stay up-to-date—always curious about who would be given command of which ship.

She decided to use the console in her bedroom and delve into what was happening in the navy as far as possible commands. From the time she discovered Admiral Smith-Clark in her quarters on *Manitoba*, Perseverance had needed to use every spare minute to maintain the documentation that eventually proved so critical. As a result, she had not kept up with the navy's comings and goings. She knew the new construction was more than two years away, so that was obviously not an option. She wondered if there were any ships in the yard for refit. She couldn't find any evidence of that in a quick look.

She reviewed the media's coverage of the battle of Ilium. There was no mention of *Manitoba*. She supposed that was good news.

The larger issue regarding Ilium on the news sites was what to do with the settlers the Chinese Republics transported there. In the midst of a war, there was no way to send them back. It might be years before the war ended. The government decided that offering them a path to become citizens was the best solution. The problem was that they currently outnumbered the Commonwealth citizens living on Ilium. So, the government was offering incentives throughout the rest of the Commonwealth to attract migration to Ilium to bring the numbers into balance.

At 16:00, she received a message summoning her to a meeting with Admiral Freshley at 08:00 the next day. Even though it would be Saturday, she did not think it unusual. On a ship underway, there was no such thing as a weekend.

Not long after that, Saint John returned her call. As she thought, the transport he was on just emerged from hyperspace into the Oregon system. He was grinning, which brought out his dimples. It was an extremely good look for him, she decided. She couldn't help but smile herself.

"What has you all happy?" she asked.

"Someone told me my girlfriend is in the clear," he said, "not that she should have needed to go through such a farce."

"Your girlfriend? Who is that?" she asked.

"You are."

"Have we reached that stage?"

"I hope so. What do you think?"

"I'm okay with that, I guess."

"Gee, I'm overwhelmed by your enthusiasm," he said sarcastically.

"Well, I've never been one to doodle initials in my little pink diary," she said. "You know that."

"If you let me be your boyfriend, I'll hold your hand and buy you ice cream," he offered.

"One scoop or two?"

"As many as you want. Sprinkles, too. You're worth it."

"Now you're talking," she said. "You still have that goofy grin. What else is going your way?"

"I got my orders," he said.

"And?"

"I'm catching a liner to Caerleon the day after tomorrow. I'll be there six days after that," he said.

"What is waiting for you in Caerleon—besides me if I don't get orders pulling me somewhere else?"

"I'm going to be XO on HMS *Deal*," he said. "Will Dallas is my CO."

"He's a good guy. When is *Deal* due to arrive?"

"It's been there, in refit," Saint John said.

"Huh," she grunted. "I was poking around this afternoon and didn't catch that."

"You probably didn't look back far enough," he said. "Remember after Alleghany, when the navy was able to eliminate the politicals? *Deal* and *Simpkin* lost their skippers. The Admiralty decided to bring the two ships in to have some work done. They haven't visited the yard since they were launched. For *Simpkin*, that's almost four years ago, and *Deal* came out of the slips a few months later. Rumor has it they received an upgrade of sorts, but I haven't received anything other than my orders so far, so I don't know. They've been in the yard long enough that an upgrade is believable."

"Huh," she grunted. "Well, I'm happy for you. Maybe by this time tomorrow I'll have my orders and know where I'm headed. Will *Deal* be shipping out immediately?"

"Between the liner's arrival and when I am ordered to report aboard, there's a gap of forty-six hours. I'm hoping to spend that time with you."

"I'll hope for that, too," she said. "I have missed you, ya know. It's just that I've been preoccupied with the other thing."

"I know. Let's hope now that you get ordered to a great assignment and that we can spend some time together," he said.

Perseverance held her crossed fingers up to the camera. Her smile now almost matched his.

"You are so gorgeous when you smile like that," he said. "I think I'll do whatever I can to make sure I see it as often as possible."

"Well, that grin you've been sporting is what my sister would call a 'panty dropper.' Whew!" she said, pretending to fan her face.

The next morning, David again delivered her to the Admiralty. After reminding her to call when she needed him to return, he opened her door and let her out. Perseverance headed for the door in much better spirits this time. She expected to receive some kind of orders, which would end the limbo-like state she'd been stuck in since Ilium.

According to naval tradition, she arrived outside Admiral Freshley's office fifteen minutes early, which meant she was on time. The yeoman recognized her and alerted the admiral to her presence. Within moments, the door opened. Hank Boyd was holding onto the doorknob and gestured her inside.

Before Perseverance reached the admiral's desk, he said, "At ease, captain. Grab a seat over there."

Boyd was already seated in an armchair, having crossed behind her. Perseverance took another armchair. The admiral took the corner of the sofa and stretched his legs out.

"Where to start?" he said with a sigh. Then, making up his mind, he said, "We just promoted Hank to command Red Fleet."

"Congratulations, sir," Perseverance said sincerely.

"Thank you. And when we're in private, it's still Hank. We've known each other too long. Your time will come, Perse," he replied.

"As long as you avoid further controversy," Admiral Freshley added. "Though this last bit is my fault. I apologize. Hank knows this, but I actually wanted you for the position a couple of months ago, but I let myself get talked out of it. That won't happen again. Unfortunately, I can't do it now. We think this whole incident will stay off the radar but need to let some time pass to be sure."

"I understand," she said.

"Time for some good news," Boyd said. "You're getting *Simpkin* and will be part of Red Fleet under my command. We'll transmit your orders before you leave. *Simpkin* and *Deal* have been in the yard. You'll take over in a week. This has been more than a normal refit. In the last two years, there have been some technological developments."

"The first development was more efficient energy transfer from the reactor bubble," Freshley explained. "The second was certain metallurgic advances that lower electrical resistance in conduit materials without needing to supercool them. This means we get more usable energy from a reactor than before and can carry more of it to where it is put to work."

Admiral Freshley shifted his position on the sofa and continued. "With the increased energy available, we decided to replace the 75mm cannons on *Simpkin* and *Deal* with 90mm guns. Cycle time is still two seconds, or thirty shots a minute. It is possible to reduce the cycle time, but it quickly causes conduit overheating and system failure—in less than a minute. The last improvement is a reconfigured nacelle for the EM drives. The new nacelles are designed to take advantage of the increased power available. They should make *Simpkin* and *Deal* the quickest ships in the fleet. Right now, every *Simpkin*-class destroyer takes twenty-three minutes and change to go from zero thrust to five hundred g. The new nacelles will enable *Simpkin* and *Deal* to reach that rate of acceleration in just under seventeen minutes."

"Admiral, a few months ago, I attended a briefing where they indicated there were new capacitors that could reduce cycle time for the cannons," Perseverance said.

"Sadly, they did not hold up in more strenuous testing," Freshley said. "They are continuing to work on them and are confident they will be able to introduce something within a year."

Boyd took over the discussion. "Obviously, these two ships are serving as a test lab for the new features. If they work here, we will include them in all the new construction. We will be seeking opportunities to try them in combat conditions. You should have an interesting time over the next year."

"What do you think?" Admiral Freshley asked Perseverance.

Her mind was already racing, thinking of what these developments might mean. She snapped it back. "I think Santa Claus put me on the 'nice' list. I've been worried I was on the other one."

"You've never been on my 'naughty' list," Freshley said, "even after Alleghany. I would also say that there are only a few members of the service who do not appreciate what you said then."

"Those few members of the service… I'm guessing it would be a good idea to inspect every container whenever I resupply, right?" she asked.

"That's not the worst idea," Boyd confirmed. "The first time you find something amiss will also probably be the last, provided you let me know."

"Hank, please be careful. Otherwise, I'll be poison," she protested.

"Perse, I've only been an admiral a few hours. I haven't forgotten how things work," Boyd said. "No one will think to connect your resupply to the visit a few weeks later by the Commonwealth Audit Division for a spot inspection of the books. The sort of people who would cheat you on supplies will also be guilty of other transgressions that a snap audit will catch. All it will take is one to be caught, and the others will straighten up and fly right pretty damned quick."

"Speaking of that kind of people," Freshley said. "Admiral Smith-Clark, on the strident advice of counsel, decided to resign her commission yesterday afternoon before a verdict was reached. On her way out, we reminded her that any violation of the Official Secrets Act would cause us to file charges of 'Failure to Engage.' We did not include that charge in what was brought forward yesterday. There is no statute of limitations on 'Failure to Engage,' and punishment of death is still an option. It is our hope that her disappearance from the service is similar to a pebble dropped into a pond without a ripple. Time will tell."

"What is the overall situation?" Perseverance asked. "Do we expect more incursions?"

Freshley shook his head. "Right now, the Republics, the Federation, and the Commonwealth are all like boxers who threw too many punches in the opening minute of the round. We're all arm-weary and exhausted, waiting for the bell to ring so we can regroup and catch our wind. All three of us are at roughly equal strength, though we might be short on destroyers compared to the others. And don't say, 'I told you so,' because we had no other options, captain. None of the three has enough ships to risk a major assault. If the Republics and the Federation trusted one another completely, their combined force could overwhelm us. Fortunately for us, they need to worry about whether their 'partner' might try to take advantage of them."

"Using your analogy, when is the next round in the boxing match?" Perseverance asked.

"When the current round of shipbuilding is complete," Freshley said. "We have a pretty good idea of what the Federation is doing. The ships they used in the recent attacks were all completed recently—only weeks before they struck. A few months before that, they began construction on five heavy cruisers, ten light cruisers, and at least ten destroyers, though some of MI-6's sources claim it could be as many as fourteen. Our information from the Republics is crap, but we are guessing they are doing something similar. The three of us are in a race to see who gets ships built first."

"If we win that race?" she asked.

"Then we assure ourselves of lasting another round—no more," Freshley stated. "With what was just approved, we won't have the numbers to go on the offensive. We should be able to defend ourselves adequately this time."

Perseverance noted his "this time" remark with a slight grimace. "Why didn't we ask for more ships, then?" she inquired.

"At the moment, we don't have the capacity to build more. Don't worry, though. We are submitting a second request to Parliament in a couple of weeks for the next cycle of shipbuilding. Already, private investors have been enticed into refurbishing or expanding the shipyard facilities in the Lincoln, Columbiana, and Ithaca systems. The next round of shipbuilding will be twice what we are doing now and should follow more quickly—less than a year after we launch what we just started. When that is complete, we might be able to consider taking the war to enemy space. We must, eventually, if we're to prevail in this conflict. If we win or tie in the current arms race, I like our chances afterward. Our economic and industrial base and the quality of our workforce will get stronger as this progresses. I doubt our enemies can make the same prediction."

The conversation did not last much longer. On her way out of the office, Admiral Freshley stopped her. He went behind his desk, opened a drawer, and pulled out the comm unit she had given Joe Sullivan to hand over to the Judge Advocate, and the paper journal.

"These are yours, I believe," he said, offering them to her.

32

B efore she left the Admiralty, Boyd transmitted her orders. He included a summary document on the enhancements made to HMS *Simpkin*. The crew roster was another attachment.

When she returned to Lord Gilchrist's, she examined the documents more carefully. Her orders were bland—just instructing her to take command of HMS *Simpkin* on the seventeenth of December, 2683, at which point she could expect further orders from Rear Admiral Boyd. She checked the date with what Saint John told her about his orders. She could not prevent the smile that appeared when she realized they would be able to spend almost two full days together.

She scanned through the documentation of the new cannons. At some point soon, she would examine it thoroughly to absorb the details, but for now, she only wanted to see the result. *Simpkin* now had four 90mm photon cannons, with one double turret on the dorsal spine and the other on the ventral, roughly midships. The cycle time of thirty shots per minute was the same as the 75mm cannons they replaced. She could reduce that time by twenty-five percent but only for less than a minute. Testing showed that the conduits would overheat and melt as soon as the fifty-five-second mark.

The new nacelles would provide quicker acceleration, as the admiral indicated. It was also possible to exceed the normal rated maximum, but that would cause the nacelles to wear out more quickly than the current design. The documents also warned that using "max boost," as it was known, could lead to the development of a harmonic tremor. That, she knew, was a warning worth heeding.

The last thing she examined was the crew roster. Her executive officer would be Commander Dave Stackhouse. She knew of him but had not worked with him before. The ranking petty officer aboard, the COB, was Henry Allen. She did not know him. She did know her new head of engineering, Commander Josh Choe. Choe had been on *Rowen* when they were nearly destroyed.

She called Saint John to share her good news. His captain had already informed him of the enhancements made to their ship, but he was delighted Perseverance was given command of *Simpkin*. The best news she shared with him, as far as he was concerned, was the forty-six hours they could spend together. His naughty grin inspired unaccustomed feelings in Perseverance. She felt desired, beautiful, and even sexy. No one in her life before had kindled these emotions.

With the court-martial over and her house arrest rescinded, she no longer needed to stay with Lord Gilchrist. While she would miss the sybaritic luxury of the shower, she knew she would feel more comfortable moving to the BOQ on Caerleon Station. She headed downstairs to inform him of her intention and thank him and Samantha for their hospitality.

She found both of them in his study. While she thanked him for his kindness, Samantha disappeared. Perseverance left him to pack her belongings, only to find Samantha already carrying her two bags and her sword downstairs.

"I'm not trying to get rid of you, dear," Samantha said, "just trying to make it easier for you. I get the feeling you're not one for lingering goodbyes. David will be here in a moment to take you to the Admiralty, where you can catch the navy shuttle. You've been no trouble at all, and if Lord Gilchrist hasn't already offered to allow you to visit us again, let me do that. You will always be welcome here."

For some reason, Perseverance felt a hug was a proper way to say farewell. She wasn't much of a touchy-feely sort ordinarily. When she finished hugging Samantha, she felt compelled to return to the study and give Lord Gilchrist a hug as well. He was still seated in his comfortable armchair and looked up with surprise.

"What brought that on?" he asked.

Perseverance shook her head and smiled. "It just seemed like the right thing to do."

"Oh," he said wistfully, "if I were even just thirty years younger..."

Perseverance laughed and went out to see David waiting at the door. Her bags and sword were gone, presumably already loaded. He held the door for her, then delivered her to the Admiralty.

She arrived at Caerleon Station in time for lunch in the officers' mess in the navy section. After a quick sandwich, she checked into the BOQ. As her departure date, she gave them the day of Saint John's arrival. She knew she would rather splurge on a luxurious hotel room.

The days leading up to Saint John's arrival dragged as slowly as the hours after his arrival sped quickly. They did not leave the suite in the hotel often. She shared with him the gory details of what happened on the bridge when *Manitoba* entered the Ilium system. He told her of commanding HMS *Lafayette*, the obsolete cruiser. He tied the point defense systems into the task force network, fired the Cyclops missiles at the enemy, then climbed into the lifepod. He admitted he always thought commanding a Royal Navy cruiser would be more glamorous.

The time came for them to part. She reported aboard and took command of HMS *Simpkin* as ordered. He went to his post on *Deal*.

Waiting for her were orders from Admiral Boyd, sending *Simpkin* to the Aries system. Immediately after dropping her belongings in her quarters, she went to engineering to speak with Commander Choe since the enhancements to the ship affected his area the most. He reported that the new-design nacelles were, as he put it, "a sonofabitch" to tune but no other problems.

When the entire ship's company was aboard, they gathered in the enlisted mess for the ceremony of reading her in as the captain. Perseverance read aloud the orders she was given to take command.

"Proceed to the station where HMS *Simpkin* may be and upon arrival, report to your immediate superior in command, if present, otherwise by message, for duty as commanding officer of HMS *Simpkin*."

Perseverance then addressed the crew with her own message.

"Not long ago, I commanded *Simpkin*'s sister ship, HMS *Rowen*. I considered it an honor and a privilege then, as I consider it an honor and a privilege to stand before you now. *Simpkin*'s recent stay in the yard resulted in some significant enhancements to her armament and her acceleration. She and HMS *Deal* are now the most powerful destroyers and the quickest ships in any navy. I suspect the Admiralty will want us to put those advantages to good use.

"The Royal Navy of the Inter-Planetary Commonwealth has succeeded in weathering a terrible storm in the last year. I predict another tempest is brewing that will prove even more challenging. What we do in the meantime has the chance to perhaps lessen the severity of the gale to come. Let us perform to the best of our ability. May God bless *Simpkin* and her crew and sow confusion amongst our enemies."

Over the next few days, Perseverance worked on getting to know her crew better. She tasked her executive officer, Stackhouse, with running various drills until specific benchmarks were met. The most important, she felt, was the ability of the crew to come to general quarters in ninety seconds or less. They reached that milestone just after emerging into normal space in the Aries system.

Simpkin, like *Rowen*, carried a crew of ninety-three, plus two squads of marines. The marines were led by Gunnery Sergeant Vince Carter. Perseverance set a personal goal to know everyone on the ship by name before reaching Aries.

She nearly achieved it. There were four people who stood in the way—a pair of men and a pair of women where one member of each pair resembled the other. If Perseverance saw them together, she had no difficulty in telling them apart. Seeing them individually, without the other present for comparison, tripped her up several times.

Before they reached Aries Station, Admiral Boyd issued *Simpkin* and *Deal* new orders. They were to leave Aries, proceed to the Hercules system, continue to system H2813, then system H2896, and then enter the Chinese Republics' Múxīng system. Then, depending on what the two ships encountered, Boyd might have them continue to the Republics' Límíng system, where it was believed there was a naval base.

They were to do as much damage as possible, though dropping kinetic weapons on the planet was impermissible. Any "target of opportunity" in space was fair game—orbital stations, orbital industrial nodes, cloud scoops, or shipbuilding facilities. Boyd added one condition—they must broadcast their intent to destroy a facility ahead of time, in order to give civilians at least thirty minutes to evacuate. Boyd encouraged them to seek engagement with any enemy force of equal or lesser strength but to attempt to avoid conflict if outnumbered or outgunned. In the briefing he held with the two captains later, Boyd outlined what the intent was.

"We want the two of you to return safely," he said. "We hope you encounter some opposition so we can see how the ships perform, but we do not want you taking on foolish risks. In addition, any damage you cause to the 'targets of opportunity' will make things more expensive for the Republics. If you cause a few billion pounds worth of damage but don't see any enemy ships, the mission is still successful. Is that understood?"

Both captains acknowledged his instruction. They set their course for the Hercules system. Though Hercules held no inhabitable planets, it was a "named" system for the same reason Automedon was. The Commonwealth eventually hoped to build a station in Hercules that, in times of peace, would serve as a freight waypoint for trade between the Commonwealth, the Republics, and the Federation. Obviously, those plans would not come to fruition in the near future.

It would take twelve and a half days to reach Múxīng. One of the reasons it would take so long is the hyper corridor between Hercules and H2813. Their time in hyperspace would be just over three days between the two systems. It was one of the longest hyper corridors in mapped space.

Perseverance was pleased the Commonwealth was trying to take the war into enemy space, even though this was a limited effort. Will Dallas was even more eager. In the initial attacks of the war, he was serving as Hank Boyd's executive officer. Theirs was the one border unit that was not attacked. He did not take part in the recapture of Southampton or Ilium, so this would be his first action.

Perseverance was in daily contact with Saint John. He was enjoying his role as Dallas' second in command. Saint John admitted he was happier being back on a ship. He had needed a break after what happened under LeFerrier but claimed the only good thing to come from his months with the Office of Public Affairs was meeting Perseverance. She chided him for being a soppy romantic but admitted to herself later that she liked hearing it.

Along their journey, they did not see any ships in the intermediate systems. Perseverance had wondered whether there would be a patrol boat in system

H2896 as a picket, positioned to warn the Chinese navy of an enemy's approach. There was nothing.

As the senior captain, Perseverance was in command of the two-ship force. She instructed Dallas on *Deal* to exit the hyper corridor three light-minutes short of the terminus. If the Chinese positioned ships at the terminus, this early entrance into the Múxīng system would give *Simpkin* and *Deal* a few minutes to prepare.

Christmas arrived while they were in transit. Perseverance wore a Santa hat and helped serve the holiday dinner in the enlisted mess. The crew seemed to appreciate it. By prior agreement, she and Saint John did not exchange presents. Instead, they decided they would make up for it on each other's next birthday.

Just under six minutes after they emerged into normal space, radar returns indicated a minefield at the corridor terminus. Equipped with plasma shielding, the Commonwealth ships were unconcerned. The ship's computer took a "snapshot" upon arrival in the system, then analyzed what it could "see." The light the computer analyzed could be hours or even days old, depending on how far away an object was.

The computer analysis indicated there were two destroyers of the shielded type and one of the older, unshielded models. This was confirmed a few hours later when the radar returns arrived. The computer did not "see" any other ships in the system.

Immediately upon receiving the initial analysis, Dallas contacted Perseverance. "C'mon! We can take 'em!" he urged.

"I feel the same way," she replied, "but I need to call it in. We have to make sure Hank agrees with us."

Perseverance sent the computer analysis of the three enemy ships to Rear Admiral Boyd. "Captain Dallas and I believe this constitutes a force of equal or lesser strength," she stated. "Your orders?"

Moments later, she received a one-word reply: "Proceed." She transmitted the intercept course to Dallas, instructing him to maintain his current speed. The two ships moved in unison toward their targets. Currently traveling at 0.23*c*, or twenty-three percent of lightspeed, it would take just over eleven hours to reach the Chinese ships if they remained stationary.

THE DEFENSE OF THE COMMONWEALTH

Perseverance reckoned they would come out to meet her or try to escape. With the Chinese at a dead stop and *Deal* and *Simpkin* already approaching rapidly, the Chinese ships had no chance of running away. The Commonwealth ships would intercept them before they reached the nearest hyper corridor.

Commander Stackhouse reported additional findings from the computer's analysis. "There are two cloud scoops working on the gas giant, an orbital station, and five orbital industrial nodes of decent size."

"Shoot it over to the admiral to let him know what we plan to do after we take care of these ships," Perseverance asked.

Even if the Chinese ships turned to approach them, it would still be hours before they reached range. Perseverance asked Commander Stackhouse to meet her in her small office. She then turned the bridge over to Lieutenant Austin, ordering the lieutenant to adjust the "time to engagement" estimate as more data arrived and to contact her immediately if anything changed.

When they reached Perseverance's small office outside her quarters, she said, "Grab a seat, Dave."

When he did, she continued. "Take a look at the watch schedule and check it against the 'time to engagement' estimates. If there is anyone in the watch rotation when we think the hammer will drop that you would prefer *not* to have on the bridge, let's make some changes. It would be better to substitute an entire watch than single out one person. If there were more time, I would ask you to finagle things so our best people are on the bridge. I reckon we have less than nine hours, so that would be too disruptive."

Stackhouse checked the watch rosters. "I'm comfortable with who will be in the seats, skipper," he said after finishing his review. "There are only two people whom I would consider as 'weak links.' I just drew up the cross-training schedule and haven't submitted it to you yet. It might be that those two are a better fit in a different area. It's too early to write anyone off."

"I agree," Perseverance stated. "When you get the cross-training program up to full speed, make sure you include the engineering officers."

"Already done," he replied. "My best friend in the service started in engineering and switched to command track as a result of cross-training on his first posting."

33

After her conversation with Stackhouse, Perseverance returned to the bridge. The "time to engagement" estimate now showed eight hours and thirty-four minutes. She checked on the current course and speed of the Chinese destroyers.

"They're awfully slow," Lieutenant Austin commented.

"They are," Perseverance confirmed. "Right now, the Commonwealth has two significant advantages over the Republics and the Federation. Do you know what they are, lieutenant?"

Austin shook her head.

"Our interface at the reactor bubble boundary is much more efficient than the Chinese or the Rodinans'. We were already ahead of them but just came up with another wrinkle that increases our advantage. That's one of the upgrades they made to *Simpkin*. We also have an edge in the metallurgic composition of electrical conduits, and that, too, was recently improved. *Simpkin* and *Deal* had all their main conduits replaced," Perseverance explained. "What does that mean?"

"I'm not sure, sir," Austin replied. "I'm not in engineering."

"Neither am I, lieutenant, but I learned to understand enough about it to make myself a more effective officer. You'll have the chance to do the same when we start cross-training between different stations and disciplines," Perseverance said. "Getting back to our discussion… It means that we get more usable power from our reactors and deliver more of it to where it's put to use. It's one of the reasons their ships are sluggish."

"I didn't know that, sir," Austin said. "I spent my first two years in BuPers before requesting transfer to a ship. We didn't do any cross-training in the two postings I had before this."

"That's not your fault then," Perseverance said. "We will begin soon. Take advantage of it. You'll become a more well-rounded officer."

"I will, sir. Thank you, sir."

Perseverance left the bridge. As she did, she heard seven bells chime in the forenoon watch. That meant it was getting close to noon, and she was feeling hungry. With action pending, she decided to find lunch in the enlisted mess. Once she was served some food, she found a table. Henry Allen, the COB, brought his tray over immediately and joined her.

Allen was tall and lanky. He looked almost too young to be a senior chief petty officer. The thinning of his blond hair was the one telltale that put the lie to his youthful appearance.

"Hi, skipper," he said. "Mind if I join you?"

"Happy to have you, COB," she replied. "How are things?"

"Finest kind, skipper. Finest kind," he said.

"That's one I haven't heard before," Perseverance admitted.

"Huh," he grunted. "It's a pretty common saying where I grew up on New Boston. You're from Alleghany, right?"

"I am," she replied. "So, when you say, 'finest kind,' does that mean things are going well?"

"It does," he said. "Folks have settled in. Not many shitbirds. I think we're on our way to having a happy ship."

"I'm really pleased to hear that," she said.

"The rumor mill says we'll be seeing action tonight," he said. "Is that why you're here—in the enlisted mess?"

"Partly," Perseverance confessed. "I'll probably do some wandering around after this. Is that a problem?"

"No, ma'am. I kind of had the sense you were the type of skipper who does that," he said. "Mind if I tag along?"

"Not at all. It will help me to get to know you better. Plus, if we see Miller or Martinelli, or DiPasquale or Scalise without the other, you can help prevent me from screwing up their names."

"No problem, skipper," Allen said.

After they finished eating and disposed of their trays, they set off. One thing Perseverance learned about Allen was his passion for the sport of rugby. Right about the time interstellar travel became a reality, American-style football ended as a sport on earth. Athletes became too big, too fast, and too strong, and the protective gear they wore became more of a weapon than a defense against injury.

When the American-settled planets joined the Commonwealth, they were reintroduced to the sport of rugby. The new members of the Commonwealth embraced rugby passionately. Most of the star players and the most powerful teams now came from non-British planets. Allen was a fanatic supporter of the team based closest to where he was raised, Gloucester. Their success over the years was mixed, but that in no way diminished Allen's enthusiasm.

After a few pleasant hours of seeing and being seen, Perseverance returned to her quarters. There was always paperwork to do. She thought about talking with Saint John, but after checking the watch rotation he shared with her, she knew he was on the bridge. She kept an eye on the course plots and the clock.

At 17:00, she thought about eating dinner but decided against it. She was full of nervous energy and not hungry. She knew she would be starving later, but she would worry about it then.

When the "time to engagement" counter reached thirty minutes, she put on her shipsuit and helmet and headed to the bridge. One other member of the bridge crew was dressed as Perseverance was. The others were leaving one by one to do the same.

At the current closing speed, there would be a gap of around sixty seconds from when they reached missile range until they were in cannon range. During that time, neither side could fire more than their initial salvo of missiles. The two Commonwealth destroyers would fire eight Cyclops missiles. The Chinese would fire at least eight of their laser-tipped missiles. If the unshielded destroyer was equipped with them, the number would be twelve.

The point defense net for the Commonwealth ships would be able to counter eight missiles, but if the Chinese fired twelve, some might survive to unleash their blasts on *Deal* and *Simpkin*. Perseverance was calm and appeared unworried. *Rowen* survived an initial salvo of five missiles in the battle in Aries.

Knowing that they would reach cannon range well before the enemy could launch another missile salvo had Perseverance almost licking her chops. She wanted to see what kind of damage the new 90mm cannons would inflict on the enemy. She doubted whether any of the enemy's ships would survive to launch a second salvo.

They reached missile range. *Deal* and *Simpkin* launched four missiles each. The Chinese launched twelve. Perseverance looked on her command console. The estimated time to missile detonation was seventy seconds and counting down. The estimated time to cannon range was fifty-seven seconds.

As the two groups of ships drew nearer, Perseverance switched her console to watch the missile tracks. Before seeing whether any of the Royal Navy's missiles would reach the Chinese, or how many of the Chinese missiles would survive to attack *Deal* and *Simpkin*, they reached cannon range.

In the thirteen seconds between coming within range and the detonation of any of the missiles, the Royal Navy's 90mm photon cannons, four on each ship, were able to fire six times. Then the missiles, both Chinese and Commonwealth, reached detonation range. Only one Cyclops missile survived to attack one of the shielded Chinese destroyers. Three Chinese missiles unleashed their deadly lasers. Two hit *Simpkin*, one hit *Deal*.

The Chinese missiles caused sections of the plasma shielding to fail but did not penetrate the hull of either ship. The one Commonwealth missile stabbed into the hull of the shielded Chinese ship it attacked. The photon cannons already caused shield failure on that section, allowing the x-ray to penetrate deep inside.

Meanwhile, the photon cannons continued to fire. Seconds after the missiles detonated, the last sections of plasma shielding failed on both of the new Chinese destroyers. Now the cannons began to rip holes in their hulls. One of *Deal*'s shots hit the mass compensator on the ship she was targeting. In an instant, the mass increased exponentially, causing the ship to collapse in on itself. One of *Simpkin*'s cannons reached the reactors of her initial target. Freed from containment, the fusion reaction bloomed out of control, consuming the ship in a nuclear fireball.

Both *Deal* and *Simpkin* then began to fire upon the unshielded Chinese destroyer. In less than ten seconds, the sections of the ship began to fly off into space under the battering of the Royal Navy's cannons. "Cease fire," Perseverance ordered. "Sensors, scan for signs of life. Prepare search and rescue teams."

"Not picking anything up, skipper," the petty officer at the sensors station reported.

"Keep looking. Damage control—report," she requested.

"Skipper, we show four failed shield generators," Commander Stackhouse replied.

"Still no life signs, skipper," sensors called out.

"Very well. Search and rescue, stand down. Astrogation, set course for Múxīng-3," Perseverance directed.

Perseverance then stabbed the comm button to connect with the captain of HMS *Deal*. His helmeted face appeared immediately. He wore a broad smile.

"Having fun, Will?" she asked.

"You bet," he replied. "You want us to take out the cloud scoops?"

"Please. Then wait for instructions," she said. "Admiral Boyd may have us continue."

Perseverance ordered the ship to stand down from general quarters. She went to her quarters and stripped off her helmet and shipsuit. With the shipsuit off, she noticed she smelled a bit ripe. She decided to take a quick shower and put on a clean uniform.

While she was doing this, she was processing her thoughts about the engagement just ended. Part of her was quite satisfied and well-pleased with the outcome. Her conscience, though, was troubled by the lopsided nature of it. Almost as soon as she thought that, she chastised herself. *Do you think the Chinese or the Rodinans were concerned about the "fairness" of what happened when they attacked Southampton or Ilium?*

She wrote her after-action report. The dry, impersonal "Navy Standard" language used in reports like these was unable to communicate concepts of "fairness." The rule was to report the facts without embellishment. Editorial comments and points of view were unsatisfactory.

Only an hour after Perseverance filed her report, Admiral Boyd sent her orders to proceed to H2813 after eliminating the assigned targets. She relayed those instructions to Will Dallas.

"We'll slow in H2896, to give you a chance to join us," he replied.

Perseverance discussed her misgivings about the recent encounter with Saint John the next time they spoke. "I applaud you for having a conscience," he said. "But you're also right to wonder how much it bothered them when they wiped us out in Southampton and Ilium. I think we both know the answer to that."

"Yeah, but you know me," she said. "It's more fun to win a fair fight."

"Understood," he replied. "That's not in the job description, though. In fact, our bosses would prefer as many encounters as possible are skewed in our favor."

Simpkin approached Múxīng-3. Within hours, the burned-out shield generators were replaced. Halfway to the planet, Perseverance ordered reverse thrust to slow their progress. When the ship was still hours away from cannon range, she started to broadcast a message. She informed the Chinese that *Simpkin* would be destroying the orbital station and industrial nodes, and everyone aboard should evacuate for his own safety. *There's your "fairness,"* she thought.

When *Simpkin* reached cannon range, the 90mm guns fired. Perseverance ordered gunnery to cease fire after less than a minute. "What's left of them, sensors?" she asked.

"Debris," was the answer.

"Astrogation, swing us around Múxīng-3, and let's head for the exit," she requested.

"Aye, aye, skipper," came the acknowledgment.

In the middle of her next sleep period, Perseverance's console woke her with an alert. She rolled out of bed quickly. Standing over her desk, she read the message.

"Gravimetric sensors indicate two Chinese light cruisers just entered the Múxīng system," it stated.

Gravimetric sensors were not subject to light-speed lag. Within their range, they would detect the entrance of ships into normal space from hyperspace or their exit from normal space. Gravimetric sensors could report the number of objects and their mass. They did not measure course, speed, or position.

"Steady as she goes," Perseverance replied, then returned to her bunk. The new arrivals could not possibly intercept her ship. Admiral Boyd guessed correctly by having them return rather than press on.

The next day *Simpkin* entered H2896. A message was waiting for Perseverance when the ship returned to normal space. It came from Admiral Boyd. *Simpkin* was to form up with *Deal* in H2813 and proceed to the Federation Venera system. Once there, they would seek targets of opportunity as before. The same restriction regarding a force of equal or lesser strength was in effect. HMS *Deal* was traveling through H2896 at 0.12c to allow *Simpkin* to catch up. Will Dallas immediately contacted Perseverance.

"We do the same thing in Venera?" he asked.

"Yes. I have to wonder if we'll run into a bigger welcoming party there," she said. "We'll see how closely these two *allies* communicate."

"Plenty of time to worry about that later," Dallas said. "You should reach us tomorrow. See you then."

34

As Dallas predicted, the two ships met up the next day. In tandem, they headed to H2813 and then neared the hyper corridor leading to the Federation Venera system. As they did when entering the Múxīng system, they would exit three light-minutes short of the terminus.

Entering the Venera system, nothing was waiting for them at the terminus of the corridor. Further in the system, however, computer analysis of the "snapshot" available when they entered showed something disturbing. Two Rodinan light cruisers equipped with shields seemed to be heading for *Deal* and *Simpkin*. Later "snapshots" taken confirmed this and provided an estimate of their speed. The cruisers were traveling at $0.28c$.

It would be nearly two whole days before radar returns came back from that deep in the system. That time lag would drop sharply as the two pairs of ships drew nearer. The same handicap affected the Rodinans as well, but the gravimetric sensors on their orbital station would have alerted them to the arrival of the two Commonwealth ships. While the Rodinan ships were probably originally heading to the corridor as a protective measure, now they had a different mission. Commander Stackhouse fed the data from the "snapshots" into the astrogation system, and Perseverance knew the result from his frown before he spoke.

"They'll catch us, skipper," he reported. "Unless we go to max boost right now and stay on it for at least twenty-four hours. From what I read of the new nacelles, I would counsel against that."

"Agreed."

Perseverance contacted Dallas. "Will, you see the same thing we do. What do you think?"

"Shit, Perse," he said, "same as last time. We can take 'em."

She laughed. "That's my gut feeling, too. I need to call it in, though. For now, reverse thrust at normal maximum. That buys us a little bit of time and, when we engage, will give the cannons a few seconds longer in range," she said.

Perseverance went to her office and quickly wrote a report documenting the situation and the orders she gave to slow their progress. She ended by stating that she and Captain Dallas shared a high degree of confidence, even though the approaching ships did not match the "equal or lesser strength" criterion. She sent the report to Admiral Boyd, then turned her attention back to the astrogation model built from the "snapshots" and her current rate of deceleration.

The more she studied the course plots, the more she liked what she saw. The initial encounter between the two pairs of ships would be relatively brief. The rate of closure between them meant only one salvo of missiles could be fired before they pulled out of range. The Royal Navy's photon cannons would also have a brief window of opportunity—they would be in cannon range for less than eight seconds.

Her console chimed, indicating a message from the Admiralty. Admiral Boyd requested a conference with the two captains at 11:00, only seventeen minutes away. Perseverance acknowledged and began to organize her thoughts in preparation. A new wrinkle occurred to her that posed a potential problem.

At 11:00 precisely, her console lit up with the conference request. She keyed the access code in. Admiral Boyd and Captain Dallas were already present.

Without preamble, Boyd asked, "Tell me what you're thinking, Perse."

She sent them both the file containing the astrographic plot she studied. "From what we can see, they're coming to engage," she said. "We have no way to avoid an encounter. We would have needed to engage max boost almost immediately after we entered the system and stay on it for twenty-four hours or more. From the documentation on the new nacelles, that did not seem to be an attractive alternative, not to mention the strain it would put on the crews. That makes engagement unavoidable."

"Do you agree with her assessment, Will?" Boyd asked.

"One hundred percent," he replied.

"Fine. Continue."

"With engagement unavoidable, our intention is to shape the terms of the action to our benefit as much as possible. For this reason, I ordered reverse thrust at normal maximum. This extends by a few seconds the amount of time we will be in cannon range but does not allow either party to fire a second missile salvo. The two Rodinan light cruisers have six missile tubes each, so their salvo is an even dozen. We faced that in Múxīng. As you know from my report, we suffered some shield failures but no hull damage. I do not anticipate significantly worse results in this situation," Perseverance said.

"Plus, we replaced all the burned-out shield generators within two hours," Dallas added.

"After the initial encounter, we would continue to pursue 'targets of opportunity,' currently the orbital station and three industrial nodes. After swinging around the system primary, we would head for the corridor leading to H2813. Here is where variables come into account."

"What variables?" Boyd asked.

"We don't know yet, but should soon, whether the Rodinans are decelerating and if they are, at what rate. If they are, at their normal maximum, that might extend the opening encounter by a few seconds—good for us, bad for them. My analysis shows that they will need to decelerate in order to engage us as we attempt to exit the system because their ships are so sluggish. If they don't, they will be past the corridor terminus when we reach it. My question for you, Hank, is whether you want us to travel past the corridor entrance to finish them off or simply leave the system? For that matter, if we disable one or both of them, do we respond to a call for assistance, knowing it will possibly delay us in the system long enough that Rodinan reinforcements arrive?"

"Hadn't thought about that," Dallas admitted.

"Crap," Boyd muttered. "I need to kick this up the ladder. You don't need an answer immediately, which is good since I don't think I'll have one. For now, plan on destroying the identified targets after your initial encounter. We should know by the time you're on your way back to the corridor. Good luck and Godspeed."

"You should be careful what you wish for, Persie," Saint John teased her when they spoke that evening.

"What do you mean?"

"You wanted a battle that was more fair. You got it," he said.

"Eh. I don't know how much more fair it is," she replied. "In a lot of ways, it's just like the last one."

"We're facing two light cruisers this time," he said. "That has to count."

"But the number of missiles we'll face is the same," she countered. "And I think our ships are that much better than theirs. It just doesn't—"

"Perse, maybe you've become an adrenalin junkie," he said.

"A what?"

"An adrenalin junkie. Someone who craves the feeling you get when you're in serious danger," he explained.

Seeing her lack of understanding, he continued. "Are you comparing everything to the opening attack in Aries?"

Saint John's remark caused Perseverance to pull back from the screen, her mouth open. She was silent while she considered it. "Maybe?" she said uncertainly.

"I'm not going to lecture you because I'm sure you can figure out what a bad idea it would be to continue to seek situations like that one," he said. "You know it's a miracle you survived. I don't want you dead—I much prefer you alive. Plus, I already went through losing someone I loved and don't want to do that again. There is already enough risk that goes along with what we do. We don't need to augment it."

Perseverance sat in silence, pondering what he said and comparing it to what she'd been feeling.

"Still with me?" Saint John asked after a couple of minutes of silence.

"Um, yeah. Let me think about this," she said as she closed the connection.

The abrupt end to the call bothered Saint John only slightly. By now, he knew her well enough to understand he might have helped her identify what was really bugging her. Perseverance liked to dive deep within herself in these types of circumstances. She would reemerge when she either figured it out to her satisfaction or realized she required outside perspective.

Commander Choe confirmed he could reduce the cycle time on the photon cannons by a half-second. The bad news was that it would require someone to access the gun turrets from outside the ship. Perseverance ordered him to make the change and requested they do the same on *Deal.*

The Rodinan ships were now close enough that the visual observations confirmed they were decelerating. From the measurements, they were now at thrust of five hundred g. The analysis showed it took the Rodinan ships more than three hours to reach that level. Compared to the less than seventeen minutes *Simpkin* or *Deal* required, that made the Federation ships incredibly ponderous in comparison.

Commander Stackhouse juggled the watch schedule only slightly to ensure there were solid people at every bridge station when they would engage the Rodinans. He confirmed to Perseverance that the cross-training program was paying dividends, resulting in some changes in assignments.

With less than two hours until *Simpkin* was in missile range of the enemy, Perseverance obeyed the rumbling in her stomach and headed to the enlisted mess for lunch. Henry Allen saw her in the service line and sought her out once his tray was loaded. He took the seat opposite her.

"Skipper, I have to say I like your style," he commented. "Some COs never eat in the enlisted mess. Some show up when it's a special occasion. On the other hand, you probably eat here as much as you do in the officers' mess. It's one of the things that makes this a happy ship. There's no sense of 'us' versus 'them' aboard. It's not just you eating with us—it's other things too."

"Like?"

"Like you know everyone by name, even Miller, Martinelli, DiPasquale, and Scalise now. Like the watch rosters for the bridge crew," Allen said. "All three watches are a mix of officers and non-comms. Most ships, they put all the non-comms on the same watch and give them graveyard. You don't seem to care as much about rank as you do about performance."

"I was lucky to have good examples to follow when I was starting out," she replied. "The officers on my first posting did it, so it's seemed like the right way ever since."

"Are you going on another walkabout today, skipper?"

Perseverance smiled at his term for it. "Not today," she answered. "Not enough time. But I'll do one soon when there's nothing exciting coming."

After she ate, she did wander just a little bit on her way back to her quarters. She didn't have an agenda, just wanted to show her face. When she reached her cabin, she put on her shipsuit and helmet, then headed to the bridge.

As the counter marking "time to engagement" ticked down, other members of the bridge crew went to put on their shipsuits and helmets. With ten minutes remaining, everyone was strapped in and ready. The Rodinan ships were still decelerating.

"Dave," Persverance called to Commander Stackhouse, "adjust course to nudge us closer. If they're going to give us a shot right up their skirts, it would be impolite to refuse."

"Aye, aye, skipper," he confirmed amid the chuckles from the others.

The two pairs of ships reached missile range and launched their salvos. The missiles erupted from their tubes and set off after their targets. All four ships began electronic countermeasures and started throwing out clouds of reflective chaff and heat flares to lure the missiles away from their true targets. As the missiles drew closer, point defense lasers and railguns commenced firing, trying to destroy or damage the missiles before they detonated.

Simpkin and *Deal* reached the point where their photon cannons were in range of the enemy. Perseverance's initial estimate of eight seconds on target was now stretched to nine because of the Rodinans' deceleration. Each Royal Navy cannon would discharge six shots. That had been enough in Múxīng to destroy the enemy.

Here in Venera, the Royal Navy cannons were as successful. On one Rodinan ship, a cannon blast hit the inertial compensator. When that happened, everyone inside the ship was instantly subject to a force five hundred times normal earth gravity. They died in a blink—their bodies transformed into strawberry-colored paste. The other ship was less damaged, except for her EM drives. Commander Stackhouse on *Simpkin* reviewed the data later and guaranteed that the Rodinan's drives were obliterated. The ship continued on a ballistic course at 0.13c, heading into deep space.

None of the Cyclops missiles reached the enemy. Three of the eight were fooled into pursuing false targets. The other five were eliminated before reaching their detonation points.

The Royal Navy defenses had similar results. Two of the Rodinan missiles were lured away, and six were destroyed. That left four that detonated, unleashing their deadly x-ray lasers. Three were aimed at *Deal*, only one at *Simpkin*.

Perseverance saw that two shield generators were overloaded and failed on *Simpkin*. Captain Dallas reported *Deal* lost seven shield generators and suffered a minor hull breach. Three members of his crew were missing and presumed dead, sucked into the vacuum of space through a hole too small for a human to fit.

Perseverance ordered both ships to accelerate and head for their targets further in the system. She instructed Commander Choe to reset the guns to the normal cycle time and replace the burned-out shield generators. After she did, the petty officer at the comms station reported the surviving Rodinans were requesting assistance. Perseverance asked him to record the message and send her the file. When she received it, she forwarded it to Admiral Boyd, asking for instructions.

It would take *Deal* and *Simpkin* over fifty-six hours to return to their current position after slinging themselves around the star at the center of the system. It would take another fifteen hours to reach the drifting Rodinans, well beyond the normal hyper corridor terminus.

35

It took nearly forty hours for Admiral Boyd to respond. Apparently, the question of what to do reached the highest levels of the government. They finally decided to offer assistance to the Rodinans.

"I understand back in earth's past, there were rules of warfare that nearly every country agreed to uphold," Boyd explained. "That's not the case now. It's something the diplomats will need to address once this war is over. For now, we'll take the high road and help them. According to the message, they have eighty-one survivors."

"Only eighty-one?" Captain Dallas asked.

"That's what they said," Boyd answered. "The photographic data you sent us from the encounter indicates that a couple of the shots *Simpkin* fired into her stern went really deep into the hull. Anyway, Will, you're coming straight back. Your hull breach needs attention, and I'm transmitting orders for you to head to Lincoln. They've just reactivated the shipyard facilities there and will repair your ship. Perse, that means you get to rescue the prisoners."

"Got it. One question, though—where the hell am I going to put them?" she inquired

"Aha!" Boyd responded. "I have an answer for that. Enlisted in the enlisted mess, officers in the officers' mess. You and your crew will need to eat standing up until you reach Aries. We will have a transport there to meet you. Use your fabricator to churn out sleeping pallets."

"What about food?" she asked.

"Will, other than what you need to sustain your folks on the way to Lincoln, send over to *Simpkin*. If that's not enough, you should have enough emergency ration bars," Boyd said.

"Rat bars? Wouldn't that be considered cruel and unusual punishment?" Dallas cracked.

"Like I said, there aren't any rules," Boyd stated. "Their basic nutritional needs will be met."

Both Perseverance and Dallas groaned. In basic training, they were forced to eat ration bars for a day. She never understood what the point of it was other than to torture them. Ration bars had the consistency of sawdust held together by glue and tasted even worse.

Boyd transmitted their new orders. Perseverance ordered *Simpkin* on an intercept course with the drifting Rodinan light cruiser. *Deal* headed for the hyper corridor at 0.23*c*.

Before *Deal* entered hyperspace, she had a conversation with Saint John. "I think you were right," she admitted. "I was comparing things to Aries. Ilium would have been a better match, but we didn't get to do anything there. Plus, I got kicked off the bridge. Anyway, what you said, helped. Thanks."

"I'm not a psychologist, but I will admit I'm fascinated with you," he said and grinned.

"You know, it's not fair when you do that," she complained.

"Do what?" he asked with mock innocence.

"Flash that skirt-lifting grin at me."

"You called it 'panty-dropping' the last time," he said.

"No, I told you that was what my sister would call it. I have a much more diverse vocabulary. And don't pretend you don't know how it affects me!"

"I miss you and love you too, Persie."

She shook her head, acknowledging defeat in this round. "Same," she replied.

After *Deal* entered hyperspace, Perseverance recorded a message that was broadcast to the Rodinans on a loop. The message informed them that help was on the way and gave them an estimate of when they could begin transferring the Rodinans aboard *Simpkin*. The necessity of slowing to the speed of the drifting light cruiser added a few hours to Perseverance's original estimate of fifteen. It now looked like twenty-one.

The next day, *Simpkin* was easing closer to the Rodinan ship. They just passed the seventy-thousand-kilometer mark, on their way to pulling up within tens of meters to make the transfer easier. The recording being broadcast was changed to inform the Rodinans to wear their shipsuits and prepare to exit their ship and travel to *Simpkin* using a tether line. Gunnery Sergeant Vince Carter and three of his marines were stationed at the main hatch and airlock. The other marines were already in either the enlisted mess or officers' mess.

Commander Stackhouse shouted, "Fuck! Skipper, they just launched!"

"Shit!" Perseverance blurted. "Strap in! General quarters!"

None of the navy personnel aboard *Simpkin* were wearing shipsuits and helmets. The marines were safe since they were clad in combat armor, primarily to look as intimidating as possible to the boarding Rodinans. The distance between the two ships was so short that it took only two seconds for the missiles to reach their detonation range. Other than her shields, *Simpkin* had no way to defend herself.

All six missiles unleashed their deadly lasers. Four of the lasers were expended in overloading shield generators. Two of them took advantage of the shield failure and tore deep into the hull. One, ironically, reached the enlisted mess where the Rodinan prisoners would be housed. The other penetrated to the bridge, exposing it to the vacuum of space. If *Simpkin* were an ill-disciplined and sloppy ship, those hull breaches might have been a disaster. As it was, hatches were properly shut and sealed. Only the two compartments were affected.

Perseverance saw Lieutenant Austin and Petty Officer Greene disappear. They had not buckled harnesses in time, and they were sucked out of the ship. As the air was sucked out of her lungs, Perseverance tried to remember how she left it with Saint John. "Same," was what she'd said. *I'll need to do better next time*, she thought, *if there is one. Otherwise, he'll be pretty pissed off at me.*

Gunnery Sergeant Carter knew something was seriously wrong. He accessed *Simpkin's* communications network using eye movements with the display on the interior of his face shield, tracked by receptors in his helmet. He found Damage Control and accessed it.

"Damage Control, Gunny here," he barked. "What just happened?"

"Missile attack, two hull breaches. Enlisted mess and bridge."

Carter and his men were closest to the bridge. The marines he stationed in the enlisted mess were beyond his help. They were in combat armor. If you have to experience a hull breach, there was nothing better to protect yourself. If it didn't protect them, they were already dead. The bridge was closer anyway.

"On me," he ordered the three marines with him. "To the bridge."

The four needed to go up one level to reach the companionway leading to the bridge. There would be three hatches they would need to open. The four marines moved quickly but not hurriedly. Their actions were smooth and practiced. Watching them, an onlooker might think it was only a drill.

When they reached the ladder to go up a level, there was no need to climb. The power assist in their combat armor enabled them to leap to the next deck. Without needing to order it, the last marine to enter the section of the companionway connecting to the bridge shut and dogged the hatch. Carter went to the hatch that opened to the bridge. He smacked the red button above it with his gloved hand. The atmosphere in their section of the companionway vented into space. Carter then opened the hatch and entered the bridge.

Four unconscious bodies were there, strapped in at their stations. Carter unbuckled Perseverance from the command chair and lifted her. The other marines each took one of the others, then exited the bridge. Once the hatch was shut and secured again, Carter hit the green button next to the red one he used earlier. Atmosphere flooded back into the companionway.

Carter was already moving. He reached the hatch that would eventually lead him to the sick bay. When the indicator light showed the return of atmosphere, he spun the dogging wheel and opened the hatch, still carrying Perseverance's limp form. He informed the sickbay he was on the way with four members of the crew who were exposed to vacuum. There were three more hatches, and they needed to drop two decks to reach the sick bay. They jumped down at the ladders, their armor cushioning the landing.

When they reached the sick bay, the medical corpsman was ready. The ship's four medical stasis pods were open and waiting, nearly filling the small space completely. Each of the marines deposited his burden in a pod. Squeezing his way around the medpods, the corpsman then placed a mask over the face of each patient. He then shut the pod and activated it. The pods would analyze what its occupant needed. If it detected no pulse or respiration, it would stimulate the heart and begin breathing for the patient.

As soon as the pod registered a pulse, needles extended and injected into the patient a cocktail of drugs that would induce a medical coma. One by one, the display on the lid of the pod showed a large green light. The only one not to light green was Perseverance's. An arm with a needle extended over her chest, then drove the needle down.

"What the hell was that?" Carter asked.

"Adrenalin, I think," the corpsman answered.

"You think?"

"Look, gunny, I'm not a doc. I just know how to run the machines," the corpsman replied, shrugging his shoulders. "I hope you don't have more. There's only the four of these."

Commander Choe was in engineering when the Rodinan missiles shot their lasers. It took him a handful of seconds to realize what had happened. He tried reaching the captain, then the XO, both without success. Then he saw a damage notification flashing, stating the bridge and enlisted mess were in vacuum, and realized why neither responded.

"Any of you cross-trained on gunnery?" he shouted.

"I am, sir," squeaked a voice.

Choe looked over to see who it was. Ensign Lee held her hand in the air. Lee was tiny, only a little over a hundred and fifty centimeters tall, and she probably weighed less than forty-five kilos.

"Ensign, you need to blow those Rodinan assholes into tiny pieces," he barked. "Got it?"

"Yes, sir," she replied in her high-pitched voice. "Tiny pieces."

It took her a few seconds to remember how to access the gunnery interface. Once the correct screen came up, she knew what to do. She highlighted the only target shown on the screen, pressed the "fire" key, and then activated the "automatic" feature.

Within seconds, the shields on the Rodinan ship were stripped away. *Simpkin*'s photon cannons raked up and down the Rodinan's hull. Chunks of the ship began to fly away as the cannons continued to fire. Choe watched as Ensign Lee destroyed the Rodinan ship. Eventually, he told her to cease fire.

"Well done, ensign. Thank you," he said.

"What happened, sir? I thought we were going to rescue them?" she asked.

"I thought so too. Someone over there disagreed with the plan and fired on us. They hit the bridge. That's all I know right now," he said.

Choe reversed *Simpkin's* course to return back to the hyper corridor entrance. Looking over the damage control reports, he saw five of the Alcubierre field generators were damaged. He ordered a work party to replace them. *Simpkin* needed to wrap itself completely in an Alcubierre field in order to shift into hyperspace.

That done, he checked the casualty report. Lieutenant Austin, Petty Officer Greene, and twelve marines were missing, presumed dead. The combat armor of the missing marines ceased to function at the time of the hull breach in the enlisted mess where they were stationed. There were a number of minor injuries, plus Captain Andrews, Commander Stackhouse, Lieutenant Herring, and Petty Officer Roscoe were listed as being in serious condition. Choe contacted the sick bay for an update.

"Sir," the corpsman responded, "I'm just a cuts and scrapes kind of guy— maybe a broken bone if it's a clean break. Past that, I'm in over my head. These medpods are supposed to be connected to the Royal Navy Medical Center on Caerleon through the kewpie. They're the ones actually monitoring them."

"Can you at least tell me if all four people are still alive?" Choe asked.

"As far as I can tell," the corpsman replied. "None of 'em look too good, though."

"Commander Choe? Hank Boyd," Admiral Boyd said when Choe appeared on screen an hour later. "I just received a flash from the Royal Navy Medical Center with a medical analysis of Captain Andrews and three others. What the hell is going on?"

"Sir, I just started writing an after-action report. I've had my hands full," Choe explained.

"What happened, commander?"

"We were easing into position to take the Rodinans aboard when they launched missiles, sir. We suffered two hull breaches—the bridge and the enlisted mess. On the bridge, no one was wearing a shipsuit. Two members of the bridge crew were not buckled in when the bridge was exposed. They are missing, presumed dead. Gunnery Sergeant Carter and three marines were stationed at the main hatch airlock to meet the prisoners. They immediately headed to the bridge and rescued the four survivors. The survivors are currently in medpods in sick bay. The corpsman knows how to activate the pods, but that's about it. He said the Royal Navy Medical Center monitors and controls them over the kewpie. We are in the process of replacing Alcubierre field generators and on the way to the hyper corridor."

"The sonsabitches launched on us?" Boyd exclaimed. "At what range?"

Choe checked his notes. "Sixty-four thousand kilometers, sir. Give or take."

"Then what?" Boyd asked.

"We destroyed their ship, sir. Completely."

"Prior to their launch, did we receive any communication from them?" Boyd inquired.

"Sir, I must admit I have not checked comm logs yet," Choe said. "From the way we were approaching, I would assume they acknowledged our offer of assistance. I will check to make certain. Sorry, sir."

"Commander, I can only imagine how crazy things have been for you," Boyd said. "Check the comm logs and add that in on the after-action report. I'm going to have my people pull your sensor data and go over it as well. Get the hell out of there and head back to Caerleon. It's nearly as close as any other system, and the medical care here is the best. I don't think the extra day or two in transit will matter as much as what happened on arrival."

Commander Choe opened the comm logs and scrolled through them until he found what he was looking for. Over twenty-four hours before, Captain Andrews had insisted that any assistance was contingent on the Rodinans surrender. The Rodinan captain confirmed their surrender.

There were broadcast messages sent after the missile launch, he saw. They were in Russian, not English. Choe did not speak a word of Russian, so he merely noted it in the after-action report.

36

Saint John learned what happened when he tried to contact Perseverance over a day later. When she did not answer his first attempt, he figured *Simpkin* was in hyperspace, returning from Venera. He was planning on contacting her again in a few hours. But, before he did, Captain Dallas asked Saint John to come to his office.

"Something happened to *Simpkin*, Saint John," Dallas said after Saint John sat down. "As she was easing in to pick up the survivors, the Rodinans launched on her. One of the warheads breached the bridge. None of the bridge crew were in shipsuits. Captain Andrews is alive, in a medpod, but she was in vacuum for ninety-eight seconds. I don't have any details—I've only seen the high-level summary."

The color drained from Saint John's face. He felt as though his wind was knocked out. A wave of nausea swept over him. He swallowed several times and managed to ride it out.

One of the first things he learned at the academy was the consequences of exposure to vacuum. The human body could withstand thirty seconds without significant damage. Up to ninety seconds was usually survivable, but there were complications. There could be brain damage similar to a stroke victim and the possible formation of scar tissue on any or all mucous membranes such as the lungs, sinuses, and mouth. Every second over ninety increased the risk of complications and decreased the chance of surviving. Being in vacuum as long as she was meant that, in all likelihood, they needed to revive her.

How badly damaged her brain and body were would not be known for weeks. The coma the medpod induced was the safest condition for her. Her pulse and respiration would be slow, and so would the rate of healing. In the case of vacuum exposure, slow was better. A slower recovery made it less likely that scar tissue would form internally. The biggest question would be brain function. That information would not be something Captain Dallas could access.

"Thanks for letting me know, skipper."

"If you need some time—"

Saint John shook his head. "I'll be better off staying busy. There isn't a damned thing I can do about it except worry. That would just make me, and everyone around me, crazy. The time she'll need me is when they..."

His voice trailed away. He was going to say, "When they bring her back to consciousness," but the second part of that statement was, "if they bring her back." Saint John tried to lock those thoughts away. He suspected that whatever time he spent agonizing over it now would by no means lessen the pain if the worst came to pass.

Saint John was as polite and civil as ever to his shipmates for the remainder of the journey to Lincoln Station. The ones he worked most closely with sensed something was off. It was as though he withdrew deep inside himself.

Simpkin replaced the Alcubierre field generators and was able to leave the Venera system. She traveled across H2813 and entered the long corridor to the Hercules system. It was only after *Simpkin* emerged back into normal space that Commander Choe learned what the Rodinans broadcast after the missile launch. Admiral Boyd shared what the translators reported.

"The commissar just killed the captain and launched the missiles. He's crazy! We could not stop him! He's dead now. Please don't kill us!"

The message was repeated twice and was cut off in the middle of the third repetition. Commander Choe read it and shrugged. He decided he didn't care if it was one of those bastards or the whole ship. The Rodinans launched their missiles, *Simpkin* responded. Simple as that.

It took a few days for the story (lacking the last Rodinan broadcast) to reach the news media, but when it did, it erupted with fury. "Rotten Rodinans Ambush

Our Persie," read a typical headline. That particular story included an "artist's rendering" of what Perseverance might look like in the medpod. The Admiralty supplied full details of the encounter, except for the last transmission in Russian.

Public sentiment was inflamed. Admiral Freshley decided it would be the perfect time to introduce the next appropriations request to fund the next wave of shipbuilding. He was planning on presenting it with a formal report to Parliament on the actions of HMS *Simpkin* and HMS *Deal* in another week but advanced the timetable a few days.

It bothered his conscience. He was fond of and admired Captain Andrews, and it disturbed him to use her this way. There was a war he needed to win, though, and he would use every weapon at his disposal to ensure victory—at least, that's how he justified it to himself.

He thought arranging for side honors to be presented when the medpod containing Captain Andrews was brought onto Caerleon Station would assuage his guilt. Of course, the media were present. Video of the occasion was transmitted across the Commonwealth.

Amid this public fervor, Parliament passed his appropriations request almost without debate. In fact, most MPs spoke only to enter into the official record how much they supported the Royal Navy in this trying time. The only dissent was mild, asking for more time to study the request.

Perseverance, Commander Stackhouse, Lieutenant Herring, and Petty Officer Roscoe were delivered to the Royal Navy Medical Center in the city of Caerleon, next to the Admiralty building. The official prognosis was guarded. All four registered some brain activity, which was a positive sign. It meant they would not be vegetables when they were brought out of their comas.

The comas in which they were placed prevented any prediction more optimistic. Brain activity was expected to be low for someone in this state. The severity of any brain damage would be determined when they were awakened.

As far as physical damage, all four presented the potential for serious complications. The consensus of the medical experts was to keep all four in deep comas for at least another six months. There was an alternative treatment using medical nanites. Nanites were tiny little machines injected into the bloodstream that accelerated the healing process and prevented scar tissue from forming on the mucous membranes. Unfortunately, nanites were outrageously expensive. The medical center rejected this treatment due to the high cost. To treat the four patients would cost between ten and twelve million pounds, with no assurance of a full recovery due to the possibility of severe brain damage. The medical center did not have the budget to afford this.

Despite the massive appropriations that had just passed, Admiral Freshley did not have money to add to the hospital budget. All the funds were allocated for building warships. He called Lord Gilchrist for advice. Part of what motivated Freshley to make the call was guilt over how he took advantage of Captain Andrews' current condition. Another part of it was due to fear of what the media might do when they learned of it.

Gilchrist listened and promised he would get back in touch soon. It took less than two hours. Gilchrist's face held a smug and satisfied look when he returned Freshley's call.

"The queen will cover the cost from her own accounts," he informed Freshley. "Everyone wins. You win because it reinforces the idea that the funds you've requested will be spent only on what you said. The queen wins because she appears caring and compassionate, and the patients win. Unless you have any objection, the queen will make an announcement this afternoon."

"As long as the queen understands the risk—that all four of them might not be able to make a full recovery—I have no problem with this," Freshley said.

"Charlie understands the risk, but part of her message will be 'that's a chance we need to take' in order to save these brave men and women," Gilchrist said. "Now, if you'll excuse me, I need to contact the Medical Center and obtain details on how much the nanites might reduce the recovery time."

The queen's secretary announced a press conference to be held at four o'clock that afternoon. The unscheduled nature of it indicated that the queen would not be speaking on a mundane topic. The different media outlets scrambled to send their most visible reporters to the palace.

At four o'clock precisely, the queen entered the reception room. She was wearing a light gray skirt suit, and her hair was in a bun. In appearance, she resembled a successful executive.

"Thank you for being here on such short notice," she said to open her remarks. "Admiral Freshley informed us today of a problem he is facing. As many of you know, four brave heroes just returned to the Royal Navy Medical Center for advanced medical treatment. They were injured while trying to aid a fallen foe who declared his surrender. As HMS *Simpkin* approached to render assistance, the enemy chose to violate every moral and ethical standard and launch a sneak attack against us.

"All four of these courageous men and women face a difficult road to recovery. In fact, there is no assurance all of them or any of them will recover fully. They were exposed to the vacuum of space for ninety-eight seconds, and statistics indicate the chances of a full recovery are not good.

"Admiral Freshley ordered the Medical Center to make every possible effort for these patients. He learned, to his dismay, that the most effective possible treatment, the injection of medical nanites into the four stricken shipmates, would cost between ten and twelve million pounds. The Royal Navy does not have the money in its budget and, if it did, would be reluctant to risk spending it on patients in such fragile condition.

"Many of you might be wondering, 'Didn't Parliament just approve massive amounts of money for the Royal Navy?' They did, but that money was granted to the Royal Navy for a specific purpose—to build new ships, first to protect our commonwealth, then to win this war which we had forced upon us. The Royal Navy does not possess the authority to divert those funds to other uses.

"Fortunately, Admiral Freshley brought this problem to our attention. His strongest desire is to help our four heroes. His strong ethical backbone prevents him from doing so. Instead, he turned to us for advice and counsel. We agree with Admiral Freshley that these brave men and women deserve the best medical treatment available. At the same time, we also feel it is unfair to ask you, the citizens of our great commonwealth, to bear any additional expenses when you have been so supportive already.

"Therefore, we decided the best solution would be for us to pay for this treatment ourselves, from our personal accounts. Whether a full recovery is possible, we do not know. Last year, we gave Captain Andrews—Dame Perseverance—a sword. We urged her 'to use your sword to the glory of God, the defense of our Commonwealth, the maintenance of your sovereign's right and honor, and for equity and justice for all, to the utmost of your power.' It is fitting and proper that we should use the utmost of our power to help her and her shipmates."

With that, the queen departed, taking no questions. Pages distributed copies of her remarks and a fact sheet on medical nanites. Included on the fact sheet was a statement from the lead physician assigned to the care of the four members of *Simpkin's* crew.

As Lord Gilchrist anticipated, media coverage was overwhelmingly positive. A typical headline was, "Queen Pledges to Save Our Persie." Most stories praised Admiral Freshley and the navy. All the coverage gushed over the queen's offer.

Aboard HMS *Deal*, moored in the shipyard attached to Lincoln Station, Captain Dallas summoned Commander Powell to his office. Saint John knocked on the door with some trepidation. Their last meeting in the captain's office was painful.

"Enter!" Dallas called.

When Saint John came in, Dallas smiled. "Good meeting this time, I think," he said.

"What's up, skipper?"

"Have you been keeping up with the news?"

"I have."

"So, you know they're hoping to bring Captain Andrews out of her coma in ten days, right?" Dallas asked.

"Yes."

"Well, someone important wants you there when it happens," Dallas said. "I just received instructions to grant you four weeks of 'compassionate leave' if you request it. In addition, there are two more weeks for 'compassionate travel.' None of this counts against your standard leave allotment. If you depart on the next scheduled liner to Caerleon, you'll make it on time. Interested?"

"Hell, yes!" Saint John answered.

"So approved. Get out of here, commander."

37

Saint John arrived at Caerleon Station the day before they were planning on rousing Perseverance from her coma. The day before, when the liner entered normal space in the Caerleon system, his comm unit indicated he received a message from "Communications Maintenance." Perseverance told him about Lord Gilchrist's unusual comm ID earlier, so Saint John knew who it was.

"Commander, it would be my very great pleasure to serve as your host for the next four weeks," Lord Gilchrist said after exchanging greetings. "I imagine you will spend most of your time at the hospital, but I would like to offer you the hospitality of my home and the services of my driver while you are here."

"Thank you, Lord Gilchrist," Saint John replied. "I will take you up on your offer. Perseverance mentioned how much she enjoyed her stay with you. As you say, I will probably spend most of my time at the hospital, but it will be nice to have somewhere to hang my hat when I am not there."

"My driver, David, will meet you when your liner docks tomorrow. You'll recognize him easily. He is a very large, imposing man," Gilchrist said.

When Saint John exited the gangway, it was not difficult for him to spot David. David recognized Saint John as well and made eye contact. Without a word, David turned away, expecting Saint John to follow. As Perseverance experienced earlier, David led him to an electric cart and then through passages not open to the general public until they reached Lord Gilchrist's private shuttle.

Almost as soon as they arrived at Lord Gilchrist's magnificent home, Saint John needed to excuse himself. "Pardon me," he said to Gilchrist and Samantha. "I have a call with Dr. Phaneuf at 17:00. He is the lead physician for the four of them."

JOHN J. SPEARMAN

Samantha led him to the same bedroom Perseverance occupied during her visit. Saint John set his bags down, then went to the desk to make the call. Dr. Phaneuf answered immediately.

"Commander," Phaneuf said, "we plan to restore Captain Andrews to consciousness around ten o'clock tomorrow morning. You will not be allowed in the room while that happens, even though I suspect that is your strong desire. We would like you to be nearby, though."

"Why will I not be allowed in the room?" Saint John asked.

"Captain Andrews was exposed to vacuum for ninety-eight seconds," Phaneuf explained. "There is undoubtedly brain damage. How it manifests and how severe remains for us to see. She probably will exhibit memory loss. How extensive it is, we will learn tomorrow. She will present with symptoms similar to a victim of a stroke. Her motor skills will be affected. Her speech center may also be impaired. We do not want you in the room because your presence would be traumatic for both of you when she does not recognize you. Seeing her in her damaged condition will also be difficult for you."

"Then why would you even want me at the hospital?" Saint John asked.

"There is a chance she regains her memory quickly, in which case seeing you should be a reassuring and comforting thing for her. Sadly, her memory may or may not return, or may remain incomplete," Phaneuf warned. "She will be undergoing psychological therapy designed to reactivate her mind. My experience has been that by the end of the third day of this therapy, that patient regains more than ninety percent of what they will recover."

"What do you think her chances are?" Saint John asked.

"Of survival?"

"Of regaining most or all of her memory," Saint John clarified.

"Impossible to predict. It depends on the state of her bloodstream while she was in vacuum," Phaneuf explained. "The drop in outside pressure will have caused any nitrogen bubbles in her blood, muscles, or tissue to expand greatly. The number, size, and location of those bubbles will determine how bad it is. This would have affected not only her brain but her muscles, her organs—everything. The nanites we gave her will have repaired the physical damage—her muscles and her organs, including the brain. With the brain, while the physical damage might be corrected, connections may have been dropped and neural pathways altered."

"So, you're saying that the nanites replaced any cards that were missing from the deck, but the deck might be shuffled?" Saint John asked.

"That's a good analogy," Phaneuf said. "I may use that in the future. Yes, the shuffling of the deck will have an effect. We will see that in her motor skills and cognitive skills. She may need to learn how to walk again. She may not know how to read. Some of those skills may never return. Given how long she was in vacuum, it is quite possible she remains afflicted by intellectual disability."

"I think I understand," Saint John said glumly.

"All four face the same dangers," Phaneuf said.

"How do you manage to stand it, doctor?" Saint John asked.

"I know I have presented a bleak picture, commander. I'm trying to prepare you for the worst," Phaneuf said. "I persist because miracles happen all the time. Small miracles—nearly every day. Big miracles—often enough that I never lose hope."

"What is a small miracle?"

"A patient learning how to walk again, or how to read, or suddenly recognizing loved ones," Phaneuf explained. "An example of a big miracle is a dock worker from Ithaca who was in vacuum for almost three minutes. It happened about fifteen months ago. The physical damage was extensive, and we kept her in a coma for over a year. When we brought her back to consciousness, she was awake and alert. She suffered no brain damage that we could find. That was a big miracle. Now I have a question for you, commander. How committed are you to Captain Andrews?"

"More committed than not, doctor," Saint John replied, "even though our relationship is less than a year old. As long as there is hope and continued progress, I'm committed. If she ends up needing to be institutionalized, with no understanding of who I am and no hope of a better life... I doubt she would want me to give up my life for her under those circumstances. I know if positions were reversed, I would not want her to do it for me. Hearing the words come out, I hate my answer, but it's as honest as I can be."

"It's a realistic view of things, commander," Phaneuf said. "I understand. If it were to happen to my wife or one of my children, I would give a similar answer. I hope I'm never asked the question, though."

After the call, Saint John returned to his host. He found them by following the sound of voices. He also heard laughing. Samantha's laugh was a high-pitched titter. Lord Gilchrist's was a low rumble. They stopped when Saint John appeared.

"Speak of the devil," Gilchrist said. "We were just talking about you. Were your ears burning?"

"No, but I heard you laughing," Saint John replied. "I hope that's a good thing."

"We were laughing because the paparazzi spotted you arriving at the station today," Gilchrist explained. "Your photo is all over the media. Some of the captions were ridiculous. My favorite is, 'Handsome Prince Arrives to Wake His Sleeping Beauty—Our Persie.' Samantha likes that one the best too."

Saint John couldn't help but chuckle and shake his head.

"When did she become 'Our Persie?' She's not going to like that one bit," Saint John commented.

"I think she became 'Our Persie' when she was put in a coma," Gilchrist said. "It comes from our common heritage. People from both British and American backgrounds like their heroes best when they're vulnerable in some way. Before this, Dame Perseverance was well-known and generally admired, but there wasn't affection. Her success in Aries showed her as the perfect combination of strategic foresight, careful planning, undeniable courage, and pluck. When she spoke out on Alleghany, she displayed perfect righteousness. The problem is, we don't like perfection—except in the queen, perhaps. If the prime minister, however, were to catch his toe on the carpet and stumble for a step or two on his way to make a speech, his approval rating would jump ten points. That Perseverance was wounded while trying to rescue an enemy who surrendered, only to have some slimy bastard fire missiles at her—now that is a cause for sympathy. She is no longer an example of unattainable perfection. She is our best and brightest warrior, laid low by the wicked deceit of a morally bankrupt enemy."

"She's still not going to like it," Saint John said.

"Doesn't that make it even better, in a way?" Samantha asked mischievously.

"It does give me something new with which to tease her," Saint John agreed.

Perseverance's first steps on the road back from oblivion were dreams—nightmares, actually—in a recurring loop. In the one, she saw an incredibly handsome man in an EVA suit turn to see an attractive blonde woman shot in the back by a fléchette pistol. The other showed two people vanish in front of her, accompanied by the sense that she felt cold and pain, along with a lingering emotion of regret.

When she returned to consciousness, she was disoriented and confused. The bright lights overhead hurt her eyes, and she shut them quickly. Her throat and mouth were dry, and her tongue felt strange in her mouth. She sensed the brightness of the lights was being blocked by something, so she dared to open her eyes just a tiny amount.

A man was standing over her, wearing a white coat. The background also appeared to be white, but she did not wish to open her eyes to make sure. Something was beeping on her left. She realized she was lying on her back. She knew the type of place where she was, but the name for it was just out of reach. She tried to think of it, but it squiggled away.

"Captain Andrews?" the man said.

Her mind spun. *Is he talking to me?* she wondered. *Andrews sounds like it might be me. In the one dream, was I a captain? How does he know about my dream?*

"Captain Andrews?" the man said again.

I didn't see anyone else in the room, but I didn't really look. Maybe I should see if there is someone else he is talking to. Nope. Don't want to open the eyes. Hurts.

"Captain Andrews?"

He must mean me. If there is someone else in the room named Captain Andrews, they should have answered him by now, damnit. "Yes," she croaked.

Sonovabitch, that hurt, she thought. *I don't really sound like that, do I?*

"Captain Andrews, my name is Doctor Phaneuf. You are in the Royal Navy Medical Center on Caerleon. How do you feel?"

Doctor? The guy in the white coat. Doctors wear white coats? In a hospital. YES! That's the damned word. Navy? Navy Navy Navy—Captain? Captain Andrews? Okaaay. How do I feel?

"Bad," she said.

"Not a surprise," the man said. "Would you like some water?"

Hell, yes! Give me some water. My throat hurts like hell, doc...

I didn't actually say anything, did I?

"Mhm."

She heard a motor and felt the bed underneath her back begin to tilt upward. As her head rose, she sensed that the light overhead was no longer glaring in her eyes. She opened them a peep. *Still bright but not as bad as before. White room. White coat. Doctor. Hospital! Score!*

The bed stopped moving. The man held a cup with a straw up to her mouth. She knew what to do. Her lips closed around the straw, and she pulled water (*Water!* she realized) into her mouth.

Oh, that water feels good. My mouth likes it. Tongue likes it. Throat wants some. How do I? C'mon! This is easy. No, it's not. Sure it is—just do that thing in the back.

"Can you swallow?" he asked.

Swallow! That's it, swallow. You can do this, Perse. Perse? Who the hell is Perse? Never mind—swallow. Who is Perse? Is Perse me? Perse knows how to swallow. Oh, that feels good. I want...

"More?" she asked.

He moved the straw to her lips again.

Oh, yeah. That's good. Perse is me. I am Perse and I am Captain Andrews. Perse Andrews? Something is missing. Swallow.

"Do you know who you are?"

Crap. I hate being wrong. I don't want to be wrong. Deep breath, then best guess. "Perse Andrews?"

He's smiling! Yes!

"Yes. Your name is Perseverance Andrews. You are a captain in the Royal Navy."

Perse<u>verance</u>—that was the missing bit. Captain in the Royal Navy? He wouldn't simply make that up, and it's not something new but... Damnit! I can't get it.

Doctor Phaneuf noticed the troubled look on her face.

"Just relax," he said.

She heard the whirring of the motor, and the top of her bed was lowering. The doctor walked away. The overhead lights dimmed. She wanted to figure out what was happening but drifted off to sleep.

"I have good news, commander," Doctor Phaneuf told Saint John, sitting in a waiting area. "She regained consciousness and is capable of speech. She's quite confused, though—in a dissociative state."

"Does that mean she has amnesia?"

"Yes," Phaneuf replied, "but she was able to recall her name. That's a strongly positive sign for now. We will be conducting a number of tests. From what I saw, I doubt we'll be needing you here today, so feel free to leave. Now, if you'll excuse me, I need to check on the others."

She woke again. The lights were still dimmed, so it did not hurt to open her eyes. She heard a door open, and a woman in a white coat entered her view.

"Hello, I'm Doctor Callsen," the woman said.

The doctor made the back of her bed rise, accompanied by the whirring noise. Perseverance heard the door open again. A white-coated man appeared, pushing something. Doctor Callsen raised her higher than before. The top of what the man was pushing slid in front of her. She looked at it. She recognized the cup with the straw.

Water.

"Captain Andrews, do you know why you are here?" Callsen asked.

Captain Andrews is me. Why am I here? No frickin' idea, lady.

"Something happened?" Perseverance said uncertainly.

"Yes. Your ship was attacked. You were on the bridge of your ship. The enemy made a hole in your ship, and all the air was sucked into space. You were in a vacuum. Someone rescued you and brought you to safety. You have been in a coma—asleep—while your body healed. Now, you are awake," Callsen said. "How much of what I just said makes sense to you? Does any of it seem familiar?"

The dream! The first part was in my dream. The second part... no.

"My dream," Perseverance said. "It was in my dream. It was cold, and I hurt. I was sad about something. No rescue in my dream."

"Your dream actually happened," Callsen explained. "It's your memory."

Okaaay.

"Please look down at the table," the doctor asked. "Can you tell me what you see?"

"Water," Perseverance answered confidently.

"Yes, water," the doctor pointed to the cup with the straw. "What else?"

There was a round thing with something in it. Next to it was a shiny thing, round on one end. On the other side from the shiny thing was something folded. They were all on a flat thing on top of a flat thing.

The doctor called one of these things "table," Perseverance thought. *Which one is that? Skip it. Shiny thing… I know that.*

"Spoon?"

"Is this the spoon?" the doctor asked, pointing to the round thing with stuff inside.

"No," Perseverance said.

"Is this it?" as she pointed to the spoon.

"Yes."

38

It took a few minutes, but eventually, Perseverance identified the bowl, tray, and table. Doctor Callsen gave her the word "napkin" for the folded cloth next to the bowl. It seemed correct to Perseverance. The trouble started when the doctor explained that what was in the bowl was oatmeal, and it would be the first solid food Perseverance had eaten in weeks.

"Would you like to eat?" the doctor asked. "Go ahead."

Perseverance knew what she needed to do. She should pick up the spoon and use it to get the oatmeal to her mouth. She knew she did things like this all the time. How she was supposed to pick up the spoon wasn't happening. She looked at her arm and her hand, just lying there. She tried to tell them to pick up the spoon. Then she tried to will them to do it by thinking extra hard. Not even a twitch.

Callsen saw tears begin to well in Perseverance's eyes. "That's fine, captain," she said soothingly. "We'll try again later. Emilio?"

The man who brought the tray in picked up the spoon, gathered some of the oatmeal, and brought it to Perseverance's mouth. She opened her mouth and closed her lips around the spoon. The man withdrew it.

Meh, she thought. *Needs something. Needs … sugar? Not just sugar…*

"Maple sugar?" Perseverance said uncertainly after she swallowed.

Callsen smiled. "I'm sure it doesn't taste like much. I'll see about getting some maple sugar next time."

The oatmeal may have been bland, but when it reached her stomach, the ache she felt there began to subside. When Emilio offered her another spoonful, she took it. Each swallow made her stomach feel better. When the ache completely disappeared, Perseverance saw the bowl was almost empty. That made her feel strangely pleased with herself.

After this, a different doctor entered and started poking her in different spots. She could feel it every time the doctor poked. It seemed to make the doctor happy. The doctor asked her to move her arms. Nothing happened. Then her legs—again, no response. The doctor could see Perseverance was getting upset, so he reassured her they would figure it out soon.

The next doctor brought in a computer tablet. He sat next to Perseverance and showed her pictures on the tablet, asking her a variety of questions about each one. Perseverance was correct more often than she was not, and she found the exercise fun.

The one she knew as Emilio returned with another tray. This time the oatmeal in the bowl had something light brown added on top. Perseverance was still unable to pick up the spoon, but when Emilio fed her, the oatmeal tasted much better. Sweet and something else.

"Maple sugar?" she asked.

"Yes."

Score!

Saint John arrived in the waiting room at 07:00 the next day. Doctor Phaneuf saw him and approached.

"How is she doing?" Saint John asked.

"Well," Phaneuf replied, "but that's a relative term. She is making strong progress cognitively. That means she is recognizing things and able to find the proper words for them. Her motor skills—in terms of control over her arms and legs—are not engaged. I am hopeful, though. She got over a big hurdle immediately by being able to swallow. That can be tricky. One of the others has not yet mastered it, though he can move his fingers and toes. We will get her out of bed today to begin physical therapy and see if we can reactivate some more of the motor pathways."

"Is there anything I can do to help?" Saint John asked.

"No. I doubt she will be ready to see you today, but things can change rapidly. If you left, how difficult would it be for you to return if that changed?"

"Not difficult, but I met the relatives of the others yesterday, and I'm fine with staying here with them," Saint John replied.

"Suit yourself," Phaneuf said.

"You said things can change rapidly," Saint John remarked. "In what way?"

"Often, on the cognitive side of things, patients reach a certain point as they progress through identifying and naming objects, when—to use your analogy—the deck reshuffles itself in something close to its original order. That usually happens in the first three days after they regain consciousness," Phaneuf explained.

"What if that doesn't happen?" Saint John asked.

"If the patient is not improving cognitively by the third day, it is unlikely they will later. They will remain intellectually disabled. That won't happen with Captain Andrews—she has already made headway. If the pieces don't fall into place for her by the end of the third day, she will probably continue to improve at the same rate she has been. It might take a few weeks or months, but there is still reason for optimism."

"What about the physical side of things?" Saint John inquired.

"We don't often see the sudden dramatic improvement as with the cognitive functions," Phaneuf said. "It generally takes months, and even then, a patient might be left with an awkward stride or an arm with limited function. This is also the area where you as her—partner?"

"Boyfriend," Saint John clarified.

"As her boyfriend, you can exercise great influence toward her recovery. I asked you how committed you are. From your answer, I reckon you would want to be a part of this?"

"Absolutely."

Saint John was again in the waiting area at 07:00 on the third day. When Doctor Phaneuf passed him, the doctor held up crossed fingers. He did not stop to talk with Saint John but did meet with family members of two of the other three patients.

Saint John spent the day waiting, occasionally chatting with the relatives of the other patients. Commander Stackhouse's parents did not return that day. Doctor Phaneuf had the unpleasant job of telling them the day before that their son would be intellectually disabled for the rest of his life.

In comparing notes with the other two in the waiting area, it seemed Lieutenant Herring had the highest degree of motor control. At the same time, Petty Officer Roscoe was still unable to swallow, even though he was regaining control over his arms and legs.

Near 11:00, an orderly summoned Roscoe's wife and took her away. Saint John looked over at Lieutenant Herring's parents and shrugged. The three of them resumed waiting.

Roscoe's wife, Amanda, returned an hour later, in tears but smiling. "He recognized me," she shared. "He still can't swallow, poor thing, but he knows who he is."

Amanda left shortly after sharing the news. Now that her husband was cognizant, Doctor Phaneuf gave her a visiting schedule. Saint John and the Herrings settled back to wait.

At 17:00, the Herrings decided to leave for the day. They wished Saint John good luck. Saint John resigned himself to another dinner in the hospital cafeteria.

After a frustrating session of the physical therapist manipulating her arms, legs, fingers, and toes, they brought Perseverance back to her room. She fell asleep, and the dreams she experienced before waking from the coma returned. There was something different this time.

In the dream of the two people in EVA suits, she understood this was not from her own experience. It was something someone told her that he experienced. In the dream about the bridge of her ship, she remembered why she felt regret. She regretted how she ended her last conversation with her lover.

She forced herself awake. *My lover*, she thought. She could see him. She remembered feeling his arms wrapped around her. A feeling of mild happiness and contentment started in her chest and flowed out. *And his name is…*

Without thinking, she grabbed the call button and began pressing it frantically. Doctor Callsen happened to be at the nurses' station. She quickly looked at the camera feed from Perseverance's room.

"That's interesting," she said.

"What is?" asked one of the two nurses there.

"As of an hour ago, Captain Andrews had no control over her arms and legs. Look."

Callsen pointed at the screen showing Perseverance rapidly pressing the call button. She then said, "I'll handle this."

Callsen opened the door and looked in. Perseverance noticed her and quit pressing the call button.

"Captain Andrews, what were you just doing?" Callsen asked.

"Trying to get someone's damned attention. I want to speak to Commander Powell," Perseverance said excitedly.

"You couldn't move your arms or legs," Callsen commented.

"That's not important right now," Perseverance snapped. "Get me a comm unit and let me speak to Commander Powell!"

"Commander Powell has spent the last three days in the waiting room. He may have left for the day, though. It's after five o'clock."

"Please have someone check. If he's here, I want to see him! If he's not, call him! And help me lower the goddamned rails on this bed!"

"I'm not sure that's a good idea, captain," Callsen replied.

"Doctor, with all due respect, I don't give a rat's ass," Perseverance said. "If he *is* here, I'll be good and goddamned if I let him see me like an invalid!"

Doctor Callsen reluctantly lowered the rail on one side of the bed. Perseverance awkwardly scooched herself and slid her legs over the side. She could barely touch the floor with her toes. In the process of maneuvering, Perseverance realized from the cool air she felt on her back that she was only clad in a hospital gown. *Screw it*, she thought. *He's seen me in less.*

Saint John did not know what was wrong. He'd just entered the cafeteria when a breathless orderly skittered in and shouted, "Is there a Commander Powell here?"

"I'm Commander Powell."

"You need to come with me, sir," the orderly panted.

"What's going on?" Saint John asked.

"Beats me, sir," the orderly gasped, still catching his breath. "My supervisor just told me to get my ass down to the caff and see if you were here, and if you were, I'm supposed to bring you back. I don't know what for, sir. I'm sorry."

Saint John did not know whether to be excited or filled with dread. He saw how devastated Stackhouse's parents were with the news about their son. Even though he was not a religious man, he began praying as they walked quickly back.

When they reached the nurses' station, one of them caught his eye and noted his worried expression. Giving him a broad smile, the nurse said, "Someone wants to see you, and pretty badly from the shouting I've heard from her room."

The wave of relief that swept over him brought tears to his eyes. He strode to the doorway of Perseverance's room. When she saw him, she stood. Doctor Callsen offered Perseverance her arm to assist, only to have Perseverance bat it away clumsily but emphatically. Barefoot, Perseverance took a couple of steps toward Saint John. Seeing her begin to wobble, he quickly crossed to her and folded his arms around her. They stood tear-stained cheek to tear-stained cheek. Eventually, Perseverance regained enough composure to lean back so she could see his face.

"What I meant to say was, 'I miss you and love you, too.' I couldn't stand that the last thing you heard from me was a smart-ass comment," Perseverance said.

ABOUT THE AUTHOR

John Spearman (Jake to his friends and colleagues) is a Latin teacher and coach at a prestigious New England boarding school in addition to writing. He began writing because his wife challenged him. His first four books, the Halberd series, have been well-received. This book takes place in the same universe as the Halberd series, though over three hundred years earlier. To learn more about the author and all his different works, please visit www.johnjspearmanauthor.com

Made in United States
Orlando, FL
14 March 2024

44773852R00189